I0612239

FRIENDS

IN

SPY PLACES

Book 14 of the NEVER SAY SPY series

Diane Henders

FRIENDS IN SPY PLACES

ISBN 978-1-927460-57-3

Copyright © 2019 Diane Henders

PEBKAC Publishing Inc.
P.O. Box 67, Station Main
Qualicum Beach, BC   V9K 1S7
www.pebkacpublishing.com

All rights reserved. No part of this book may be used or reproduced in any manner whatsoever without prior written permission, except in the case of brief quotations embodied in critical articles and reviews. For information, address PEBKAC Publishing Inc.

NO AI TRAINING: Without in any way limiting the author's and/or publisher's exclusive rights under copyright, any use of this publication to "train" generative artificial intelligence (AI) technologies to generate text is expressly prohibited. The author reserves all rights to license uses of this work for generative AI training and development of machine learning language models.

This book is a work of fiction. Names, characters, places and incidents are either the product of the author's imagination or are used fictitiously, and any resemblance to actual persons, living or dead, business establishments, events or locales is entirely coincidental.

First printed in paperback May 2019 by PEBKAC Publishing Inc.

v.2.1

Books in the NEVER SAY SPY series:

More books coming! For a current list, please visit
www.dianehenders.com
Or sign up for my New Book Notification list at
www.dianehenders.com/books

Humour by Diane Henders

Probably Inappropriate

Definitely Inappropriate

Totally Inappropriate

Completely Inappropriate

Unabashedly Inappropriate

More books coming! For a current list, please visit
www.dianehenders.com
Or sign up for my New Book Notification list at
www.dianehenders.com/books

Since You Asked...

People frequently ask if my protagonist, Aydan Kelly, is really me.

Yeah, you got me. These novels are an autobiography of my secret life as a government agent, working with highly-classified computer technology... Oh, wait, what's that? You want the *truth*? Um, you do realize fiction writers get paid to lie, don't you?

...well, shit, that's not nearly as much fun. It's also a long story.

I swore I'd never write fiction. "Too personal," I said. "People read novels and automatically assume the author is talking about him/herself."

Well, apparently I lied about the fiction-writing part. One day a story sprang into my head and wouldn't leave. The only way to get it out was to write it down. So I did.

But when I wrote that first book, I never intended to show it to anyone, so I created a character that looked like me just to thumb my nose at the stereotype. I've always had a defective sense of humour, and this time it turned around and bit me in the ass.

Because after I'd written the third novel, I realized I actually wanted other people to read my books. And when I went back to change my main character to *not* look like me, my beta readers wouldn't let me. They rose up against me and said, "No! Aydan is a tall woman with long red hair and brown eyes. End of discussion!"

Jeez, no wonder readers get the idea that authors write about themselves. So no, I'm not Aydan Kelly. I just look like her.

Oh, and the town of Silverside and all secret technologies are products of my imagination. If I'm abducted by grim-faced men wearing dark glasses, or if I die in an unexplained fiery car crash, you'll know I accidentally came a little too close to the truth.

I hope you enjoy the book!

For Phill

Thank you for being my technical advisor and the most
tolerant husband ever. Much love!

**To my beta readers/editors, especially Carol H.,
Judy B., and Phill B., with gratitude:** Many thanks for
all your time and effort in catching my spelling and grammar
errors, telling me when I screwed up the plot or the
characters' motivations, and generally keeping me honest.

To everyone else, respectfully:
Canadian English is an unholy hybrid of British and
American English, so I apologize if spellings in this book look
odd to you. But if you find typos, please send an email to
errors@dianehenders.com. Mistakes drive me nuts, and I'm
sorry if any slipped through. Please let me know what the
error is, and on which page. I'll make sure it gets fixed as
soon as possible. Thanks!

CHAPTER 1

As I slid into a chair at the meeting table, Clyde 'Spider' Webb hid a cavernous yawn behind his hand.

"Are we keeping you up, Webb?" Greg Holt inquired sarcastically. "We wouldn't want you to sacrifice your beauty sleep over trivial little things like international espionage and murder."

A blush stained Spider's cheeks, making him look more like a guilty teenager than the brilliant twenty-seven-year-old analyst he was. "Sorry," he mumbled. "I was up really late last night. I wasn't expecting a Sunday morning meeting."

The contagious yawn overtook me, too, in spite of my best attempt to smother it.

Holt shot me a look, his steel-blue eyes glinting with contempt. "Christ, I'm more alert than you and Webb put together; and I was interrogating Grandin all night."

Yeah, yeah. Holt The Magnificent.

I was biting my tongue so I wouldn't say that aloud when Spider sprang to my defence. "You didn't get attacked and drugged yesterday like Aydan did!" His pale cheeks flushed with indignation. "She was barely out of the hospital when she flew down to Calgary last night! And then she had to drive back to Silverside this morning for this meeting; and I bet the roads were still awful after that blizzard, weren't they, Aydan?"

"Yeah, they reopened an hour before I left Calgary this

morning," I agreed, trying not to sound as exhausted as I felt. "It took me nearly three hours instead of the usual two." I gave Spider a little 'thank-you' smile and turned back to Holt. "So did you get anything from Grandin?"

Holt scowled. "He'll crack soon."

"So that's a 'no'." I tried not to sound snotty, but Holt's scowl deepened anyway.

Director Charles Stemp strode in, quelling our exchange of unpleasantries. As he took his seat at the head of the table, he said, "Agent Kelly, your mother wishes to speak with you."

"Tough," I snapped. "She can rot in hell."

"Allow me to clarify," Stemp said in his usual dispassionate tone, but something in his voice made the small hairs rise on the back of my neck. "Your next mission is to visit your mother."

It seemed like a bad idea to voice the retort that quivered on the tip of my tongue, so I stared at Stemp in silence.

After a chilly moment, he went on, "When we released her last night she begged me to arrange a meeting with you, to allow her a chance to fully explain herself. I agreed. She is staying at the Silverside Hotel in Room 106, and she is expecting you this afternoon."

I pressed my lips together to hold in an explosion of profanity. Meddling bastard. Just because he'd finally reconciled with his parents, now he thought there should be a happy ending for everybody? Bullshit. *His* mother hadn't faked her death and run off with some sleazy criminal only to turn up thirty years later pretending to be dear old Mom.

Spider gave me a sympathetic look across the table. Holt just smirked. Asshole.

"I realize this is an uncomfortable situation for you,"

Stemp went on. "But we need to know whether your mother was involved in Sam Kraus's espionage and treason, and this is our only chance to investigate her before she returns to the United Kingdom to resume her work with MI5. Although it is not optimum for you to return to active duty so soon, your personal connection makes you the only logical choice for this mission."

I forced myself to see past his impassive façade to the understanding in his eyes. He wouldn't do this to me unless it was necessary.

And Nora was only here for two weeks. Surely I could tolerate her for that long. Make nice, and find out for sure whether she truly was the conniving bitch I thought she was.

Who knew? Maybe I'd gotten it all wrong. Maybe she loved me as much as she claimed, and she had been protecting me the only way she knew how by leaving all those years ago. My heartstrings quivered with painful hope.

I squashed it. The woman was a liar, an adulteress, and probably a criminal. Not worth getting my hopes up.

"I'll do my best." My voice came out flat.

"Good. Dr. Rawling is available to do your psych clearance interview today. Do you foresee any difficulty obtaining it?"

Suppressing a groan, I muttered, "No." I didn't bother to add, '...as long as I lie to him as usual'.

"Why can't we just question Nora under the lie detector again?" Spider asked. "If she's innocent, she wouldn't mind doing that, would she?"

"She has refused to answer any more questions," Stemp replied. "And as long as the UK continues to grant her diplomatic immunity, Canada has no authority to hold her or question her."

"If she's innocent, you'd think she'd want to help out her daughter," Holt growled. "Sounds guilty to me."

"Perhaps. Or she may simply be observing standard MI5 security protocols." Stemp turned back to me. "We are exploiting a grey area, since your mother has completed all activities directly covered by her diplomatic immunity. We have a bug in her hotel room, taps on the hotel phone and her cell phone, and analysts are monitoring her email and internet usage. They have also prepared a dossier including her financial records and other pertinent documents. Those records have been forwarded to you."

Holt snorted. "That's a hell of a so-called grey area, since the Vienna Convention flat-out says 'the premises of the mission shall be inviolable'."

"My point exactly," Stemp replied. "Nora Taylor's hotel room in Silverside is not 'the premises of the mission'. Her mission is complete, and its premises were her hotel room in Calgary. She is officially on vacation."

Holt smirked, clearly enjoying the opportunity to show off his knowledge. "Except that Article 30 says the diplomat's private residence and papers and correspondence are also inviolable."

"Which is why this is a clandestine op," Stemp said coolly. "The potential for a catastrophic worldwide security breach is of larger concern to the chain of command than the possibility of a slap on the wrist for a technical violation of the Vienna Convention."

I read between the lines: 'Don't get caught.'

Stemp went on, "Of equal priority to the investigation of Nora Taylor is the investigation into who paid former CIA agent Grandin to abduct Agent Kelly. Holt, did you make any progress with your interrogation last night?"

"No," Holt mumbled. "But he'll crack soon. I'm sure of it."

Stemp turned to Spider. "Webb, do you have any new intel?"

Spider rubbed bloodshot eyes and sat up straighter, squaring his bony shoulders. "As soon as Holt arrested Grandin yesterday afternoon I got the team to comb the internet for any connections between Grandin and Aydan, but they didn't find anything. I also got them to infiltrate the CIA's network and check Grandin's personnel file, along with anything else they could find, but it looks as though the CIA has already given us everything they have on him." He sent a questioning glance toward Stemp. "I didn't tell Brock and Tammy to work on it today. Should I?"

"No," Stemp replied. "You were right to make the attempt, but there is no need to expend further resources. An experienced agent like Grandin would be unlikely to leave behind any kind of digital or physical evidence."

"But..." Consternation creased Spider's brow. "If he won't talk, we'll never know whether he's blown Aydan's cover. And we'll never know who was paying him to abduct her, either. Somebody else could be hunting her already."

Tension seized my shoulders. I had been carefully avoiding that thought.

Deep breath. Calm...

"Grandin will talk," Holt said tightly. "Just give me a bit more time."

Stemp inclined his chin in my direction. "Kelly, Webb is correct. Consider your Arlene Widdenback cover burned until further notice." He transferred his attention to Holt. "The United States government has cancelled Grandin's diplomatic immunity so that we can question him, but they are pressuring us to release him to their custody. Breaking Grandin is your top priority. This morning we'll shake him up by having Kelly take over the interrogation."

"But he's *my-*" Holt blurted, then pressed his mouth shut, muscles rippling under the unshaven bristles that darkened his prominent chin.

Caught between dismay over facing Grandin and petty satisfaction at Holt The Magnificent's discomfiture, I squashed my reaction and nodded like the professional I was supposed to be.

I should cut Holt some slack. He was a good agent and he'd saved my ass. And he was actually an okay guy when he wasn't playing superhero...

"*She* won't get anything out of Grandin." Holt's arrogant words shattered my attempt at a charitable attitude adjustment. "He won't strike a deal with a loser agent that let him capture her."

My fist clenched with the need to grab Holt's bullshit attitude and shove it straight down his throat.

Holt added, "No offense, Kelly; but I know how these guys think."

"Well, we'll see," I growled. In my mind I added, "...asshole."

"Yes," Stemp agreed, making my lips twitch with secret amusement. "We shall see." His expressionless gaze drifted over Holt's rampant five o'clock shadow and rumpled hair. "Go home and get some rest, and come back to relieve Kelly in the interrogation room at thirteen hundred hours."

His reptilian gaze snapped to Spider. "You may go home for now, too, though we may need you to come back later today if we gain any time-sensitive intel from Grandin. Dismissed."

As we all pushed back our chairs Stemp added, "Kelly, stay."

Holt shot us a frown as he rose, clearly wondering why I merited special attention.

I kept my expression neutral to hide my rising anxiety. Oh, God, dealing with my shitty excuse for a mother was bad enough. What other bombshell was Stemp about to drop on me?

When the door had closed behind Holt and Spider, Stemp spoke again. "I have a second assignment for you."

Great. I'd barely survived my last mission, and now he wanted me to do two at the same time. So much for 'not optimum to return to active duty so soon'.

Stemp went on, "In each of your last two missions, you involved John Kane."

My stomach tightened.

"It is undesirable to involve civilians in clandestine operations." Stemp's cool precise voice felt like a scalpel poised over my jugular. "Furthermore, it was undesirable for the Department to be forced to accept Kane's resignation in the first place."

I resisted the urge to close my eyes before the killing blow. Instead, I stared past Stemp's left ear, keeping my gaze on the wall behind him as he went on, "So, since you have a close personal relationship with Kane..."

Shit, shit, shit...

"...your assignment is to recruit him back into the Department. An agent of his calibre is wasted in civilian life. We want him to return to active duty."

"No!" The word leaped from my mouth despite my best attempt to bite it back.

Stemp's eyebrow rose a fraction of an inch. "Pardon?"

"No! I won't. Can't. Don't you see..." I sucked in a breath and attempted to marshal my objections into something more coherent. "Ever since I've known him, Kane has said that active agent status isn't an appropriate role for a parent. Now that he has Daniel, he won't go back to being an agent no matter how much he might like to." I drew a slow breath. This was where it was going to get ugly. "And I won't manipulate him into it."

"So he *wants* to return to active duty."

"For shit's sake, that's the one irrelevant part of what I just said!" With an effort, I managed not to wave my arms in frustration. "It doesn't matter if he wants to be an agent again, he won't. Done. Over. End of story."

Stemp's deadpan façade never altered, but I sensed his satisfaction as the trap snapped shut around me. "If you are already certain he will not compromise his principles, then there is no reason for you to refuse the assignment on moral grounds."

"You..." I was trying so hard not to yell '*dickhead*' that words failed me completely. I knotted my fingers together and squeezed, wishing his throat was between them.

He gave me a look as level and emotionless as his voice. "I suggest you do not refuse this assignment."

After allowing a moment for the veiled threat to trickle ice water down my spine, his stone-hard eyes softened. "I understand Kane's objections, and yours. However, it is not your place to make that decision on behalf of either Kane or the Department. We are not asking you to coerce him, merely to highlight the potential benefits. If he truly has no desire to return, he will not."

I met Stemp's bland expression with a glare and countered, "Then you don't need me at all. If you don't plan to use sneaky persuasion or emotional blackmail, just send a recruiting officer to talk to him."

We eyed each other in silence. Stalemate.

Stemp sighed. "Please don't make me give you a direct and specific order."

His odd phrasing registered just as I was opening my mouth to tell him where, how high, and how hard he could stick it.

I shut up, my mind accelerating to maximum RPM.

'*A direct and specific order*'.

Before I had gotten to know Stemp, I would have assumed he was only trying to threaten and manipulate me; but now...

Shit. It was a warning. I was already on thin ice with the chain of command for involving Kane. If I refused the assignment or disobeyed orders now, I could end up in prison. I replayed the conversation in my mind. So far Stemp had only given me an assignment, not a direct order.

He had left me a loophole. Don't force him to plug it.

Unclenching my jaw, I muttered, "Okay. I'll talk to Kane. But I can't promise it'll work."

The faintest hint of a smile quirked Stemp's mouth. "That is all we can ask. Go and question Grandin now. Dismissed."

Heading for the door, I didn't bother to wonder which of us had won that round.

Stemp, no contest. As usual.

CHAPTER 2

Standing in the cramped time-delay chamber that led to the underground secured area, I felt every one of my forty-eight years and then some. Only a small quiver of claustrophobia shook me. Hooray for sleep deprivation.

Hell, maybe if I stayed permanently exhausted I could nap my way through captivity. That might be a handy skill if the chain of command found out I had no intention of trying to recruit Kane.

Sweat slicked my palms at the thought of being in a prison cell for the rest of my life. Never seeing the light of day...

Don't think about it.

The lock released, and I hurried down the stairs into the bright white subterranean corridor.

When I opened the door to the observation booth a few minutes later, I pulled up short at the sight of Holt's glower.

"What are you doing here?" I demanded. "I thought you were supposed to go home and sleep."

"What are you doing here?" Holt retorted. "You're supposed to be in *there*, questioning him." He jabbed a finger at the bank of video screens displaying various angles of Grandin sitting shackled to a steel table in a featureless room.

"And I will be," I snapped. "I just wanted to scope him out first. But since you're here anyway, you can tell me what you've asked him so far."

Holt snorted. "Doesn't matter. He hasn't said a word. Ask him anything you want."

"Hm." I studied the video screens, noting Grandin's headdress of electrodes and the electronic case on the small table near him. "Was it a good idea to leave the lie detector in there with him? It's classified techn-"

"Fuck, Kelly, you think I'm a fucking idiot?" Holt jerked forward in his chair, his fists clenching. "He's shackled to the fucking table so he can't reach it. And just in case he somehow got free, I've had security personnel watching him the whole time I was in Stemp's fucking useless briefing. That was a total fucking waste of my time. There was no damn reason for me to be there at all." His jaw jutted as if daring me to piss him off again.

I dared.

"You should say 'fuck' one more time. You missed using it in that last sentence."

"Fuck off," he snarled.

I grinned. "Nailed it."

A grudging smile fought its way onto his craggy features. "Not bad, eh?"

"Yep, you looked feral." I lifted my upper lip with a fingertip to display my teeth in a parody of his snarl. "You should have shown Grandin that face. He would have talked for sure."

"Wouldn't have done any good," Holt grumbled. "That asshole knows he's sitting pretty while he's under surveillance. Give me a few minutes off-camera with him and I'll have him begging to tell us whatever we want to know."

I sighed. "Yeah, it doesn't seem fair that he should be able to murder an FBI agent in cold blood and then hide behind the laws he was supposed to be upholding."

"Murder an FBI agent, shoot an MI6 agent with intent to murder, and drug and kidnap one of ours," Holt corrected. "Which reminds me, how did you get back here this morning? I thought you weren't supposed to drive for twenty-four hours after you'd been drugged with ketamine."

"I drove. I'm fine." I changed the subject. "So did you really question him all night?"

"I grabbed a few naps between sessions, but I had the guards make sure he stayed awake all night. He's tired now. He should crack any time."

A glance at Grandin's slumped posture gave me a pang of unwanted sympathy. "Looks like he's sleeping now, just sitting in the chair. Has he had anything to eat or drink? Bathroom break?"

Holt rolled his shoulders, massaging the back of his neck as if to ease aching muscles. "Yeah, the guards gave him breakfast and took him to the can. Not that he deserved it. You going soft or something, Kelly?"

"I just don't want to be in there when he shits his pants."

Holt barked out a laugh. "As if you're going to scare the shit out of anybody."

"I have," I said shortly. "It's overrated."

Holt scowled. "Then stop wasting time and get your ass in there. I'll be here to take over when you give up."

"I thought you had orders to go home."

"Quit stalling, Kelly." Holt gave me a narrow smile. "Unless you're too scared to go in."

"You're such an asshole." I yanked the door open and marched out.

Back in the corridor, I hesitated at the door to the interrogation room and tried to ignore the quizzical scrutiny of the guard stationed beside it.

Dammit, I didn't have any idea how to make Grandin talk. I had studied the Department's interrogation resource guides, but I didn't have the kind of real-life experience Holt had. My interrogation experience came from cajoling expense reports out of my bookkeeping clients.

And extracting intel from criminals under threat of torture. Guilt twisted my guts at the memories.

Worst of all, Holt the Magnificent would be watching my every move. If I made some rookie mistake, he'd never let me hear the end of it.

Dammit.

I clenched my teeth and walked into the interrogation room. Grandin stiffened awake but didn't raise his head.

"Good morning," I said.

His head jerked up, surprise flickering across his face before he schooled his expression to blankness and stared at the wall.

Pulling out a chair across the table from him, I eyed him for a moment before dropping into it so he wouldn't see my knees trembling.

Shit, what should I do? What question could I ask that Holt hadn't already hammered at him umpteen times through the long night?

I stared at Grandin.

Grandin stared at the wall.

Maybe he'd start talking if I said nothing.

After several minutes of silence, he hadn't moved or

spoken. Had barely even blinked.

A furtive itch crept up my leg.

Shit, please tell me there isn't a spider crawling on me.

I resisted the urge to scratch my leg.   Be silent.
Motionless.

The tickle climbed to my knee.

My nose itched. My arm itched.

Patience…

Itchy prickles skittered across my scalp like tiny bug feet.

Oh God, Skidmark had borrowed my car. What if he had
head lice? Those revolting little creepy-crawlies had three
long hours to creep up out of the upholstery and burrow into
my long thick hair, *GROSS!*

I convulsively scratched my scalp.

Okay, outwaiting Grandin wasn't an option.

"So…" My voice came out in an uncertain croak. "Um…
I hear you like Gummi Bears."

Grandin's gaze twitched in my direction, his eyes
pinching in confusion.

"You like them a lot. 'Way too much, in fact," I went on,
warming to my story. "That was a pretty disgusting video of
you masturbating with them. What's so special about the red
ones, anyway?"

"What the hell are you talking about?" After a sleepless
night of disuse Grandin's voice was a dry rasp.

Got him. I hid my surge of triumph.

"Oh, come on, don't be coy," I prodded. "You obviously
have an exhibitionist streak, since you filmed yourself doing
it."

"You're nuts." He pressed his mouth shut and resumed
staring at the wall.

I smiled and relaxed, clasping my hands behind my head

and stretching out my legs. "Seriously, you're not even going to own it? We know it's you in the video. We can see your face, and we captured a digital fingerprint from the corner of the footage when you grabbed the camera to pull it in for a closeup of your dick."

His gaze flicked to me again before returning resolutely to the wall.

"It was pretty funny the way you humped that bag of red ones." I dropped my hands to my lap and did some pelvic thrusts, half-closing my eyes and grunting, "Gummi. Gummi. Oh baby..."

A muscle twitched in Grandin's cheek.

I leaned down to peek under the table at his crotch. "Wow, you're getting a hard-on just thinking about it. Those red ones must be really something."

"I am not!" he barked. "And you don't have a video, because it never happened."

"Sure it did. But the red Gummi Bears must not be as special to you as..." I dropped my voice to a seductive singsong. "...the *yellow* ones." Resuming my normal tone, I went on, "That was some sick shit you did with them. Literally. How long did it take you to wash the yellow goo off your ass when you were done?"

Grandin said nothing, but the muscle jumped in his cheek again.

Leaning forward, I whispered, "But even that wasn't as sick as what you did next. You're gonna be famous when *that* hits the internet."

"THERE'S NO VIDEO!" Grandin's sudden bellow and jerk at his shackles made me rock back in the chair despite the knowledge that he couldn't get to me.

Giving him a slow smile, I purred, "Oh, you're so wrong.

Do you know how long it takes to fake a porn video? Any recreational hacker worth his salt can do it overnight. And a true professional? Ha. By now you've got a whole series. You're the Great Gummi-Fucker. Just wait 'til you see the episode where you lick up your own-"

"Kelly!" Holt's sudden bark made me twitch as he strode through the door.

"Damn, don't startle me like that," I complained.

"What the hell are you doing?" he demanded, but under his scowling brow I spotted the devilish glint in his eyes.

"Nothing." I gave him an innocent look.

"You're supposed to be questioning the prisoner."

I leaned back in my chair with a dismissive wave. "Fuck him. I don't want him to talk. If he does, we'll have to keep him here; and we don't have the death penalty. But in a few more hours the FBI will come for him, and then I'll get to watch him fry in the electric chair."

"Huh." Holt leaned a shoulder against the wall, crossing his arms as if in thought. "I think they use a lethal injection in most states."

"That's okay. I hear it can be pretty slow and painful."

"Yep," Holt agreed. "I heard about this one guy that took more than an hour to die; and they'd screwed up the anaesthetic, too, so he felt every second of the poison burning inside him."

I shrugged. "That'll be fun to watch. But not as much fun as the videos. Whichever prison he ends up in, I'll make sure those videos get there first. The other prisoners are gonna love the Great Gummi-Fucker to *death*." I gave Grandin a wolfish grin.

Grandin slumped in his chair. "Okay, fine, you can cut the crap. I just needed some time to think things through, and The Mouth there..." He shot a glare at Holt. "...wouldn't shut up long enough so I could hear myself think."

"So who's your contact?" Holt demanded.

Grandin sat back with a smile. "Not so fast, Mouth. First you cut me a deal."

Holt snorted. "I don't deal."

"Then I don't talk."

"Suit yourself," Holt snapped. "Come on, Kelly. I want to see those videos."

"You're going to laugh your ass off," I said as I rose. "The look on his face is just priceless while he's fucking those red ones."

Holt laughed as we exited the room, closing the door behind us.

Out in the hallway, I muttered, "You know we'll likely have to negotiate with him."

"Probably, but let him sweat a bit first. We can't cut a deal without Stemp's say-so anyway."

"Well, at least he's talking now."

Holt grinned. "Yeah. Are we good or what? Boo-yah!" He held out his fist for a fist-bump, which I reciprocated. As he lowered his hand he pulled his brows into a mock frown. "But seriously, Kelly. The Great Gummi-Fucker? Lame."

I smirked. "It was the best I could do on short notice. But it's okay. The only thing worse than having the world know you perform unnatural acts with Gummi Bears is having the world know you perform unnatural acts with Gummi Bears *and* you've chosen the lamest nickname ever."

Holt eyed me, grinning. "You're one sick puppy, you know that?"

"Thank you." I sketched a bow.

He turned to face the guard's open-mouthed expression.

"Watch the prisoner. We'll be back." Turning back to me, he said, "Come on, let's go report to Stemp." As we walked down the corridor, Holt added, "You didn't actually have time to fake any porn videos, did you?"

"No." I considered for a moment. "But I know a guy who's tapped into some major kink. I could probably get some pretty fast. Videos," I added hurriedly before Holt could misconstrue my meaning. "Get some videos. Not 'get some'. I wouldn't touch this guy with a ten-foot rubber-coated pole boiled in antiseptic."

Holt's lip curled. "Nice. Anyhow, I figured you'd be getting yours from Kane. Or that Hellhound guy that was all over you. You doing him, too?"

"None of your business." Hoping I wouldn't blush, I held my head high and stared straight ahead.

"You're blushing." Holt let out an incredulous laugh. "Well, shit. Never thought Kane would be pussywhipped enough to share his main squeeze with another guy, but what the hell; I learn something new every day."

Damn my telltale redhead's skin. My cheeks burned.

I kept my gaze trained forward. "You're such a disgusting prick. I'm not going to respond to any of that."

"No need. Your face says it all." He nudged me with a lascivious elbow. "Hey, Kelly, if the two of them can't keep you satisfied, I can-"

I spun, flinging out my palm in a 'stop' gesture only millimetres from his face. "Now you're over the line."

Holt jerked to a halt and backpedalled a step. "Sorry."

I waited for the next gibe that would force me to rip out his tongue and strangle him with it, but he said nothing. We stood staring at each other from close range.

After a moment, I said, "Okay, then."

We walked up the stairs to the time delay chamber in silence.

CHAPTER 3

Inside the hushed confines of the time-delay chamber, Holt spoke again. "I *am* sorry, Kelly. I didn't mean to push it that far. I know I can be an asshole sometimes, but..." He grimaced. "...I start joking around with you and forget you're not just one of the guys."

Deadpan, I said, "So you're saying you hit on all the guys?"

At the sight of his popeyed expression, I couldn't suppress a snicker.

"No, I don't hit on guys, for fucksakes!" Holt scowled, but I could see the worried sincerity in his eyes. "I'm just saying I didn't mean to-"

"Forget it," I interrupted. "We're good. But you can stop being an asshole any time. Sooner would be better."

He snorted. "Easy for you to say. Being an asshole is my life's work." We shared a wry grin as the chamber door opened into the main floor reception area.

When we arrived outside Stemp's office, the door was closed.

I peeked through the sidelight. "He's gone."

"Huh. I can't believe the guy actually takes a piss every now and then like a normal human being."

I glanced behind us, expecting Stemp to materialize with his usual impeccable timing, but the corridor remained empty.

"Maybe he left for the day," I suggested.

"Stemp?" Holt gave me an 'are-you-kidding?' look. "The guy's a robot. The only reason he ever goes home is so we don't catch him plugging himself into the wall and going into hibernation mode until work starts again."

Another glance down the hallway assured me that Stemp wasn't returning from the men's room.

"It's Sunday, and his parents are in town for a visit," I said. "He might have gone home. I'll check with the security desk."

As I stepped into the nearby conference room to use the phone, Holt snorted. "Parents? You mean those hippy-dippy nutcases that call him 'Cosmic River Stone'? No way those are his real parents. He was created by some unholy union between a snake and a cyborg."

"Lay off, would you?" I shot Holt a frown, then transferred my attention to the phone as the security guard picked up.

"Hi, Leo, it's Aydan," I greeted him. "Has Stemp left for the day?"

"He's just signing out. Do you need him?"

"Oh. Um..."

Damn, for once in his life Stemp was trying to take some time off. I hated to spoil that for him...

"Never mind." Leo's voice interrupted my deliberations. "He's already on his way back to his office. He'll be there in a minute."

I sighed. "Thanks. 'Bye."

"He's on his way up," I told Holt.

We waited in silence for several minutes.

"What the hell's taking him?" Holt asked, but before I could reply Stemp appeared at the top of the stairs.

His gaze sharpened as he strode down the deserted corridor. "Developments?" he asked as he unlocked his office and motioned us inside.

"Yep," Holt said smugly as Stemp closed the door behind him. "Grandin's ready to talk."

"Well done, Kelly," Stemp said.

A muscle ticked in Holt's jaw and I hurriedly corrected, "Greg and I tag-teamed him. Now he wants to negotiate."

"Excellent."

"I told him we won't deal," Holt said. "I figured we can let him sweat over that for a while."

Stemp lifted one shoulder in a fractional shrug. "Don't take too long. Let me know when you've negotiated a deal that satisfies you and I'll pitch it to the chain of command. You'll also head up the investigation into who paid him to capture Kelly. Dismissed."

Holt drew himself up, his ego visibly inflating along with his chest. "On it." He strode out of the office, a rock-jawed steely-eyed action hero trailing an invisible cape blazoned with 'Holt The Magnificent'.

Somehow I managed not to groan. "Will I be assisting Holt?" I asked without much hope.

"No."

Feeling inexplicably slighted, I blurted, "Why not?"

A moment later I bit my tongue. What the hell was wrong with me? I should be thrilled that Holt was handling it.

"You have yet to file your reports from your last mission. You also have your own assignments, which will require all your time; and which are less likely to be dangerous." Stemp gave me an incisive look. "When you have completed your post-incident psych evaluation, I will re-evaluate your status."

"Holt hasn't done his psych evaluation yet, either," I protested, reasonably secure in guessing that he wouldn't have had time.

"Holt is not required to undergo post-incident evaluation. He experienced no violence or fatalities." Stemp's disturbing amber gaze dissected me. "You did."

"It wasn't a big deal..." I trailed off in the face of his implacable expression and sighed. "Okay, I'll go and do my report."

"And make your appointment with Dr. Rawling," Stemp prompted. "And, after you obtain your psych clearance, visit your mother."

Gritting my teeth, I nodded. "Yes, I'll see Dr. Rawling and visit my..." I hissed out a breath. "Can we please just call her Nora? Every time I hear the word 'mother' I want to punch somebody. And I won't call her Nola Kelly, either. She chose 'Nora Taylor' thirty years ago, so she can have it."

"Very well. Nora it is," Stemp agreed. "And you should discuss your conflicted feelings about her with Dr. Rawling."

"Not until I've finished my investigation. When I know what really happened, I'll know how I really feel." Silently congratulating myself on a clever evasion, I eased a step toward the door. "Well, I'd better get to work on that report."

"One more thing." Stemp's voice halted me.

God, now what?

He went on, "I received a call from the Silverside Hospital as I was leaving the security desk, which was why I was delayed. Agent Rand wants to see you."

"He's still in the hospital?"

"Yes. He didn't divulge why he wanted you to come, but he said it was a professional matter." Humour glinted in Stemp's eyes. "Although with the amorous Agent Rand, the distinction between professional and personal may be subtle if not completely nonexistent."

I grinned. "True. I don't think Ian even has a purely professional mode; but if his concussion is bad enough to keep him in the hospital, he's probably not feeling very frisky."

Stemp nodded. "One last thing. My parents have vacated your home and will be staying with me for the remainder of their visit. They asked me to convey their thanks to you, along with this." He handed over the chunky wristwatch that doubled as the monitoring receiver for my farm's security system.

"Thanks." I strapped it onto my wrist.

"They also hoped that you might have time for a social visit later. However, they do understand how busy you are..." He trailed off as though hoping I'd agree that I was much too busy to subject us both to any awkward social interaction.

"I'd love to," I said sincerely. "I'll call your mom and set something up after I've talked to Ian and, um... Nora."

"Very well," Stemp said. I was trying to decide whether he was pleased or annoyed when he added, "Dismissed."

In my office, I slumped in front of my computer and poked at the keys for a few minutes but my eyes kept falling closed. After my third head-bob, I abandoned the half-finished report.

It would keep. There was nothing that I hadn't already reported verbally; and Ian was waiting. Maybe he had some important intel that I could use as an excuse to postpone my visit to Dr. Rawling.

Or maybe I should go and see Rawling right away. Get it over with, get my psych clearance, and see Nora right afterward. The sooner I finished investigating her, the sooner I'd know whether she was really my loving mother who had sacrificed everything for me, or just a cold-hearted lying cheating bitch who also happened to be my mother.

My stomach twisted.

Right. Ian first, then. I logged off the computer and headed for the door.

At the hospital, I cleared the retinal scan and let myself into the secured wing. As I strolled down the hall, an elfin brunette clad in pink scrubs waved to me from behind the nurse's station.

"Hey, Aydan, it's great to see you!" she chirped with a sparkling smile.

"Hi, Linda." I eyed her perkiness with envy. "You look a lot more wide awake than your other half."

She giggled. "Uh-oh. Did you go by the house and wake him up?"

"No, we got called to a nine o'clock meeting. He could barely keep his eyes open."

"Ohmigosh, poor Spider." Her amused smile belied her words. "Last night was his once-a-month World of Warcraft marathon with the guys. He was just crawling into the house when I was leaving for my shift."

I chuckled. "Stemp sent out the meeting request at six AM. Spider must have figured it wasn't worth going to bed."

Linda shook her head, her eyes soft. "No, he never comes home on World of Warcraft nights until he knows I'll be out of bed and he won't disturb me. He's such a sweetie."

Her glow of happiness put a smile on my face. "He really is," I agreed. "Anyhow, I know you're busy. I'm just here to see Ian."

"Oh, sure. He's two doors down." She pointed, lowering her voice to a confidential murmur. "He's been very restless. Maybe it would help if you sat with him a while." Her brow furrowed. "I feel sorry for him, suffering and alone here in a strange country."

I grinned. "Don't feel too sorry for him. Canada isn't that strange compared to the UK, and he's an expert at manipulating other people's feelings. He'll be milking it for all he's worth with you."

Her brows drew together. "Aydan, he's in pain! The poor man has thirty-one stitches in his scalp, and a terrible concussion."

Holding up a conciliatory hand, I backed away. "Okay, okay, I'll be nice to him." Her indignant nod of approval made me smile and add, "This is why you're such a good nurse."

Her cheeks went pink as she beamed at me. "Thanks!" A soft chime sounded and she added, "Oh, gotta go!"

She hurried off toward another room, and I headed for the half-open door she had indicated earlier.

When I poked my head into the room, Ian's gaze snapped to me. Even in the dimness of the curtained room, I was struck anew by his attractiveness as he lay on his side facing the door. Green eyes rimmed with thick dark lashes, chiselled features, broad shoulders and muscular physique...

"Storm," he murmured. "You came. Thank you."

"I thought we agreed you weren't going to call me that," I chided as I slipped into the room and shut the door behind me.

He made a mute 'what does it matter?' gesture and let his hand drop back to the bed as though it had taken all his strength to raise it.

Approaching the bed, I studied him with concern. Despite the handsomeness that had momentarily distracted me, his face was unusually pale. Hard lines of pain crimped his mouth, and his beautiful eyes were dark-shadowed.

"You look like hell," I said.

"I feel like hell." He eased his head cautiously on the pillow. "I'm glad you're here. I can't..." He squeezed his eyes closed. "I can't... *rest* here, never knowing who's going to come through that door. They've taken my weapon and I feel..." He opened those gorgeous green eyes again, sucking my heart in. "...helpless. Naked."

Fighting the urge to put my arms around him and comfort him, I leaned close and whispered, "Bad news. You *are* naked." As his eyes widened, I added, "Under your gown and blanket."

"Oh, very funny," he grumbled, but a smile twitched his mouth. He sobered. "Seriously, though... would you please sit..." He cocked a thumb behind him. "Over there? I've been lying on this side for hours because I can't bear to turn my back to the door, and my shoulder feels as though it's been worked over by a gang of dockers. If you'll watch the door for me, I can turn over for a while."

My heart clenched with sympathy. "Of course."

As I rounded the bed and pulled up a chair facing the door, Ian closed his eyes and eased onto his back, moving his head in small increments. At last he completed the rotation onto his right side with his back to the door, and a half-sigh-half-moan escaped him as his body settled. His eyes stayed closed.

"So much better," he murmured. "Just a moment 'til the vertigo subsides..." Soon his eyes opened and he inquired anxiously, "You're armed, aren't you?"

"Yes, but you're safe here in the secured wing. Nobody can get to you in here."

"I've heard that before." He gave me a pained smile, his pale face vulnerable against the white pillowcase. "You'll excuse me if I don't find it as comforting as you might hope."

"I know what you mean. I'd feel the same if I were you." Ignoring the cynical suspicion that he was only playing me, I reached over and stroked his arm. "Just relax. I've got your back."

"Oh, that's heavenly. Thank you." His eyelids sank closed again. As I withdrew my hand, he added, "Please don't stop."

Okay, he was definitely playing me.

But despite that knowledge, I shuffled my chair a bit closer and stroked his arm some more. I'd seen the patchwork of stitches on the back of his head, and if his concussion was severe enough to keep him hospitalized, he must have a terrible headache. And with the vertigo he'd already mentioned, he was surely suffering nausea. All because he'd helped Holt save my ass.

Ian's breathing slowed and deepened, his body relaxing while my palm made gentle passes up and down his arm. His skin was hot under my hand, and I wondered if he had a fever. That would be bad.

"Storm..." he whispered.

Unsure whether he was awake or asleep, I leaned in and

murmured, "It's okay, I'm here. You're safe."

The arm I had been stroking hooked around my neck, drawing my face down to his as his eyes popped open.

"You faker!" I growled. "I *knew* you were playing me!"

As I tried to sit up, his arm tightened. "Please," he whispered urgently.

I froze, studying him. This wasn't his usual lighthearted flirting.

Letting him draw my lips close to his, I whispered, "What?"

"Is this room bugged?"

"It shouldn't be, but I can double-check." I unzipped my waist pouch and pressed the activation button on the bug detector I always carried. "All clear," I announced when the green light shone.

"Good." He closed his eyes again, apparently fighting another wave of pain and vertigo. "I didn't tell you everything before... about Nora Taylor," he whispered. "She could be dangerous. And if she knows I'm suspicious of her, she might try to bump me off."

Cold fear doused my heart.

A moment later the soft click of his door jerked me upright, my Glock already in my hand.

CHAPTER 4

"Is... everything okay...?" Linda stared wide-eyed from the doorway, frozen with a tray of pills in her hand.

I let out a breath and holstered my weapon. "Fine. Sorry."

"What's going on?" She moved cautiously into the room. "Ian, are you all right?"

"Fine," he mumbled. "We were just snogging. You took us by surprise."

"Oh..." Colour suffused her face. "I just... brought your pain and nausea medication... I didn't mean to..." She gave me a flustered glance before pulling herself together and approaching the bed. "I'll give you some privacy in a minute," she said firmly. "But I need to check your vital signs now."

After recording his temperature, pulse rate, and blood pressure, Linda handed over his medication. As she turned toward the door I stopped her and spoke quietly. "Don't let anybody come into Ian's room without clearing them with me first, okay?"

She stepped back, eyes widening. "Is he in danger? Is that why you had your gun drawn?"

"I don't know, and I don't want to find out the hard way.

How well do you know the staff here?"

"Really well. We've all worked here for years."

"Including the cleaning people and support staff?" I probed. "Delivery people? Food services?"

Linda frowned. "Nobody gets in here unless they have a security clearance. We prepare the food and drink ourselves to make sure nobody tampers with it. Support staff and delivery people are always escorted by a security guard, and the guard stays with them every second they're inside the security perimeter. Even the cleaners are watched by a guard the whole time they're here. I literally know every person who has access to this area. It's part of my job."

"Did you hear that, Ian?" I asked. "You're safe here."

A noncommittal mumble came from the bed, and I turned back to Linda. "Still, I don't want anyone but Stemp or Holt in here without my permission. And I mean *nobody* else, not even if they have a security clearance. Can you do that?"

"Yes, I'll put a note in the system."

"And can you give Ian's gun back to him?"

Linda's brow furrowed. "Not without authorization from Director Stemp or General Briggs. But if you're worried, we could put a guard outside his door."

"Yes, let's do that. Thanks."

"You're welcome." She hurried out, still frowning.

I closed the door behind her and rounded the bed to face Ian again, fists on hips. "Snogging?" I demanded.

"Of course." He gave me a passionate look from under suggestively drooping eyelids. "And who could blame you for mixing a little pleasure with business? I'm irresistible."

Dropping into the chair, I snorted. "Don't flatter yourself, pretty-boy."

"You're a cruel woman. I'm crushed." He gave me a ghost of his usual grin before sobering and reaching out a beseeching hand. "Won't you please come closer so I don't have to crane my neck to see you?" As I hitched my chair toward the bed he gestured me closer still.

When I leaned in, he snagged my neck and drew me down until we were face to face again. "I'm sorry if my cover story gets you in trouble," he whispered. "But even though there may not be an electronic bug, I don't want to take a chance that someone might be using a passive listening system."

"Okay, but I can't twist over the chair arm like this. I'll be crippled in ten seconds or less." Slipping out from under his embrace, I straightened from my awkward position with a breath of relief.

A quick survey of the situation convinced me that hospital beds are not designed for the sharing of confidences. My options were to kneel on the hard floor beside the bed, lean over from the chair and risk walking like Quasimodo for the rest of my life, or...

"Move over, Mr. Irresistible," I said.

Smiling, Ian scooted backward with an alacrity that made me suspect his earlier suffering-hero performance. As I stretched out cautiously on the narrow bed facing him, he tucked his arm over my waist and pulled our hips into contact.

"That had better be your Walther PPK in your pocket," I warned.

His smiling lips were nearly on mine. "I already told you they confiscated it. But I do happen to have a particularly large... gun."

"Uh-huh." I shifted backward, hovering my butt

precariously over the edge of the bed. "And I've heard you'll shoot anything that moves, so I'm sure you'll understand if I keep my distance. What did you want to talk about?"

"I'm deeply wounded by your mistrust." He gave me a look that was probably supposed to be beseeching; or maybe seductive. It was hard to tell when our faces were so close together that all I could see was a cross-eyed blur.

"My heart pumps purple piss for you." I eased a bit farther away, then had to clutch ignominiously at him when I almost fell off the bed.

"See? Irresistible," Ian said with satisfaction as he pulled me close again.

"You wish, Rand," I growled, trying to ignore the firm pressure of his body against mine. And the way his fingertips were tracing small exquisite circles on my lower back.

And his minty-fresh breath. And the hint of spicy aftershave wafting off his smoothly-shaven cheek...

Bedridden and barely able to move, my ass. The bastard had been well enough to shave and brush his teeth. He'd been playing me all along.

Unsurprised, I added, "You have three seconds to give me some intel that will keep me from twisting Walther and the boys into a half-hitch."

"Storm, how could you even-"

"Three," I interrupted. "Two."

"All right." Ian sighed and lowered his voice to a ghost of a whisper again. "You recall that I said Nora Taylor has been employed with MI5 since 1983..." He hesitated with a wry quirk of his lips. "...which I now know was about a year and half after she faked her death in a fiery car crash so that she could leave Canada without anyone knowing."

"Don't remind me," I muttered.

"Anyway, I told you her employment records were complete and unremarkable, which was true."

"But...?" I prompted.

"But there's something that's been nagging at me. Not enough to make accusations; but just... a feeling. You know how you get a hunch sometimes for no apparent reason?"

I was far too comfortable in the warmth of his arms. His fingertips were still making those soft circles on my back. My eyelids dipped, my body melting against him.

Shaking myself awake, I snapped, "Yeah, I know what you mean. Stop stalling and tell me what you suspect."

"But you're exhausted," Ian soothed, brushing a kiss over my lips as his hand curled around the back of my neck to coax me closer. "Just relax and have a lovely little rest, nice and safe here with-"

"Three!" I snapped. "Two!"

"Oh, fine." He sighed and eased himself into a more comfortable position, his hand resting on my shoulder, fingertips skimming the side of my neck in the lightest of caresses.

I considered pulling away again, but he lowered his voice to a whisper, making me strain to hear him.

"When I checked MI5's records, I discovered that there had been a confidential investigation into Nora last year, at the behest of your Department. Since they provided only sketchy details as to their concerns, we provided a rather noncommittal clearance in return. Would you care to tell me the real reason for that investigation?"

"Um..." I pondered for a moment. What could I tell him that wasn't classified? "Her husband was involved in espionage and treason."

"Yes, that's what your Department told us," Ian said patiently. "What was the real reason, and how does it connect to you personally?"

"Well, she's my... mother." I couldn't quite prevent my lip from curling when I said the m-word. "And she dumped my dad for that treasonous asshole Sam Kraus."

And she had abandoned me. I had been seventeen, not exactly a child; but still not ready to lose my mother.

Ian chuckled softly. "But you still haven't answered my question. Nora said you had worked with Dr. Kraus. Perhaps 'worked with' was a polite euphemism for 'investigated', or maybe you were actually working together before he showed his true colours..." He hesitated before going on thoughtfully, "...and something he did made you investigate him and discover he was a spy." His lips firmed in a satisfied smile. "Yes, that fits." He widened his eyes at me. "Am I right?"

"Yes," I said reluctantly.

"Oh, very good." Ian considered for a few more moments. "So Dr. Kraus was involved in classified research and development."

"Nora told you that days ago," I pointed out. "You're wasting time. Tell me why you think Nora might be dangerous."

He ignored the question. "You're not a researcher, are you?"

"No."

"So if you were working with Dr. Kraus, it was because he was studying you."

Shit.

I hid the uptick of my pulse in a cool tone. "Hardly. I'm just an agent. I was his bodyguard."

Ian gave me one of his flirtatious smiles. "It's always such a pleasure to work with you. You're an excellent liar. I would have believed you if not for my lie detector here." He tapped gently on the side of my neck where his fingertips had been caressing the skin over my carotid artery. "Your heart rate spiked when I hit on the truth."

Shit, I had *known* I couldn't trust him. And I had let him get the better of me anyway. Idiot.

I batted my eyes and gave my hips a seductive little wiggle against him. "Maybe there was another reason for my pounding pulse."

His smile widened. "Oh, lovely. I'd like to continue that conversation when the slightest movement of my head doesn't make me feel like vomiting."

I pulled away a few inches, trying to bring his face into focus. "Good Lord, I've never known you to turn down a chance like that. You really are in rough shape."

"I feel like death," he admitted. "But don't think you'll be able to distract me. So Dr. Kraus was studying you. Nora said his work was classified. Ergo, *you* are classified, which makes you very important to someone. Probably several someones; hence Grandin's attempt to abduct you and sell you to the highest bidder." He smiled. "I won't ask if I'm right. I know I am; and you wouldn't tell me the truth anyway."

I shrugged, holding onto my poker face despite the obvious futility. "Nice try; but Grandin's buyer wanted me because of my cover as an arms dealer. And you're still wasting my time. Last chance. In ten words or less, why would Nora want to kill you?"

"She wouldn't, unless she knew my suspicions."

Clenching my teeth, I braced both hands on his chest. "If

you don't tell me what you found out about Nora *right now*," I gritted, "I'm going to shove you off this bed and laugh when you hit your head and bust open your stitches and puke your fucking guts out."

"All right, all right!" He clutched my arms as if to keep himself from falling in case I carried out my spurious threat. "Howard Coleman might not have died of natural causes." He eyed me as though that should mean something.

At the end of my patience, I snapped, "Who the *hell* is Howard Co-" Realization struck. I finished, "...oh. MI5's former Weapons Director. The guy Nora replaced."

"Yes."

"Hang on." I arched backward in a useless attempt to get far enough away that my aching eyes could focus on his face. "When we talked about him before, you said he had retired."

Ian shrugged easily. "Death does tend to enforce one's retirement."

"You lying asshole," I said without venom. "Okay, so Howard Coleman died. Were you also lying when you said he was in his late seventies?"

"No, he was nearly seventy-eight; but he was as hale and hearty as you and me when he died of a sudden heart attack."

Irritation made me forget to whisper. "Big deal. A heart attack at seventy-eight isn't exactly a shocker. And I'm sure they did an autopsy and found everything normal, or there would have been an investigation. You'll have to do better than that."

"Shhh. All true," Ian agreed almost inaudibly, forcing me to lean closer again to hear him. "But you didn't know Howard Coleman. He was a marathon runner, and he even did ultra-marathons. He always placed first in his age class, and he often beat the times of the winners in the younger classes. The man was indestructible."

"Athlete or not, anybody can have an unexpected heart attack," I argued. "And an elderly man training for an ultra-marathon, well..."

"That's what the medical examiner said, but Howard hadn't been pushing himself when he died. And the timing has been niggling at me. Nora made her annual suggestion to the chain of command that they should put Coleman out to pasture; they disagreed as usual; and then, bang, he died. I didn't have time to investigate before we left the UK, but when I put it together with what I know now..." He trailed off, frowning.

I sighed and let my head fall back on the pillow. "So let me get this straight. After pissing around for..." I consulted my wristwatch. "...twenty minutes; lying to me; coaxing me into your bed; kissing and feeling me up... you finally get around to telling me that you fear for your life because an elderly man died of a heart attack. You're so full of shit." I disengaged myself from his arms and got off the bed to glare down at him.

"That's not it at all," he protested. "I needed some information from you in order to process my thoughts; and thank you for sharing it, however unintentionally you might have done so..."

I flipped him my middle finger, but he went on without acknowledging the gesture. "...and with what I know now..." He dropped his voice to a whisper, making me lean close to hear him again, dammit. "I realize that Howard Coleman was almost certainly murdered. Due to his age, the autopsy was likely cursory at best. And I know of at least one undetectable drug that can cause a heart attack a few hours after it's been administered, when the victim exerts himself only slightly more than usual."

A deluge of memories froze me to the spot.

My second husband's still-warm body slack in my arms. My frantic call to 911; the desperate efforts of the paramedics to revive a healthy athletic man who'd suffered a sudden fatal heart attack...

"...Storm? Storm! What is it? What's wrong?"

Ian's urgent voice penetrated my mind and I shook off my paralysis. "Nothing. Just thinking." My voice came out in a dry croak.

"You look as though you just saw a ghost." He peered up at me with concern.

"I did." Ignoring his worried expression, I patted him absently on the shoulder. "I have to check on some things. Don't worry, you're safe here; and I've assigned a guard to your room."

I headed for the door.

"Storm, wait-aagh-oh-*Lord!*"

I spun in time to see him half-turned to face me, his head clutched in both hands while sweat sprang out on his bone-white face.

"*Shit!*" I sprang toward him shouting, "LINDA! COME QUICK!"

CHAPTER 5

"Not so loud..." Ian moaned. He gulped, his eyes squeezed shut and face contorted.

The hospital room door burst open. "What happened?" Linda demanded as she hurried to the bed. "Did he have a seizure?"

"I don't know; I didn't see..." I trailed off uselessly.

Fingers pressed to Ian's pulse, Linda snapped, "Ian, open your eyes. Don't move your head, but follow my finger with your eyes."

Index finger extended, she moved her free hand up and down, then side to side.

"I'm all right..." Ian ground out between clenched teeth as he obeyed. "Just turned... too fast." He gasped a couple of quick breaths, his pallor turning greenish. "Oh bugger it, not again..."

"Close your eyes," Linda advised. She whisked an empty disposable bowl off the nightstand and pressed it into his hands, then stroked his sweaty forehead, crooning reassurances. "You'll feel better soon. Just relax and breathe. Nice and slow. In... two... three... four... out... two... three... four..."

He followed her directions, clutching the bowl in a

white-knuckled grip.   After several tense moments he gradually relaxed, perspiration trickling down his face and darkening his hospital gown.

"Better..." he whispered, eyes still closed.

"Good. Just concentrate on your breathing. I'll get you a cool cloth." Linda shot me a meaningful frown. "Aydan has to go now."

"No, we're not finished..." Ian began.

Linda widened her eyes fiercely at me.

"Sorry, Ian, I really do have to go," I said hurriedly. "Don't worry, you'll have a guard outside your door and you'll be safe. I'm going to take care of that thing we talked about, and I'll come back later."

Linda seized my arm and propelled me out into the hallway almost before I had finished speaking. "Wait here," she snapped, and went back into the room.

Loitering awkwardly, I listened to the sound of running water and the soft murmur of Linda's voice as she presumably applied the cool cloth she'd promised.

A few minutes later she stepped back out into the hallway, swinging Ian's door shut behind her. "Stay," she said, pointing to the floor in front of my feet as though I was a disobedient puppy. Then she hurried to collar the security guard who was striding down the hall toward us. As soon as he took his place beside Ian's door, Linda strode back to me and took my arm again, her face tight.

She ushered me down the hall without speaking, turning us into a supply room just inside the exit.

"What were you thinking?" she demanded. "He has a concussion! You were supposed to calm him down, not make out with him!"

Half amused and half impressed by her fierce

protectiveness, I leaned down to speak softly so we wouldn't be overheard. "We weren't making out. He had some important classified intel, and even though I'd checked for electronic bugs, he didn't want to take a chance on being overheard by a passive listening device."

"Oh, you... *agents!*" Linda threw up her hands, her expression lightening. "So you got into bed with him as a cover story?"

I blinked. "How did you know I was in bed with him? Do you have surveillance in the room?"

"Yes, but it wasn't active. I saw a smear of dirt from your boots on the foot of the bed, and two dents in the pillow. And one dent had one of your long red hairs in it." She grinned. "Never try to fool a nurse."

"I would never dare. You had me shaking in my dirty boots."

"Good." Her smile faded. "Are you going to have to do that again? It really isn't good for him. He shouldn't be overtaxing himself by trying to think too much; and certainly not by..." Her lips quirked. "...snogging."

"That was just his wishful thinking," I grumbled. "I had nothing to do with it."

Linda sighed, her eyes going dreamy. "You live such an exciting life. Handsome agents wanting to kiss you..."

I cut her off with a loud snort. "I'll take a boring life any day, thanks. And that handsome agent is just a cheap man-whore looking for his next lay."

"Ohmigosh, Aydan." She laid a hand protectively over her heart, making big sorrowful eyes up at me. "Way to kill my fantasies." She hesitated. "Is... Is that really true...?"

I took pity on her. "That's only what I've heard. Ian's an incorrigible flirt, but I don't know how often he follows through." I didn't mention that the times he'd rounded third base with me, he'd seemed pretty eager to score a home run. "It might be just another cover story. But I wouldn't get too close to him if I were you."

Linda drew back, frowning. "I wouldn't! I love Spider with all my heart and soul and I'd never cheat. I just... I guess... I know how many sacrifices agents make, and I wanted him to be... you know, a perfect hero." Her cheeks went pink. "Spider and I both... we think you're all heroes, every one of you."

It was my turn to blush. "Thanks, Linda. That means a lot to me. And I know you'd never cheat on Spider; I was only teasing."

"So you really are looking into something for Ian? You weren't just trying to distract me from the two of you making out?"

Ian's words came back to me in sobering rush, and I sighed. "Yeah, I have to do some digging. I'd better get going. If Ian asks, tell him I'm investigating and I'll let him know if I uncover anything new. And keep that guard on his door."

"I will."

When I stepped out of the hospital, the glare of sunshine on snow nearly blinded me. Squinting, I hurried to my car and slid in. The temperature sensor reported -15C and I let out a breath of relief. Finally the weather was warming up. Maybe we'd even get a chinook thaw.

Pulling out a secured phone, I punched the speed dial. As usual, it rang only once before a crisp voice snapped, "Stemp."

"Hi, it's Aydan. Ian suspects Nora might have murdered the Weapons Director she replaced. I put a visitor restriction on Ian's room and posted a guard outside his door because he's afraid that if she finds out he suspects her, she might try to kill him, too."

"Evidence?"

"None. Just a hunch."

"But you are taking precautions nonetheless?"

I sighed. "I don't dare ignore it. Howard Coleman was elderly, but he was an athlete who'd just finished a marathon the previous week. If he'd been due for a heart attack, he should have had it while he was racing. But if Nora slipped him the same drug that Kane used to kill my second husband..." I trailed off, imagining Nora smiling her sweet motherly smile while she trickled the lethal poison into poor Howard Coleman's food.

Uncharacteristically, Stemp hesitated before replying, and I wondered if he felt guilty about issuing the kill order for my husband.

Apparently not. When he spoke again it was with his usual decisiveness. "I will contact Nora and tell her that unforeseen circumstances will prevent you from meeting with her today, and that you will speak with her on the telephone instead. I don't want to place you in a potentially hazardous situation until Dr. Rawling clears you for full active duty."

Despite my relief at avoiding Nora for another day, my pride stung. Holt would never let me hear the end of it if he found out Stemp didn't think I could hold my own against a petite seventy-two-year-old woman.

"I'm fine," I argued. "You don't need to coddle me; and anyway, Ian's the one who's potentially in danger from her, not me. She *loves* me. She wants to be my *darling Mommy*." The last two sentences came out in a bitter snarl despite my effort to maintain a dispassionate tone.

"I am not coddling you; I am merely acting within the parameters laid out by our chain of command," Stemp replied coolly. "How much sleep did you get last night?"

"Uh..."

A late night at my best friend's wedding, followed by a brief but extremely satisfying interlude in Hellhound's bed before I'd finally fallen into a sodden slumber; and Stemp's text had dragged me rudely awake at six AM...

"...five hours," I mumbled, padding the truth by an hour or so. "Give or take."

"So you have had inadequate sleep on top of the trauma and fatigue from your previous mission, plus the aftereffects of being drugged with ketamine," Stemp said. "Until Dr. Rawling clears you for a potentially hazardous mission, you will avoid Nora. He will also evaluate your fitness to head the investigation into Nora. If your objectivity is compromised by your personal feelings, perhaps Holt would be a better choice."

Fuck, I was *not* going to give Holt another chance to play Superman.

"Holt is a f-" I bit off my incipient epithet and substituted, "...awfully busy. And like you said earlier, I'm Nora's daughter so I'm the best choice to get close to her."

And to send the conniving old bag straight to jail as soon as I discovered what game she was playing.

Idiot hope raised its head and wagged its tail like a pathetically eager puppy. Maybe I'd discover that Nora had been telling the truth all along. Maybe I'd get my mother back.

Somehow I managed not to scoff audibly. And maybe pigs would fly.

Assuming a brisk tone to hide my reluctance, I added, "I'll make an appointment with Dr. Rawling as soon as he can see me. I'm sure everything will be fine."

"Very well. Until then, concentrate on recruiting Kane. There should be no danger involved in that. Keep me posted."

He hung up, and I let the phone drift down from my ear as my heart sank at the same pace.

I wouldn't be in physical danger with Kane, but there would be more than enough emotional danger.

Dammit.

Flopping back in the driver's seat, I stared at the roof liner. Could I lie? Tell Stemp I'd tried to call Kane but couldn't reach him and didn't want to leave a voicemail on such a delicate subject?

Or would Stemp check my call records and find out I'd lied? I wouldn't put it past the suspicious bastard to check up on me.

Then again, if I hadn't been stupid enough to make a big stink about the assignment, he wouldn't have had anything to suspect.

Shit.

But if I did actually call Kane, even getting his voicemail wouldn't let me off the hook. As soon as he saw that he'd missed my call, he'd call back. Maybe I could call from one of my burner phones so he wouldn't recognize my number...

My waffling was interrupted by the vibration of my cell phone. A glance at the call display made me groan aloud. Kane.

"Oh, for f-" Biting off my reflexive profanity, I punched

the 'Talk' button and summoned a cheery tone. "Hi, John!"

"Good morning." His velvet baritone warmed me. "I hope I didn't wake you. I didn't know whether you conformed to Hellhound's sleep schedule or vice versa, but I thought it should be safe to call this close to noon."

I barked out a short laugh. "I wish. I'm not at Arnie's anymore, I'm in Silverside. I got a text at six AM telling me to be back here for a nine AM meeting."

"Ouch. I'm surprised the highway was open."

"Ministry of Transport opened it at five AM, the bastards. They could have at least kept it closed for a few more hours so I could have gotten some sleep."

"You should lodge a complaint," Kane joked. "How was your drive?"

"Shitty. The road was open, but it wasn't great."

"The highway reports say it's clear now." Kane hesitated. "Is it still all right for me to bring Daniel over so we can work on your Chevy this afternoon? Or are you assigned to another... project now?"

"Um..."

As far as I knew, I wasn't in any more danger than usual. It should be safe enough for Kane to bring Daniel. And if I talked to Kane in person, Stemp couldn't know whether I'd actually carried out my recruitment mission. And I could ask Kane about lethal untraceable drugs, too.

But was I ready to deal with a six-year-old? Or... shit. Was Daniel seven now? I didn't know when his birthday was...

I jerked my mind back to the conversation. "I'm not really on another project yet," I said slowly. "But... isn't it getting pretty late for you to leave Calgary? Even if the drive only takes the normal two hours, it'll be nearly two o'clock by the time you get here; and if you have to get Daniel home for bedtime, that doesn't leave much time for wrenching."

Kane chuckled. "We'll have lunch before we leave so it will probably be after two-thirty when we arrive. But a couple of hours in the garage will be more than enough. Seven-year-olds don't have a long attention span."

"Oh." My stomach clenched. "Right. Come if you want, then. Give me a call when you're about half an hour out, and I'll head home and meet you there."

"Great. See you then."

I disconnected and fell back in the seat.

No more leisurely hours of automotive tinkering, cold beer, and comfortable bullshitting. Daniel's wide eyes would notice my every gesture and avid ears would soak up any accidental profanity. And no matter how tidy and organized I kept it, my garage would never be child-safe. He would need constant supervision. Constant attention.

Tension gripped my shoulders at the thought.

Closing my eyes, I took a few calming breaths. Relax. Kane wasn't asking me to parent his son.

There was no commitment. No terrifying inescapable bond of need and duty...

My heart attempted to climb out of my chest and I patted it back into place with another long breath.

Not my child; not my responsibility.

If only I believed that.

Hands quivering on the wheel, I put the car in gear and headed for the saloon.

When I strode into Blue Eddy's, Eddy gave me a smile and wave from behind the bar. The gritty lowdown blues music slowed my still-pattering heart to match its earthy tempo, and my shoulders relaxed as I dropped into the chair at my usual table with my back to the wall.

The usual handful of hard-bitten elderly men were bellied up to the bar, imbibing in slow motion with their eyelids already at half-mast; and several well-dressed couples occupied tables, enjoying brunch on their way home from church. All the small-town Sunday regulars.

Including me. Stretching out my legs, I let the comfort sink into my bones.

"What can I get you, Aydan?" Eddy asked as he hurried over.

"I want a beer so much I can almost taste it, but I'm driving." I sighed. "Just water, I guess."

Eddy chuckled. "Well, if you *really* want a beer, you can always crash on my crappy couch upstairs and sleep it off before you drive."

Wincing at the memory, I shook my head. "Nope, as much as I appreciated your couch that time, I'd better not do it again." I gave him a grin. "If I get too comfortable here, you'll never get rid of me."

"I wouldn't mind." He shot an amused glance at the dead-eyed men propped on their barstools. "You're much prettier than the other regulars. Would you like some food?"

Unsure whether he was joking or actually complimenting me, I avoided the issue. "Are you waiting tables today as well as bartending? Is Darlene sick?"

"No, I gave her a paid vacation day." He shrugged as though it was something any employer would do. "She's a single mom, and Christmas is coming. She needs the time as much as she needs the money, and Sundays are never very busy anyway."

Impulsively, I reached over and squeezed his hand. "You're a good guy, Eddy."

He flushed and made a self-deprecating gesture. "No big deal. So what can I get you? The cook did a great job on the Hollandaise sauce today. It's her best Eggs Benedict ever."

"Sold." As he turned away, I gently snagged his sleeve and added, "Hey, I've got a bunch of meetings coming up this week. So far it looks as though I'll be okay for our usual Tuesday at eleven; but if things look like they might go sideways for me, could I come in some other time?"

"Sure, whatever works for you. My door's always open." He grinned. "A good bookkeeper is worth her weight in hamburgers."

I settled back smugly in my chair as he hurried away. Now I had an excuse if I needed to avoid anybody. Like Nora.

My satisfaction ebbed away, leaving an ache in my stomach. I couldn't waste time avoiding her. Ian's life might be on the line.

I blew out an unhappy sigh and dialled Dr. Rawling's number.

CHAPTER 6

A soothing male voice spoke on the telephone line. "Good afternoon, you've reached Dr. Henry Rawling."

Silence fell.

"...Hello?" he added.

"Oh! Shi... I mean jeez, sorry; I didn't expect you to be answering the phone on a Sunday afternoon. I was expecting your voicemail," I babbled. "Hi, it's Aydan."

I could hear the smile in his voice. "I normally don't answer the phone on Sundays, but Director Stemp said you would be calling."

"Oh. Right." Keeping my voice warm and friendly, I added, "Thank you for picking up. So I guess you know I'm looking for an appointment."

"Yes, and I'm taking the upcoming week off for Christmas vacation, so I'm glad we can do this today. Would two o'clock work?"

"Um... Actually, I'm expecting company at two-thirty..."

"Do you have time now?"

"N-Now...?" Overcoming my panicky impulse to evade and delay, I metaphorically yanked up my big-girl panties and added, "I'm having lunch right now, but I could meet you around twelve-thirty."

"That would be fine. I'll see you then."

He disconnected, and I fell back in my chair with a groan. Now I really needed a beer. Or three.

Instead, I sipped my water and pressed the speed dial for Hellhound's number.

After a couple of rings, his cheerful rasp tickled my ear. "Hey, darlin'. Did ya get to Silverside okay?"

"Yeah. I'm sorry I didn't call you earlier. It's been a busy morning."

"Is that good or bad? How'd your meetin' go?"

"The meeting went okay, I guess. We made some progress with, um..." I hesitated. Unsecured line. "...the guy we were interviewing." I sighed. "But I have to go and see Dr. Rawling this afternoon. God, I hate that."

"Yeah, I know, darlin', but it's for your own good." Hellhound hesitated. "Wish ya could trust some shrink enough to really talk to 'em. Not hold anythin' back."

I grunted. "Even if I wanted to, Rawling isn't the one. His goals aren't the same as mine. And it creeps me out knowing that the whole time he's sitting there smiling and nodding and acting like my best friend, he's trying to worm inside my brain and judge me. Doesn't that bug you, too?"

"Dunno. Never talked to him."

"*What?*" My yelp of outrage made Eddy glance over in concern, and I gave him an 'it's-okay' wave as I settled back in my chair and lowered my voice. "What the hell? Stemp's blowing smoke up my ass about how I have to do this every goddamn time..." I trailed off, unable to think of a discreet way to say 'somebody gets killed'. Instead, I finished, "...and you've *never* had a psych evaluation? With *your* job?"

Hellhound's sigh carried clearly over the line. "Hell, darlin', nobody wants to know what's in my head. *I* don't even wanna know. S'long's I get the job done, they leave me the fuck alone."

"That's... that's..."

Words failed me as my anger rose. What the hell? Agents had a mandatory psych evaluation if so much as a drop of blood got spilled, but the Department completely ignored the mental state of a professional assassin?

After a moment of sputtering, I managed words again. "That's the stupidest thing I've ever heard! That's not fair!"

"It ain't stupid," he countered gently. "It's good that they're makin' sure you're okay."

"No, that's not what I meant. I meant, it's not fair that they're ignoring you! You could be... you could have *been* talking to somebody years ago! Things could have been so much better for you."

"Don't think so, darlin'. An' anyway, it doesn't matter," he added before I could protest. "I'm doin' pretty damn good these days. Kane an' his folks saved me when I was a kid; an'..." His voice softened. "Ya saved me all over again. Two chances is more than most guys get."

"Oh, Arnie..." I swallowed hard against the tightness in my throat.

"Just don't get any ideas about commitment," he warned before I could get completely maudlin. "'Cuz I'd hate to hafta run for Tijuana this close to Christmas. It'd be a fuckin' pain in the ass tryin' to get a flight."

I laughed. "You know I'd run just as fast in the opposite direction. Besides, I figure I've pushed my luck about as far as I dare, dragging you to Nichele and Dave's wedding last night."

"Jesus, darlin', stop sayin' that 'W' word. You're givin' me the cold sweats."

Eddy slipped a plate of food in front of me, and I smiled my thanks at him as Hellhound went on, "Ya gonna be back in Calgary for Christmas? Dad Kane'll be here in a few days an' he'll wanna see ya if you're around."

"I'd like to see him, too, but I've got a few things happening right now and I don't know yet how it'll all shake out. I'll keep you posted." The mouthwatering aroma of bacon drew my attention to my plate, and I added, "Eddy just delivered my food so unless you want to listen to me chewing in your ear, I'd better go."

Hellhound chuckled. "Figured ya were at Eddy's; I could hear the blues. Maybe I'll run up there for the jam on Thursday." His voice coasted down into a sexy growl. "An' a little R an' R, if you're up for it."

"Mmm." A hot memory from the previous night made me smile. "You know I am."

"See ya soon then, darlin'. Take care. Love ya."

"I love you, too."

Still smiling, I stowed my phone in my waist pouch and dug into my delicious meal.

Smiling was the last thing on my mind when I tapped on Dr. Rawling's open door at twelve-thirty.

He looked up from his desk with his usual pleasant expression. "Hello, Aydan. It's nice to see you. Please come in and sit down." He rose and gestured to the comfortable leather sofa and chairs in the corner.

I entered, already second-guessing myself. Should I stride decisively? Stroll casually?

Shit, now I couldn't remember how to walk.

By some miracle I managed to make it across the room

without tripping over my own feet. I lowered myself into a chair with its back to the wall, and arranged myself in an open friendly posture. Feet slightly apart, elbows comfortably on the chair arms, neutral expression...

My nose itched, and I hurriedly rubbed it with the back of my hand before rearranging myself in my 'hello-I'm-perfectly-sane-and-normal' pose.

God, this was far worse than interrogating Grandin. At least I hadn't given a shit what *he* thought. Rawling, on the other hand...

My nemesis took a seat on the sofa diagonally from me, smiling his mild little smile.

I wasn't fooled.

"So, Aydan, how have you been?" he asked.

"Fine."

He smiled. Waited.

Jesus, I hate psych evaluations.

"I've completely recovered from being drugged with ketamine," I volunteered in my best bright positive voice. "The hallucinations were really upsetting, but they only lasted for an hour or so and I've been fine ever since."

"That's good to hear. How are you feeling about the experience?"

"Disinclined to ever try street drugs," I snapped.

Dr. Rawling chuckled as though I'd made a joke. "Understandable. And how are you handling the emotional aftermath of Grandin's attack?"

"Fine."

That didn't sound too cooperative, so I shrugged and added, "It sucked, but getting drugged was better than getting beaten up. Nice change, actually."

"And witnessing him murdering Agent Dirk?"

The scene played again behind my eyes. So much blood. So horribly bright on the white snow...

"That sucked, too." My voice came out completely emotionless. "But there was nothing I could do."

"How do you feel about that?"

Somehow I managed not to spring to my feet and yell 'How the hell do you think I feel?'

"I'm pissed off," I admitted, surprising myself with my own candour. "There was no reason for Dirk to die. He shouldn't have even been there. And there was nothing I could do to stop it. And now Grandin's sitting there in the interrogation room all smug because he knows he's going to get a deal."

"So I'm hearing that you feel angry and helpless." Rawling gave one of his patented understanding smiles. "Let's explore that." Behind his benign expression I imagined him rubbing his hands together like a giant spider salivating over the juicy contents of my brain.

I gave myself a mental shake. Stop being so paranoid. He was only trying to help. But despite my best efforts, I couldn't help mentally adding, 'Trying to help the Department, not me'.

Get on with it.

"I feel angry because an agent was murdered in cold blood by a scumbag who was supposed to be on our side." I gave Rawling a hard look. "I don't feel helpless, because we're going to figure out what Grandin was up to, and who he was working for."

Anticipating his next questions, I added, "And I don't feel guilty, because I couldn't have changed that situation no matter what I did. And I hate to say it, but I'm not grieving Dirk, either. I didn't even know him. I'm just glad Grandin didn't manage to kill Ian, too. It sucks that Dirk died, and it especially sucks that I had to watch it, but sometimes shi-" I bit off the four-letter word and substituted, "...stuff happens in our line of work."

Rawling's accepting expression never changed. "Unfortunately, that's true. And how are you feeling physically?"

"Tired. I didn't get much sleep last night."

"Nightmares?" he inquired sympathetically.

"No, I slept like the dead; just not for long enough." I conveniently omitted the fact that the safety of Hellhound's embrace had ensured my dreamless sleep. I added, "I was up late celebrating my best friend's wedding, and then Stemp texted me a meeting request at six AM this morning."

"Ah, yes. He informed me that he has assigned you to investigate your mother." Dr. Rawling paused just long enough for me to say the next words in my mind right along with him. "How do you feel about that?"

I feel like I really fucking hate that question.

"I'm eager to start my investigation," I lied.

Rawling gave me a small smile that made it clear he'd noted my evasion. "And how do you feel about your mother's deception and her return?" he clarified.

Okay, into the minefield.

I trod cautiously. "I'm not sure yet. And I don't think I will be sure until my investigation is complete."

His bland expression said 'I'm noting another evasion' just as clearly as if he'd spoken the words aloud. I fought the childish urge to yell 'Get out of my head!'

That's the whole point of this, idiot. He's supposed to be inside your head.

"It sounds as though you have some conflicted feelings

about your mother," Rawling persisted.

No shit.

I shrugged. "If she hadn't lied last week and told me Sam Kraus implanted subconscious programming in my brain, I might have been more receptive to hearing why she faked her death and left thirty years ago. She says it was all a noble sacrifice to protect me; but I don't trust her."

"Director Stemp said you seemed quite angry with her."

Bastard. He'd tattled on me.

I hid my irritation behind a grave face and a restrained nod. "I won't judge what she did back then until I know the whole story; but last week she lied just to serve her own agenda, and she put me through hell as a result. That's going to be hard to forgive even if it turns out she's been telling the truth about why she left in the first place."

"Sometimes well-intentioned people make errors in judgement when the personal stakes are high," Dr. Rawling said gently.

"Yeah." I gave him a level look. "And sometimes even the most accomplished sociopath slips up and shows her true colours. Which is why I'm reserving judgement until I've finished my investigation."

"That sounds like a wise decision." He smiled, and I held my breath.

Did that mean we were done? Could it be that easy?

"Now, about your other mission," he said.

My gut clenched.

Shit, shit, shit. I had thought talking about Nora was a minefield, but it hadn't occurred to me that Rawling would broach a much more dangerous topic.

I heard his next words as if from a great distance.

"Let's talk about John Kane."

CHAPTER 7

"Okay." I offered Dr. Rawling a smile that I hoped would look disarmingly relaxed. "What would you like to know about John?"

Braced against the tornado of thoughts whipping around inside my brain, I clung to the most important: Ian had said I was an excellent liar.

Lies, don't fail me now.

"Well, let's start with how you feel about him personally." Rawling leaned back on the sofa, comfortably crossing his legs and holding me captive with his pleasant little smile.

"Okay," I repeated, and prevented myself from sucking in a deep breath before I took the plunge. "John and I are good friends. He's... he was an excellent agent, and I trust him with my life."

Rawling nodded, his too-perceptive gaze pinning me to my chair. "So you respect him as an agent. And how do you feel about him personally?"

He knew, the bastard.

Well, fine. Just say it.

"As I said, we're good friends. We're also occasional lovers," I added as matter-of-factly as I could.

"And do you foresee your relationship becoming more serious in the future?"

Somehow I managed not to twitch. "Um... define 'serious'."

He did, of course. "A deepening commitment leading to an ongoing or permanent relationship such as cohabitation or marriage."

"No." The word popped out of my mouth almost before he'd finished speaking.

"No?" Rawling parroted as though he couldn't quite believe what I'd just said.

"No," I repeated firmly. "John and I agree, that type of relationship isn't in the foreseeable future for us. Particularly not now that his son Daniel is part of his life. Neither of us is willing to expose Daniel to the risks that come with being an agent. That's why John quit the Department. And I can't quit." My voice came out hollow in spite of my effort to conceal my feelings.

Dr. Rawling leaned forward as though I'd revealed something significant. "Why do you feel you can't quit?" he inquired mildly.

"The reason is classified." Despite my best attempt at a poker face, my lips twisted in a wry grimace. "My only options are to keep working for the Department until it kills me, or rot in prison for the rest of my life."

"Those seem like very black and white choices..."

No shit. But explaining that I was an unstoppable cyber-spy was far above his security clearance.

He was still talking. "Let's explore-"

"Those are my only two options," I interrupted before he could get started. "Ask Stemp. He's the one who laid them out for me last year."

"I see." Rawling eased back on the sofa, his eyes sharpening. "Is this because of something in your past...?" He let the question dangle delicately.

I went for brutal bluntness. "If you're asking whether I committed some crime or indiscretion and Stemp's using it as leverage to force me to work for the Department, the answer is no. The reasons have to do with my work, which, as you might recall, is *classified*."

Oops, snarky.

I gave him an apologetic smile. "Sorry. It's a sore point. I don't really want to be doing what I do, but I don't have a choice."

"No need to apologize." Rawling returned to the original topic. "So your career is keeping you and John apart."

Fuck this shit.

"No, *I'm* keeping us apart," I snapped. "Contrary to popular belief, not all women are desperate to get married. John and I are good friends who sometimes have sex, and that's all I want from him. Do you have any questions that are relevant to my mission?"

Snarky again. This time I didn't apologize.

"It sounds as though your relationship with John might be a sore point, too. Let's talk about that." Rawling gave me one of his little smiles, making me clamp down on the desire to lunge out of my chair and rip his lips off.

"No need." By some miracle, my voice came out calm and reasonable. "That's not why I was short with you. My relationship with John is fine, but I'm feeling impatient because I don't see the point of your questions about it."

How's that for touchy-feely, dipshit?

I went on, "This morning I discovered some intel with potentially life-threatening consequences, so I'm impatient to get to it. I need to talk to Nora, and Stemp won't let me do that until you sign off on my psych evaluation."

"So the intel you discovered is related to the investigation of your mother." Rawling gave me a searching look. "Are you prepared to recruit John back to the Department, too?"

Holding steady eye contact with him, I said, "Stemp told me to talk to John about coming back, and that's what I'll do. I have no control over what John ultimately decides."

"And how would you feel about him returning to work with the Department? Considering the potential complications if things should change in your personal relationship?"

Finally, the real point of his questions. Protecting the Department's interests, as always.

I gave him my best fake-genuine smile. "When John and I were both agents, we agreed that lives could depend on our ability to work together regardless of our personal feelings, and we're both committed to making sure we can do that. Nothing would change if he came back to the Department."

"So you don't feel strongly about his decision one way or the other?" Rawling inquired.

"No, I don't have a preference. I want what's best for John, but he's the only one who can decide what that is. I'll support his decision no matter what."

"That's good to hear." Rawling gave me another kind little smile.

He was probably a very nice man.

I probably shouldn't be fantasizing about pulling out my tranquilizer pistol and shooting him so I could escape.

"Do you have any other concerns you'd like to discuss?" he asked, as though I'd been eagerly spilling my guts instead of pretending not to begrudge the tidbits of information he'd squeezed out of me.

"Nothing I can think of at the moment. But I'll be sure to give you a call if anything comes up." I topped off that heap of bullshit with a plastic smile.

Rawling eyed me as though he'd caught a whiff, and I exerted all my will to stay relaxed and smiling.

Come on, buddy, say we're done. I promise not to let the crazy leak out on anybody if you'll just *let me the hell out of here...*

"All right, Aydan," he said as though he'd read my mind. "I'll sign off your evaluation as long as you get a good night's sleep tonight. If you find yourself struggling in any way..." He gave me a look that would have made me twitch if I hadn't been projecting 'normal and sane' for all I was worth. "...with nightmares or anxiety..." he went on. "...insomnia, intrusive thoughts or feelings, self-medicating with food or alcohol..."

Christ, did he have to list *all* the things that made up my usual existence?

"...please call me immediately," Dr. Rawling finished. "I'm here to help you; and please don't feel as though you shouldn't bother me while I'm on vacation. I'll be staying in town for the holidays; and your mental and emotional health is my top priority."

"Thank you." I tried not to let my relief show, but I was pretty sure my smile betrayed me. "That's very kind of you." Squashing the urge to leap out of the chair and sprint out the door, I rose unhurriedly. "I hope you have a wonderful vacation."

"I hope you are able to enjoy time with your loved ones, too," he said as he stood to walk me to the door. "I know your job often makes personal time scarce. As a civilian, I appreciate all the sacrifices you and the other agents make to keep us safe. Thank you."

He gave me another warm smile.

"You're welcome," I mumbled, and strode away before the weight of guilt could buckle my knees.

Using all my self-control, I made it to the ladies' room without actually breaking into a run. Inside, I shut myself into a cubicle and did a whole-body shudder, shaking off the feeling of being naked under a magnifying glass.

I'd done it. I hadn't had to tell any direct lies about insomnia or claustrophobia; and the topics of commitment and children and dependent relationships hadn't come up at all.

I was safe. Just breathe...

After taking a few more minutes to regain my composure, I glanced at my wristwatch. Only a quarter to two. I had enough time to file my reports and then slip into the network for a bit of research.

I washed my hands and headed for the door.

Back in my office, I dialled Stemp's number. When he answered, I said, "Hi, it's Aydan. I'm sorry to bother you again, but I wanted you to know that I saw Dr. Rawling and he cleared me for duty. I'm still at Sirius Dynamics and I want to go into the virtual reality network to do some research on Nora and Howard Coleman. Will you have time to post my clearance this afternoon?"

"Already done," Stemp replied crisply. "You have full access."

"You're amazing." The words popped out uncensored and I winced in embarrassment. Then I straightened my spine, shaking off the reaction. I couldn't take my words back; and anyway, he *was* pretty damn amazing. I probably should have told him that long ago.

I could hear the smile in his voice. "Thank you. I'll assign Webb to anchor you."

"That's okay, I don't want to drag him back to the office," I demurred, but Stemp overrode me.

"He is on his way already. Holt is nearing a deal with Grandin and expects to begin interrogation soon, so Webb will be available to assist you until Holt begins relaying intel. You are not to enter the network without supervision. That's an order."

"Okay, I'll wait for Spider," I agreed, secretly relieved that I wouldn't have to make the descent to the subterranean secured area to retrieve my network key, nor brave the vastness of the internet alone. "Oh, and I'll be seeing Kane this afternoon, so I'll talk to him then," I added, hoping to forestall any questions. "And I'll call Nora and set up a meeting for tomorrow. That should give me time to finish my research before I see her."

There. Competent and mission-ready. No need to ask any probing questions...

I held my breath.

"Very well," Stemp said. "Thank you."

He disconnected and I let out my breath in a whoosh. So far, so good.

I fired up my computer, updated my reports, and then switched to the dossier on Nora.

Hmm. Mommy Dearest was a shopaholic. Her credit cards were nearly maxed out, showing frequent large purchases at Harrods, Chanel, and other fancy places. Her bank account hovered near overdraft and she had no savings; although the analysts noted they were still checking for offshore accounts.   Her paycheques kept the creditors satisfied, but barely. No wonder she was still working at age seventy-two.

Switching to the surveillance logs, I discovered that she hadn't done much since arriving in Silverside. Besides her calls to and from Stemp, there was no other activity on her hotel phone. She hadn't used her cell phone, and her email showed only one communication with the UK branch of Sirius Dynamics. She had requested an archived copy of the corporate financial records dating back to before Sam had died, so she was probably using her downtime in the hotel room to get up to speed with her new responsibilities as owner. Most likely hoping to find some cash in Sam's estate to pay her bills; or buy more designer shit.

I sighed. Why couldn't she have been emailing people and offering them national secrets?   Then I could have simply arrested her and erased her from my life.

But the financial records might be interesting, whenever they arrived.   I calculated the time difference between Silverside and London. If somebody responded to Nora on Monday morning at nine AM London time, it would be two AM tonight...

Spider strode by in the hall, whistling.

"Hey, Spider!" I called.

He backtracked to poke his head through the doorway. "Oh, hi! I didn't expect you to be here. I thought you'd be home sleeping."

"I wish." Eyeing him with envy, I added, "You look all bright-eyed and bushy-tailed."

"Yes, I got a few hours of sleep and I'm ready to go." He smiled, as fresh and cheery as ever.

Oh, to be twenty-seven again. I held in a sigh and put on

an answering smile. "I'm glad, 'cause I'm about to sidetrack you. I just got off the phone with Stemp and he said I could borrow you for a while, until Holt has new information for you."

"Sure." Spider came inside and dropped into my guest chair. "What do you need?"

"I want to go into the virtual reality network for a while. I've got some snooping to do."

"Okay..." he said slowly. "But why don't you get Brock and Tammy to do that for you? That's their job; and it doesn't hurt Tammy the way it hurts you."

I sighed. "I know, but I have to check a few things that I don't want to share with anybody else just yet."

"Is this about your mom?" Spider hesitated, his cheeks turning pink. "I mean, should I even call her that? I don't want to be rude, but... I can't imagine how I'd feel if I found out my mom had faked her death and just... left and never came back." His colour deepened. "I'm sorry, that sounded really awful and I didn't mean to rub it in, but... are you okay? If you want to talk or anything, I'm here."

His sweet awkwardness warmed the cold knot that had constricted my heart since Nora had dropped her motherhood bombshell on me.

"Thanks, Spider." I gave him a smile. "I'm not really going to know how I feel until I've finished investigating. But if we could just call her 'Nora' for now, that would be more comfortable than 'Mom'."

"Okay, no problem. When do you want to start?"

"Right now, if that's okay with you. I'm probably going to head home around two-thirty, so I've only got about half an hour."

"Sure." He sprang up. "I'll be right back with your

network key."

Several minutes later I was slouched comfortably in the corner of the small sofa in my office, clutching the tiny electronic cube that gave me access to the brainwave-driven network as well as all the digital secrets of the world.

I gave Spider a nod and closed my eyes to concentrate. The white void of virtual reality materialized around me. Visualizing my familiar system of corridors, I walked my avatar toward the Sirius Dynamics file repository.

"Have you got me, Spider?" I asked the virtual ceiling.

"Yes, I've got you anchored with my software. Go ahead whenever you're ready," he assured me. "And if I lose you, I'll send out searches for..." He hesitated. "...um, how about 'unified string theory'?"

"I don't even know what that is, but it'll be fine. Just as long as you don't ever call me home with a search for 'cameltoe' again," I teased.

"That was so embarrassing!" His voice quivered and I could imagine his blush. "I honestly never meant to do that, I was just so frantic and it came up in the auto-search and I just hit 'enter'..."

"It's okay, I know you didn't mean to," I reassured him, feeling guilty over his discomfort. "You were brilliant to get me back that time, and I didn't mean to embarrass you. I just have a weird sense of humour."

"You kind of do," he agreed, and I could hear the smile in his voice. "But you always make me laugh. So we're okay with 'unified string theory'?"

"Yep. And if I'm not back in half an hour, give me a pull, okay?"

"I will. Happy hunting."

Instead of replying, I faded into invisibility and slipped

through the simulation into the busy data streams of the network.

Still inside Sirius's firewall, I bobbed gently in the currents of data. I wanted to infiltrate the servers at MI5 and MI6 to cross-check Ian's information, but that would take too long and I was too tired.

But maybe Sam had left something encrypted here at Sirius. Spider had probably already scoured our network, but it wouldn't hurt for me to look.

And if I could find any of Sam's communications with Nora I might be able to find out whether he had told her I could invisibly breach any network security and break any encryption.

Okay, Sam, you traitorous bastard; let's see if you left me any breadcrumbs.

I dissolved into the file structure, extending questing tendrils in all directions.

CHAPTER 8

With my senses alert for the taste/feel/smell of Nora Taylor, Sam Kraus, or Nola Kelly, I slipped inside Sirius's archive server.

And found my own name.

I hesitated.

There was a lot of data. According to Canada's privacy legislation I was fully entitled to read everything the Department knew about me, but it seemed wrong somehow. And eavesdroppers never hear anything good about themselves...

If I could have drawn a deep breath in my bodiless form, I would have.

Screw it.

I plunged in.

It was all there. Everything about Sam's work, right back to his original Wetware project back in the 1960s; when he was trying to find a way to use the human brain instead of silicone-based computer processing; then on to the mid-1970s when Project Wetware had diverged into the earliest concept of brainwave-driven networks.

There was a list of eight women's names, including mine. All red-haired, brown-eyed, and conceived during the three-day window between October 29 and November 2, 1963: The eight women in the world believed to be the only candidates whose minds would supercharge the virtual reality simulations.

There was no mention of the darker side of Sam and the other seven Knights of Sirius. No hint that they had been using us, their 'mages', to harvest top-secret information from all the countries of the world.

But copious notes showed Sam's obsessive desire to recruit me to Sirius Dynamics, and he recorded increasingly frequent visits to our family farm 'to monitor Aydan's development'.

To seduce my mother.

Traitorous asshole.

I didn't bother to clarify to myself whether I meant Nora or him.

Then Sam's notes abruptly stopped in November of 1981, notated only with a terse 'Project on hold'.

'On hold'. Such innocuous words for such a cataclysmic life change. After Mom died, Dad and I had been paralyzed with shock and grief, suspended like insects in amber while the rest of the world went on without us.

Only a few weeks later, the Department had sent another man to our farm. Calling himself a college recruiter, he had attempted to persuade seventeen-year-old me and my shattered father that computer science was my ideal career. His failure was duly noted in the files.

Then, several months later, a handsome young agent had been assigned to my case. Robert Carver. My heart clenched as I read his words from so long ago; dispassionate accounts of his attempts to woo me away from my college boyfriend, whom Robert noted as 'manipulative, narcissistic, and potentially abusive'.

Seemed like everybody had known about Steven's personality except me. At least until after we were married. Then I'd discovered his true colours pretty damn fast; and too damn late.

I skipped the rest of Robert's notes. I didn't want to read the emotionless official version of his long and dedicated courtship after my divorce, and our later marriage. I had believed he loved me. Maybe he had. I would never know.

And I didn't want to see the kill order Stemp had issued for Robert; nor Kane's report of his assassination; nor the Department's ultimately successful attempt to lure me to Silverside with my dream farm and a deluxe garage.

They'd won in the end, after all those years.

My heart burned with grief for the path I'd never been allowed to follow. Nora claimed to have been protecting me by diverting Sam from his recruitment plans; but how many decades of misery could I have avoided if I'd gone to work for Sirius right out of high school?

What if I had never been so desperate to fill the void of my mother's loss that I committed to the first serious boyfriend I'd ever had?

What if I had never spent long harrowing years learning that marriage was a prison and love its most vicious torture?

What if I hadn't experienced firsthand how convincingly a top agent could fake loving devotion?

Pushing aside my self-pity, I focused on the only positive side I could find. If I had been recruited by Sirius right after high school, Sam would still be using me to steal secrets without my knowledge, just like the rest of the innocent mages. I would never have discovered that the virtual reality simulations were nothing more than a front for treason, and

Sam and his Knights would still be alive and selling the world's classified secrets.

At least my suffering hadn't been for nothing.

Get over it.

I moved on to Dr. Rawling's psych reports.

Apparently I hadn't concealed my weaknesses as cleverly as I'd thought. But at least the word 'resilient' kept cropping up in his reports. 'Denial' and 'avoidance' made frequent appearances, too, along with 'repressed anger' and 'need for approval'. Ouch.

The remaining documents were Stemp's and Kane's. Unlike Dr. Rawling's clinical language, Stemp named my deepest vulnerabilities with brutal directness, along with the actions he'd taken to exploit them.

Even though I knew he maintained files like this on everyone, the callousness of his words made my heart flinch. In these cold assessments there was nothing of the complex man I knew; only an ugly litany of all the ways he'd tried to manipulate and break me.

And failed.

Grim amusement warmed me while I read the words 'unexpected outcome' over and over. And I was pleased to see that there were no recent entries. He must have discovered what he needed to know. Despite the fact that I should probably be furious with him, I felt a small glow of pride.

I had passed his tests. He trusted me.

Or at least, he trusted me more than he trusted most people; which was precious little indeed. Still, I'd take whatever compliment I could find.

Following Stemp's timeline backward, I found copious notes from when he had taken over as Director of

Clandestine Operations three and a half years ago. Most of the intel about me seemed to have been gleaned from Robert's reports, but some...

My mind froze.

He knew.

That fucking *bastard!*

He had known right from the start that my mother had faked her death and left the country.

CHAPTER 9

Heartsick, I let my consciousness float aimlessly in the sea of data surrounding me. How could Stemp have looked me in the eye and pretended he hadn't known Nora was my not-so-dead mother?

Realization dawned. He hadn't pretended at all. He had simply said 'We discovered that your mother is a British citizen' and I had assumed he had investigated her and found out.

But that hadn't been necessary. He had known all along.

And that meant Kane probably had, too.

I had left Kane's notes for last, hesitating to violate his privacy and afraid to read what he'd reported about me. Not anymore.

I dove into the data, heedless of the hazards lurking beneath its surface.

Fighting the gut-wrenching memories of Robert's lifeless body still warm in my frantic embrace, I memorized every detail of the drug Kane had used to assassinate him. A colourless, odourless, tasteless liquid, administered in food or drink and causing no immediate symptoms. Robert might have noticed a headache increasing over the next hour or two, but he wouldn't have thought to seek medical attention for it. Meanwhile the drug was silently raising his blood pressure sky-high and increasing his blood's clotting factor until even mild exertion would precipitate a fatal heart attack. And if the heart attack hadn't killed Robert, a massive stroke would have finished him only hours later; or worse, imprisoned him inside a mute paralyzed husk.

I shuddered. The heart attack was more merciful.

Was that how Howard Coleman had died, too?

I read on.

Even though I knew Kane had been ordered to pretend he was in love with me to lure me into Department, reading the dispassionate report of his emotional manipulations still filled my virtual gut with queasy doubt. How much of our so-called friendship was based on lies?

Something tugged to the left of where my midsection would have been if I'd had a body. Spider, reminding me that my time was up.

I eased out of the archive servers and snapped back into my avatar in the virtual file repository. Even though it wasn't necessary to travel any distance at all in virtual reality, the walk back to the portal felt far too long. Standing beside it, I braced myself.

When I stepped out, the usual agony crashed through my head.

"*Aah!* God... damn..." I fought the pain and the urge to vent profanity for only a few moments before giving in.

"Snotsucking-motherfucking-*syphilitic-goat-cocks!*" I rained a volley of punches on the sofa cushions, hissing through my teeth until the pain subsided enough for me to open my eyes.

When I did, Spider was hovering a few feet away, prudently out of reach. His eyes looked concerned, but his lips twitched as though he was fighting a smile.

"Are you okay?" he asked. "That seemed worse than usual."

"Yeah." My voice creaked like an unoiled gate. "It's always worse when I'm tired. The headache's easing now. Thanks."

He surrendered to the smile. "Syphilitic goat cocks...?"

"Sorry." I gave him an apologetic grimace.

"Don't be. It's been too long since I've learned any new curses from you." His smile widened. "Wait 'til I tell Linda that one; she'll laugh herself silly. She loves your vocabulary as much as I do."

I fell back on the sofa, massaging my temples and smiling in spite of my pain. "Have I told you lately how much I like working with you?"

He flushed. "Um... no."

"I love working with you. You're the best co-worker ever, and the nicest person in this whole damn building. May blessings rain down on your pointy little head."

Spider's cheeks turned bright pink. "Thanks!" He beamed at me. Then his smile faded to a fake-anxious expression as he reached up to feel the top of his head. "I think...?"

"It's just a figure of speech," I assured him.

He grinned. "Just checking. So did you find out what you needed to know?"

My good humour drained away. "I found out far more than I wanted to know; and not nearly as much as I needed. I'll have to go in again." I glanced at my watch. "Later. I have to go home now. John's bringing Daniel over to work on my '53 Chevy for a while, and it'll likely be suppertime before they leave."

"Oh, that'll be great! You're so lucky to get to spend time with Daniel." Spider's smile softened. "You'll have so much fun together!"

I pasted on an answering smile that was supposed to look enthusiastic.

My attempt must have been plausible, because Spider went on without questioning my response. "If you want to go back into the network after they leave tonight, just give me a call. I'll be here anyway."

"Thanks. I might do that."

Or I might hide in my closet and have a nervous breakdown. Could go either way...

The phone rang, and Spider made for the door with a wave. As he went out, I picked up the call.

Kane's delicious voice rewarded my 'hello'. "Hi, Aydan. We're in Drumheller, and the roads have been good all the way. We should be at your farm in about half an hour if that's still all right."

"Sure, that'll be fine. See you... oh, wait!" I added as a thought struck me. "Do I need to do anything... or is there anything Daniel needs... I mean, should I... I don't know, buy something or put anything away in the garage...?"

"Don't worry," Kane said. "I brought everything that Daniel could possibly need, and your garage is always so organized that I'm not worried about child-proofing it. Daniel is smart and careful and always pays attention if I tell him something is off-limits..." His voice softened as though he had turned to face his young passenger. "...don't you, Daniel? I know I can count on you to follow instructions."

A small voice said, "Uh-huh! Just like a soldier!"

"That's right," Kane said warmly. "A good soldier follows instructions. And what else does a good soldier do?"

"Think. So he doesn't follow bad orders."

"Right again," Kane said, and I could hear the smile in his words. His voice gained volume as he returned his attention to the phone. "So, Aydan, don't worry about anything. We'll see you soon."

"Okay, great."

I hung up before he could hear my heart sinking. After only four months of fatherhood, he was already a great dad.

But what did I have to offer a child? Tips on developing a debilitating fear of commitment? Top techniques for undetectable murder? Advanced swearing lessons?

I sighed and trudged out.

As my car slithered around the snowy corner into my driveway, my lips curved into a smile despite my worries. My neighbour had been hard at work with his snowblower as usual. The lane and turnaround at my house were all clear, and a heap of snow beside the garage marked Tom's hard work at clearing access to all four overhead doors.

What a guy. I didn't pay him enough. I kept trying, but it was a struggle to get him to accept even a pittance for his tractor's gasoline, and he wouldn't take a penny more.

Guilt nagged at my heart. Was that just normal generosity, or was he still hoping we might become more than just friendly neighbours?

I shook off the thought. Nothing I could do about it. And it was damn nice to come home to a clear driveway. I got out at the gate, straightening my tired shoulders as I inhaled the crisp cold air.

It was damn nice to come home, period. After five days of chaos and fear in Calgary, the endless acres of snow sparkling under a flawless blue sky were balm to my soul.

I breathed deeply, catching a whiff of pine from the direction of the frozen creek. Rainbow-tinted shards of reflected sun glittered off the snow, but already the shadows were lengthening. In only a few hours we'd be plunged into darkness again, nearing the shortest day of the year.

After one more satisfying breath, I unlocked the gate and drove through, leaving it open for Kane and Daniel.

Even though I knew the gate offered no protection from armed enemies, I still felt exposed leaving it open. But dammit, I was not going to go back and lock up. That was just too paranoid.

I parked my Legacy in its usual spot in the garage and went into the house, resolutely ignoring the open gate.

Only a few minutes later the crunch of tires on snow made me hurry to the window. To my relief, the arriving vehicle was Kane's black Expedition, and he had closed the gate.

I pasted on a smile and strode over to open the door.

Kane got out and waved as he came around the vehicle to open the back door. Inside, Daniel eyed me with obvious trepidation.

I stayed on the porch.

"You can get out now," Kane encouraged him. "You remember Aydan; she's the one who found you when you were kidnapped."

I hid a wince, expecting Daniel to completely melt down at the memory. Instead he nodded, studying me wide-eyed.

Kane said nothing more, just waited patiently. After another moment's hesitation, Daniel unbuckled his seat belt and slid out of the tall vehicle. The way he reached for Kane's hand gave my heart an unexpected twist.

Such trust.

Surely I must have trusted my mother that much, once.

The two of them advanced to the bottom of my porch steps, and I cleared my throat, hoping my voice would come out sounding normal. "Hi, John. Hi, Daniel."

"Hi," Kane replied with a smile.

Daniel eased closer to Kane's side, his gaze dropping. His free hand clutched a toy soldier, his chubby fist tucked close to his chest in the fearful gesture I remembered from four months ago.

"Say hi to Aydan," Kane prompted gently.

"Hi," Daniel whispered, still staring at the ground.

Oh, God. I was SO not equipped to deal with children.

"So, let's head for the garage," I said in a falsely hearty tone. "Unless, um... you want to come in? Do you need to... uh, go to the bathroom, or want a drink or something...?"

"We went to the bathroom in Drumheller," Kane replied, unfazed. "Daniel, do you need to go to the bathroom now?"

Daniel shook his head, his gaze glued to the snowy step.

"And we brought a cooler with drinks," Kane added. "We'll get our things and meet you in the garage."

"Okay," I agreed. "The door's open. I'll put on my boots and be there in a minute."

They turned back to the Expedition and I swung the door shut to grab my boots from behind it, wishing with all my heart that I could just lock the door and hide in the basement until they left.

I dawdled through putting on my boots and jacket, then hesitated behind the door for a mental pep-talk.

You've faced deadly gunmen, enraged bikers, crazed terrorists, and exploding geese. You can face one seven-year-old supervised by his dad. It's only for a couple of hours.

And you need to talk to Kane.

So get your cowardly ass out there.

I was just squaring my shoulders when the sound of a powerful engine swelled in the distance. A moment later the monitor on my wrist vibrated.

When I toggled the video display and saw Tom's big four-wheel-drive half-ton coming down my lane, I wasn't sure whether to be relieved that it was only him, or worried that he and Kane would clash as they usually did.

Deciding to err on the side of caution, I toggled the display back to its normal wristwatch mode and waited by the front door until I heard the clump of Tom's boots on the front porch.

I swung the inside door open just as he was opening the screen door to knock.

"Oh, hi! I wasn't sure whether I'd find you here or in the garage." His handsome weathered face creased in a smile, but the seriousness in his sky-blue eyes set off my alarm bells. "Company today?" he asked with a nod at Kane's Expedition.

"Yes, John's here to work on my Chevy." I didn't get into any complicated explanations. "What's up? Would you like to come in?"

"No, that's all right, I can see you're on your way out so I won't keep you." His smile disappeared. "I just wanted to let you know that we might have some trouble."

"What's wrong?" I asked as I stepped outside, shooting a wary glance at our surroundings. The man-door to the garage was partly open, and Kane and Daniel were investigating my big floor-standing tool chest. Daniel was engrossed by the shiny tools, but Kane gave me a questioning look.

I gave him a tiny nod of reassurance as Tom replied, "Be careful around your farm. Don't step into any snow that has been disturbed, and watch out for human tracks."

A chill that had nothing to do with the outdoor temperature trickled down my spine. "Why? What's happened?"

"This morning I nearly stepped on a leghold trap that had been placed outside my barn door."

"*What?*" I stared up at him. "Who would do that? Who would even have a leghold trap? Aren't they illegal?"

"Yes, but there are lots of old ones around, even if they haven't been used in years. And as to who would do it..." Tom shrugged, vertical lines deepening between his brows. "I don't know. Somebody that didn't like me much, I guess."

"But everybody likes you!" I protested. At his smilingly raised eyebrow, heat rushed to my cheeks. "I mean, um... do you have any enemies?"

"Well..." Tom said slowly. "I ruffled a few feathers when I was young and stupid, but I haven't had a problem with anybody in years." He hesitated. "The only person I've really tangled with lately is..." He didn't finish the sentence, but his gaze drifted to the open garage door, where Kane had led Daniel over to the transmission bell housing I'd dragged out to the middle of the floor for easier access.

Outrage stiffened my spine. "John would never do something like that! And anyway, if you found it this morning, he couldn't have done it. The highways were closed until five AM, and he was in Calgary."

Tom raised a placating hand. "I'm not accusing him. I'm just saying I can't think of anybody else I've riled up enough to make them want to cripple me."

"Anybody from your past?"

He shrugged, the self-deprecating smile tugging at his lips again. "My past is all right here, except for when I was on the rodeo circuit; and that was only for a couple of years. I got married and moved home when I was twenty. Anybody with a beef could have found me here in the past twenty-eight years. It's hard to believe they'd wait this long."

Sudden fear chilled my blood. What if the trap had been meant for me? It would be easy enough for a stranger to mix up two farms side by side. Oh, God, what if my enemies had targeted Tom's farm by mistake?

Tom's hands closed gently on my shoulders, his blue eyes troubled. "You're as white as a ghost. I'm sorry, I didn't mean to scare you. I don't think you're in any danger; I just wanted you to be careful. I called the police and they took the trap away and said they'd investigate."

"Th-thanks..." I hugged my arms around the icy hollow that had replaced my stomach at the thought of him in agony, alone in the country winter. He could have lost his leg, or even died if the cruel jaws of the trap had severed an artery.

And if my enemies tried again...

CHAPTER 10

My voice trembled. "Be careful, Tom. Carry your shotgun whenever you're outside. And always keep your cell phone with you, even when you're inside your house. Promise me you will, okay?"

His eyes warmed to the colour of summer sky. "Don't worry about me." He folded me into a hug and I slid my arms around his lean work-hardened body, pressing my face against his broad shoulder and inhaling his clean-cotton and woodsmoke scent.

A moment later my brain caught up with my hormones and I pulled away.

Worst thing I could have done, dammit. Idiot.

Tom let me go, his palms coasting down my arms to gently capture my hands. "You feel good in my arms," he said softly.

"I'm sorry." I backed away a step, disengaging his grip. "I didn't mean to give you the wrong idea."

He smiled, an engaging mixture of humour and ruefulness warming his handsome weathered face. "It felt like the right idea to me." Before I could respond, he added, "It's okay, I'm not reading anything into it. Thank you for being worried about me. I'll let you know if the police find anything." His smile flattened. "And you be careful, too. If you find anything out of place, or even if you just have a bad feeling, call me and we'll tackle it together. Or call the police. Don't take chances because you're afraid you'll feel foolish if it turns out to be nothing."

"I won't. Thanks."

"You're welcome." He gave me another of his attractive crooked smiles. "I'll talk to you later." He tipped his cowboy hat and headed for his truck.

Lingering on the porch, I gave him a final wave and watched until his truck disappeared behind the trees that separated our farms. When I turned, Kane and Daniel had their heads together over the housing, but Kane's penetrating grey gaze was pinned on me.

Damn, from there he would have been able to see my entire exchange with Tom, including the hug.

My teeth clenched reflexively. He would be jealous and angry...

Forcing the thought away, I headed for the garage.

No, he wouldn't. He had promised that everything was fine between us and he was okay with me seeing other men.

I swallowed chagrin.

No, dammit, he hadn't said 'other men'. He'd said he was okay with me loving Arnie, his best friend since childhood. Not Tom, who had been a bitter rival from the start.

Oblivious to my desire to turn and flee, my feet carried me inside the garage and over to the wrench-wielding father and son. As I shed my jacket, I plastered on a smile. "Looks like you guys are getting the job done just fine without me."

Kane returned my smile, looking perfectly relaxed except for the sharpness of his eyes. "Yes, we're hard at it. We'll have this thing apart in a jiffy." He cracked another bolt loose. "Here, Daniel, this one's ready for you to take off now."

Daniel hunched over the housing, frowning with concentration as his small hands fumbled a wrench onto the bolt head.

"I need a beer," I blurted, and hurried for the fridge in the corner. "Do you want one?"

"Yes, please. I'll come and get it." Kane rose and followed me.

Not meeting his eyes, I handed over an icy bottle and concentrated on opening one of my own.

"Are you friendly with Rossburn now?" Kane inquired.

Oh, God, here we go.

I gulped a large slug of beer. The bubbles fizzed unmercifully, and I barely managed to smother a giant belch. Way to set a good example for a child.

"No," I muttered. "It was only a hug. I just found out somebody sabotaged his farm and he could have lost a leg." I sucked back another mouthful of beer. Come on, suds, work your magic on my nerves...

"Aydan." A gentle touch tipped my chin up to look into Kane's serious grey eyes. "That wasn't meant as a demand or a criticism. Just a request for information. Has the status of your cover changed?"

"No. I'm just an idiot." I gulped another swallow.

"Of course you're not an idiot." Kane frowned. "What's wrong? You seem on edge."

"I... I'm, um..." My gaze strayed over to Daniel, who had stopped working on his bolt and was observing us with a disconcertingly solemn gaze. "I've got some stuff on my mind."

"You're uncomfortable with Daniel." Kane's tone held no accusation, but I could read the disappointment in his eyes.

"Of course I'm n..." I bit off the lie. "Um..." I let out a breath of resignation. "Yeah. I'm sorry; I don't know how to act. I mean, what have you told him about... us? What have you told Alicia? If I hug you, will he go home and make it sound like we were making out, and get you in shit? Or... hell, I don't know! What do you want me to do? How do you want me to act?"

"Just be yourself-"

"Daddy," a small plaintive voice interrupted. "I can't get this one. Will you help me?"

Kane gave me a twisted smile. "I'm sorry. We should have talked about this before I brought Daniel here."

He strode back to his son and reached into the cooler they'd brought. "Here's your root beer, Daniel." He twisted the cap off a brown bottle and passed it over. Holding out his own untouched beer with a smile, he clinked bottles with Daniel and they each took a drink.

"Beer is yummy, Daddy." Daniel beamed up at him.

"Yours is root beer," Kane corrected gently. "Real beer has alcohol in it, so it's only for grown-ups."

"May I please taste your alcohol beer?"

Kane smiled at him. "Just a little taste."

Daniel nodded eagerly, and Kane offered him a tiny sip. Daniel's face screwed up. "Yuck! I like root beer better."

"That's good," Kane said gravely. "That's why beer is only for grown-ups."

"Does beer taste better when you're a grown-up?" Daniel inquired.

Kane chuckled. "Not really." At his son's puzzled frown, he added, "I'll get some bolts started for you, and then Aydan and I are going to have a grown-up talk for a few minutes. You can work on the transmission if you want; or if you'd rather play with your toys, that's fine, too."

"His hands are covered with grease," I pointed out. "Alicia won't thank you if he gets it all over everything."

"We didn't bring any toys that can't be cleaned," Kane said as he loosened a few more bolts and then rose to wipe his hands on a shop towel. "There you go, Daniel. Now..." He nudged me gently toward the opposite side of the garage. "Let's talk."

'Let's talk'. My least favourite phrase in the world.

Well, okay, my second-from-least-favourite. 'I'm going to kill you now' would be my *least* favourite. But still...

I swallowed more beer, hoping for some liquid courage.

"Are you planning to get drunk?" Kane inclined his chin at the half-empty bottle in my hand.

"Maybe," I muttered. "I'm deciding."

Kane reached for my bottle as if he intended to take it away, but sensibly desisted when I tightened my grip and gave him the stink-eye.

He smiled. "I promise this isn't the kind of talk that requires sedation."

"I'll be the judge of that," I mumbled. "What do you want to talk about?"

"I wanted to apologize. It wasn't fair to spring Daniel on you without talking about it first. I'm sorry. How can I make you feel more comfortable?"

"You don't have to apologize." I hugged my beer bottle. "It's good to see you and Daniel getting to spend some quality time together. I just... I don't see how I fit in. I'm sure as hell not any kind of decent mother-figure. I just know I'm going to swear or belch or fart or something and he'll go home and tell Alicia, and then she'll run off to court and tell them you're an unfit father for exposing him to such a bad influence..."

I trailed off as Kane burst out laughing. He sobered fast, but his eyes still sparkled with amusement as he said, "Can you envision a judge's face while Alicia says, '...and he allowed a woman to *break wind* in front of my child!' She'd be kicked out of court so fast it would make her head spin."

A small snicker escaped in spite of my discomfort. "Okay, fine; bad example. But you know what I mean. We're drinking beer. I'll slip up and swear, I know it. And if I give you a hug or something and then he tells Alicia all about his day, it wouldn't take much for her to twist it into some great story about how we got absolutely shit-faced, started talking dirty, and screwed each other's brains out in the middle of the floor with Daniel watching."

"Well." The twinkle in Kane's eye had turned into something considerably hotter, and a smile quirked the corner of his mouth. "There's a scenario worth exploring. Minus the drunkenness and the seven-year-old onlooker."

"Cut it out." I shoved his shoulder playfully, then regretted it when the contact of my palm against those hard muscles swept a wave of heat over me.

Fuck, I was half-drunk already. This whole playdate had been a bad idea from the start.

"Be serious," I admonished us both.

"I was being serious; but I'll also address your concerns." Kane's smile dwindled. "I'm not worried about your behaviour. Daniel is old enough to understand that adult language isn't appropriate for him to use, and I know you'd never do anything to harm him or endanger him. But you do have a good point about physical contact. What boundaries would you like to place?"

"Me? Hell, it doesn't matter what I want. What's going to get you in hot water?"

"Of course it matters what you want." Kane gave me a slow smile. "And I'm quite encouraged by your concern that you might accidentally hug or kiss me."

Oh, God. Me and my big mouth.

I slugged more beer to prevent myself from saying anything else inappropriate.

After waiting a few moments for a response I didn't provide, Kane went on, "Don't worry about it. Children aren't bothered by displays of physical affection. Families hug. Friends hug." His voice deepened, his gaze holding me. "Lovers hug. And I don't care what Alicia thinks we're doing."

"Oh. Well, that's good, then." My voice came out feeble, and I took another mouthful of beer.

"And Daniel already has a mother," Kane went on. "He doesn't need that from you. But I think it's important for him to have strong, smart, independent women in his life." He smiled, his eyes softening. "Women who know which end of a transmission is which."

"Thanks," I mumbled, heat rising in my cheeks.

Don't let him sweet-talk you. He lied to you before. He might still be lying. Last night at Dave and Nichele's wedding I had felt so comfortable with him. But now...

Kane frowned. "There's something else bothering you, isn't there? You said you had 'some stuff' on your mind."

I glanced over at Daniel, hoping he would suddenly demand his father's attention; but the child seemed perfectly content mumbling to himself while he trekked his toy soldier up and down the bulge of the bell housing.

A sigh escaped me. Might as well just dump it out. "When you told me last year that you'd called in some favours and found out that our government hadn't killed my mother, did you know she'd actually faked her death and left the country?"

Kane's eyes widened. "No," he said promptly.

"Bullshit." Lubricated by beer, the accusing word slipped out before I could stop it.

Kane frowned. "I didn't lie to you," he repeated. "I really didn't know she was alive."

"Where did you get your intel, then?" I demanded. "What favours did you call in? Who did you talk to?"

It was Kane's turn to sigh. He took a drink of beer as though hoping it would give him strength, and replied, "Stemp. I should have known he wouldn't tell me the whole truth."

"Stemp?" I let out a bark of bitter laughter. "He never tells anybody the whole truth. What favour did he owe you?"

Kane hung his head. "He didn't owe me any favours. That was when I was still under orders to manipulate you. I told him I needed the information to gain your trust, and that was what he gave me: 'Our government did not kill any of your family, directly or indirectly'. True, but not the whole truth."

"As usual." I drained my bottle. "Fine. Tell me about how you killed Robert."

Kane winced. "You weren't kidding when you said you had a lot on your mind."

"That's just the tip of the iceberg," I said gloomily, eyeing my empty bottle. "I need another."

As I turned toward the beer fridge, Kane laid a restraining hand on my arm. "Maybe you should wait. That one went down pretty fast."

I fought back a prickle of irritation.

"Probably right," I agreed, faking reasonableness for all I was worth.

Hell, he *was* right. My tongue felt thick and my eyelids were heavy. God, if only I could lie down and sleep for a week...

"There's not much to tell," Kane said, returning to our previous conversation. "Robert had been undercover as your husband for years by the time I joined the Department. My early missions were mostly overseas; and after I got shot it took nearly a year before I could resume active duty. That's the only reason I got the assignment: Robert didn't know me. The analysts supplied me with his schedule. The Weapons lab gave me the drug. I poured it into his drink at a business dinner..." Kane hesitated uncomfortably. "...and the rest you know."

Pushing away the horrible memories, I persisted, "Did he show any signs that he wasn't feeling well as the dinner went on? Did he seem like he had a headache? Was he rubbing his forehead or anything?"

Kane frowned. "Why are you asking me this? Do you really want to revisit that time in your life?"

I sighed. "Not even a little bit. But somebody else might have been killed with the same drug. I'm collecting all the information I can."

"He didn't have any visible reaction. I'm sorry, but that's all I can tell you."

I spotted the weasel-words immediately. "All you can *tell me*, or all you *know*?" I demanded.

"All I know," Kane clarified without rancour.

But he could still be lying. He was an excellent agent;

and agents had to be good liars.

"Which reminds me," I said. "Stemp assigned me to recruit you back to the Department. They want you to be an agent again."

Kane nodded. "I wondered how long it would take."

I stared at him, his words slowly penetrating my beer-fogged mind. "You were expecting this?"

"Of course. I thought you were already working on me when you involved me in your last two missions. Weren't you?"

"No!" Indignation made my voice too loud, and I lowered my volume as Daniel glanced over worriedly. "What kind of a shitty friend do you think I am? Stemp just gave me the assignment this morning."

"I wouldn't think badly of you if you were only following orders."

My heart sank. If he wouldn't think less of me for following orders instead of honouring our friendship, that meant he wouldn't think twice about betraying my trust if our positions were reversed.

"So how will you entice me to rejoin?" Kane asked, grinning. "I hope you have a honey trap planned."

"I wasn't planning to entice you," I said stiffly. "I told Stemp I'd talk to you but I was sure you wouldn't be interested now that you have Daniel to consider. So... that's it. I just talked to you. I won't try to influence your decision."

"Oh." His smile drained away, leaving a pucker between his brows. "Don't you want me to come back to the Department?"

"I don't care whether you come back or not."

Hurt flashed across his face and I backtracked hurriedly.

"I didn't mean that the way it came out. I just meant it doesn't matter to me... fuck, no, that's not what I meant, either!" I squeezed my eyes shut in an attempt to kickstart my aching brain and tried again. "I want what's best for you and Daniel and I'll support your decision no matter what it is. It would be great to have you back, but I don't want you to come back if it compromises your relationship with Daniel."

When I opened my eyes again Kane was studying me, his cop face impassive. "Which of those was actually the truth?"

I clenched my fists in my hair, fighting annoyance again. "The last one! If you don't believe me, ask Stemp. And Dr. Rawling. I told them it was wrong to pressure you, and that I'd support whatever decision you made."

"If you felt that strongly about it, why didn't you decline the assignment?" The hint of accusation in Kane's question fanned the sparks of my annoyance into instant anger.

"I tried!" I glared at him. "Stemp basically said that if I refused the assignment the chain of command would chuck me in prison. So if anyone asks, I damn well hope you'll pretend I'm doing my best to influence you!"

"I will." He frowned. "Why are you angry with me?"

"*I'm not fucking angry!*"

We stared at each other in silence while my stomach twisted into a slow sick knot. Now he would be angry at me in return, and with good reason. Oh, God, just let this shit end...

"Aydan, stop," Kane said firmly. "I can tell by your expression that you're falling back into your destructive thought patterns." His voice softened. "I'm not angry or hurt. I won't hurt you in return, and I'm not demanding anything from you. It's all right if you're angry with me for some reason. I just want to understand why, so I can make it better."

I didn't need this. I couldn't trust him. Every one of my old defensive instincts screamed to pick a giant fight and throw him out.

But dammit, I *wouldn't* let my fucked-up past make my decisions for me...

Kane gently interrupted my thoughts. "It's all right if you don't want to talk about this now, but are you in danger? Is that what's bothering you?"

"No. Hell, maybe." I groaned. "I don't fucking know. I'm so tired I can't think straight, and that beer isn't doing me any favours." I sucked in a deep breath and took the plunge. "And you're right, I was angry earlier, but it was just my default reaction. Nothing you did."

"It's your default reaction when you feel threatened," Kane clarified. "And I guess you have a lot of reasons to feel threatened." He gave me a rueful smile. "When I put myself in your shoes, I can't imagine how you stay sane. On top of all the usual pressures of being an agent, you're also dealing with the fact that I, the man who murdered your last husband, now want to be..." He hesitated and his voice deepened. "...considerably more than friends."

"That doesn't bother me as much as the fact that you had standing orders to lie to me and manipulate me, right up to the day you quit the Department," I said, avoiding the emotional danger lurking in his words. "It's pretty hard not to second-guess that."

"I can-" Kane began, but a small voice interrupted.

"Daddy?"

"Yes, Daniel, can you be patient for a few more minutes? Aydan and I-"

"Daddy..." Daniel's voice rose.

"Just a few-"

"*Daddy, I have to go pee!*"

I grinned at Kane. "I guess we're done here. You can take him into the house or let him write his name in the snow behind the garage. Doesn't matter to me."

He gave me a rueful smile. "Alicia would be furious if she found out I had encouraged public urination. We'll go into the house." He hurried over to help Daniel into his jacket, and moments later they hustled out the door.

Released from the stress of their presence, I made a beeline for the beer fridge and cracked another cold one. Soon they'd be gone, and I could gobble a bowl of cereal and go straight to bed. A nice little alcoholic buzz might even take the edge off my inevitable nightmares. I tipped up the bottle for a long swallow.

By the time Kane and Daniel returned, another half a bottle was soothing my belly while I contentedly spun bolts off the transmission housing. I gave them a smile, all warm and fuzzy with beery goodness.

"Is that a wrench, too, Daddy?" Daniel asked, hunkering down beside me and directing an inquisitive gaze at the tool in my hand.

"It's kind of a wrench," Kane explained, crouching opposite me with a smile. "The handle part is called a ratchet, and it uses different sizes of those metal tubes. Those are called sockets. A socket fits over a bolt to turn it the same way as a wrench."

As I tackled the next bolt, Daniel giggled. "It makes a funny noise. Creeee! Creeee!" He imitated the tool's metallic chirping.

"Yes, that's the ratchet making that noise," Kane agreed.

"Ratchet is a funny word!" Daniel giggled again. "Ratchet! Ratchet! Creeee! Creeee!" He sprang up and galloped a circuit around the garage, waving his toy soldier between high-pitched shouts of "Ratchet! Creeee!"

My beery goodness fading rapidly, I sucked back another swallow and concentrated on the last bolt.

"There we go," I said a moment later. "Give me a hand?"

Kane nodded, and together we pried the heavy housing apart.

The next hour dragged interminably. As I emptied the dregs of a third bottle into my mouth, I realized there wasn't enough beer in the world to maintain my usual state of wrench-turning zen under the auditory assault of an energetic seven-year-old.

And now I was shit-faced on top of my stress and exhaustion. Bad combination.

Kane had nursed his single beer as long as possible and declined a second, so in addition to my grumpiness I felt vaguely guilty about being a poor hostess. Or about being drunk. Or something.

"Whatever," I muttered.

"I'm sorry, what did you say?" Kane asked.

"Noth-" I began just as my phone dinged.

Incoming message. Saved by the phone. I squinted at the display and deciphered 'Call home'.

Turning the screen toward Kane so he could see the message, I said, "Sorry, I have to call in. I'll be right back."

I made a grateful escape from the garage, leaving Daniel singing, "*Eighty-six bottles of root beer on the wall, eighty-six bottles of root beer...*" The first fourteen verses had been more than enough for me. If he sang eighty-five more, I might have to draw my Glock and put myself out of my misery.

Shivering in the icy darkness outside the garage's bright warmth, I momentarily regretted leaving my jacket behind; but not enough to go back for it. I wrapped my free arm around myself to conserve body heat and pulled a secured phone out of my waist pouch.

Gazing up at the black clouds devouring a brilliant moon, I drew a deep breath and punched the speed dial.

When Stemp answered on the first ring as usual, I said, "It's Aydan", and waited.

"I received a call from Nora," he said. "She is feeling discouraged that you haven't called her and is considering returning home immediately to the United Kingdom."

The censure was clear in his voice. I had promised to call her, and I hadn't. And now she might leave the country before I could investigate.

Shit!

"Sorry, I didn't get to it because I've been working on my other assignment with Kane," I mumbled. "I'll call her right now."

"Very well."

Stemp didn't add 'see that you do', but I heard it in the momentary silence before he disconnected.

"Fuck," I muttered. "You fucking bitch, you're not going to screw me over that easily." In case the moon had gotten the wrong idea, I glanced up at it and added, "Nora, I mean; not Stemp. He's not a bitch. He's jush..." I got my inebriated tongue under control and finished, "...just a bastard."

Wrapping my other arm around myself, I stood shivering

in thought. I didn't want to face Nora until I'd finished researching her, so I couldn't meet her tonight. And anyway, I was drunk. That wouldn't go well.

But if she was thinking of leaving, I'd damn well better get there bright and early tomorrow morning.

Which meant I had to go back to Sirius tonight.

I let out a long tired breath that plumed silver in the cold moonlight. The steam dissipated as rapidly as my happy dream of creeping into my warm bed.

Hell.

I stuffed the secured phone in my pocket for later disposal and brought out my personal cell phone. Squinting through my alcoholic haze, I scrolled to the Silverside Hotel's number and punched it.

When the desk clerk answered, I said, "Please connect me with Room 106", proud that my words came out precise and crystal-clear.

The phone rang only once before Nora's eager voice said 'Hello?'

She had been right beside it. Guilt softened the cold bedrock of anger and betrayal in my heart. How shitty would it be to sit alone in a hotel room all day, waiting for a call that never came?

I stiffened my spine. Not as shitty as facing the life-shattering words, 'There's been a bad accident'. Not as shitty as finding out that your mother was never coming home.

And especially not as shitty as finding out that she'd chosen not to.

"It's Aydan," I snapped.

"Oh, Dani-dear." Her voice trembled. "I thought you were never going to call."

My guts twisted with renewed guilt, but I fought it back.

Dammit, I wasn't going to let her play me.

"Sorry," I said shortly. "I'm on assignment. This was my first chance today."

"Do you... Will you come to see me tonight?"

"I can't. I'm working right now, and I'll have to work late on another job tonight." I forced some warmth into my voice. "But I'll have time tomorrow morning, if that would work for you."

"Oh, yes! You can pick me up and we can go for breakfast! Surely there must be someplace nicer than the hotel restaurant, even in a crummy little town like this."

Despite the fact that I shared her low opinion of the hotel's restaurant, defensiveness stiffened my shoulders. "Yes, there are some great little restaurants here, but I won't be able to make it in time for breakfast." More to the point, I couldn't deal with her on an empty stomach. "How about if I come around ten?"

"Oh, that would be fine! We could have a visit and go for an early lunch at one of your little restaurants; and then maybe we could-"

"I have to work tomorrow," I interrupted. "I don't know if I can get away for long."

"But Dani-dear, I've come all this way to see you." Disappointment filled her voice. "And we haven't seen each other for over thirty years."

"And whose fault is that?" I barked. I clenched my teeth before I could launch the tirade that begged for utterance. "I'll pick you up tomorrow morning at ten," I gritted instead. I punched the disconnect button and stomped back into the garage.

Kane glanced up, his smile turning to concern. "You look half-frozen." He rose from his crouch beside Daniel and an empty cardboard box that had apparently become a toy-soldier barracks. Thank God the root beer song was over, at least for now.

Kane pulled me close, rubbing hot hands over my arms and back. "Is everything all right?" he whispered for my ears only.

I slid my arms around him and huddled into his warmth. "Fine. Just another annoying twist to an annoying day. I have to go back to Sirius tonight."

Kane pulled away far enough to study me. "You're not planning to drive, are you?"

I sighed, pointing my face away so I didn't blow a gust of beer-breath into his face. "No, of course not. I don't even like to get behind the wheel after one beer, and I sure as hell wouldn't do it after three on an empty stomach. I'll..." I hesitated.

I wouldn't risk driving; but walking six miles into town in the middle of winter wasn't an option, either. "...I guess I'll see if Tom will drop me off," I said slowly. "And maybe Spider can give me a ride home when I'm done."

"Don't call Rossburn," Kane said immediately. "I'll drive you."

"But Silverside is in the opposite direction to where you're headed."

"It's not, actually." Kane smiled. "I had intended to take you to dinner anyway, and I need to check my house. I haven't been inside it for over a month; and even though I hire someone to keep an eye on it, I still like to look in whenever I'm in town."

My spirits lifted at the thought of a nice dinner. "Okay, perfect. Thanks!"

Keeping an arm around my shoulders, Kane turned to

Daniel. "Are you getting hungry for supper yet?"

Daniel looked up from his soldiers. "Uh-huh. My tummy's grumbly."

Kane smiled. "Well, let's go and get some pizza for your grumbly tummy."

Daniel sprang up. "Pizza! Yay!" Hopping from one foot to the other, he sang, "Pizza-pizza-pizza-pizza..." in time with the hopping.

I bit back a small moan and plastered on a smile for Kane's sake.

CHAPTER 11

Fortunately Fiorenza's offered crayons and paper placemats. With Daniel absorbed in colouring, Kane and I exchanged a tentative smile.

"How are you feeling?" he asked. His sidelong glance at Daniel made his meaning clear.

"Okay," I lied. "I was expecting tears and tantrums; but everything went pretty smoothly, considering."

Kane's fond gaze slipped to Daniel again before returning to me. "Yes, he's quite even-tempered most of the time, unless he's over-tired or stressed."

I faked surprise. "Oh. I was talking about myself. But Daniel did pretty well, too."

Kane laughed. "Yes, you were very good. Maybe I should give you a lollipop."

A vision of his hot hard lollipop drove every other thought from my head. The air between us crackled with sudden sexual tension.

Kane's voice deepened to a panty-vibrating bass. "Oops. How's that for a Freudian slip?"

"Um." I cleared my dry throat. "Good. Really good."

Under the table, Kane's hand slid over to find mine. Hot fingertips traced seductive circles on the sensitive skin inside my wrist. "Maybe..." he rumbled, "...you should come to my house with us."

Without conscious thought, my hand turned palm-up and opened for his touch.

"You think?" I croaked.

"Oh, yes. Definitely." His velvet voice seduced my ears.

His fingertips traced the sides of my fingers, slipping intimately between them to caress my soft places...

I shook myself back to the present. "Um... about that seven-year-old onlooker..."

"He's getting tired," Kane murmured. We both glanced at Daniel as he laid down his crayon and screwed his fists into his eyes. "If I settled him on my couch he'd be asleep in minutes."

"Without Alicia?" I came back to reality with a snort. "Not a chance. He'll wind himself up and scream bloody murder if you're not both there."

"No, he's finally over that stage," Kane said. "He's been doing really well lately. So..." He leaned closer, filling my senses with the spicy gun-oil-and-leather scent that was his alone. His hot gaze held me immobile. "What do you say?"

My brain bobbed helplessly in a sea of beer-infused lust. My lips were opening to say something irrevocable when the waitress arrived with our pizzas and a clatter of serving utensils.

Sucking in a breath that was half relief and half disappointment, I retrieved my hand from Kane's and used it to serve up my pizza instead.

Hoping to soak up some of the alcohol still coursing through my veins, I gobbled a couple of pieces of pizza at light-speed. Kane ate more decorously, slowed by the necessity of cutting up Daniel's pizza and damming a small tidal wave of milk when Daniel accidentally upset his glass.

By the time Daniel's wedge of pizza had dwindled to a few bites remaining on his plate, I had stuffed down four pieces and was heartily regretting my excesses. The overload of pizza had done nothing to mitigate my earlier beer, and I was not only still tipsy but also uncomfortably distended.

I faked enjoyment, sitting back in the banquette with a smile and a sigh. "Wow, that was amazing as usual. Fiorenza's makes the best pizza."

"Yes, I still haven't found a place in Calgary I like as-" Kane began, only to be interrupted by Daniel's small voice.

"Daddy, I don't want any more."

"That's all right, Daniel. You don't have to finish it if you're full."

"My tummy doesn't feel good." Daniel rubbed his eyes again, then clutched his midsection. His cheeks were flushed and his forehead moist, and all my instincts went on high alert. I might not know anything about children, but I was pretty sure I knew the look of pre-projectile pizza. I readied myself to dodge.

Kane swept a swift assessing gaze over Daniel. "I think we'd better get to the bathroom." Scooping an arm around the child, he manoeuvred them both out of the banquette and hurried for the back of the room.

Afraid to watch, I slid down in my seat and concentrated on my water glass. I relaxed at the distinctive squeak of the men's room door hinges, but a moment later an '*Urp-splat*' made me wince. At least he'd made it to the tiled floor instead of blowing chunks into the hallway carpet.

I whipped out my phone and cued up a game of Solitaire, studiously pretending everything was fine.

Less than thirty seconds later, the plump elderly waitress

arrived at my table, her broad face creased with concern. "Your son is being sick in the men's room."

She looked like the motherly type. I was pretty sure she'd take offense to anything that came out sounding like 'Not my kid; not my problem'.

"Um..." I said instead. "But his dad's with him, right?"

"Yes, but the poor wee tyke needs his mother." The waitress gave me a 'how-could you?' frown. "Dads just can't cut the mustard when a little one is sick."

I tried an apologetic smile. "I'm afraid his dad is it. Daniel's mother is in Calgary. This is only the second time I've met him, so I doubt if I'd be any comfort." Waves of her unspoken disapproval crashed over me, and I sighed. "I'll go and see if his dad wants my help, though."

Her grudging nod seemed like the only encouragement I was likely to get, so I hauled myself reluctantly out of my seat and plodded to the men's room. Outside, I tapped on the door and opened it a crack to call softly, "John? Do you need me to do anything?"

"Yes, please." He sounded relieved, although it was hard to tell over Daniel's sobbing. "Would you please bring a glass of ginger ale, and if they have any plastic bags, that would be..."

Another gut-twisting retch interrupted him, and the sour smell of vomit wafted to my nose.

"Be right back," I yelped, and fled.

Small towns are both a blessing and a curse. By the time I returned with ginger ale, extra paper towels, and a plastic bag, Daniel had acquired a set of surrogate grandparents. A pleasant-faced sixtyish man took the supplies from me and ferried them into the bathroom while his well-upholstered wife guarded the door, issuing decisive instructions to Kane and cooing soothing nothings at Daniel.

I faded gratefully into the background. Thank God for people who love kids.

Nearly an hour later Kane and Daniel emerged from the men's room, both looking worse for wear. A pungent aroma rose from the plastic bag that apparently contained Daniel's pants, shirt, socks and shoes. Wearing only Superman underwear, Daniel huddled miserably in Kane's arms, his face pressed into Kane's neck. Kane looked white and strained, and flecks of paper towel clinging to the wet stains on his T-shirt and jeans indicated that he'd only managed a cursory cleanup.

"I think he's over the worst of it," Kane said. "Let's get him back to my place. Would you please bring our jackets?"

"Right here." I tucked Daniel's jacket around him, trying not to disturb him. Draping Kane's jacket over his shoulders, I added, "The bill's paid. Give me your keys and I'll warm up the Expedition."

"They're in my right pants pocket." Kane nodded downward.

When I slipped my hand into the heat of his jeans I momentarily considered a joke or a playful grope, but a glance at his expression assured me that now was not the time. I snagged his keys without fanfare and hurried out.

Daniel whimpered as Kane did up his seatbelt, and I eyed him worriedly. "Do you think he needs to go to the hospital?"

Kane frowned, his eyes dark in the streetlights. "I don't know. The lady in the restaurant seemed to think this was only a normal childhood bug, but..." He swung the door shut and lowered his voice to a fierce whisper, his fists clenched by his sides. "I've only been a father for four months. How should I know? How does any parent ever know?"

My heart twisted. "I don't know. Maybe you should take him to the hospital anyway."

Kane nodded, a single decisive jerk of his chin. "You're right. I'm not equipped for this, and I'd rather look like an anxious overprotective idiot than take a chance on..." He didn't complete the sentence. "Get in," he said instead. "I'll drop you at Sirius on the way."

"It's okay, just go straight to the hospital. I'll walk to Sirius."

"I'm not going to abandon you in the middle of winter..." he began.

"You're not abandoning me," I interrupted gently. "It's only a ten-minute walk, and it was only a few degrees below zero when we left the farm. You get going. I likely won't be able to answer my phone for the next few hours, but if you need to get a message to me, call Spider."

"I will. Thank you." Kane seized me in a short fierce hug before hurrying around to the driver's side. A moment later his Expedition accelerated out of the parking lot, and I drew a breath of relief mingled with worry and started walking.

By the time I arrived at Sirius I was feeling better. The fresh air and exercise had dissipated the last of the alcohol and given me a small surge of energy. My carb high was sure to crash down into amplified fatigue as soon as I sat in a comfortable chair, but I appreciated it for the moment.

I even managed a cheerful greeting for the security guard as I signed in. "Hi, Leo. Do you know if Spider is still here?"

"Hi, Aydan. You're here late for a Sunday." At my nod and grimace, he added, "As far as I know Spider's still here.

Let me check..." He consulted his computer. "Looks like it."

"Great. Thanks." I accepted my security fob and headed for the stairs, only to trail to a halt as a thought struck me. I reversed direction and bellied up to the security wicket again. "Is Reggie Chow still here?"

Leo shook his head with a smile. "He used to hang out here pretty much 24/7, but now that he's seeing Dr. Travers..." Leo said her title with reverence. "...he doesn't spend nearly as much time at work." Apparently bored and ready for a chat, Leo shot a quick glance around the deserted lobby before leaning forward and lowering his voice. "How about that, eh? Who would've thought cranky old Reggie would end up with somebody as beautiful as her?"

I sidestepped to a different topic. "Reggie's not that old. He can't be more than thirty-five, is he?"

"Well, no; he's only thirty-three. But he's such a hard-ass, he seems a lot older." Leo's expression turned reflective. "Guess I can't blame him, though. After what he's been through." His face lit up. "Maybe getting together with Dr. Travers is some kind of cosmic payback. Kind of like a 'Sorry, Buddy' from heaven."

Unwilling to gossip about either of my friends, I gave Leo a smile. "Who knows?" I consulted my watch. "Guess I'd better get to work. Do you know if Holt's still here?"

"Yep," Leo replied without checking his screen. "But not for long." He nodded across the lobby.

When I turned to look, Holt had just come out of the secured area. He looked as tired as I felt, and as he trudged over to the security wicket I asked, "Calling it a day?"

He grunted assent, slapping his security fob into the rotating tray for Leo to collect.

"Any luck?" I added.

Holt shot a pointed look at Leo, an unspoken rebuke to me for asking about classified information outside the secured area. I was trying to summon enough energy for annoyance when Holt jerked his chin in a 'follow-me' gesture and headed for the door.

When I fell into stride beside him, he muttered, "Grandin's still bargaining. He's dropped a few tidbits and says he'll give me the good stuff when I cut him a good deal, but so far it's just been the usual bullshit: 'They know how to get to Kelly; my intel is the only thing that can save her; yadda, yadda'. I'm really starting to hate that fucking asshole."

I snorted. "Starting? That's a first. You usually hate everybody on sight."

Holt barked out a laugh. "Too fucking right. Well, let him rot 'til morning. I'm going home to bed." He gave me a narrow-eyed assessment. "You should, too. You look like shit."

"Fuck you very much," I said mildly, and he grinned and tossed me a casual salute as he strode out.

I headed for the stairs, my brain shifting into work mode as I climbed.

Seven-thirty. With any luck I could finish my search for Sam's documents, then zip across the globe to infiltrate MI5's servers and still be home in bed by ten.

After a quick trip to the ladies' room, I headed for Spider's office. The lights were on, and I tapped on the open door as I poked my head in. "Hi, Spider. How's it going?"

"Fine," he said without looking up, his fingers racing over the keyboard. A moment later he blinked and surfaced, sitting back in his chair and giving me a smile. "Sorry, I was just chasing a lead." He indicated the computer screen.

"No problem." Hope and fear quickened my pulse. "Are you finding anything? Do you know who Grandin's buyer is?"

Spider's brow furrowed, his gaze returning to the computer screen as though irresistibly drawn there. "Not yet. Grandin's not being very cooperative. He's given us a few little teasers, but..." His voice faded, fingers twitching as if in eagerness to type, and I smiled in spite of my anxiety. Spider on a cyber-trail was just as inexorable as Kane on a mission.

With Holt's words lingering in my memory, I asked, "Have you discovered anything about, um... anybody who might be out to get me? Not necessarily capture me, but hurt me?"

Spider's attention snapped to me, his brow furrowing with worry. "No. Why? Did something happen?"

"Not to me; but to my neighbour. Somebody set a leghold trap outside his door, but it doesn't make sense for anybody to want to hurt him. He's such a nice guy and he doesn't have any enemies, so I was afraid maybe the trap was meant for me and somebody just mixed up our farms."

"Ohmigod, that's awful!" Spider shuddered. "Leghold traps are barbaric! I don't even want to imagine anybody getting caught in one. I haven't got anything concrete, just Grandin's vague threats. Holt thinks he's only trying to rattle us, but I'll tune into the chatter just in case."

"Thanks. I know you're busy, but I'm in a bit of a time crunch tonight. Do you have time to spot me in the network, or should I call Holt back?"

"Don't call Holt!" The undisguised dismay in Spider's voice brought a smile to my lips, and he flushed. "He's really tired," Spider explained. "And really grumpy. I can help you tonight. Holt said I didn't need to stay late to work on this; I just..." Spider's gaze drifted back to the screen before jerking resolutely back to me. "Are you ready to start right now?"

"Yes, but I can wait if you're in the middle of something."

"No, I can do this while you're in the network. I only have to keep an ear open in case my monitoring software pings." He closed the screen and rose. "I'll go and get your network key from the secured lab."

While I waited for him to return with the network key, I checked my computer for any updates from the surveillance on Nora. The only new activity on the hotel phone was her whiny call to Stemp and my irritable response to her. She wasn't even surfing the internet. The bugs in her room had picked up a few minutes of channel-surfing before the TV went silent. After that, the only sounds were soft movement, the quiet flip of book pages, and an occasional toilet flush.

Still nothing incriminating.

Whatever. I logged off the computer and went over to flop onto the small sofa.

When Spider arrived a few minutes later, he asked, "How long do you think you'll be?"

"I don't know. If I'm gone for more than two hours, signal me, okay? I drank a bunch of beer earlier and I'd hate for my body to pee my pants while I'm gone."

"Oh..." Spider blushed. "Sure, no problem. What search term should I use if I lose you?"

"Um... let's do something really easy for me to find, because I'm headed for some high-security places. I'm pretty sure I'll get scrambled." I held my voice steady so he wouldn't realize how much that prospect frightened me.

He paled. "Oh, no! D-Do you really have to? It totally freaks me out when we lose our connection and your body goes comatose and brain-dead. I'm always afraid you'll get lost in the internet forever and never regain consciousness."

Remorse twisted my heart. I had been so focused on my own upcoming misery, I'd forgotten how upsetting this was for him.

"I'm sorry," I said. "I really hate doing it, and I know it must be awful for you, too. But I have to."

"I know; I just..." He sighed. "How about if I just run continuous searches for your name? You'll be able to find it easily, and if anybody else is watching for your name, it might attract their attention and then I can reel them in."

"Perfect. Wish me luck."

"Good luck. And Aydan..." His forehead scrunched with worry. "Be careful."

"I'll try."

But I knew it wouldn't help.

I closed my eyes and slipped into virtual reality.

CHAPTER 12

Putting off the terrifying trip to MI5's servers, I sniffed around inside the Sirius network for a while. No whiffs of Nola Kelly, Nora Taylor, or Sam Kraus rewarded me, and at last I had to admit defeat.

After another moment of hesitating in the foolish hope that I would somehow be spared the ordeal of fighting my way past MI5's security, I stiffened my resolve and oozed into the internet. As usual, I obsessively dropped tiny data markers along my path even though the shifting IP addresses would obscure most of my trail by the time I tried to return.

MI5's servers were well-hidden, but I found them at last. Hovering in the data stream, I sent tentative feelers in their direction. The storm of data at their firewalls made my virtual stomach twist.

Oh, shit. I'd never tried to breach this level of security before.

I gathered my nerve. I could do this.

Really, I could. I'd be fine. My consciousness couldn't actually get trapped forever in the internet.

Could it?

Shut up.

I launched myself at the firewall.

All my data bits exploded into a chaos of ones and zeroes. The tiny remaining spark of my consciousness tumbled helplessly.

No up, no down, no left or right.

No *out*.

Stripped to the barest semblance of self, I could only let the storm fling me where it would.

At last I hurtled across a slim ribbon of smoother flow, like a trickle of water leaving an angry ocean. I thrashed frantically backward to regain the tiny stream and let it carry me to the safety of the nearest internet data tunnel.

Clinging like a spent swimmer, I could neither pant nor sob, but I would have done both if my bodiless form had been capable of it. My few remaining data bits vibrated with sheer terror.

Did my complete consciousness still exist? Spider would be firing search after search into the internet to call me home, but I knew with cold certainty that I couldn't make it without collecting the rest of my virtual self.

I was trapped here.

My worst nightmare was coming true...

Something whisked by me, a flavour I knew.

One of my own data bits. I seized it, hugging the glorious familiarity close.

That tiny addition lent me strength enough to extend a cautious feeler into the data storm. Soon I captured another piece of my consciousness, then another. Each new assimilation replenished my strength.

With more confidence, I fashioned a net of feelers, sweeping it through the turbulent data again and again to capture the remaining fragments of myself.

At last I was whole. I was vibrating with terror and

exhaustion, but I was finally, gloriously, whole.

All perception of time had fled. It might have been minutes, hours, or days since I left Sirius. Or longer.

Would my body still be waiting for my return?

What if I had been declared legally dead? *What if they had pulled the plug and cremated my body, leaving me trapped in here forever?*

With an inaudible scream, I rocketed down the data tunnel flinging questing tendrils in all directions.

Where were my markers? Where were Spider's life-giving searches?

Aydan Kelly.

There!

Aydan Kelly. Aydan Kelly. Aydan-Kelly-Aydan-KellyAydanKelly*AydanKelly*…

I catapulted my consciousness along the stream of searches with such velocity that when I burst into Sirius's virtual file repository my avatar crashed through two walls before rolling to a sobbing halt in the corridor.

Sprawled facedown on the virtual floor with my arms and legs spread wide to take in the maximum amount of glorious sensation, I gasped my terror and relief into the sim.

"Aydan! Aydan! Omigod, say something! *Aydan!*" Spider's avatar hurtled down the corridor toward me. He flung himself to his knees, sliding the last couple of feet to lock his arms around me. "I'll get you out!" He struggled to lift me, apparently forgetting that in virtual reality his avatar could be as strong as he chose.

Paradoxically, his near-hysteria calmed me. I sucked in a shuddering breath and sat up.

"I'm okay," I croaked.

"Thank *God!*" Spider buried his face in my shoulder. "I

thought I'd lost you. I th-thought I'd lost you..."

I patted his back while he clung to me, trembling violently.

"What *happened?*" he demanded a few seconds later.

"I..." Even though I was only an avatar, I still had to stop and swallow. "I thought I'd lost me, too. How long was I gone?"

"Nearly two hours. You were brain-dead and comatose for nearly *two hours*! I called Jack, and the hospital, but we were afraid to move your body out of the building in case you were still trying to come back..." He trailed off with a gulp and hugged me tighter.

"I was. Believe me, I was." I hugged him in return. "Let's get out of here. I'm completely creeped out and I just want to get back into my body."

"Okay." Spider relinquished his grip on me and sat back on his heels. A frown formed on his forehead.

"What?" I demanded, my voice cracking. "What is it? What's wrong now?"

"Nothing," he assured me. "I was just thinking. You're probably going to be in terrible pain when you step through the network portal, aren't you? Because you're so tired."

"Probably." I dragged myself to my feet. "I don't care. Any amount of pain is better than what I just went through."

As I turned toward the portal, Spider sprang to his feet. "Hang on. Can you wait here in the virtual network just a few seconds longer? I have an idea that might help with the pain."

"I'm listening."

"Are you carrying a trank pistol? Like, in real life? On your real body?"

"Yes..." I said slowly. "In my left ankle holster. Why?"

"Because if I go out of the network first, I can pop one of the darts open to release the aerosolized tranquilizer. Your body will breathe it and pass out, and that should snap your consciousness out of the sim and back into your body. You'll wake up in about five minutes, and that's about how long it usually takes for the pain to go away, right? So you shouldn't feel a thing."

Hope dawned, but I squashed it. "But you just said I've been comatose for the last couple of hours, and I'm still in the network. Unconsciousness shouldn't be any different."

"But... it kind of... *is* different," he said slowly. "Because your coma was caused by you being in the sim, not by something that affected your physical body. It's like... a push instead of a pull."

I shrugged, still trying not to hope. "Well, I've got nothing to lose. If it works I'll be forever grateful; and if it doesn't, it only means I'll have to come out of the network normally and have my usual amount of pain. Let me know when you're ready."

"Okay, I'll have to get everybody out of your office. Then I'll do a countdown and break open the capsule. I won't be able to say anything after that because I'll have to hold my breath and leave, too, until the aerosolized trank dissipates. I'll be as quick as I can." He scurried down the corridor and disappeared.

I followed slowly, then jittered beside the portal. Oh, please, let this work...

A few minutes later, Spider's voice spoke from the virtual ceiling. "Are you ready?"

"Yes."

"On the count of three. One. Two. Three."

I swam up through murky depths, fighting my way to the surface. A steady beeping sounded next to my head, and I dragged my eyelids open to squint in that direction.

"You're back!" Spider's joyful voice coaxed my sluggish gaze in his direction, and I blinked a couple of times to make the two smiling Spiders coalesce into a single one.

"Uh," I said. "Wha'th fug?"

"It's all right, Aydan, you're just waking up from the tranquilizer." A soft female voice spoke from my other side, and I hauled my heavy head over to focus on an angel. Flawless ivory skin, a cloud of celestial-blonde hair, big blue eyes...

"Hi, Jack," I mumbled. "Thanksh." Blinking and squinting, I struggled to sit up and failed. "Dam trank," I added thickly. "Brain's work'n bu' bodysnot w'th' program yet."

"Bodysnot?" Spider laughed. "That's a new one."

"Body's... not," I enunciated with great care. "With... the... program. Yet."

With nothing to do for the next couple of minutes until my muscles came under my control again, I took stock of my crowded office. In addition to Spider and Jack, two paramedics stood near the door, frowning. The beeping noise came from the heart monitor that was attached to me via several wires, and the headdress of electrodes that belonged to Jack's brainwave-monitoring system was secured around my forehead.

I lay on an ambulance stretcher in the middle of the room. I was warm and comfortable and, miracle of miracles, I hadn't peed my pants.

Hallelujah. Although I was definitely going to head for

the bathroom as soon as my legs deigned to support me.

Should be any minute now...

I tried to sit up again and was rewarded when my body actually responded.

"Stay on the stretcher," one of the paramedics instructed, but I shook my head and disentangled myself from the blanket to swing my feet down to the floor.

"I'm fine now," I said. "You can unhook me and take out the IV line."

"You're not fine," the other paramedic snapped. "You were in a coma."

"Yeah, but I'm fine now." I gave Jack a 'help-me-out-here' glance. "Dr. Travers knows I'm fine."

Jack frowned. "My doctorate is in neuroscience, not medicine." When I scowled at her, she added reluctantly, "But I have seen Aydan experience this before, and she was fine all the other times." She consulted her instruments. "And her brainwave tracing has returned to normal."

"See? I'm fine." I held out the hand with the IV attached to it. "So could you please unhook me? I need to go to the bathroom." As the paramedic took my hand grudgingly, I said, "Spider, you won't want to watch this."

He hurriedly turned his back. "No, I'm feeling queasy just thinking about it."

"By the way, you're absolutely brilliant," I added, hoping to distract him so he wouldn't faint at the thought of blood. "That didn't hurt a bit. I want to do it this way every time from now on."

"You want to be comatose?" The paramedic eyed me with concern.

"Um, no. I was talking about something else," I said.

No matter how high his security clearance might be, it

wasn't high enough for the truth. Hell, I wasn't even going to tell Spider and Jack where I'd been.

After several more minutes of wrangling and reassurances, the paramedics produced a waiver for me to sign and departed. Jack disconnected my electronic headdress and I hurried to the bathroom, profoundly grateful for my dry pants and unwilling to take a chance by waiting any longer.

When I returned to my office, Jack fixed me with an accusing frown. "Was that wise?"

"What, peeing? Yes, absolutely." I gave her my best disarming smile.

"No," she replied with exaggerated patience. "Sending the paramedics away. By which I deduce that you have no intention of going to the hospital."

"Well, you said yourself this has happened to me before; and I've been fine every other time."

She sighed. "All we know is that we haven't been able to pinpoint any anomalies in your brain scans *thus far*. That doesn't mean you aren't incurring hidden damage; nor does it preclude the possibility that this may be the time when you actually develop an observable problem."

I hid the chill her words caused. "Spoken like a true scientist, but..." I tried my disarming smile again. "I feel fine. Better than usual, actually; thanks to Spider's idea. My exit through the portal was completely painless. It was wonderful!" My smile widened. "This is going to make my research *so* much easier!"

"No." Jack's tone was implacable. "You are not going to sniff tranquilizer darts every time you come out of the network."

"But why not?" Realizing I had just whined like a five-year-old, I attempted a mature argument. "I researched the trank pistols when I first started using them, and their safety sheet said the inhaled tranquilizer is short-acting and completely harmless. You wake up after about five minutes, and in another five minutes it's completely cleared from your bloodstream. The injected trank is the heavy-duty part of the dart."

Jack gave me a look that made it clear I wasn't going to win any science arguments with her. "That's true; but the gaseous tranquilizer's safety wasn't tested over repeated usage. There's no data on what might happen to you physically or cognitively if you inhaled it over and over, day after day."

I sighed and pretended to capitulate. "Okay, you win. Thank you for coming in on a Sunday to take care of me, Jack. I really appreciate it, but you should head home now. It's getting late and your kids will be missing you."

She gave me a radiant smile. "Oh, no; the children are fine. We had just tucked them in when Spider called, and Reggie is home in case they wake up."

"Wow. He's really diving into this relationship, isn't he?" The words popped out of my mouth before I could stop them. "You only announced yesterday that you were together."

Jack's eyes sparkled with devilish humour. "The key word being 'announced'. In reality our relationship has been developing for some time." Her smile softened. "Reggie loves children, and he's so good with Brendan and Ivy. And they adore him."

Spider chuckled. "I can't imagine Reggie loving anything. He's terrifying."

Jack drew herself up, her blue eyes turning glacial.

"Reggie's scarring is a normal result of physical trauma from a catastrophic explosion and extensive burns. It most certainly is not terrifying; and I don't want to ever hear you say such a thing in front of my children." Frost formed in the air around her. "Or ever again to anyone, for that matter."

Spider went white, then beet-red. "Ohmigod!" he stammered. "No, I'm sorry, I didn't mean it that way! I just meant he's... his *personality* is terrifying. He scares the bejeebers out of just about everybody at Sirius. Me included. I'm sorry, I didn't mean..." He trailed off helplessly, his ears purple with mortification.

"Oh." Jack thawed immediately, and a flush stained her cheeks, too. "I'm sorry, I should have realized you would never say anything so insensitive. I'm just..." She gave him a sheepish look. "Oversensitive about it myself, I suppose. The children were afraid of Reggie because of his appearance at first, and we've been working hard to help them understand that disfigurement isn't anything to fear or shun or ridicule. They've absorbed the lesson far better than most adults, so I'm very careful not to let anyone undo that." She reached out to him. "I'm so sorry. Will you forgive me?"

"Of course." He squeezed her hand, his flush draining away. "I get it. It's okay."

"Well." Jack gave us a wry smile. "I think I'll withdraw before I put my foot in my mouth again." She packed up the metal case that contained her equipment and headed for the door. "Goodnight, Spider; Aydan. And again, please forgive my outburst."

"No problem," I said at the same time as Spider said, "It's fine. Thanks again for coming in."

She smiled and left with a small wave.

I fell back on the sofa cushions with a long breath.

"Whew. Don't ever rat me out to Jack, okay?"

"I won't," Spider said fervently, then paused. A crease formed between his brows. "Wait, what would I have to rat about?"

"Nothing, yet. But she'll be unbelievably pissed if she finds out I went back into the network again tonight and sniffed tranks to get out painlessly."

CHAPTER 13

"*What?*" Spider's voice came out in a high-pitched yelp that made me wince and shoot an anxious glance at the doorway in case Jack wasn't out of earshot yet. "No, you can't! You were comatose for nearly two hours! Jack would kill me if I let you..." He trailed off, then finished, "Never mind; *I'd* kill me if I let you go back in there tonight!"

He assumed his sternest expression, which was approximately as intimidating as a newborn puppy growling. "Aydan, you are not allowed to go back into the network tonight."

With an effort, I managed not to coo 'Aw, you're so cute'. Instead, I hid my gut-dropping fear in a firm decisive voice. "I'm sorry, I know how awful that was for you; but I have to do this tonight. I have a meeting with Nora tomorrow morning that I can't miss; and I absolutely have to gather intel before then."

"But..." Spider looked as though he might cry. "What if..." He drew a deep shaky breath and squared his jaw. "Okay. I know it's your job. I just... I really hate that this is so dangerous for you. What can we do to make it safer this time?"

My heart warmed. "You're the best."

"Thanks," he mumbled. "But if this is what 'the best' feels like, I can do without it." His voice firmed. "So where are you trying to go?"

"Um..."

I wanted to tell him. But I was pretty sure that hacking into one of our allies' servers was an international incident waiting to happen; and if it ever came to light I didn't want him caught in the shitstorm.

"I can't tell you," I said. "Sorry. But it's a really secure server and I got totally thrashed." The thought of trying again chilled my blood, and I shivered. What if I couldn't rebuild my consciousness this time?

"There has to be another way," Spider insisted. "Some back door to the server that you haven't found yet, or..."

Revelation struck, and my mouth fell open.

"What?" Spider demanded. "What did you just think of?"

A slow smile stretched my lips. "You're brilliant!" I beamed at him. "What would I do without you?"

"Um..." He eyed me uncertainly.

"A back door." I couldn't stop grinning. "Why didn't I think of that?"

"What do you mean?"

"I mean..." I stopped, replaying the last horrifying attempt in my mind. "I've been brute-forcing my way into servers all this time because I was thinking that I had to breach their firewalls. I'm an idiot! There's always another way in."

"Well, not always," Spider countered cautiously. "If that server is as secure as you say..."

"It's not. None of them are. *That's* what that little calm current was! Ha!"

Spider looked worried, and I hastened to explain. "I got caught up in the usual data storm outside their firewall. The first time you explained it, you said it was probably a proxy server rejecting unauthorized data packets. So it's this giant cement-mixer of data, and that's where I got scrambled."

"Okay..." he said slowly.

"So the proxy server is bouncing back all kinds of traffic that's trying to come in." I jabbed a finger at the air for emphasis. "But something has to come out of that server, right? Or they wouldn't have any internet connection at all."

"Right..."

I grinned wider. "So I found it. All this time I've been trying to push through or surf over that ugly mess, when I should have just been sitting at the edge watching for the little stream of data coming out. Because if something's coming out, that means there's a way in!"

"Um..." Spider frowned. "It doesn't really work that way. But you don't seem to be bound by the usual laws of network topology anyway, so... if you think it'll work, it probably will."

My enthusiasm subsided, overcome by bone-deep weariness. I sighed. "It had better work. Because if it doesn't, it's going to be one hell of a long night."

"Should I, um..." Spider hesitated. "If you go comatose again, do you want me to call Jack and the paramedics?"

"No," I said hurriedly, flinching at the thought of Jack's wrath. "I mean, not unless I've been unconscious for hours. My heart rate and blood pressure and everything stays normal, doesn't it? So the paramedics don't really do anything except stick an IV in my hand and monitor me?"

"That's right." Spider gave me an anxious frown. "So far. But what if..."

I held up my palm in a gentle 'stop' gesture. "We can 'what-if' all night long, but if I haven't died yet I probably won't tonight."

Spider pressed his lips together, but they trembled anyway. "You *were* dead. Your brainwave tracing was flat. Your heart was still beating, but your... whatever it is that makes you 'you'... was gone."

The urge to shudder was strong, but I managed to suppress it. "Right," I said in the most matter-of-fact tone I could summon. "Because my consciousness was in the internet. My brainwaves went flat because my consciousness lost its anchor to this network, but I wasn't dead. I was just... away. For a while."

Spider wrapped skinny arms around himself. "That doesn't make me feel any better." He sighed. "We'd better get started before I completely lose my nerve."

"Okay." I closed my eyes and stepped into virtual reality before he could voice any more objections that would make me lose my nerve, too.

After we'd done our usual pre-flight check and I had faded into invisibility, I hesitated for a long moment inside the safety of Sirius's network.

Was this really worth risking my life?

Maybe I should just pretend I wanted to reconcile with Nora, and subtly question her in the guise of 'catching up'.

Anger vibrated my data bits. Yeah, I could ask questions all day long, and she could lie to me over and over; just like she'd already done.

And if she killed Ian, his death would be on my conscience if I hadn't done everything I could to investigate.

Not an option.

Before I could change my mind, I dove into the vast

tunnels of the internet.

A handful of my original markers still remained, and I found MI5 quickly this time. Of course. Some small cowardly part of me... okay, fine; the giant cowardly majority of me had been hoping I wouldn't be able to find it at all.

But there it was, its deadly data storm churning up ripples all the way to the tunnel where I hovered fearfully.

Clinging to the data tunnel, I extended delicate tentacles, letting them tumble in the maelstrom. After a few minutes one tentacle-tip found...

There.

That calm little stream. Pulling the rest of my tentacles into it, I mapped its course and dimensions.

Now, ease into it...

After a brief terrifying bobble I released my hold on the tunnel and slipped into the stream, concentrating on staying in its centre.

Turbulent data churned on all sides. Fighting fear, I concentrated on a ridiculous image of myself as a sperm with a squiggly little tail, wriggling madly upstream toward my goal. Gross; but at least the adolescent part of my mind was snickering instead of screaming.

Ahead I sensed the router port opening and closing, emitting stream after stream of data. If I had been capable of breathing, I would have drawn a deep breath. Closer... closer...

The port opened and suddenly I was through, floating in the relative peace of an internal network.

Well, hello, MI5. You've just been screwed.

My anchor to Sirius was only a whisper of sensation, but it was there. My body wasn't in a coma, and I'd be able to find my way home.

Fortunately I wasn't capable of actual physical movement, since my victory jig wouldn't have been pretty.

Settle down. Make this count.

Swallowing my triumph, I surged forward.

Personnel files were my first stop. There, I discovered Nora Taylor's original interview and the records of her aptitude tests when she had applied for a position as an analyst in 1983.

She had been brilliant. She had no experience at all, but her aptitude tests were nearly off the charts. They had offered her the position the very next day.

Subsequent decades showed her meteoric rise through the organization: Commendation after commendation; raise after raise. She'd started from nothing at the age of forty-four, and built a career that made it clear she deserved her current position as Weapons Director despite her lack of scientific background.

For the first time, I wondered what it must have been like for her as a young woman. Married to my father straight out of high school, she took on the never-ending job of farm wife and did bookkeeping for friends and neighbours as well. Then the miscarriages had started, and when she finally gave birth to me at twenty-five I became her world.

After that came years of grinding farm labour, topped by the additional burden of motherhood. Planting and harvest, calving and butchering, gardening and picking and preserving fruit and vegetables; and none of it had used more than a fraction of her intellect. Had she secretly resented it?

Resented me?

What if she had felt the same as I did about children? What if she had gritted her teeth and done her duty until her child was old enough to survive without her; and then fled for her own sanity, never looking back?

Gut-deep sympathy welled up, squeezing my heart with equal parts pity for her and pain for myself.

But if that was the case, why would she suddenly change her mind after thirty years?

She wouldn't. If she had hated her life with me that much, she'd still be hiding.

Unless she had something to gain by returning.

Shit.

I switched to Howard Coleman's file.

His qualifications were impressive, too, and his file ended with a copy of his autopsy report. Interesting. Was that a standard procedure if an employee died while still in MI5's employ, or had someone suspected something?

And was Ian that 'someone'?

I examined the report but the complicated medical terms only seemed to translate to 'Fatal heart attack of unknown cause'. No surprises there.

A quick survey of the rest of the files showed that nobody had died before Nora took over any of her previous positions. No sign of promotion-by-murder.

Maybe Ian had only been bullshitting to lure me into his bed. That seemed a whole lot more likely than him fearing that a petite seventy-two-year-old woman would sneak into his hospital room and kill him.

Time to investigate Ian.

But his data would be with MI6, the Brits' foreign intelligence branch; not here in MI5. Thank God I'd finally figured out how to breach high-security servers without getting thrashed.

Slithering back into the internet, I sought out MI6's

servers and the telltale trickle of data that offered me easy access. Moments later I found Ian's personnel file.

Reading between the lines of his commendations and promotions, I recognized the brash young agent who had slowly matured into Ian's current James Bond persona. His early ops were full of breath-taking risks that somehow turned out well, often through sheer luck. If I'd been his director I would have wanted to slap him in the head.

Sure enough, notes in his personnel file showed multiple rebukes from Ian's commanding officers; but they were mere formalities when stacked against his success rate.

As I skimmed through his later mission reports I noted the development of Ian's devious nature: Lies and half-truths exploited for maximum benefit, successes achieved through deception of such jaw-dropping magnitude it seemed that nobody should have believed him; but clearly they had. He was remarkably convincing, the bastard.

My attention snagged on his mission report from the hippie commune last year, and I slowed to read it thoroughly. All the details coincided with what Moonbeam and Karma and Skidmark had told me and what I had experienced myself, except...

If I'd had a mouth in my current bodiless state, it would have fallen open. That sneaky *bastard*.

He'd lied to me again.

CHAPTER 14

Granted, Ian's lie wasn't a huge one, but as far as I could see he'd had no reason to lie to me at all. Last week he'd told me that he'd taken all the credit for subduing the terrorists at the commune in order to keep our names out of his official report. His words echoed in my mind as though he'd just spoken them: *'My official report states that I singlehandedly eliminated sixteen terrorists.'*

The report didn't say that.

Instead, it said that Ian had killed one terrorist before being shot himself, and that other undercover operatives had killed the remaining fifteen terrorists. As he had promised, our names weren't mentioned in his report. But had he simply placed that information in a different file?

I flung virtual feelers in all directions, letting go of my conscious mind and opening myself up to feel/smell/taste/listen for any familiar names.

Long minutes later I came up empty. If Ian had recorded our names somewhere, it wasn't in any official files.

So far, so good.

And what about his claim that he had investigated Nora himself when she had mentioned my name?

Another long search netted no results; but that didn't

mean much, dammit. If Ian had secretly investigated Nora, he wouldn't have left any records behind.

So had he lied to me about his investigation or not?

If I could have blown out a frustrated sigh, I would have. This was a waste of time. Ian was a good agent and I believed he was loyal to his country and had kept his promises to me... so far.

But no matter what I found or didn't find here, I could never trust him to tell me the whole truth. Or hell, even part of it. He had his own agenda, and all I could do was hope my wellbeing didn't conflict with it.

Heartily sick of other people's deception, I allowed myself a wistful thought of Hellhound. I knew with absolute certainty that he would never lie to me or compromise my safety or happiness, even if it meant sacrificing himself.

Even Kane couldn't match that level of integrity, despite our red-hot chemistry. He probably did love me; and I knew he would lay down his life for me if necessary. But it wasn't the grand gestures that really mattered in a relationship; it was the mundane daily details...

Hang on.

Details.

My drifting mind snapped into focus while Kane's voice spoke in my memory: *'The Weapons lab gave me the drug.'*

A deadly classified drug would be tightly controlled. If the Brits had any of it, the records should be part of their domestic security branch in MI5. And if Nora had stolen some, the shortfall should show up somewhere.

I rocketed back through the data tunnels, sniffing for weapons or drugs.

When I found their internal Weapons server, my mind recoiled.

So much deadly technology. For someone like Reggie Chow who ate, drank, and breathed weapons, this would be a glorious bonanza. For me it was stomach-churning. So many ways to injure and maim and kill...

I jerked my mind back to the job at hand. Concentrate.

After a lengthy search during which I tried not to absorb too many graphic details, I discovered Substance X: '*A colourless, odourless, tasteless drug undetectable except by specialised analysis; induces acute hypertension and thrombotic embolism resulting in death from acute myocardial infarction or cerebrovascular accident.*'

Pushing aside the horrible memories of the real-life consequences of those clinical words, I concentrated on the drug's chain-of-custody reports. As I had suspected, it was only manufactured in tiny quantities. Only one or two doses were kept on hand at any time. The records were complete and no doses had gone missing.

Ever.

So unless Nora had somehow managed to procure a highly classified and extremely rare drug from somewhere else, which seemed unlikely in the extreme... Ian was full of shit.

I had already suspected that; but disappointment scored my heart nevertheless. He had only been playing me, as usual.

I was backing out of the chain-of-custody reports when another detail caught my eye. To maintain freshness, the drug's stored doses were destroyed annually and new doses were created to replace them. A notation from six months ago indicated that a dose had failed during a mission, and the entire batch had subsequently been discarded and remade. The chemist attributed the failure to the fact that the dose had been nearing its expiration date and the survivor had been young and healthy.

Inspiration sparked through me.

What if Nora had pocketed one of the discarded doses instead of destroying it? The drug might still have been potent enough to work on an elderly man.

Their protocol required two people to observe and sign off on the destruction of each dose, but someone as smart as Nora could undoubtedly figure out how to circumvent the safeguards...

A tiny tug on my consciousness shook me out of my train of thought. Spider, signalling me to return.

Dammit, I wasn't done here. Maybe I could stay a bit longer and pretend I hadn't noticed his summons.

No. I'd ravelled poor Spider's nerves enough with my first disastrous trip. And what if he had some urgent news for me?

Oh God, what if Daniel had taken a turn for the worse? The thought of Kane pacing alone in the barren corridors of the emergency room had me rocketing out of MI5's servers without another thought.

The distant thread of Spider's connection guided me unerringly through the convoluted internet connections. Less than a second later I was outside Sirius's firewall, closing the last millisecond gap to-

A blinding explosion of data pulverized my consciousness.

Chaos.

Drowning.

I was lost in...

Sam Kraus.

Nora Taylor.

Sirius.

Who the *hell* was Rebecca Stile?

She was the owner of all these memories.

Panicked comprehension flared. I'd collided with another mage. Shit, no! This couldn't happen!

It *was* happening.

Yanking my consciousness together with all my strength, I flung myself against the data storm.

It surrounded me, its frantic data bits stinging like electronic wasps while I pried Rebecca Stile's consciousness away from my own. Creating a virtual net, I deposited bit after bit of her into the net, snapping it shut after each addition to capture her pulsating data.

The task was gargantuan. Fear and exhaustion weakened my grasp.

She fought me, her consciousness clinging with such ferocity that detaching each piece of her felt like peeling off a layer of skin.

God, what if I couldn't do this?

But I couldn't fail. Couldn't allow a single one of my memories to remain in her mind.

My world contracted to three dogged steps on an unending treadmill. Pull off another piece of her, slip it into the data net, snap the net shut. Pull off another piece...

When suddenly there were no more pieces, I wavered uncertainly in the data tunnel.

Was that all of her?

My net vibrated with the wild oscillation of her data bits. Straining to hold her, my consciousness dragged itself through one final inspection.

Nothing. That should be all of her.

But now what?

How could I protect everyone from this woman who shouldn't exist? This woman who had access to all the world's secured data, but lacked the knowledge and ability to deal with it?

My grip on the net slipped and nearly failed. Quivering on the verge of panic, I poured every ounce of my strength into the effort of keeping her contained.

If I let her go, we would be doomed. Nobody could stop her.

And I couldn't hold on much longer.

Only one option remained.

Overcoming sickening guilt, I did what I'd sworn I would never do.

I altered her memories.

Just a tiny insertion. An absolute certainty that she could never have developed on her own.

Done.

Snapping my consciousness into an impervious cannonball, I released the net.

Rebecca Stile's explosion blasted me through Sirius's firewall. My avatar crashed through the virtual file room, smashing into a chair and sending it flying.

Tumbling helplessly.

Floor-ceiling-floor-*oh-shit*...

My back slammed into the edge of the table. Agony flared through my spine and ribs.

Motionless in a crumpled heap, I lay panting and whimpering at the pain that blazed through my chest with each breath.

"*Aydan!*" Spider sprinted through the door. "*What happened?*"

My back was broken. I couldn't feel my feet...

The shock of panic slapped some sense into me. This is virtual reality. Get it together.

As soon as the thought registered, my pain and paralysis faded into the bone-deep ache of fatigue that I knew my physical body would be experiencing.

Spider was still firing questions at me with machine-gun speed. Kneeling beside me wild-eyed and trembling, he looked absolutely terrified.

That made two of us.

I held up a hand to deflect his questions, and a groan escaped as I hauled myself into sitting position.

"Sorry to scare you," I croaked. "I'm okay, but we have a really fucking big problem."

CHAPTER 15

I hadn't thought Spider could get paler, but virtual reality had no limits. His avatar went paper-white.

"What's wrong?" His voice came out in a squeaky whisper.

"There's another mage. One that only Sam knew about. And she's in the internet right now."

"Oh, *crap!* What happened? Tell me everything!"

"I will, but I need to tell Stemp, too. Might as well tell you both at once." Suppressing a groan of sheer exhaustion, I hauled my avatar upright. "What time is it?"

"Three-fifteen AM." Spider followed me as I plodded out of the virtual file room toward the portal. "I signalled you at midnight because I thought you'd need a break," he went on anxiously. "I was pulling and pulling on your anchor, but nothing happened. I was afraid to pull too hard in case I broke the connection, but it's been hours and I didn't know what to do..."

"You did everything right." I patted his shoulder. "I was busy separating my data from the other mage's and I couldn't leave until I was done, but I'm really glad you didn't break the connection."

As I stepped toward the portal, Spider halted my avatar

with an outstretched hand. "Let me go through first and break open a tranquilizer for you."

Tears of abject gratitude prickled my eyes, and I blinked them into invisibility before he could see them. "Thanks," I whispered.

He stepped through the portal, and I waited for his 'Three... two... one'.

I was so comfortable here in the warm friendly darkness. Everything was fine. So easy and safe...

"Aydan."

Something jostled my shoulder and I grunted and pulled away, retreating into my interrupted slumber.

"Aydan, wake up."

More shoulder jostling.

I growled and flailed out a defensive arm.

The resulting smack and cry of dismay jerked my eyes open to see Spider clutching his face.

"Shit!" I sat up so fast my head spun and the edges of my vision darkened ominously. "I'm sorry!" I exclaimed. "Are you okay?"

"I'm fine." He lowered his hand, revealing a reddening mark on his cheek. "You just startled me."

"No, I hit you." Guilt twisted my stomach. "I'm sorry, I was dreaming, and I didn't know what I was doing. I'm so sorry!"

"It's okay, I figured you were dreaming. You were unconscious for five minutes like I expected and then you started to, um... snore." Pink rose on his cheeks and he hastened to add, "Just a little bit. Not loudly or anything, but..."

I smiled despite the anxiety corroding my stomach. "It's okay, you don't have to be tactful. Thanks for the trank, and thanks for waking me up. If you hadn't, I'd have snored the night away right here on this couch."

When I sat up, my neck cramped viciously. "Oh fuck, ow... ow..." Cautiously rotating my head, I eased the kinks out and staggered to my feet. My bladder responded with a painful spasm and I let out an involuntary gasp. "Holy*shit*gotta*go*!" I scuttled for the door, every muscle in my body clenched with the effort of not peeing my pants.

When I returned from the ladies' room at a less urgent speed a few minutes later, Spider was pacing worriedly in my office.

I flopped into my desk chair and reached for the phone receiver. "Are we the only ones here?"

"Um..." Spider frowned. "As far as I know. I haven't heard anything in the past five hours, and nobody's walked by in the hallway."

"Okay, good. Then I'll put my call to Stemp on speaker so we can both talk to him. I'll just check with the security desk to make sure we're really alone."

A quick scan with my bug detector reassured me that we were secure, and the security desk confirmed that we were the only staff remaining in the building besides security personnel. I disconnected with a sigh of relief and punched the speaker button before dialling Stemp.

His wide-awake 'Yes?' after the first ring made me feel even more exhausted than I already was. I managed not to groan, but my voice came out sounding as though I was at the bottom of a barrel.

"Hi, it's Aydan. Spider's here with me and we've got you on speaker. The building's secure, so we can talk." I didn't expect or receive a response, so I kept going. "I'm sorry to bother you in the middle of the night, but we have a serious security issue. I just encountered another mage in the network."

As always, I envied his nerves of steel. He didn't suck in a horrified breath. Instead, his voice sharpened to a scalpel-edge. "From the U.S. program?"

"No. Totally new. She wasn't even in any of the Knights' records."

A muffled word that might have been an expletive floated over the line. Any other time I might have been shocked at the breach of Stemp's icy self-control, but under the circumstances it seemed like a perfectly appropriate reaction.

"What did you get from her?" he snapped. "And more importantly, what did you disclose?"

"I didn't disclose anything. She doesn't know I exist. And I got everything from her." I rubbed my aching forehead, trying to ease the too-full sensation of someone else's lifetime of memories squeezed into my mind along with my own. "She doesn't know that the brainwave-driven network exists and she doesn't know anything about the other mages or the network keys. She's basically in the same situation as I was a year and a half ago, stumbling into something she doesn't understand. And she has even less frame of reference to deal with it than I did."

"Which could be beneficial or disastrous," Stemp said tightly. "What else?"

"Her name is Rebecca Stile and she works for the UK branch of Sirius Dynamics. I think that's why she was hanging around near our servers; she was thinking of Sirius and must have subconsciously followed my markers here without realizing what she was doing. I have her home address and phone number and email..." I reeled them off before the memory could fade while Spider recorded the information on his laptop, his fingers flying.

I went on, "Sam discovered her at the same time as the rest of us, but he didn't add her to the official list so the other Knights never knew about her. He gave her all the same tests while she was growing up, and when she turned eighteen he offered her a dream job as his personal assistant. In exchange for complete confidentiality, keeping her hair dyed *any colour but red* for the rest of her life, and relocating to Britain, he would give her lifetime employment with the UK branch of Sirius Dynamics with raises and an indexed pension, an apartment of her own, and glamorous European holidays a couple of times a year. She's been working for Sirius UK ever since."

A moment of silence floated on the line, and I imagined Stemp's incisive mind coming to the same conclusion I'd already reached.

"She was Kraus's insurance policy in case he lost control of Sirius Dynamics," Stemp deduced. "He kept Rebecca Stile secret from the rest of the Knights so he could access classified information for his own purposes without their knowledge."

"Yeah, I think so." I let out a breath of pure fatigue. "She doesn't know anything about it; but that scenario fits. Up to now I've thought Nora was lying about getting Sam to move away with her, because he was so obsessed with getting me into his program that I just couldn't see him giving up. But if he had a fallback plan..."

"Rebecca Stile could have been it," Stemp agreed. "If so, Kraus's delay in leaving Canada makes sense. He had to wait until she was legally an adult so he could offer her the job."

"Right." Bitterness twisted my heart. "So he got everything he wanted. He got my mom and a new life in the UK, and he got Rebecca so he could continue his so-called research. And he got me in the end, too. That fucking bastard."

"There will be time for anger later," Stemp said. "Right now our priority is shutting down Rebecca Stile. How did she get into the network? And how can we contain her if she has the same abilities as you?"

"We can't," I said, weariness dragging at my bones. "But I think I've bought us some time."

"How?"

"Her cushy lifetime job kept her from developing any useful skills beyond basic clerical work. She doesn't know much about computers, and she hasn't a clue what just happened to her or where she is. She thinks she nodded off at her desk and she's having a horrible nightmare. So I..." I hesitated, guilt twisting my guts all over again. "I added a thought to her mind. A... certainty. She knows, or thinks she knows, that if she stays exactly where she is and ignores everything around her, she'll wake up soon and everything will go back to normal."

"Risky," Stemp objected.

"Yeah." I sighed. "But I don't think she's going to pop out of the network and blab."

"Why not?"

I squeezed my eyes shut and suppressed a shudder. "She's been bouncing around the internet since about four o'clock PM yesterday, London time. She got an email from Nora asking for some financial files and even though it was Sunday over there, she went to the office. The last normal thing she remembers was looking in one of Sam's desk drawers for the USB thumb drive that contained the financial archives. She found a thumb drive and plugged it in..."

"I bet it was one of the brainwave-driven network generators, wasn't it?" Spider interjected eagerly. "And if her network key was anywhere nearby and her mind wandered for a few minutes, she would have slipped into the network without realizing it, just like you did the first time, right?"

"Right," I agreed without opening my eyes. "And she's been floating around in the internet for over eighteen hours." I held my voice absolutely flat, hoping to hide the nausea churning in my stomach. "Her body will have lost bladder and bowel control after that long. And it's nearly ten-thirty in the morning over there. Somebody will have found her by now and rushed her to the hospital, where they'll discover she's in a coma with no brain activity. As long as they tube-feed her body, she'll survive..."

I swallowed rising bile. "...but if somebody doesn't take her network key and the network generator to the hospital and go into virtual reality to guide her out, she'll be trapped in the internet forever."

CHAPTER 16

"Ohmigod." Spider's voice came out strangled. "Ohmi*god*! That's horrible! We have to get Rebecca out of the internet!"

"No." Stemp's tone was coolly analytical. "We do not. Well done, Kelly. She may be privy to a great deal of damaging information at the moment, but as long as she is ignoring it and incapable of communicating it to anyone..."

"We can't just leave her there!" Spider burst out. "That's *sick!* I won't stand by and-"

"You will," Stemp interrupted. "Because you are currently incapable of altering the situation."

I opened my eyes in time to see furious spots of red blaze into Spider's pale cheeks. "*You*..." he began.

I clamped a hand on his wrist, making him sputter into silence. I wasn't sure whether he would actually yell obscenities at Stemp, but now wasn't the time to find out.

"We'll have to get her out," I said firmly. "Because until she's out, we can't go in. We can't risk Tammy encountering her, and if I'm exhausted I can't deal with another collision, either. And as for the idea that she can't communicate..." I shrugged, feeling the ache of tension in my shoulders. "...if she realizes where she is and what's happening, she could send emails or create data files on any server in the world. So the sooner we get her out, the better. I just hope the memory I implanted will keep her calm until then."

And keep her from realizing that she was living my worst nightmare. I shuddered.

"If her physical body died, that would solve the problem, would it not?" Stemp's clinical tone sent a shiver of nausea through my guts.

If he issued a kill order, Rebecca Stile would be dead within hours; maybe less. And he'd do it, too. I knew it with absolute certainty.

"I wouldn't want to count on it," I said hurriedly. "When my physical body was comatose it didn't matter a bit to my consciousness in the internet. I came out of the network when my physical body was tranked unconscious; but I knew what was happening and I *wanted* to come out. What if her body died but her consciousness didn't know it had been separated? And if her consciousness stayed in the internet, we'd have no way to ever get her out. She could exist in there forever, learning more and getting crazier and more dangerous all the time."

My voice quivered at the end of the sentence. I had only been trying to prevent Stemp from killing Rebecca in cold blood; but now that I'd thought it through, her destructive potential was horrifying. Not to mention the possibility of her eternal captivity.

"So we have to get her out," I finished, my pulse thumping. "The sooner the better."

Spider's fists clenched. "We have to do it now while we can still find her! Even if she stays right where she is, the IP addresses will shift and the route you used to find her will be gone."

My heart plummeted. "Shit, I didn't think of that. What if she's already lost? Tammy or I could run into her anytime. I can handle it if I'm rested, but when I'm wiped out like this..." I trailed off, too tired to even finish the sentence. "And Tammy wouldn't have a clue," I went on. "She'd give away every scrap of classified data she knows without even realizing it..."

I considered the possibilities for a moment, but my worn-out brain rebelled. I shot Spider a questioning look. "Maybe Tammy's mind would be shielded because she goes in with Brock controlling her the way the original Knights did...?"

"I doubt it," Spider said. "I think the Knights purposely designed the system so the mages would do a complete memory-sync every time they met. Brock might be able to override it with his control chip, but we've never attempted it..."

"That is an unacceptable risk," Stemp snapped. "Webb, I thought you had developed a way to allow Kelly and Ms. Mellor to coexist inside the network if they collided. Can't we do the same in this situation?"

"No." Spider knotted his bony fingers together but they trembled anyway. "It was never really a solution; only a workaround. The problem is that mages are, um..."

He hesitated, obviously searching for an explanation that would make sense to non-techies. He blew out a breath and dove in. "Okay, so you know about bandwidth, right? How any given connection can only handle a certain rate of data transfer?"

"Yes," Stemp replied. "And the bandwidth varies with the type of connection. Sirius's optical-fibre backbone allows us maximum bandwidth."

"Right," Spider agreed. "And that's what makes the mages so unique. When they're in the internet they're like... super-compressed data bursts. Their consciousness squishes billions of megabytes of data into a crazy-efficient format so they can travel through connections that normally wouldn't handle even a tiny fraction of that bandwidth."

Enlightenment dawned, and I fell back in my chair. "So that's why it's such a data storm whenever I meet another mage. I'm just happily floating along in the regular data flow; and then all of a sudden, wham, I'm completely overwhelmed."

"Yes," Spider agreed. "So my workaround is to throttle Tammy's data connection down to practically nothing whenever I know you're both in the network." He sighed. "And that's why it won't work with Rebecca, or with any other external mage. I can't throttle a signal that doesn't originate here." His voice rose with urgency. "But we have to go and find Rebecca right now, or we'll lose her..." He gulped. "Omigod, what if the hospital takes her off life support because she's brain-dead? What if Rebecca's body dies but her ghost lives on forever in the internet?"

Stemp's reply was as dispassionate as always. "Unavoidable. You have done all you can do tonight. Kelly is, by her own admission, exhausted and unable to risk another contact. File a report containing all of Rebecca Stile's pertinent data, before her memories fade from Kelly's mind. Then both of you go home and sleep. When Kelly is rested, you may attempt to find Ms. Stile..." His tone sharpened. "...but you are not to re-enter the network under any circumstances without my explicit permission. I will notify Brock that the covert decryption program is on hold and that he and Ms. Mellor are to stay out of the network until further notice."

"But at least let me check to see whether she's been admitted to a hospital," Spider begged. "I could-"

"No," Stemp said, his voice hard as iron. "I will assign one of the on-duty analysts to check hospital records. You are to file your report, return Kelly's network access key immediately to the secured area, leave the building, go to your respective homes, and go to sleep. Both of you. That's an order. Understood?"

Spider and I exchanged a helpless glance.

"Understood." Spider's and my acquiescence came out on a groan and a sigh, respectively.

"Good night." Stemp hung up.

My eyes fell shut and I let out a long sigh. When I dragged my eyelids open again, Spider was watching me with an expression of fearful anticipation.

"So..." He glanced over his shoulder at the open door as if afraid to be overheard. "Are we going to..."

"Disobey a direct order?" I finished. "No. Not this time, anyway." Defeated, I hauled myself out of the desk chair and trudged over to fall onto the couch, burying my head in my hands. "Stemp's right," I said to the floor. "I couldn't handle another collision right now. And if I go back to where I left her and she's still there, we'll collide for sure and I'll end up giving away classified information that could kill a lot of innocent people. I feel sick about leaving her in there, but there's nothing more we can do tonight."

"Oh..." Spider's voice trailed off into a minor key.

I didn't want to see the hope dying in his eyes, so I kept my face in my hands.

"Well, that's a relief," he said.

"What?" My head popped up.

He was watching me with a bittersweet smile. "I hate that we can't do anything right now; but I'm glad you're not going to risk your life trying." He poised his fingers over his laptop keyboard. "Tell me, as best you can, where in the internet you met Rebecca. An IP address, some kind of recognizable data; anything. And tell me everything that might be important about Rebecca Stile."

It didn't take long. My mind was crowded with her memories, but most of them were irrelevant. I sighed and fell back on the sofa. "I wish she'd known more about what was going on with the UK branch of Sirius Dynamics. And especially whether Nora knew about what Sam was doing. All those happy memories of vacations with Nora and Sam are completely fucking useless."

I tried not to sound bitter, but Rebecca's memory of calling Nora 'my second mom' made my stomach ache. Especially since Nora had never told Rebecca about me, her real daughter.

Not one word.

Spider closed his laptop, rose, and stretched before coming over and reaching down to help haul me off the sofa. "Come on, let's call it a day. Or a night." He grimaced. "Or, heck; a morning, I guess. At least we can still get a few hours of sleep."

"That sounds like heaven..." I trailed off as a thought struck me. "Oh. Actually, never mind. You go on home. I'm going to sleep here in my office."

"But..." Spider's brows drew together. "Wait, you're not sending me away so you can try to save Rebecca without getting me in trouble, are you?"

"No, I'm not that noble." I gave him a grimace. "Or that stupid. It's just that I don't have my car tonight. Things got complicated earlier and John ended up bringing me in. Which reminds me, have you heard from him?"

"No. Should I have?"

"No; no news is good news. Daniel got sick and John wasn't sure how serious it was, so he took him to the hospital. I told him to call you if anything went wrong, so that must mean it's only a normal childhood bug."

Spider's frown deepened. "I hope Daniel's okay. But you don't need to sleep here. I'll drive you home."

"No, that's okay, it's the middle of the night..." I began.

"And that's why you need to go home and sleep in your own bed," he said firmly. "Come on. I'll take your network key down to the secured area on the way out, and then I'll drive you home."

I surrendered. "Thanks, you really are the best!"

Crossing the parking lot toward his tiny Smart Fortwo a few minutes later, I shot a worried look up at the fat snowflakes floating down from the dark sky.

"I don't think you'd better try driving on the highway." I shuffled my feet through the fluffy accumulation. "There's a good four inches of new snow here and my road wasn't great to start with. Your little tires aren't designed for this."

Spider frowned. "I hate to admit it, but you're right. I'll be lucky to make it into my own driveway. But that's okay, you can stay at our place." His expression brightened. "And you don't even have to sleep on the couch! You'll get a room all to yourself because we just finished cleaning all our crap out of the spare room for-" He stopped speaking abruptly. "...um..."

Even in the pallid streetlights I could see the flush rising on his cheeks. He avoided my gaze with a theatrical glance at the sky. "Wow, look at the size of those snowflakes! They're as big as golf balls!"

"Never mind, I'll stay here," I said. "I don't want to put you out."

"No, it's fine! Of course it's fine," he insisted. "We've got tons of room and it's no trouble at all..."

"Spider." I halted him with a hand on his parka sleeve. "You can't lie to me. I know you're uncomfortable about having me stay with you, it's written all over your face. I'm perfectly fine in my office; you don't need to-"

"We've cleaned out the spare room to make a nursery!" he blurted. "We're having a baby!" A grin split his face and he clutched my sleeve, his eyes sparkling. "Linda's eight weeks pregnant and we aren't telling anybody until she's past the first trimester, but it's been killing me not to say anything 'cause I'm so excited!" A laugh bubbled out of him as he bounced on the balls of his feet, shaking my arm in jubilant emphasis. "We're having a *baby*, Aydan! How totally awesome is that?"

Spider's joy ignited a wide grin of my own despite my exhaustion, and I threw my arms around him. "That's wonderful! Congratulations! I'm so happy for you!"

"I'm so happy I think I'm going to burst!" He pulled back, sobering. "But you can't tell anybody. Not a soul, okay? And especially not my mom or Lola. We don't want to..." He hesitated, his eyes darkening with worry. "I mean... the first trimester is big, you know? If anything's going to happen..." He squeezed his eyes shut. "Oh, God, I hope nothing happens..." He reopened his eyes to gaze down at me. "It would be awful if... if Linda miscarried. But it would be so much worse if our families were looking forward to having a new baby and then we had to tell them..." He trailed off. "I'm sorry. I shouldn't have told you, either."

"It's okay, don't apologize." I squeezed his mittened hand. "I'm thrilled for you; but I promise I'm not one of those baby-crazy women. If anything bad happened..." I squeezed his hand harder. "...and it *won't*, everything's going to be just fine... I would only be sad for you and Linda; I wouldn't be disappointed for myself."

He slumped with relief, smiling again. "Okay. Thanks." He turned back toward the car. "Come on, let's get home before the snow gets so deep we have to walk."

It was only a five-minute drive to Spider's house, but my eyelids kept closing of their own volition every few seconds. His tiny car churned heroically through the snow on the street, but the small incline of his driveway defeated it. After a few attempts that ended in fruitless wheel-spinning, I said, "Why don't you just park it at the curb tonight?"

Spider frowned. "We're not allowed to park on the street if it's snowing. The plow goes by first thing in the morning. I'll just try again. I almost made it last time."

As he reversed into the street, I said, "I'll get out and push. It only has to be on the driveway, right? We don't have to get all the way up to the garage?"

"That's right, but you drive and I'll push," he countered.

I grinned. "I don't want to be a smartass, but... which of us do you think is heavier and stronger?"

"Oh, I know I'm heavier," he said hurriedly, flushing. "I'm four inches taller than you..."

"And as big around as a toothpick," I finished fondly. "Trust me on this. You drive. I'll push." I got out of the car before he could argue.

Our first attempt landed the small car safely on the

bottom of the driveway, clearing the sidewalk by several inches.

Spider hopped out and hurried around to inspect its position. "That's good enough," he said. "Come on."

We plodded up the snowy drive and he let us quietly into the house. Several minutes of whispering and tiptoeing later, I was installed in the nursery-to-be, warmly cocooned in blankets on a makeshift bed made of scavenged sofa cushions.

Sweet darkness and blessed silence enfolded me.

Every exhausted muscle relaxing, I floated into...

Hell.

Trapped in a cage barely bigger than my own body, my arms pinned by my sides. Beyond the bars, faceless things shrieked evil laughter, stabbing me over and over with bright steel-

My first strangled cry woke me and I bolted up to sitting position, panting and clutching the blankets.

A tap at the door preceded Spider's quiet voice. "Aydan? Did you call? Do you need something?"

"No, I, um... I just sneezed," I lied. "Sorry about that. I hope I didn't wake Linda."

"No, she's a pretty sound sleeper. I wouldn't have heard you myself if I hadn't been on my way by. Sorry to bother you. Good night."

"Good night." I fell back on the pillow, fists pressed to my forehead.

Thank God I hadn't been so deeply asleep that I did my usual crazed screaming. Poor Linda's sleep would have been shattered; and so would Spider's nerves.

I stifled a groan. I knew from long experience that this wouldn't be the last of my nightmares. And the harder I tried to suppress them, the worse they got.

Dammit all to hell.

I couldn't sleep here.

CHAPTER 17

Fists still grinding into my forehead, I stared wide-eyed into the silent darkness of Spider and Linda's nursery-to-be.

Damn, damn, damn.

I didn't dare fall asleep again, but I was too exhausted to stay awake.

Trapped. Just like Rebecca inside the internet...

My chest tightened, panic skittering under my skin.

I sucked in a breath and sat up. Settle down. It was only a short walk back to the office. Fifteen or twenty minutes, tops. I could leave Spider and Linda a note and go back and sleep in my office...

Shit.

I didn't have a key to their house. I couldn't just wander off in the middle of the night leaving the door unlocked.

Trapped.

Fighting claustrophobia, I sprang up to pace the small room. Three strides. Turn. Three strides. Turn...

Like being in a prison cell.

Dammit, stop thinking like that.

Maybe a drink of water would help. And I'd step outside for a breath of fresh air.

Nerves twitching, I got dressed and eased the door open.

I tiptoed down the hall to the kitchen, navigating easily in the dim illumination coming from the streetlight outside the front window.

As I headed for the sink, a small object on the kitchen table caught my eye. Memory flared. Spider had let us into the house and put his keys on the table while we wrangled sofa cushions.

My muscles went limp with relief. I could leave a note, let myself out, lock the door, and drive Spider's car to the office. I was already reaching into my waist pouch for a pen when a closer look at the key fob made my heart sink.

It was only the car key. No house key.

Fighting the urge to punch something and scream, I checked the kitchen counter and hallway table. Even the front closet yielded no house key. He must have pocketed it.

After a moment of frantic frustration, I blew out an irritable breath.

Fine. To hell with it.

Silverside was a small town and the crime rate was practically zero. In another two or three hours the neighbourhood would be awakening, and any potential burglar would be thwarted. And what were the chances that somebody would choose to break into this particular house on this particular night, in the next three hours?

Returning to the table, I scribbled a short thank-you note and added that I had Spider's car and keys before snatching them up and heading for the door. A few moments later I was standing in the soft hush of nocturnal snowfall, sucking in deep breaths of cold air and freedom.

I slid into the driver's seat of the Smart car and fired it up, but my hand hovered over the shifter.

Sure, the crime rate was low here. But what if the person

who had left the trap outside Tom's door had been targeting me?

Holt's words echoed in my mind.

They know how to get to Kelly.

Anybody who knew Arlene Widdenback would know her reputation. People who attacked her simply vanished. So the best way to get to her would be through her friends. What if that unknown enemy had seen me go into Spider's house but hadn't seen me leaving?

Or worse, what if they *did* see me leaving my friends unprotected? What if they came in through the unlocked door and attacked Spider and Linda?

Fuck, I couldn't leave.

With a whimper, I let my head fall back against the headrest.

Wait a minute.

Slow inspiration oozed into my exhausted brain, and relief eased my shoulders.

I could sleep here in the car, where I could scream my fool head off without disturbing anyone. The heater was already wafting warmth into the cabin; and the car's tiny engine could idle for hours on a teaspoon of gasoline. And I'd hear the crunch of snow if anybody tried to sneak past the car to the front door.

Thank God.

Flipping up my hood and zipping my parka up to my chin, I laid my head back and gave myself to the nightmares.

Smart Fortwos are not designed for comfortable sleeping.

By the time the snowplow roared past an hour later, I

had woken myself screaming twice, and my back and knees ached from their enforced immobility. When I tried to straighten my legs I accidentally kicked the gas pedal, making the little engine yelp in protest.

Groaning, I dragged myself out of the car into the cold and did a few stretches before creeping back into the cramped interior. Squirming in the seat, I sighed. Five AM. I probably wouldn't sleep any more now anyway...

The sound of approaching footsteps jerked me awake.

But the footsteps were coming from the direction of the house...

I groaned and powered down the fogged-up side window.

"Is everything okay?" Linda frowned in at me. "Your note said you'd gone to the office. Did you get stuck?"

"What time is it?" I mumbled.

"Six-thirty." She shivered, hugging Spider's parka around herself. It skimmed her knees and she wore tall snow boots, but her legs were bare between the boots and parka. "I just got up and found your note," she went on. "But then I looked out and saw the car idling here. What happened?"

"Shit, I'm sorry. You're freezing out here. Go back inside and I'll be there in a minute to explain."

I turned off the ignition and pried myself out of the seat as she hurried back into the house.

Trudging up the driveway at as slow a pace as I could reasonably use, I racked my brain for a plausible explanation for my bizarre behaviour. Nothing came to mind.

I sighed and stepped into the house. The truth would have to do, embarrassing though it was.

"Would you like coffee?" Linda offered as I shed my boots and parka. "I just put some on."

"No, thanks..." My words trailed off into a groan as I stretched the kinks out of my shoulders and back and knees.

"So what on earth were you doing out there?" Linda demanded, her expression a mixture of amusement and concern.

"Long story. Um..."

My tired brain refused to manufacture a usable lie.

I sighed. "Okay, no; it's a short, stupid story. Spider and I worked late and I don't have my car; he was going to drive me home but couldn't because of the snow, so he invited me here; and then I-was-having-nightmares-and-didn't-want-to-wake-you-so-I-slept-in-his-car." I spoke as quickly as possible but no matter how fast I spoke, it didn't get any less humiliating.

"Oh, Aydan..." she began, but I kept babbling.

"So I'm sorry for being so weird and I'll get out of your hair now; John will be up and he can come and get me-"

"Aydan!" Linda planted her hands on her hips in her 'authoritative-nurse' pose. "I can't believe you thought you had to sleep outside! I'm sorry you were having nightmares, but it wouldn't have bothered us, honestly."

"Well, um... yeah, it would have." I concentrated on tracing a seam in the flooring with my toe, my face on fire. "I... kind of... scream. A lot."

"Oh, Aydan." She flung her arms around me and held me tightly. "I'm sorry you have such awful nightmares, and thank you for being so nice and trying not to disturb us; but you look exhausted. Go back to bed, and just don't worry about it, okay?"

"Thanks." I hugged her in return before disengaging and

backing toward the door. "But Spider's still sleeping, and I really need to get home. I'll just call John and get him to come and pick me up."

"At least let me give you some breakfast," she coaxed.

My stomach responded with a ravenous growl, and I managed a smile. "Okay, sold. Thanks. I'll call John and get him to pick me up in twenty minutes or so."

When I dialled his number, the phone rang several times at the other end without an answer. Worry rose. What if they were still at the hospital? What if something terrible had happened-

"Hello." Kane's voice was a painful croak, and fear seized me.

"What's wrong?" I demanded.

"Nothing. Just sick."

"Oh, no! Did you get what Daniel had?"

"Has. We're both sick... *Berightback!*" After a lengthy pause he returned to the line. "The hospital said it was only the stomach flu, but I'm willing to swear I've been poisoned-" An ear-splitting clatter indicated he'd dropped the phone.

"John! *JOHN!*"

The unmistakable sound of vomiting drifted through the line, and my heart battered my chest. What if he was dying while I stood here uselessly? What if my enemies were attacking everyone around me? Should I call 911, or rush over there myself?

"Sorry." Kane's voice returned to the line in a raw rasp. "Now's not a good time. Can we talk later?"

"Could you have actually been poisoned?" I demanded. "You and Daniel ate the same pizza..."

"Not poisoned," he croaked. "Only joking. Ha." He gave up his dismal attempt at laughter after only one syllable.

"The doctor assured me it's only a flu bug that's been going around-"

He broke off again and I waited on the line for several long minutes while sounds of misery floated faintly to my ear.

"I'm back." He sounded even worse.

"Can I do anything?" I asked. "Bring you anything? Ginger ale, or Pepto-Bismol or anything?"

"Thank you, no. Just stay away from this plague house. Trust me, you really don't want to be anywhere near this."

"But you said last night that you hadn't been in your house in a month. You won't have any food..."

"I have electrolyte drink so we'll stay hydrated; and I have soda crackers, which is more than either of us can face at the moment. Thanks for calling I-have-to-go-now-'bye!" He hung up.

As my phone floated uncertainly down from my ear, Linda gave me a concerned look. "That didn't sound good."

"No. Daniel got a flu bug so he was throwing up last night, and now John's got it."

"Oh." Her face crinkled in sympathy. "*That* flu bug. It's making the rounds of the schools. It's a nasty one, but at least it doesn't last too long. They should be feeling better by tomorrow."

"Could... is there any way it could be... poison?"

Linda frowned. "Why? Were they having other symptoms like numbness, tingling, dizziness, convulsions, passing blood...?"

Fear clutched my chest all over again. "I didn't ask. John said the hospital told him it was only a flu bug..."

"Oh." Linda relaxed into a smile. "Well, if they've been checked at the hospital then I'd say there's nothing to worry about. The doctor would have told John to watch for any escalation in symptoms, and he was coherent when you spoke to him just now, right?"

"Right," I agreed, easing my shoulders down from around my ears. "Okay, then. I'll try not to worry."

"Don't worry!" she commanded with a smile. "Sit down and eat some breakfast." She indicated the table, where she had placed orange juice and whole-grain bagels with cream cheese. "And then you should go back to bed. If you're run down, you'll be more susceptible to catching that bug yourself."

"I know; but the desire to sleep in my own bed is taking on epic proportions," I countered. "I'll call my neighbour to come and pick me up. That way I'll be gone from here about the same time you have to leave for work, so you can lock up."

She agreed, and after a quick call to Tom, I helped myself to a hot and crispy toasted bagel.

Twenty minutes later Tom's big half-ton growled into the driveway, and I gave Linda a hug and a fond 'goodbye and thank you'. "Could you please leave a note for Spider?" I added as I hesitated in the doorway. "Tell him not to rush in to work. I have a ten o'clock meeting, um... elsewhere; and I don't know how long it'll take." I sighed, wondering whether the queasy sensation in my stomach was anxiety and fatigue or an oncoming flu bug. "I won't likely get to the office until at least noon, maybe later."

"I'll tell him. Now go home and get some sleep. Take care, Aydan." She waved a cheery goodbye from the doorway as I plodded down the drive.

When I hauled myself up into the passenger seat of Tom's truck, he gave me a smile. "Good morning..." His smile faded as he took in my exhausted slump. "What's wrong? It's more than just car trouble, isn't it?"

I sighed and buckled my seat belt. "Not really; it's just a little more complicated than what I explained over the phone. There's nothing wrong with my car, but it's at home. John took us out for dinner last night but his son Daniel got sick and John had to take him to the hospital, so I stayed the night with friends."

"Why didn't you call me last night?" Tom asked as he backed out of the driveway and headed for home. "I would have come to get you."

"I know you would have, but it was three o'clock in the morning before everything settled out. I didn't want to wake you at that hour." He frowned and began to speak, and I added, "I would have called you if it had been an emergency; but it wasn't. Just an inconvenience."

"So is Daniel all right?"

"Still sick, but the doctor thinks it's just stomach flu. John's got it now, too, and he told me to stay away."

Tom nodded approval. "No point in everybody suffering."

"Speaking of suffering... have you had any more problems at your place?"

I held my breath, afraid to hear the answer.

"No. And the police called to let me know that the trap actually wasn't as dangerous as I'd thought. It had been welded open, so it couldn't have hurt me." He gave me his attractive crooked smile and my stomach clenched.

The trap hadn't been an attack; it had been a message. A threat.

They know how to get to Kelly...

"Oh." I tried to make my unpleasant enlightenment sound like relief. "Thank goodness. So do you have any more ideas about who might have left it?"

Tom shrugged. "Probably just kids horsing around. I'm not worried."

Somehow I managed not to say, "You should be."

CHAPTER 18

"Just be careful anyway, okay, Tom?" I said. "Even if that trap couldn't have hurt you, having it left outside your door is just a little too creepy for my taste."

He smiled. "Don't worry; I'm still keeping my eyes open. And I'll check everything at your place when we get there, too."

Christ, that was all I needed. Another way for him to end up in my enemies' crosshairs.

"Oh, that's okay," I said as reassuringly as I could. "The sun won't be up for another hour so you wouldn't be able to see much anyway; and I'm not worried. In fact..." I didn't bother to stifle the giant yawn that nearly cracked my jaws. "...I didn't get much sleep last night and I'm going straight to bed, so as long as I make it from the door of your truck to the door of my house, everything will be fine."

He chuckled and dropped the subject, and we made small talk all the way back to my farm.

It seemed as though my eyes had barely closed when my alarm sounded. Groaning, I buried my face in my pillow. Maybe I could call Nora to say I was sick and couldn't make it.

I sighed. I could; but after my avoidance yesterday and my ungraciousness on the phone last night, she probably wouldn't believe me. And Stemp would have my ass if she gave up on me and left the country.

Reluctantly easing one limb at a time over the edge of the mattress into the unkind chill of the room, I momentarily debated slithering to the floor and crawling to the shower to avoid the effort of standing, but that seemed a little too pathetic.

I hauled myself to my feet and shuffled to the bathroom, trailing invective all the way.

In the parking lot of the Silverside Hotel, I yawned and shivered as I plodded toward the building. What the hell was I going to say to Nora? 'So tell me, Nora, are you a lying murdering adulterous self-centred bitch?'

No, the direct approach was definitely out.

But she wouldn't believe me if I flung my arms around her and proclaimed my joy at the return of my long-lost mother. And how could I ask about things she wasn't even supposed to know?

"Dani-dear!" Nora carolled from the front steps of the hotel, her cultured British accent grating on my ears now that I knew it was fake. "I'm so glad to see you!"

"Hi." I yanked my lips into a smile-like grimace as I climbed the stairs to meet her. "I'm sorry it's taken me so long to come and see you. Work's been crazy." Eyeing her parka and boots, I added, "Can we go up to your room and talk...?"

"Oh, I'm sick of that hotel room!" she exclaimed. "Let's

go to one of those little restaurants you were telling me about."

"I'd really rather talk to you..." I lowered my voice as a man emerged from the hotel door, giving Nora a smile and nod as he passed. "...somewhere we won't be overheard."

"Oh, piffle." Nora smiled and waved off my words with an insouciant hand. "We'll have lots of time for that later. Let's go. I'd kill for a decent cup of coffee right now!"

I pressed my lips together so I wouldn't blurt out, 'Did you kill for the job as Weapons Director?' and motioned her toward my car.

"Isn't this a lovely day?" She gazed around at the sparkling whiteness with a smile. "London is so grimy in winter. I've missed the sight of sunshine on clean snow!"

The bereft girl hidden in my psyche cried out at the stab of pain. My mother had missed the snow, but not her only daughter.

I slammed the door on my inner child. Cry later. Do your job now.

"I guess it must have been a big change for you," I said. "Talk about culture shock, moving from a Saskatchewan farm to London, England."

"Oh, it was wonderful!" Nora beamed, then sobered. "Except that I missed you terribly, of course."

Too little, too late. I hardened my heart and did my job.

"We missed you terribly, too." I forced my lips into a bittersweet smile. "Everyone did. It's too bad you didn't get to hear all the nice things people said at your funeral."

"You're trying to make me feel guilty, aren't you?" Nora snapped as she yanked open my car door.

I didn't have to fake my surprised blink. "Um... no. Sorry, I thought you'd want to hear how much everybody loved you and missed you."

"Oh." Her smile came back. "Thank you, dear, that was very thoughtful." She slid into the passenger seat and closed the door, leaving me standing uncertainly beside the car.

What game was she playing?

I got into the driver's seat and buckled up, literally and metaphorically. This was going to be a seriously weird ride.

"So did you find a place to live right away in London?" I asked as I put the car in gear. "Or did you wait until Sam arrived so you and he could pick out a place together?"

She gave me a sharp glance, but I had kept my tone innocuous. She replied in the same carefully-neutral tone, "Sam already had a country estate in the Cotswolds. We lived there for a couple of years, but it was almost as boring as living on the farm in Saskatchewan. I was thrilled when I got my first job with MI5 and we had to move to London."

Injecting a note of incredulity that I hoped wouldn't sound too insulting, I exclaimed, "How on earth did you end up working for MI5? I wouldn't think that being a farm wife and occasional bookkeeper would prepare you for anything like that."

Nora sniffed. "Yet here you are, a bookkeeper living on a farm; and you're a government agent."

"That was an accident," I muttered. "I never wanted this job."

"Then you're a fool," she snapped. "Women as smart as you and I shouldn't waste our intellect on..." She waved a derisive hand at the small-town scenery around us. "...backward hicks."

"Wow, *Mom*." Despite my best efforts, my words came out loaded with bitter sarcasm. "I'm surprised you didn't murder Dad and me in our beds if you were that fucking desperate to get out of Dodge."

Her chin lifted. "Watch your language, young lady. I'm still your mother, and you will treat me with respect."

I braked to an abrupt halt in the Melted Spoon's parking lot. "With all due *respect*, you can blow that right out your ass," I snarled. "I'm not young anymore; I've never been a lady; and you sure as hell don't get to show up here expecting to be treated like the fucking Queen of England just because you gave birth to me forty-some years ago and fucked off for thirty of them."

"I did *not* 'eff off'!" Nora faced me, eyes blazing. "I gave you *everything*! My love, my full attention, seventeen years of my *life* when I could have been developing a career instead! And it was a sacrifice I was happy to make because you were *everything* to me! You were my child, my world, my reason for living!" Her eyes brimmed with sudden tears as she reached out to caress my cheek with trembling fingers. Her voice fell to a choked whisper. "My one and only daughter."

My throat squeezed shut and my face tilted into her touch despite my best efforts.

Dammit, stop acting like a kid desperate for affection.

I began, "But why did you-"

"Let's talk about this later." Nora pulled away and reached for her door handle. "First I need coffee. You know how I get when I'm not properly caffeinated. You used to be such a love, bringing me my first cup in bed. Come, Dani-dear."

As she got out of the car, a memory-flash of the child I had been obscured my vision.

Carefully balancing the hot mug so none of its precious contents would escape while I tiptoed down the hallway.

Eager for her extravagant praise and radiant smile when I delivered it, fearful of her wrath if I spilled a few drops on the sheets...

I got out of the car, locking it behind me with the electronic fob as I headed for the coffee-shop entrance. Damn this stupid childish hope that she would give me her smile and approval when she tasted the Melted Spoon's custom-blended house brew.

When we stepped inside Nora stopped and inhaled deeply, the familiar smile spreading across her face. "Oh, I think I'm going to like this," she exclaimed. "What's your favourite coffee, Dani-dear?"

"I don't actually drink coffee..." As a frown wrinkled her forehead, I spotted a saviour ahead of us in the lineup. "...but we can get advice from a connoisseur," I finished hurriedly before Nora could express her disappointment. "Hey, Lola!"

A tiny figure in a neon-orange parka topped by vibrant purple hair turned at the sound of my voice, a smile splitting her wrinkled face.

"Aydan!" She vacated her spot in line to hurry back to us. "It's great to see you, honey!" She hugged me warmly. "I missed you last week."

"Yeah, I'm sorry I had to skip out on your bookkeeping," I replied, hugging her in return. "I missed you, too."

"Big John was disappointed that you didn't show up," Lola deadpanned with a wicked twinkle in her eye. "He was looking positively... droopy."

I sucked in a breath of mock horror. "Oh, no. Well, I'll be there tomorrow at the usual time to perk him up."

Nora had watched our exchange with a frown. "Excuse me," she said, extending her hand to Lola. "I'm Nora,

Aydan's mother. And you are...?"

Lola gaped at her, then turned a confused face up to me. "I thought you said your mother had, um... passed away when you were seventeen...?"

"I thought she had," I said, hoping Lola wouldn't notice that my words came out through clenched teeth. "I was wrong."

"I had to go into witness protection when Aydan was seventeen," Nora lied glibly. "Believe me, it was the most difficult thing I've ever done, leaving my child behind."

Lola's frown deepened. "I can imagine," she said slowly. "And... you never contacted her? In all this time?"

Nora drew herself up. "Her life was at stake. It was the only way."

"And you couldn't take her with you? Or at least tell her what was happening so she knew you weren't dead?" Lola demanded. "Seventeen is old enough to keep a secret."

"I wish that had been possible," Nora said stiffly. "But it wasn't."

Lola stared at her.

I broke the chilly silence. "Lola, we need your coffee expertise. What's the best brew here?"

She followed my redirection gracefully, turning a polite smile on Nora. "That depends on what you prefer. I love the espresso here, but if you just want good regular coffee you'll probably like their house blend. It's robust but not bitter." She turned back to me. "I'm sure you and your... mother..." Her gaze slid sideways to Nora, her usual cheerful expression darkening. "...have a lot of catching up to do. I'll see you tomorrow."

"Absolutely," I assured her. "Thanks, Lola."

"Any time, honey." She slipped an arm around my waist

to give me a one-armed squeeze, turning a benign smile on Nora as if daring her to make something of it.

Fortunately Nora said nothing. A catfight between Lola and Nora might be fun to watch, but only if I knew for sure Lola would win. And if Nora was actually a cold-blooded murderer, I sure as hell didn't want to take the chance.

"Well, how nice to meet one of your... friends," Nora said coolly as Lola walked away. "Now I *really* need some coffee."

"Lola's a bit protective," I mumbled. "She's one of my favourite clients, and she always looks out for me."

"Charming. It's a bit of an insult to you, though, considering that she's twice your age and half your size."

My temper flared and I clamped my teeth on my tongue before I could explode. "She's the same age as you," I said. "And even if she can't actually protect me, it's nice to know she's there." As soon as the words left my mouth, I realized how they would sound to Nora, but it was too late. "I didn't mean..." I began, but Nora's eyes had filled with tears.

"I had forgotten how cruel you could be," she said softly. "I know you're only thinking of your own pain, but imagine for a moment how much I suffered. You knew I was dead, so you had closure and you went on with your life as best you could. I had to live every day, every month, every year, knowing that you were here but I couldn't contact you without risking your safety. Can you imagine how that made me feel?"

My heart twisted despite my efforts to harden it. "I'm sorry, I didn't mean that as a dig."

"Oh, maybe not consciously, but some part of you definitely meant it the way it came out." Nora sighed. "I was hoping you'd be more understanding; but it's all right. I know what a shock this has been for you, and..." She gave me a wobbly smile. "I'm your mother. I will always love you and forgive you, no matter what. Now, let's get some coffee and talk about more pleasant things." She turned away and headed for the coffee counter.

Feeling like a rebuked ten-year-old, I hid behind the neutral mask I'd perfected through years of practice and followed her.

A few minutes later we sat at my favourite corner table, eyeing each other warily over the rims of our mugs.

Do your job. Get her talking.

"I'm sorry I've been so prickly," I said. "I'm just... having a really hard time with all of this. Would you please start from the beginning? Tell me all about what happened with you and Dad and Sam when I was young?"

She hesitated. "Are you sure you truly want to know?"

"I really do." I leaned forward and lowered my voice. "I grew up without a clue. I never knew that my whole childhood was this weird double life, and I'm only beginning to piece together the real story. Stemp might know part of it; but he won't tell me. Sam and Dad are dead. You're my only hope." I had intended to fake earnestness, but the need behind my plea took me by surprise.

"Please." My voice trembled. "Please tell me."

Nora hesitated again, and my fist clenched on the handle of my mug.

Tell me, dammit!

Eyeing my whitening knuckles, she let out a sigh. "You're right. I owe you that."

"Thank you." I gulped some tea to hide my emotion.

"Can I speak freely?" she asked.

I unzipped my waist pouch and consulted my bug detector. "Yes."

"Then I'll begin at the beginning." Nora took a swallow of her coffee as though to fortify herself for the task ahead.

"When I was pregnant with you," she said, "I was terrified."

CHAPTER 19

"Why were you terrified?" I demanded. "Was someone threatening you?"

Nora gazed back through time. "No; no one was threatening me; but I had miscarried so many times. I barely breathed for nine months, always wondering 'what if I do something to cause another miscarriage'." She grimaced. "Barely breathed; and vomited the rest of the time. If I had known how awful pregnancy was, I might not have been so eager for it."

"That sounds horrible," I said sincerely.

"It was. And then you were born. The culmination of my dreams." She sighed and sipped again, gazing into the past. "You were a colicky baby. You used to scream for hours and you never slept more than an hour or two at a time. And you were so stubborn and quick-tempered as a toddler. Your tantrums were just... I wanted to walk out the door and never come back."

My heart clenched. "And you did."

She sat up quickly, her hand flying over to squeeze mine. "Oh, Dani-dear, no! Never believe that my leaving had anything to do with you! You outgrew your health problems, and I outgrew my mothering problems. By the time you were four, we were inseparable." She fell back in her chair. "And then Sam appeared. The cause of some of the worst days of my life..." She sighed, and smiled. "...and the best."

I clamped down on the urge to tell her exactly what I thought about her days with Sam.

Let her talk.

Nora leaned closer and lowered her voice below the hum of conversation around us. "When Sam first told us he thought you would grow up to replace a super-computer, we pooh-poohed the whole idea. It was ridiculous. Computers were the size of entire buildings; and they were only used by places like NASA. But... he persisted. And your father and I didn't see the harm in going along with his tests. After all..." She smiled at me, her face softening. "All parents want to believe their children are special."

"When did you start to believe him?"

Nora frowned. "When you turned twelve Sam introduced the idea that we should move to Alberta to be closer to his lab. Your father would never consider leaving the farm that had been handed down to him through three generations; and when he told Sam that, Sam began to hint that perhaps the government might take an active role in relocating you. As if they might... take you away." She sighed. "We panicked."

"So Sam hadn't mentioned the government before that?" I asked. "He made it sound as though it was just him and his research?"

"Well, yes. And he seemed like such a nice man..." She smiled, her eyes softening. "He *was* a nice man. Your father and I both liked him, and you adored him and called him Santa Claus. We believed we were helping him with his research, and we included him in our social circle. He was always welcome in our home."

Yeah, she'd welcomed him with open arms. And open legs, the cheating bitch.

I swallowed my anger along with another mouthful of tea and managed to keep my tone neutral. "Until he threatened to take me away."

"He never *threatened*, but your father and I became frightened when he mentioned government involvement. That was when your father got the government job to try to protect you, and I took on the responsibility of deterring Sam." She gave me a twisted smile. "I had nothing but good intentions in the beginning; but Sam was so sweet, and so smart. Worldly and wealthy and attentive. He made me feel intelligent and beautiful and... worthwhile."

She fell silent, and I reluctantly considered what it must have been like for her to glimpse the big world beyond the farm. To be valued for her intellect. To find a new sense of purpose at an age when most farm wives were resigned to another couple of decades of hard labour in the fields and barn and garden.

"And that's when I realized there was only one solution," Nora went on. "I had to lure Sam away from you. Convince him to leave Canada forever. It was the only way to save you."

Bullshit.

Furious accusations fought to escape, but I clenched my teeth on them.

Stay detached.

Move in for the kill.

"So when you left with Sam, was that when he told you what he was really doing?" I asked.

"Yes." She blinked. Almost a twitch. Hesitated as

though realizing she had said too much...

She knew.   A caustic mixture of triumph and disappointment stung my soul.

"Yes," she repeated firmly, leaning forward and lowering her voice even more.   "That was when he told me that the project to turn you into a super-computer had been diverted into research on brainwave-driven networks, and that he was studying how you could be used to power virtual reality simulations instead."

Shit, maybe she didn't know.

Keep her talking.

"So, did Dad know you were still alive?" I blurted.   "Was he in on it, too?"

"Oh, Dani-dear, don't be silly.   Of course your father didn't know.   I had to protect him, too.   I would never have hurt him by leaving him for someone else."

"And you thought it would hurt him less to *fake your own death*?"   I barely managed to keep my volume below an incredulous half-shout.

Nora's cheeks coloured.   "Keep your voice down, for heaven's sake!   It was the kindest thing I could do for him. Imagine how the neighbours would have talked about him if they had known I'd left him for another man."

My spine stiffened with outrage.   "Our neighbours were great!   They were always there for us, and they certainly wouldn't have thought badly of Dad because you..."

I bit off the words 'were screwing around on him'. Enlightenment dawned even as my sentence faded away.

"No, they wouldn't have thought badly of him," I added slowly.   "But they would have thought badly of you.   And you couldn't bear the thought of that, could you?"

"Nonsense, Aydan," Nora said briskly.   "Of course the

neighbours would have thought badly of him. Everybody knew your father had been treated for prostate cancer, and you know what that does to a man's ability to perform. They would have realized he couldn't satisfy me anymore, and he would have been the laughingstock of the town."

Speechless, I sat with my mouth gaping for a long moment. "You..." I shook my head and tried again. "You..." Somehow I managed not to say 'piece of shit'. "Dad beat *cancer*, for God's sake!" I sputtered instead. "He loved you, and you should have admired him for being brave enough to go through the surgery and chemo! What did it matter if he couldn't get it up anymore? There are lots of other ways for a couple to-"

"Aydan, please." Nora halted me with an out-facing palm. "I certainly don't need sex advice from you. And I didn't say that's why I left him; I said that's what the neighbours would think. Your father and I had been having marital difficulties long before his cancer diagnosis."

I clenched my fists around my mug and throttled my anger down to a vicious whisper. "So pretending to die was neat and tidy, wasn't it? You got a new life and a new lover and a new career and everything you always wanted; and to hell with all the people who loved you and needed you."

Tears welled up in Nora's eyes and trickled down her cheeks. "I did it for *you*," she choked. "To keep you out of Sam's clutches. To give you a chance at a normal life. I should have *known* you wouldn't understand; you were always a selfish child."

Selfish child.

Selfish bitch.

Different voices; the same words.

Slow realization set my insides like icy concrete. "You," I

whispered, barely finding the breath in my frozen lungs to speak. "You're the one who set me up."

"What?" Nora stared at me, tears glistening on her cheeks. "I didn't set you up for anything. I was *protecting* you."

"No, you were fucking me up." My words echoed out of the cold distant place in my chest. "All those years of manipulating me when I was a kid. Withholding affection whenever I did something you didn't like. Jerking me around with your emotions. You set me up for an abusive relationship, and like a good little daughter I walked right into one."

Rage thawed the ice in my heart, sending it boiling out in a corrosive torrent of words. "All this time I've been blaming my first husband for the way he fucked me up, but he never would have gotten his hooks into me in the first place if you hadn't made me believe that's how love works. No wonder Dad never remarried!"

Nora went bone-white. "Now you listen here..." she began in a furious hiss.

"Hello, Storm Cloud Dancer, how nice to see you." A soft voice and feather-light embrace around my shoulders made me twitch violently.

Yanking my attention back to my surroundings, I forced a smile onto my face at the sight of Moonbeam standing beside my chair, looking like a weathered angel with her serene wrinkled features and long silver braid.

"Hi, Moonbeam Meadow Sky." Somehow my voice came out warm and welcoming. "It's nice to see you, too. Are you having a good visit?"

"Yes, dear. Wonderful, thank you." She turned her luminous smile on Nora. "Please forgive my interruption.

I'm Moonbeam Meadow Sky. My son works with Storm Cloud Dancer... or Aydan, as I'm sure you know her. Storm Cloud Dancer is the special name I've given her. It suits her, don't you think?"

"Yes, it does." Nora had composed herself as rapidly as I had, erasing tears and anger from her face with a swipe of her paper napkin. "She can be very stormy indeed. As her mother, I can attest to that." She smiled. "I'm Nora Taylor. It's a pleasure to meet you."

"Her mother?" Moonbeam faked surprise.

Skidmark had undoubtedly told her about Nora's return, but nobody would have known it from Moonbeam's puzzled expression as she turned back to me. "Dear, I must be misremembering. I thought you'd said your mother had passed on."

"I thought she had," I said through teeth only slightly gritted.

"I had to go into the witness protection program when Aydan was seventeen," Nora lied again with grim determination. "It was a heartbreaking decision to let her believe I had died, but I had to do it to protect her."

"Oh, how devastating for you." Unlike Lola, Moonbeam's face softened with sympathy for Nora. "What a dreadful situation. I was estranged from my own dear son for many years as a result of a silly misunderstanding, so I can only imagine how difficult it must have been for you to leave your family behind." Moonbeam turned to me. "And I can imagine what a terrible shock the truth must have been when you discovered it. I hope you can put aside your hurt feelings long enough to empathize with your mother's point of view."

Her gentle words hit me like a slap. *Selfish bitch.*

My anger vanished, my heart shrivelling to a small painful lump at the bottom of the void that remained.

"I'll try," I croaked.

"I do hope you succeed." Moonbeam's smile bathed us in radiance. "Life is too short to hold grudges. Now, Nora, I beg your forgiveness, but I must speak to Storm Cloud Dancer privately."

"Of course," Nora said graciously, and rose. "I'll just zip to the ladies' and repair my makeup." She turned a long-suffering smile on us. "Tears and motherhood go hand in hand."

"That is very true," Moonbeam agreed ruefully.

As soon as Nora disappeared into the washroom, Moonbeam closed her arms around me, the strength of her hug a startling contrast to her earlier light embrace.

"My poor child," she whispered. "I saw the pain in your aura at my words, and I am so sorry! I didn't intend to hurt you; I only interrupted your conversation with Nora because it looked as though your conversation was becoming heated. If that was part of your strategy, I do apologize for my interference…"

"It wasn't. Thanks," I mumbled.

Her arms tightened around me and she spoke in a fierce undertone. "You have built yourself into a strong, competent, loving, and lovable woman without her. You needed her when you were a child, but you don't need her now. Don't let her push your buttons."

Overcome, I hid my face in Moonbeam's jacket and squeezed her in return. After a moment, the tightness in my throat eased enough to allow me a choked whisper.

"Thanks."

"You are most welcome, dear." The touch of her hand on

my hair was like a benediction.

Getting my emotions under control, I pulled away to look at her. "I'm glad you showed up when you did. How did you know we were here?"

"I ran into Lola in the grocery store. She was most indignant on your behalf. She opined that Nora was 'a stone-cold bitch'." Moonbeam's lips turned up in the gentle smile that concealed her backbone of steel. "Despite my urge to side unconditionally with you, I am attempting to reserve judgement on Nora. She may not have been an ideal mother, but she may have been doing the best she could under the circumstances." She sighed. "I have made too many parenting mistakes of my own to judge harshly. In any case, when Lola told me she had seen the two of you here, I thought perhaps you could use some moral support."

"You were right," I said gratefully. I almost blurted, 'I wish you were my mother', but fortunately Moonbeam spoke again before I could embarrass us both.

"I would like to extend a dinner invitation to you, for tonight at five PM at Cosmic River Stone's home. Preferably to you only; but if you must include Nora, we will all understand."

"I'll ditch her. What can I bring?"

"Only yourself and your appetite, dear." Moonbeam patted my cheek. "Now I will make myself scarce before Nora returns. Goodbye for now. And remember..." Her soft blue gaze held me in its compassion. "...you are strong. You can do this."

I watched her slim figure move gracefully toward the entrance, and sighed.

What if Moonbeam had been my mother instead of Nora? Where would I be now?

Shaking myself back to reality, I tamped down a cynical smile. I'd be Stemp. Probably not an improvement.

But maybe I could think like him. Close down my feelings and coldly evaluate Nora's emotional manipulations; and manipulate her in turn.

I straightened my spine.

Yes. I could do that.

CHAPTER 20

Nora slid into the chair opposite me again, and I gave her a contrite smile. Time to slip back into my old approval-seeking role.

"I'm sorry I was so rude," I said. "You're right; it was selfish of me not to think of what you've been through. Can we start again?"

"Of course, Dani-dear." She smiled. "You know I've always forgiven you, no matter how badly you treated me."

I hid my snarl behind a slightly-too-toothy smile. "I know. Thanks." I didn't sound particularly grateful; but at least I wasn't spewing venom. Yay, me.

"So..." I added, widening my smile to face-aching dimensions. "...we've got so much catching up to do! Tell me all about your life. You've said you were part of the witness protection program. Is that how you got out of the country?"

"I really can't discuss the details." She gave me a warm smile. "And how about you? You became a bookkeeper just like me. That's so flattering. And you said you were married. Do I have any grandchildren?"

"No." The word fell flatly on the table between us, and I hesitated. 'I'm sorry' would be a lie that I probably couldn't carry off convincingly, but...

"Are you married to that horrible man who was holding you after you were attacked at the weapons conference?"

A surge of fury blotted out all other thoughts. Goddammit, I was so fucking sick and tired of people judging Arnie by his appearance.

"I'm not married." My voice came out strangled by my effort to control my temper. "And Arnie's not horrible. He's the best thing in my life."

Nora blinked. "Oh, dear. I didn't realize your life was so awful."

I rocketed to my feet. "Pee break," I grated, and strode to the bathroom before I could rip her head off and jam it up her ass.

Breathing deeply, I washed my hands in ice-cold water hoping it would cool my rage.

Don't react. She's purposely pushing your buttons. If she was any other slimeball criminal, her words would roll right off your back.

Locking eyes with the murderous-looking woman in the mirror, I muttered, "She's just another slimeball. Treat her that way."

My reflection agreed with a single jerk of its chin and turned for the door.

Nora looked up with a smile as I returned to the table, and I reminded myself all over again: Just another slimeball.

"I could use a warm-up," I said, gesturing at my mug. "I'm going to get some more hot water. Would you like a coffee refill?"

"Yes, please. Thank you, Dani-dear." She sat back in her chair and rewarded me with a radiant smile.

No, dammit, not 'rewarded'. 'Manipulated'. Like the

slimeball she is.

When I returned with our beverages, I took my seat determined to control the conversation.

"So you didn't answer my question earlier," I said. "I know you can't tell me all the details; but did you go through government channels, or did you leave privately? I don't mean to pry, but I don't want to get you in trouble by saying something I shouldn't to the wrong person, either." I gave her a bland smile.

She out-blanded me. "Don't worry, Dani-dear. You can say anything you want to the authorities. Everything about my relocation was legal and properly documented."

And Stemp had never breathed a word about it. Bastard.

I bared my teeth in what I hoped was a smile. "Oh, good." As Nora opened her mouth to speak again, I added, "So did Sam set up the UK branch of Sirius Dynamics after you moved over there permanently?"

Her expression chilled. "Don't bother digging for that information, *Agent Kelly*. The UK branch is beyond your government's greedy reach. And I will regain control of the Canadian branch, too. I've hired the best lawyer available, and we will overturn that ridiculous 'proceeds-of-crime' seizure."

I didn't have to fake my shock. "What the hell are you talking about?"

Dammit, the last I'd heard, she hadn't known that Sam's Canadian assets had been seized. Either my intel was faulty, or she'd discovered the truth in the last day or two.

"You mean you don't know?" Nora eyed me with a mixture of curiosity and suspicion. She leaned forward and lowered her voice to a murmur below the hum of conversation in the coffee shop. "How long have you been an agent?"

"Not long." I cast my gaze down to study my tea as though embarrassed to make the admission. "They promoted me after Sam died," I mumbled, then glanced up to watch her reaction. "Before that I was only doing... stuff for him on his project." I hesitated as if reluctant to divulge any other information. "Do you know, um... how much do you know about what he was doing?"

Come on, Nora, confess.

She matched my quiet tone. "I knew that you would be powering virtual reality sims in the brainwave-driven network. Sam had never made any secret of his intentions for you, even when you were only a child. That's why I had to get him away from you."

I sat back and faked a confused frown. "Why? The pay's good, and it's easy work. Just sitting there all day long. It's pretty much a dream job." Watching her over the rim of my mug, I let my lie settle between us.

Admit it. You knew Sam and the Knights had been using us to steal classified intel.

Nora gave me a pitying smile. "I think we both know it was a little more than that."

I tamped down my surge of adrenaline and managed a puzzled expression. "What do you mean?"

She blew out a small impatient breath. "Please don't play dumb, Dani-dear; it's unbecoming. He was conducting experiments on your mind to further his professional career; and that put you at risk to be held prisoner in a government lab for the rest of your life. I couldn't bear to see that happen, so I intervened in the only way I could."

Shit.

I baited my next trap. "How much did you know about

those experiments? Because it didn't seem that bad to me. He just put electrodes around my head and monitored me. Was he doing something else that I should know about?"

If I hadn't been expecting it, I might have missed the twitchy blink of her eyes. An instant later the furtive expression was gone, replaced by a look of wide-eyed sincerity. "As I told you last week, Sam and I didn't discuss the classified details of our work. I simply didn't want him to exploit you like... like a lab rat."

I suppressed my urge to growl 'bullshit!', then reconsidered. She'd know something was up if I seemed to accept everything she said now.

I scowled. "Okay, so let me get this straight. You were so desperately afraid that Sam might 'exploit' me..." I made sarcastic air quotes around the word. "...that you uprooted your own life and everybody else's to get him away from me. And then you stayed married to him for nearly thirty years even though you say you couldn't trust him. But last week you dripped tears all the over the place telling me how much you loved him and missed him. Which time were you lying? 'Cause I'm just not buying it."

She tensed. "I *wasn't* lying. I didn't say I was afraid Sam would exploit you; I said his research was putting you at risk to be exploited by our government. And I did love him..." Tears glistened in her eyes and her voice wavered. "...and I miss him terribly."

Unmoved by her performance, I countered, "But when I got into the government program last year and Sam came back here and resumed his experiments, I didn't see you rushing back here to protect me then."

"I couldn't leave my job-" she began.

I talked over her. "And anyway, the government knew

about Sam's research all those years ago, before you left with him. So you basically just abandoned me to their clutches. If you had really wanted to protect me, you would have stuck around to make sure the government didn't get me."

"That was your father's job," she snapped. "We had agreed that I would handle Sam and he would protect you from everyone else."

My rage tried to escape in a fiery torrent, but I fought it back with words of ice. "So Dad knew about you and Sam after all."

"Aydan!" Nora's eyes blazed. "*Listen* to me! I have not lied to you! Your father didn't know Sam and I were in love; and he didn't know I faked my death! When you were only twelve, your father and I agreed that we had to safeguard your future. I took charge of all the interactions with Sam; and your father stopped farming and took a job with the Department of Agriculture so he could develop government contacts and protect you from that side."

I froze with my mouth already open to blast her. Then I slowly closed my gaping jaw. "So *that's* what Aunt Minnie was talking about," I muttered.

Nora sat bolt upright. "When did you talk to Minnie?" she demanded. "What did she tell you?"

Icy fear trickled down my spine at her intense expression. She didn't look like a nice elderly lady anymore. She looked like a cold-blooded killer who wouldn't hesitate to wipe out anyone who got in her way.

Like Howard Coleman, who had held a job she wanted.

And like her former sister-in-law, who might know too much.

I had to protect Minnie.

"She's dead," I blurted. "I went to see her last year,

hoping to find out more about what had happened when you died... um, I mean..." I let out a breath. "Whatever. When we thought you'd died."

"What did she tell you?" Nora repeated, an edge in her voice.

I shrugged, aiming for a blend of futility and regret. "Nothing. At least, nothing I didn't already know. She was mostly blind, and she had dementia and didn't have a clue who I was."

"You said 'that's what Minnie was talking about'," Nora insisted. "What did you mean?"

"Oh, she said she couldn't understand why Dad had quit farming and started working for the government. And she said she saw a gun in his briefcase once. That's all," I said truthfully. "She was completely out of it. She thought your accident had just happened last year, and that Dad and Uncle Roger were still alive and I was still a teenager. She was really frail and I wasn't surprised when she died a couple of months later."

"I didn't hear about that." Nora eyed me levelly. "I kept track of everyone. I knew when Roger died, and your father. I didn't see any obituary for Minnie. As far as I know, she's still in that nursing home in Victoria."

My throat constricted. Shit, she knew exactly where to find her victim.

I shrugged, putting everything I had into looking disinterested. "There probably wasn't an obituary. Cousin Janice called to tell me her mom had died; and she only called me because she found out I'd visited Aunt Minnie recently. They did a small family get-together for her memorial because pretty much everybody who had known her was dead."

"I see." Nora eased back in her seat.

She's off-balance now. Keep up the pressure.

"So what were you talking about earlier, when you said something about a proceeds-of-crime seizure?" I asked. "I thought Sam owned all the civilian branches of Sirius Dynamics, so I just assumed it would all go to you."

"And it should!" Her chin rose in the stubborn expression I knew so well. "It's ridiculous! The government seized his Canadian assets as proceeds of crime; but Sam was never convicted of any crime. And when I demanded to know what crime he supposedly committed, they said 'treason' and wouldn't tell me anything more. No charges, no evidence, no conviction. It's completely spurious. My lawyer sees no reason why we shouldn't be able to overturn this ridiculous ruling quite easily."

"So that's why you're here." Despite my attempt to stay detached, disappointment bruised my heart. "It's nothing to do with me; you just showed up to fight for Sam's money."

"That's not true!" Her indignant frown softened into a motherly smile. "Dani-dear, I didn't have to reveal my identity to you or anyone. I have just as many rights of ownership as Nora Taylor, Sam's legally married spouse."

"Legally married," I echoed with disgust. "I seriously doubt that. I'm pretty sure Dad would have noticed if he'd signed divorce papers after you supposedly died. You were never legally married to Sam because you were still legally married to Dad."

Nora shrugged, unperturbed. "Regardless of my marital status, I am the sole beneficiary of Sam's will. If his assets had been my only concern, I certainly wouldn't have done anything as messy as revealing myself to you." She leaned forward, reaching imploring hands toward me. "Dani-dear, why can't you believe that I truly love you and couldn't bear to be parted from you any longer?"

My heart clenched, my most heartfelt question bursting out in spite of my efforts to stay detached. "But why now? After thirty damn years, *why now?*"

"Because, dearest, my last reason to stay away died with Sam.   And you had already been swallowed up by the government.   My lifelong crusade had failed.   And... I thought... I might still be able to help you by revealing myself." Her voice trembled. "If... if you can find room in your heart...?"

I stared at her in silence, not sure whether it was tears or vomit climbing my throat.

"Dani-dear..." Nora reached across the table to pry my fingers loose from their deathgrip on my mug.   She slid her hand into mine, and my fingers betrayed me by closing tightly around hers.

"I love you," she said softly.   "I've always loved you. More than anything or anyone else in the world."

The lost child in my soul cried out, reaching desperately for her mother.

I fought my voice steady. "This... is... You've given me a lot to think about.   Is it okay if I drop you off at the hotel now?"

She sighed and fell back in her chair, her shoulders sagging with disappointment.   Every old instinct lashed my mind, driving me to make it better; to fix things no matter what it took.

Selfish bitch.

I braced my heart against the old vicious memories and added, "I'm sorry; I'm not trying to hurt you.   It's just that I need some time to work through all this, and..." I tried for a firm tone but my voice came out small and lost. "...I don't want to fight with you."

I'm sorry, Mommy. I'll never, ever spill your coffee again; I'll be so careful, I promise...

I surged to my feet. "I have to be in a meeting at..." I glanced blindly at my watch, completely failing to register the time. "...in fifteen minutes. I'm sorry. Let's go."

She was trying not to cry, her eyes brimming while a single tear trickled artfully down her cheek. Her face twisted into the heart-wrenching expression of hurt that had never failed to bring me to my knees...

I turned and strode for the door.

CHAPTER 21

I was half relieved and half disappointed when Nora followed me out of the coffee shop. The short drive to the hotel was accomplished in silence, and when I pulled up in front of the building Nora turned a tentative expression toward me.

"When will..." She hesitated, then tried again. "Will you... call me later? Or... may I have your phone number?"

"No." Sheer reflex jerked the refusal out of me.

She flinched as though I had slapped her.

"I'm sorry," I added hurriedly. "I didn't mean it to come out like that. Of course you can have my home phone number. I just meant that you won't be able to reach me. I've got back-to-back meetings for the rest of the day and I likely won't even have time to check my messages. But I'll call you when I can."

"T-Today?" Her voice trembled.

Guilt and yearning and anger churned inside my chest. Somehow I managed to keep my voice steady. "I'll try. But it might be pretty late in the evening."

"Any time at all. A few minutes. That's all I ask." Her tears overflowed and trickled down her cheeks. "Oh, Dani-dear, I know how hard this is for you, but please give me a chance. I love you so much."

She stretched over the centre console to hug me, and my throat closed. Of their own accord, my arms rose to hug her in return.

"My dearest," she whispered against my hair.

I forced myself to let go. "I'll call you later," I croaked. "I really have to go now. I'm late."

"All right." She gave me a watery smile and got out of my car. Leaning down, she repeated, "I love you", then closed the door.

Throat burning, I watched her climb the stairs. Waiting for one last smile and wave, and despising myself for it.

At the top of the stairs she turned. There was her radiant smile; her hand lifting...

My stupid heart was already warming before I realized the gesture wasn't for me. A well-dressed man jogged up the stairs with a jaunty salute for Nora, and the two of them went into the hotel together, already engrossed in conversation.

It shouldn't have hurt that much.

I held myself rigid, refusing to fold over the slice of pain in my chest. Refusing even one lapse into raw grief before I turned off my emotions and buried them so deeply that nobody could ever hurt me again...

The vibration of my cell phone made my locked-up muscles jerk painfully. The call display showed Hellhound's number, and a rush of longing for his embrace nearly shattered me. I gulped hard, then gulped again. The phone was already on its third ring. It would go to voicemail in a few seconds...

I tapped the accept button and attempted a cheery tone. "Hi, Arnie."

"Shit, what's wrong?" he demanded.

My traitorous breath hitched, and I held my voice steady with every ounce of control I possessed. "E-Everything's fine. Is everything all right with you?"

"I'm fine; an' don't bullshit me," he growled. His rasp softened to a warm rough rumble that soothed my battered soul. "Come on, darlin', give. Ya sound like hell. Talk to me."

I closed my eyes, imagining his battle-scarred brow creased with concern for me, his gentle arms holding me warm and safe against his bulky chest, his hand stroking my hair...

Shit, that wasn't helping.

I blew out a hard breath and forced a level tone. "Nothing bad is happening. I'm just wiped out because I worked really late last night and didn't get much sleep, and then this morning I had to deal with Nora."

"That bitch." He spat the epithet. "Fuckin' waste a' skin. Why's she still here? Thought they were gonna deport her."

"They can't. She has diplomatic immunity, and anyway, she hasn't done anything wrong."

"She sure as hell did," he snapped. "She abandoned ya when ya were only a kid, an' now she's waltzin' back into your life like nothin' fuckin' happened. She's a fuckin' worthless shitbag!"

I sighed, wishing it were that simple. "She hasn't done anything illegal. And after talking to her today, I'm seeing that she might have had good reasons for what she did..." My half-hearted defense trailed off into silence. The silence lengthened, and I added, "Arnie? Are you still there?"

"Yeah," he said. "Just thinkin'. Tell ya what; I'm gonna come up there this afternoon. Can I stay at your place, or would ya rather I got a room at the hotel?"

Biting back the sob of gratitude that tried to escape, I held my voice steady. "Thanks, but I'm okay. You don't need to drive all the way up here."

"I know, but I'm comin' anyway. So should I head for your place or the hotel?"

"My place. But I don't know when I'll get home tonight."

"I'll come to Silverside an' call ya when I get there." He hesitated. "Sounds like ya got more than enough shit on your plate right now, but... the reason I was callin' in the first place, um... have ya talked to Kane lately?"

He was trying to sound casual. I didn't fall for it.

My grip on the phone tightened. "I talked to him this morning. Why, what's wrong? Did they get sicker? Are they at the hospital?"

"So he really is sick? An' so's Daniel? An' they're at Kane's place there in Silverside?" Anxiety tinged his voice.

My pulse sped up to an uneasy lope. "Yes. Why? What's wrong? Should I go over there?"

Hellhound let out a breath. "Couldn't hurt. When did ya see 'em last?"

"Last night. Arnie, what the hell's wrong?"

"I'm pretty sure it's nothin', darlin', but... Lish called me a few minutes ago, freakin' the fuck out. She thinks Kane kidnapped Daniel."

"Oh, for..." I bit off my incipient profanity. "Of course he didn't. Daniel got sick at supper last night, so they stayed at John's place here in Silverside. Surely he called Alicia last night to tell her they wouldn't be home."

Hellhound blew out a breath. "Yeah, he did; but when she tried to call him at his house this mornin' an' he didn't answer, she completely fuckin' lost it. I told her there was no fuckin' way Kane'd kidnap Daniel." Worry tightened his voice. "But I tried to call him right after I hung up from her, an' he didn't answer. I thought he might just be screenin' his calls from her; but he woulda picked up for me, an' I called both his numbers."

"Shit! He must have gotten sicker! Dammit..." I switched the phone to speaker and tossed it onto the passenger seat. "I'm going over there now!" I slapped the car into gear and accelerated.

As I neared Kane's street only a few minutes later, the sound of sirens chilled my blood. "Shit!" I muttered.

"What? What's happenin'?" Hellhound's voice rattled my phone speaker from the passenger seat.

"Sirens." I rounded the corner, adrenaline sizzling through my veins as I spotted their source. "Shit, a cop car at Kane's... no, two; there's one circling around behind the house as well. Shit-shit-shit..."

"Stay calm, darlin', don't get in the middle of it," Hellhound warned. "Stay in your car."

"But he was so sick; he said he felt like he'd been poisoned..." My voice was rising, my foot pressing the accelerator despite the obvious wisdom of Hellhound's advice.

"Stay put!" His voice snapped out of the speaker. "If he's that sick, the cops'll call the ambulance, an' you'll only be in the way. An' if some other shit's goin' down, you're just gonna make it worse by chargin' in there!"

I jammed on the brakes and skidded to a stop at the curb. "I'm not going to charge in there. I'm just going to go over to the cruiser and ask-"

"Aydan, *NO!*"

"Oh. Um... okay," I said meekly.

"Aw shit, what're ya doin'?" Dread edged Hellhound's

voice. "I know ya ain't just doin' what I said."

"Actually, I am." I powered down my window before replacing my hand on the steering wheel, both hands in full view and heart thumping. "There's an RCMP officer headed for my car, and he doesn't look happy."

"Shit!" Hellhound fell silent, apparently listening for my exchange with the officer.

The uniformed man strode up to my car, frowning. "Are you aware that you were speeding-" He broke off, eyes widening and hand dropping to his gun. "Aydan Kelly?"

"Y-Yes...?" Suddenly I was having a hard time getting my breath.

The cop drew his weapon, stepping back a couple of paces. "Please step out of the car. Slowly. Keep your hands where I can see them." He wasn't pointing his gun directly at me, but it would only take a tiny adjustment of his stance to do it.

I forced my voice strong and level. "My name is Aydan Kelly. I'm a government agent, and you can check my ID with my Director, Charles Stemp. I'll give you his number. I'm armed, but I won't cause any trouble. I'll sit here and keep my hands on the wheel if you'd like to call the Director now."

"Already talked to him," the officer said shortly. "Get out of the car, slowly, and keep your hands where I can see them."

My heart pounded in my throat, making it hard to hold onto my calm voice. "Would you like me to take my hand off the steering wheel to open the car door, or would you rather do it yourself?"

"You do it. Slowly."

"Okay. I'm going to open the car door now." I moved

my hand carefully off the steering wheel, down to the door latch, and eased the door open. Raising both hands, I added, "I'm going to get out of the car now. I'll step to the side and stand beside the rear door."

Keeping my hands at eye level, I did as I had described. As soon as I was standing, the cop barked, "Turn around and put both hands on the car."

I obeyed, trying to look as non-threatening as possible. "I have a Glock in my right ankle holster," I said. "There's a pistol in my left ankle holster, too, but it's classified technology. If you take it off me, please secure it where nobody can see it."

"What's going on here?" an authoritative female voice demanded.

I sneaked a peek over my shoulder and drew a breath of cautious relief. "Hi, Constable Peters."

Her lips quirked. "Aydan. We have to stop meeting like this."

Unsure whether that had been a smile or a sneer, I ventured, "I really hope this isn't another strip-search situation."

Her lips quirked again, and this time I was pretty sure it was a smile. "Me, too." She glanced at the young male officer, who was still bristling and glaring, then turned back to me. "We have some questions for you. Are you willing to answer them?"

"I guess that depends on what they are." My neck protested its awkward twist over my shoulder and I faced the car again, rolling my shoulders in an attempt to ease the cramp without removing my hands from the vehicle. "Ask away."

"Please turn and face me."

With a sigh that was half relief, half nervous tension, I lowered my hands slowly to my sides and turned.

The young male officer was still gripping his gun in a white-knuckled hand, but Constable Peters looked calm and contained as usual. "Daniel Kane is missing," she said. "Witnesses placed you with him and John Kane, yesterday evening around seven PM at Fiorenza's restaurant. Do you know anything about his disappearance?"

Despite her unemotional words, I could see the apprehension in her eyes. She'd been the one to break the news to Kane that he had a son he'd never met. She and John had been co-workers before he started working for the Department, and as far as I knew they were still friends.

"Disappearance?" My voice came out strangled by my thumping heart. "You mean Daniel's not here at John's place?"

Her expression jabbed a cold knife of fear into my chest before she even uttered the words.

"No, he's not. They're both gone."

CHAPTER 22

"Oh, *shit!*" Momentarily forgetting the twitchy young cop, I knotted both fists in my hair. His weapon jerked up, and I slowly released my hold on my hair and kept my hands high.

"Stand down, Rice," Constable Peters said tiredly. "Aydan, what can you tell us?"

"Like your witness said, I was with John and Daniel at Fiorenza's last night." I eased my hands down again. They were shaking, and not because I was afraid of the young cop. "Daniel got sick. He was vomiting. John took him to the hospital to make sure it wasn't anything serious. After that, he took Daniel back to his place and put him to bed. I called around seven this morning, and by then John was sick, too. That's the last time I talked to him. If they're not here, John must have taken Daniel back to the hospital."

"Rice, check it," Peters snapped, and the young cop gave me one more suspicious glance before hurrying away. "When did you actually see them last?" she asked me.

My guts twisted at her inference.

Kane wouldn't lie to me.

Okay; he would. But not about something like this. And he'd never kidnap Daniel.

Would he?

What if the stress of living with Alicia had finally gotten too much and he'd decided to take Daniel and run? Dammit, I should have asked how things were going with him instead of dumping out my own problems.

Selfish bitch.

I yanked my mind back to Peters. "We parted outside Fiorenza's around seven last night. I walked to Sirius Dynamics because John was taking Daniel directly to the hospital..."

"So you're saying John drove away from Fiorenza's alone with Daniel," Peters clarified worriedly.

"In the direction of the hospital," I insisted. "Daniel was vomiting. I seriously doubt John would seize that moment to abduct him."

"Did you see whether John handled Daniel's food?"

My heart sank. "Well... yeah. He cut up Daniel's pizza for him. And he handled a milk glass after Daniel accidentally tipped it over."

Peters stiffened. "Did you call his home phone or his cell phone this morning?"

"His home phone. They were definitely here this morning."

She hissed out a breath between her teeth. "Or he forwarded the home number to his cellphone to buy time while he vanished with Daniel."

"I really don't think so," I said, hoping desperately that it was true. "John sounded awful. He was throwing up. He said he felt like he'd been poisoned..." The fear rose again, dark and deadly at the edges of my mind. "I'm sure they're at the hospital," I repeated, but I didn't sound sure at all.

"Hey!" Rice's jubilant shout from the cruiser snapped

both our heads in that direction. "Found them!" The young cop was beaming. "They're at the hospital!"

"Thank God," Peters muttered, her posture easing.

"Are they all right?" I called.

Rice jogged over, his step light. "Kane brought Daniel into Emergency this morning around nine-thirty. They're rehydrating him, and he's on the mend. Kane is still sick but he refuses to leave Daniel's side. He had his cell phone turned off to comply with the hospital regulations, so he didn't know anybody was trying to call him."

"False alarm," Peters said as a smile spread across her face. "And I can't even be angry with his ex for dragging us out here. After having her son kidnapped once, I can only imagine how frightened she must have been. I'm sorry to have bothered you, Aydan. Thanks for your help."

Relief was making my knees wobble. "No problem." I drew a deep breath and let it out slowly. "Thanks for not strip-searching me."

Peters laughed. "We really do have to stop meeting like this." She raised a hand in farewell and strode off to her cruiser, followed by Rice.

I half-sat, half-fell into the driver's seat of my car and laid my head back, trembling. "Arnie? Are you still there?"

"Yeah." His voice rasped out of the speaker. "What the hell's happenin'?"

I explained, and when I was finished he blew out a long low whistle.

"Christ, what a clusterfuck. Glad everythin's okay." He let out a breath. "Guess I'll slow down then, 'fore I get the mother of all speedin' tickets."

"You're driving already?"

"Hell, yeah." His chuckled sounded a little less

humorous than usual. "I was haulin' ass before the cop even got to your car."

My heart squeezed. "I'm sorry you were so worried. But everything's okay. You don't need to come now."

"Yeah, I do," he countered. "I ain't leavin' ya to face the mother-bitch all by yourself. I know ya, darlin', an' I bet you're already thinkin' maybe the whole damn thing was somehow your fault. It wasn't your fault thirty years ago, it ain't your fault now, an' I sure as hell ain't gonna sit around down here knowin' she's mind-fuckin' ya up there."

"Thanks, Arnie, but I have to deal with her. Orders. There's really nothing you can do here."

"I can be on your side. An' I can give ya a reality check if she starts playin' mind games." He hesitated. "But... it's okay if ya don't want me there; I can just-"

"I want you," I interrupted. "Of course I want you. But I don't want you to drop everything to come and rescue me again."

Hellhound's voice softened. "I ain't rescuin' ya. I know ya can handle any shit that happens. But it never hurts to have a friend around to cover your back, right?"

I lowered my voice to a seductive purr. "And cover my front."

He chuckled. "It's a tough job, but somebody's gotta do it. Hey, wanna get a late lunch at Eddy's? I'll be there around one."

"Around *one?* That's only an hour and a quarter from now! Shit, how fast were you driving?"

"If ya don't wanna know, don't ask."

I shook my head even though he couldn't see me. "See you soon. Drive carefully. At the speed limit!" I added severely.

"Yes, ma'am."

I was still quivering from the adrenaline overdose when I parked in the Sirius Dynamics lot five minutes later. My stomach growled, reminding me that breakfast had been far too long ago. I growled back, irritable with ravelled nerves and hunger.

My anger rose as I strode across the parking lot. I managed to sign in at the security wicket without biting Leo's head off, but my boots pounded an aggressive beat as I strode down the hall toward Stemp's office. This time that fucking bastard was going to tell me *everything* he knew about me and my family. And while he was at it, he could damn well explain why he'd sicced the RCMP on me.

When I marched into his office without knocking and stood glowering at him, Stemp greeted me with an infinitesimal eyebrow raise.

I snapped, "You knew all along that Nora was my mother!"

Stemp leaned back in his chair, his face revealing a flash of weariness before his usual impenetrable façade closed down. "Please close the door."

I spun on my heel and complied, rage making my breath come as hard as if I'd been running. Returning to my rigid stance in front of his desk, I glared at him in silence.

"Please have a seat," he said mildly.

"I'll stand." The words ground out between my teeth.

"Very well." His emotionless amber gaze flicked over my face, a cool appraisal that did nothing to soothe my temper. "You are angry," he observed.

"No shit, Sherlock!"

He sighed. "I would be, too, if I were in your place."

His empathy was so unexpected that my anger vanished.

Its absence left hollow exhaustion behind, and I dropped into the chair.

"Why?" My voice came out flat and tired. "Why didn't you tell me?"

"To what end?" Stemp regarded me with an expression that looked a lot like compassion. "What if I had told you that she was alive, and that she had chosen to cut all ties with you? That knowledge would only have brought you pain."

"But at least I wouldn't have been blindsided."

He shrugged. "I did not expect her to ever make contact with you."

Pain twisted my heart, sharper than it should have been, and I held my expression impassive with all my will.

I might have fooled a civilian, but not a former agent of Stemp's calibre. "I did not mean that as a judgement of your worthiness," he said quietly. "Her actions are a reflection of her own character, not yours."

My throat went tight. Dammit, I could have handled his indifference, or even anger. But kindness?

Dammit.

I swallowed hard. "I... um... thanks." I sucked in an unsteady breath and changed the subject. "So you talked to the RCMP about me this morning?"

"Yes. I confirmed that you had an ironclad alibi between nineteen thirty yesterday and zero four hundred this morning. I told them I was unsure of your current whereabouts, but they declined my offer to summon you until such time as they had searched Kane's house. I presume they found you?"

"Actually I found them, when I went over to John's place."

"And was the situation satisfactorily resolved?" Stemp's

words were dispassionate, but I read the concern behind his mask. His secret daughter overseas was around the same age as Daniel.

"Yes, everything's fine," I assured him. "Daniel got the stomach flu last night so they stayed at John's house instead of driving back to Calgary; and this morning John took Daniel to the hospital, so that's why he wasn't answering his phone. Alicia just panicked."

"Understandable, given that Daniel was kidnapped less than six months ago."

"Yeah. I can't even imagine what that must have been like for her." I shuddered. "God, I'm glad I never had kids."

A moment later I realized how heartless that must sound to a man who had been forced to live half a world away from his daughter for the entire seven years of her life.

"I'm sorry, I didn't mean-" I began, but Stemp raised a dismissive hand and changed the subject.

"Since you are here... I received a report from the analysts this morning. Rebecca Stile was hospitalized in London around zero two hundred our time, which was zero nine hundred over there. Although her vital signs are strong, she is in an unexplained coma. She is being monitored in the intensive care unit, and her parents in Halifax have been notified. They are currently en route to London."

Guilt turned my stomach to lead. "Oh, God, I didn't even think of Rebecca this morning. And her poor parents; they must be going through hell. Is Spider in yet? We need to-"

"You do not 'need to'," Stemp interrupted. "You will not be entering the network today. Ms. Stile's condition is stable, but yours..." He raked a gaze from my finely trembling hands to my bloodshot eyes, which sported bags big enough to store a spare sandwich or two. "How much sleep did you get last night?"

"Um..."

"The truth," he added. "If necessary, I will hook you up to the lie detector." His hard level gaze made it clear that he wasn't kidding.

"It's a long story..." I began, scrambling for ways to evade the question.

"It is not a long story," Stemp countered. "It is a simple question requiring a single-word answer. How many hours of sleep did you get last night?" His eyes narrowed. "Actual sleep. Excluding time spent lying awake or fighting nightmares."

Shit, had Spider ratted me out?

"Um, I don't know, exactly," I equivocated. "I slept for a while at Spider's place, and then I got a ride home and went straight to bed until it was time to leave for my meeting with Nora-"

"How many hours of actual sleep?" Stemp repeated. "Take the time to count them up. I'll wait."

Cornered, I lashed out. "I got as much as I got, okay? If I hadn't had to suck up to Nora this morning, I'd have gotten more. I'll catch up on my sleep tonight. My meeting with Nora was interesting, by the way. I think she's hiding something."

"As are you," Stemp said with exaggerated patience. "How many hours of sleep did you get?"

"Oh, for chrissake!" I flopped back in the chair like a petulant teenager.

Stemp remained unmoved, watching me with the predatory stillness of a snake sizing up its prey.

"Okay, fine," I said into the lengthening silence. "We got to Spider's place a little before four AM. I had breakfast with

Linda around six-thirty-"

"True, but incomplete," Stemp interrupted. "Webb said that you did not, in fact, sleep in his house. I questioned him at length."

My irritation returned full force. "Seriously? You interrogated Spider about my sleeping habits? Don't you have better things to do?"

Stemp's impassive mask dissolved into impatience. "Yes, I do. And you are wasting my precious time. Now. How... many... hours?"

A chill chased down my backbone. If Stemp's legendary patience was wearing thin, I was in deep shit.

"Um..." I did some rapid mental math. "About three and a half. What's the big deal? I've been sleep-deprived lots of times before and I've always gotten the job done."

"It is important because I want you to have at least eight hours of quality sleep before risking another collision with Rebecca Stile in the internet." Stemp eyed me narrowly. "And, more to the point, it's important because your psych clearance for active duty has just been rescinded."

CHAPTER 23

A deluge of ice-cold adrenaline raised my voice to a squawk. "*What?* But Rawling already approved my clearance! He can't rescind it, he's on holidays! Why would he..."

Stemp cut off my babbling. "He granted your clearance on the condition that you got a good night's sleep. You did not. Therefore your clearance is rescinded until such time as you do."

Oh, God, could they lock me up just because I was tired? Was this some creative way to chuck me in the secure facility and bury me forever?

My faulty emotional wiring short-circuited fear into rage. "That's bullshit!" I lunged to my feet. "It wasn't like I *chose* to get waylaid in the internet last night! What did Rawling expect me to do, just let Rebecca Stile wander off with all our classified intel because..." I assumed a bitterly sarcastic child-like voice. "...it's getting late and I have to go home to beddy-byes now?"

"You could have followed your Director's orders and gotten adequate sleep after you emerged from the network," Stemp observed coolly.

"No, I fucking couldn't!" I glared at him, jamming my

fists against my hips as an inadequate substitute for punching him. "Because my *Director* had just given me shit for discouraging Nora. I didn't get out of the network until nearly four AM, I had an appointment with Nora at ten AM, and there's no math in this universe where ten minus four equals eight! And if I'd called Nora and postponed our meeting and she'd gotten discouraged and left, you'd have been chewing my ass for that, too!"

"Kelly." Any hint of compassion was gone from his voice. "Sit."

Fear choked me all over again. My freedom was in his hands. Pissing him off had been colossally stupid.

I dropped back into the chair, largely because my trembling knees wouldn't hold my weight any longer. "Sorry," I whispered.

Stemp studied me without speaking. Was he making mental arrangements for my transfer to the secure facility? Or was he only bringing his own temper under control?

Or maybe he was just waiting to see if I'd crack. Dammit, what did he want from me?

Fighting the urge to babble confessions and pleas, I pressed my lips together and sat in silence.

The silence stretched, and my bratty inner child dug in her heels. Go ahead and try to wait me out, asshole. I settled deeper in the chair, schooling my breath to a slow easy rhythm and easing the tension out of my muscles.

To my surprise, Stemp spoke a moment later. "I apologize if it seemed to you that I was 'chewing your ass'." His precise diction made the phrase sound ridiculously vulgar. "That was not my intention. I was merely informing you that your active-duty clearance is rescinded until such time as you achieve eight consecutive hours of sleep. Dr.

Rawling did not rescind your clearance personally. Adequate sleep was a written condition of his approval; and as your director, it is my responsibility to ensure that all conditions are met."

Shit, now I was embarrassed as well as scared.

"I'm sorry," I mumbled. "I overreacted."

"Yes, you did," Stemp said mildly. "Why?"

I shrugged and attempted a self-deprecating smile. "Because I'm very tired?"

His lips quirked. "Ah." He sobered, inspecting me with such intensity that I had to suppress a squirm of discomfort.

"You only react with anger when you feel threatened," he observed clinically. Before I could respond, he added, "Why would you feel threatened by a temporary and easily-remedied suspension of your active-duty status?"

Terror froze my insides. Oh God, he was realizing how fucked up I was. They'd lock me up and throw away the key.

I catapulted beyond panic to icy calm. If he wasn't already thinking of locking me up, I sure as hell wouldn't put it into his mind by naming my fear aloud.

My shoulders rose in an easy shrug and my voice came out tinged with wry humour. "It might be a teeny bit important to me to find out whether my mother is a flawed but well-meaning person who truly loves me, or a treasonous killer who's lying her ass off."

The corner of Stemp's mouth tugged upward. "Plausible." The hint of a smile vanished as if it had never existed and he studied me again.

Trying to see inside my mind.

He had only said it was plausible. He hadn't said he believed me.

If he demanded to know what else was bothering me,

should I lie? But what if he put me on the lie detector? Would it be better to just admit I was still desperately and irreversibly claustrophobic and terrified of imprisonment, and throw myself on his mercy?

But regardless of any sympathy he might have for me, he would never compromise his duty...

When Stemp spoke, I held myself very still so I wouldn't flinch.

"Very well. When you can truthfully..." His eyes narrowed to emphasize the word. "...report a minimum of eight consecutive hours of restful sleep, I will restore your active-duty status." His expression softened. "Why don't you go home now? Mother is expecting you for dinner at seventeen hundred hours, but you could rest between now and then."

"Um... thanks..."

Too easy. Where was the catch?

"So, um..." I gave him a questioning look. "Does this mean you don't want me to talk to Nora until tomorrow?" Suspicion flared. Was he trying to keep me away from Kane? "Or you don't want me to talk to John?" I prodded.

"Given that Nora is under suspicion of murder, personal contact with her would be considered an active-duty scenario and therefore off-limits; although you may speak to her via telephone. Your recruitment of Kane is not considered to be dangerous, so I encourage you to proceed with that assignment. The chain of command is eager to expedite his return."

His last sentence set off alarm bells in my mind. "You mean they're eager to hear his decision, right?" I prompted, trepidation rising.

Stemp eyed me levelly. "Only if his decision is to return."

I slumped. "This isn't going to go away, is it? Even if he says no, they won't give up."

The warm human Stemp vanished, replaced by a chilly reptilian robot. "Your assignment was to convince John Kane to return to active agent status. That assignment remains unchanged."

I licked suddenly-dry lips. "And if I fail?"

"I recommend you don't."

Nausea rolled in my stomach as I stared at his remote expression. Not only was I doomed to failure because of Kane's devotion to Daniel, but I had also set myself up to be convicted of defying orders when he ultimately refused to come back.

Dammit, why had I opposed the assignment so vehemently? Now no matter what I said or did, they would accuse me of subverting the mission.

Fuck-shit-damn, I *knew* better than to reveal my true feelings to anybody. Ever.

Idiot.

"Do you have any other questions regarding your duty status?" Stemp asked.

"No." The word came out as hollow as my heart.

"Very well. You said earlier that you suspected Nora was concealing something. Report."

My tired brain slowly shifted gears. "Um. Right. I met her for coffee this morning. I was trying to get a handle on her motivations for coming back into my life." To my surprise, an analysis popped out of my mouth. "The way I see it, there are only two reasons why she would blow her cover after never saying boo to me for thirty years." I ticked off the points on my fingers. "One: She always wanted to stay in touch but something prevented that; and that 'something' has recently changed. Or two: She was thrilled to be gone and never intended to come back..." I hid the stab of hurt that accompanied that thought. "...so she would only return if she had something to gain."

"Logical," Stemp agreed.

I went on, "So I was asking questions about why she left and why she didn't get in touch with me before now; and she had plausible answers... well, plausible coming from her, anyway. I hadn't realized until now what a manipulator she was. Is." I didn't mention that she'd managed to twist my so-called interrogation into an emotional bloodbath. Blowing out a breath, I added, "There's nothing like thirty years of perspective to figure out your childhood issues."

Stemp gave me a twisted smile. "So I discovered."

An unexpected smile tugged my lips in return. "Yeah, I guess you did. How's that going for you?"

His stiffening was so subtle that I might have thought I had imagined it if I hadn't known him.

"Sorry, I didn't mean to pry," I added hurriedly.

His shoulders eased, and I realized that his defensiveness was as much a reflex as my own.

"There is no need to apologize," he said. "My reconciliation with my parents is going well and has been extremely gratifying; although we are all struggling to overcome entrenched attitudes and behaviours that are no longer necessary or desirable. Thank you for asking."

My heart warmed. "I'm so glad it's going well."

"I am, too." Stemp sobered. "And how are you handling the emotional component of your assignment with Nora?"

It was my turn to stiffen. Not going to fall into that trap again.

I grimaced. "About as well as can be expected. Like I

said, it's been enlightening. She didn't say anything that I could nail as an outright lie, but she looked..." I searched for the right word. "...shifty... when I asked how much she knew about Sam's research. She said she knew I could power the VR sims, but it seemed as though she knew more than she was admitting.   And if she does know that Sam was skimming classified data and passing it around..."

"Then she was complicit in the Knights' espionage and treason even if she didn't actually participate," Stemp said flatly.

"Yeah." The weight of my exhaustion seemed to double and I sagged in the chair. "And I really don't see any situation where she wouldn't have known. I mean, she knew everything about the brainwave-driven network and the sims right from the start. Wouldn't you think that after being married to Sam for thirty years, she'd ask some questions about why they were getting a stream of unexplained income through Sirius Dynamics?"

Stemp tipped his hand one way and the other in an equivocating gesture. "Perhaps; but perhaps not. The day-to-day operations of all branches of Sirius Dynamics were and are handled by a management company; and unlike the rest of the Knights, Kraus never did sell secrets for profit. Even though the others were cashing in personally, he simply handed over the sensitive intel where he thought it would do the most good.   No dirty revenue flowed through the company."

Massaging my aching temples, I let out a sigh. "Damn. Just when I was starting to convince myself that it was an open-and-shut case and she was guilty."

But the stupidly hopeful part of my heart perked up. Maybe I'd been wrong. Maybe Nora's little twitches were a normal reaction to discussing classified information in public. After nearly thirty years with MI5, her reluctance to divulge anything would be deeply ingrained.

Maybe she was on the up-and-up. Maybe she was really a selfless, dedicated woman like Moonbeam...

I slapped that thought down and kicked it into a corner. And threw a mental rug over it, just to be sure it wouldn't jump up and bite me later.

"I'll try to manipulate her into answering more questions under the lie detector," I said. Stemp's raised eyebrow prompted me to add, "After I get some sleep. By the way, she knows that Sirius Canada has been seized. She's got a lawyer working on it. Considering her financial situation, she's probably pretty motivated to get it back."

Stemp nodded. "It is her last resort. According to the analysts, Sirius UK is barely solvent; and the U.S. branch was sold to the United States government ten years ago for pennies on the dollar. Apparently Kraus bulldozed all the profits back into the research division, which is a black hole from where dollars never return."

"And Nora likes to spend money."

"Yes, and Sirius Canada is profitable." His mouth flattened. "For now. That may change if Nora has her way. Her lawyer contacted us this morning, and we may have to choose between divulging the true nature of Kraus's activities or relinquishing the company to Nora. And since divulging his activities would result in the release of highly classified intel..." His shoulder rose in a fractional shrug. "We will likely have to return Sirius Canada to Nora's control."

"Shit."

"Indeed."

I dragged myself to my feet. "Then I'd better find a way

to nail her. I'll file my case updates and talk to Reggie about that heart-attack drug, and then I'll drop by the hospital and talk to Ian again."

"Or you could go home and rest," Stemp said pointedly.

"I'll do that, too. But John's still at the hospital as far as I know, and I want to at least make a show of support."

"To further your recruitment mission." Stemp's expression was inscrutable.

I offered him a businesslike nod and a bald-faced lie. "Right."

"Very well, then. I will see you at my home at seventeen hundred. Dismissed."

My exit from Stemp's office was considerably less energetic than my arrival. As I plodded past Spider's office, his call stopped me.

"Hey, Aydan!"

I reversed direction and leaned against his door jamb. "Hi, Spider. What's up?"

His gaze flicked behind me to the empty hallway and he lowered his voice. "Come in for a second."

Prying myself away from the welcome support of his doorway, I stepped inside and swung the door shut behind me. "What's up?" I repeated quietly.

"Is everything okay with..." He tilted his head in the direction of Stemp's office. "I had a totally weird conversation with him earlier. He was asking about you sleeping at my place. Does he think we're..." His thin cheeks flushed crimson. "Um... I mean... did he ask you whether we..."

I couldn't help it; I laughed. "No, it's okay, it was nothing like that. It was just that Dr. Rawling had approved my active-duty status with the condition that I got enough sleep last night. Stemp was checking with you about how many hours of sleep I'd actually gotten so he'd know whether I was lying about it."

"Oh!" Spider's word came out on a released breath and his blush subsided. "That's a relief! I mean, um..." His colour returned in a flood. "Not that I'd be embarrassed or ashamed if we were, um, you know... because I think you're great and any guy would be proud to... um... I mean, not me, because I'm, like, totally happily married to Linda and you know I'd never cheat on her, but if I wasn't... I mean... I wouldn't..."

He trailed off helplessly, his blush deepening to a shade of purple that made me fear for his capillaries.

Despite the belly laugh that threatened to burst out, I managed a straight face and a palm-out 'stop' gesture. "It's okay, I get it. Thank you."

I didn't bother to add that even if the thought of a dalliance with him had ever crossed my mind, it would have been immediately nixed by the knowledge that I was the same age as his mother.

He hurried on to a more comfortable topic. "So I found out that Rebecca's parents won't get to London until about ten o'clock tonight our time, which is about five AM London time. And they'll be tired and jet-lagged so they probably won't make any decisions about whether to discontinue her life support until tomorrow morning at least."

"I doubt if there's too much risk of them making a snap decision," I reassured him. "Stemp said her vital signs are strong, so her parents won't likely arrive and immediately decide to pull the plug on their otherwise-healthy daughter."

"But her body's condition could deteriorate fast with her consciousness gone," Spider said worriedly. "What if her organs start to shut down? The hospital could keep her alive with machines for a while, but if the doctors decide there's no hope of recovery..."

I hid my own anxiety in a comforting tone. "If you were in Rebecca's place, do you think your mom and dad would pull the plug on you if there was even the tiniest bit of hope?"

"Oh." Spider sat back in his chair, the tension easing from his face. "No. I keep forgetting that Rebecca and her parents are just normal people, not the freaks we usually deal with."

"Try not to worry," I soothed. "I'll be ready to go back into the network tomorrow and I'll check on her then. And I'll put some more reassurances into her mind to keep her calm until we can figure out a way to get her consciousness back into her body."

Spider nodded, looking more cheerful; and I didn't voice my fear that Rebecca might not be sane enough to comprehend anything at all by the time I found her again.

CHAPTER 24

I had just gotten down to the lobby when Reggie and Jack emerged from the secured area, hand in hand. Taking advantage of their absorption in each other, I studied them with pleasant warmth rising in my chest.

Beside Jack's angelic blonde beauty Reggie's scars looked even more horrific, but it was the undamaged side of his face that captured my attention.

He was smiling.

A warm, genuine smile; not the sardonic smirk he usually wore. His muscular shoulders were relaxed, and his easy gait belied the prosthetic legs concealed by his khaki slacks. For the first time I realized how rigidly he usually held himself, as though braced for the inevitable reactions of horror and pity and curiosity that confronted him outside the safe haven of his lab and trusted co-workers.

Realizing I was standing there grinning like an idiot, I got my face under control and hurried across the lobby to intercept them.

"Hi," I greeted them. "Where are you going?"

"Lunch," Jack replied. "Would you like to join us?"

"Sorry, I don't have time." My stomach underscored my regret with a loud rumble. "Now that you mention it, though,

I'm starving!"

"Well, it is nearly one o'clock," Jack pointed out. "You need to eat. Come with us; we're just going to the Melted Spoon."

"Thanks, but Arnie's on his way and we're going to grab a late lunch when he gets here. Reggie, do you have time to meet this afternoon? I need to pick your brain-"

"Kelly!" Holt's demanding voice interrupted from across the lobby. He jerked his chin in an arrogant 'come here' gesture that made my middle finger itch to flip him the bird.

Lowering my voice, I spoke for Reggie's and Jack's ears only. "Holt The Magnificent has issued his summons. Guess I'd better go see what he wants."

Reggie snorted. "Like you ever obey anybody."

I grinned. "This is enlightened self-interest. He has information I need."

"So do I," Reggie countered.

"Yeah, but I like you better, so I'm going to let you go for lunch."

He gave me his usual mocking half-smile. "I'm touched." He sobered and added, "I'll be in the lab all afternoon. Drop by whenever you want."

"Thanks, Reggie. See you la-"

A short shrill whistle interrupted me, followed by Holt's impatient shout. "Hey, *Kelly!* Get your ass over here!"

Like calling a none-too-obedient dog.

My temper flared.

Reggie took in my expression, his face twisting into an unholy grin. Through the static of rage that jangled in my ears, I barely heard him stage-whisper to Jack. "Wait for it. This is going to be awesome."

With an effort, I wrangled my temper under control.

Deliberately turning my back on Holt, I said to Reggie, "Sorry, you're not getting a show today. I'm pretty sure I couldn't get away with shooting him in front of three witnesses." I inclined my chin in the direction of the security wicket, where Leo watched with interest from behind the bulletproof glass.

"No witnesses here," Reggie drawled. "Leo likes you. He'll keep his mouth shut. And I can't see anything." He gestured toward his prosthetic eye, smirking. "I'm blind. It sucks, but what can you do?" He turned to Jack. "Do you see anything?"

She shook her head, her prim expression at odds with the wicked glint in her eyes. "At the moment I'm quite distracted by mental calculations for my latest research. My observations would be unreliable at best."

Suddenly recalling that she had been the unenthusiastic recipient of Holt's romantic overtures a few months ago, I grinned. "What do you say, Jack? Should we double-team him?"

She shook her head. "It's not fair to engage in a battle of wits with an unarmed man. Anyway, you know what his temper's like; and you said you needed information from him."

"Oh, he'll get over it, he's just a-"

The widening of her eyes was the only warning I got.

A hard hand clamped onto my shoulder and jerked me around.

Shock and rage exploded adrenaline into my veins. I spun in the direction of the yank, multiplying its force as I uncoiled and slammed an elbow strike into my attacker's jaw.

Holt absorbed the blow, hitting the floor and rolling

instantly back to his feet. For a bare second he rocked precariously, legs straddled and eyes glazed.

My stomach plummeted to my toes. I'd just hit a top martial artist. He was going to beat the living shit out of me.

Holt shook his head like an infuriated bull, his eyes snapping back into focus as his lethal fists clenched.

"Is there a problem?" Stemp's cool voice was the most beautiful sound I'd ever heard. Standing at the edge of the lobby, his hard amber gaze measured us. His posture was easy, but his hand rested casually close to his concealed holster.

"No problem," I croaked through a paper-dry throat.

"No problem," Holt growled, his cold steel gaze eviscerating me.

"What happened?" Stemp asked. When nobody said anything, he prompted, "Kelly?"

"I didn't hear Holt coming up behind me," I mumbled. "He grabbed my shoulder and startled me, and I spun around and hit him before I realized who it was."

I secretly crossed my fingers. Please let Stemp believe that mixture of truth and lie.

"She knocked him ass over teakettle!" Reggie contributed gleefully. "Rattled his brains but good!"

I threw him a 'shut-up' look and said, "It was just a lucky shot. I didn't know what I was doing."

"Holt?" Stemp inquired, one eyebrow rising.

"No big deal. She didn't hurt me," Holt grated, scowling and fingering the reddening mark on his prominent jaw. "I thought she knew I was there. I shouldn't have grabbed her."

"Shouldn't have pissed her off, you mean," Reggie said under his breath, still grinning. Jack gave him a quelling look and squeezed his hand hard enough to make him wince.

"Do I need to review the security footage?" Stemp asked ominously.

Holt shrugged, exuding confidence and honesty. "Go ahead if you want, but you won't see anything but what we told you. Ask him." He cocked a thumb in Leo's direction.

As Stemp approached the security wicket, Leo shot a questioning look at me. I gave him a nod and stepped over to stand beside Holt, hoping Leo would get the message.

"Well?" Stemp inquired. "What did you see?"

"Um..." Leo eyed Holt and me standing side by side. Despite the painful-looking mark on his jaw, Holt wore a calm and pleasant expression. I did my best to match it.

"Just... what they said," Leo said slowly. "Aydan had her back to Holt, and he came up behind her fast and grabbed her shoulder. She spun around and hit him once. That's all."

"See? No big deal," Holt said easily. "Nice elbow strike, by the way, Kelly. Have you been studying martial arts?"

I managed a laugh that didn't sound too false. "Nope. Like I said, just a dumb-luck shot."

Nobody needed to know about the heavy bag I'd installed in my basement, or the muay thai training videos I'd been studying.

Stemp gave us a look that made it clear he could smell bullshit, but he turned back to Leo without comment. We stood in silence while he signed out at the security wicket, and when the exit door closed behind him I let out a breath of relief.

"Show's over, folks," I deadpanned to Jack and Reggie. "Just move along. Nothing to see here."

Reggie snorted amusement, but the smile didn't stay on his face long. Taking a couple of steps forward, he stood toe to toe with Holt, staring up into the taller man's face with deadly intensity.

"Don't manhandle Aydan again," he said quietly. "Or I will fuck you up in ways you can't even imagine." His fire-ravaged features lent the words spine-chilling menace, and he gave Holt one last glare before turning his back and stalking away. Jack gave us a tentative smile and a little finger-wave before hurrying after him.

"Christ, that fugly sonofabitch gives me the creeps," Holt muttered. "What'd you do to get on his good side? Suck his-" His eyes widened at my expression, and he snapped his mouth shut so fast I heard his teeth click. "Sorry," he mumbled. "That was Holt The Asshole talking."

I fought my anger under control. "I thought I recognized that voice," I said lightly. "I'm glad he's gone now."

Holt's posture eased. "Yeah. Listen, I need to talk to you. Not here." He indicated the public lobby with a jerk of his chin.

"Let's go up to my office," I said, hoping this wasn't just a ploy to get me alone so he could kill me at his leisure.

We walked upstairs without speaking, and when we entered my office he swung the door shut behind him.

"So what's up?" I asked, holding my voice steady and wondering whether I could grab my gun out of my ankle holster before he could twist my head off.

Holt dropped onto my sofa and propped his boots on my coffee table with a weary sigh. "Fucking Grandin."

"Um... would 'fucking' be a verb or an adjective?" I inquired cautiously. "Because if it's an adjective I'm right there with you; but if you're talking about literally fucking Grandin, he's all yours."

Holt barked out a laugh. "Don't tell me; let me guess. You were an English major."

"Nope. Bookkeeper. Accuracy is very important, especially if it keeps me from ending up in bed with guys like Grandin."

"True." Holt's grin vanished, his jaw hardening. "So... things just got a whole lot more complicated. Grandin's claiming he was under official CIA orders the whole time."

"To kill an FBI agent and an MI6 agent and sell me? How stupid does he think we are?"

"That's what I thought." Holt frowned. "But... the lie detector corroborates his story. He said he had orders to have the U.S. scientists fake their weapon demo; so he coordinated that with them and their Weapons director. That whole thing was just a ruse to frame you and extradite you."

"Yeah, we'd already figured that out," I agreed. "And somebody in the U.S. government has a lot of explaining to do to Five Eyes about that. But there's no way Grandin had orders for the rest of it."

Holt rubbed his forehead, frowning. "He swears he got a second set of orders after he framed you at the conference. The orders said Dirk and Rand were dirty and he was authorized to use deadly force against them; and he'd get a cash bonus if he abducted you and handed you over to a contact instead of waiting on the official extradition. Then he was supposed to pretend you'd attacked him and escaped."

My stomach tightened as I processed that. "So they intended to bury me. Extradition would have taken too long and left a paper trail, but this... it would look as though I'd gone rogue and vanished. The U.S. could claim ignorance of the whole thing, and nobody would ever know where I'd ended up."

"Yeah. And Grandin's orders said if anything went wrong he should sit tight, claim diplomatic immunity, and they'd have him safely back on U.S. soil within twelve hours. That's why he wasn't talking earlier, but now the twelve hours is long past and the U.S. government is denying they ever issued those orders. Grandin says he got set up."

"But... hang on." I planted my fists on my hips. "When he kidnapped me he said he had a better market, and he called me Arlene Widdenback. And I seriously doubt the CIA pays cash bonuses to agents just for following orders. He's bullshitting. He might have gotten so-called 'orders' from somewhere, but he had to know they weren't legit."

Holt scowled. "Maybe. He's been careful about the way he answers my questions. But the Arlene Widdenback thing is probably a dead end. Grandin knew about your cover identity from your dossier with U.S. Customs, so he just assumed that's what it was about. He says nobody specifically told him to abduct Arlene Widdenback."

I grimaced. "Great. Nothing like narrowing the field."

Holt grunted agreement and went on, "So Grandin finally coughed up the phone number for his contact. He was supposed to call the number and arrange a drop as soon as he had you. He's never met the contact in person, but we have to assume they know who he is. So it looks like our only option is to set up a sting with you as bait."

I fell into my chair and buried my head in my hands. "Absolutely fucking marvelous."

My voice came out thin and tremulous, and Holt snapped, "Have you got a problem with that?"

I had been teetering on the edge of admitting I was in no shape mentally or physically to undertake that kind of mission; but the contempt in his tone prodded my stubborn pride.

I raised my head from my hands and gave him a level look. "*We* have a problem with that. Stemp just rescinded my active-duty status."

"What the hell? What did you do?" Holt demanded. "Couldn't you game the psych evaluation? I thought you had that covered."

Still prickling with irritation, I snapped, "I passed my psych evaluation."

"But?"

"Stemp nailed me on a technicality." Before Holt could dig for details, I went on, "It's no big deal. I should be back to active duty tomorrow."

"Oh." He relaxed. "Okay, good. I won't have anything set up before then anyway." He removed his feet from my coffee table and rose, stretching and flexing his neck. "Christ, did you have to go to town on me like that?" He touched the swollen spot on his jaw and winced. "You knew damn well it was me."

"I'm sorry," I said sincerely. "I did know it was you, but you startled the hell out of me and by the time my brain caught up with my reflexes it was too late."

"Huh." He gave me a narrow look. "Lucky for you Stemp showed up when he did."

"I'm still thanking my lucky stars."

Holt must have heard the profound truth in my voice. He laughed. "Way to suck up, Kelly. Don't worry, I probably wouldn't have killed you outright. Remember, I'm gaming my psych evaluations, too." Heading for the door, he added, "I'll run the sting mission by Stemp and bring you into the loop as soon as we have a strategy. Catch you later."

As he vanished down the hall, I fell back in my chair with

a whimper of sheer despair.

CHAPTER 25

My cell phone vibrated as I stepped out of Sirius Dynamics into a bitter wind that whipped my breath away. The call display showed Hellhound's number, and I accepted the call with a smile.

"Hey, darlin', wave at me," he said. "I'm lookin' at ya from the parkin' lot."

My grin widened as I waved in the direction of the Subaru Forester idling across the street. "Hey, you creepy stalker," I teased. "Are you planning to take me to the bar, get me drunk, and take advantage of me?"

"Sounds like a helluva plan." His voice deepened. "Hey, little girl, come here. I got candy."

"Mm, I bet you do. Be right there." I crossed the street and hurried over.

He got out of the SUV as I trotted up, and a moment later I was engulfed in the gentle strength of his hug. Burying my face in his parka, I closed my eyes and let the hurt and fear and anger of the day fall away.

"Hey, darlin'," Arnie rasped softly, his lips against my hair. "It's okay. Everythin's gonna be okay."

Somehow I managed to stop myself from saying 'everything's okay now that you're here'. Instead, I gave him an extra squeeze and pulled away with a smile. "Thanks for coming. I'm really glad you're here."

"Glad I am, too. Hey..." He stroked my quivering hand with frown. "You're shakin'. Are ya cold? Come on an' get in the SUV an' get warmed up."

"No, I'm just tired and hungry." I sighed. "And I've got one more stop before we go to Eddy's. Why don't you head over there and I'll meet you as soon as I can?"

He frowned. "If you're so hungry you're shakin', ya oughta eat first. 'Specially if ya think ya might run into trouble." He studied me worriedly. "Are ya gonna be safe, where you're goin'?"

"Yeah; no big deal," I assured him. "I just have to stop in at the hospital to check on John and Daniel and Ian."

"That doesn't sound like a big enough emergency to skip a meal for."

"No, but I just..." I trailed off as his words filtered through the fog in my brain. "Shit, you're right. It can wait. I'm too tired to think straight."

Hellhound grinned. "An' that's why I'm here. Hop in, darlin'. Let's get ya fed an' watered."

"Maybe even beered," I said hopefully as I hurried around to the passenger side.

The lunch crowd was trickling out when we arrived at Blue Eddy's, and my favourite table in the corner had just been vacated. Hellhound and I slid into the two chairs with their backs to the wall.

"Ah," Hellhound said with satisfaction as he shed his jacket and dumped it on one of the remaining chairs. "Best table in the place."

Darlene hurried over to take our orders, returning with our beer in minutes. I sucked back a cold crisp swallow with a groan of satisfaction. "Damn, that's good."

Hellhound grinned. "Hope I can make ya moan like that later."

"You always do." I hitched my chair closer to his so I could lean into his shoulder with a contented sigh.

My sigh trailed off into a frown and I sat up again.

"What, darlin'?" Hellhound followed my sightline with a frown of his own. "Uh-oh."

Our table gave us a commanding view of the entire bar, including the private corridor that led to Eddy's office. Eddy and another man stood in the hallway talking, their body language tense.

The other man wore a suit that was too expensive for the atmosphere at Blue Eddy's and he loomed threateningly over Eddy, scowling. Eddy faced him squarely, fists clenched by his sides. I could only see his back, but there was more than anger in his posture.

"I never saw Eddy pissed off before," Hellhound said.

My pulse sped up as I assessed Eddy's jerky gestures and the withdrawn angle of his body. "He's not just pissed off. He's scared." I leaned back, resting my ankle on my knee. A quick survey of the bar assured me that nobody was looking, and I slipped my trank pistol out of my ankle holster and into the back of my pants. "I'm going over there. Watch my back."

"Right behind ya," Hellhound growled.

We strolled toward the two men. The man in the suit gave us a hostile glare, and Eddy turned to face us.

"Oh. Hi, Aydan; Hellhound. Um, can I talk to you later?" He glanced at the other man, anxiety in his eyes. "I'm just in the middle of something here."

"Yeah, I can see that," Hellhound rumbled. "Doesn't

look like a good somethin', either." He shot a look at the suit-clad man that would have made any sensible person turn tail and flee.

"Uh..." The man eyed Hellhound's shit-kicker boots and bearded battle-scarred face, and took an uncertain step backward. Then he squared his shoulders and summoned a sneer. "Strong-arm tactics, Carlson? That's not going to win you any points with AHS."

"No, no." Eddy spread his hands in a placating gesture. "That's not it at all. These are my friends..." He gave us a look that implored us to back off.

"Sorry, we didn't mean to interrupt," I said hurriedly. "It's just that I'm Eddy's bookkeeper, and I have a quick question for him. It'll only take a minute."

"Take as long as you want," the stranger snapped. "I'll be in the kitchen." He strode in that direction, pulling out his phone as he went.

"Sorry, Aydan, now's not a good time," Eddy said rapidly. "I'll talk to you later, okay? Gotta go." He hurried after the other man.

"AHS. Alberta Health Services," Hellhound said as we sat down at our table again. "That ain't good."

"I can't imagine Eddy would ever have a problem with the health inspectors," I replied. "I've been in that kitchen. It's spotless. And Eddy's kitchen staff have been with him for years. He treats them like family. There's no way they'd get sloppy and risk a health violation."

"He sure looked nervous, though," Hellhound pointed out.

"Yeah..." I frowned and gulped some beer. It didn't taste quite as good anymore.

Darlene arrived a few minutes later with our burgers and

a strained smile.

"What's with the health inspector?" I asked quietly as she placed the plates on the table.

She glanced anxiously over her shoulder. "I don't know," she whispered, her face tense. "We had a routine inspection a few months ago, but this guy's acting like he expects to find rat poison in the soup or something. Our kitchen is clean, it's always been clean, and the food's always fresh. Eddy loves his customers and he'd never serve bad food!" She gave us a desperate look. "Don't tell anybody, okay? If Eddy ever went out of business, I'd... I'd just..." Her voice choked off and she blinked rapidly as her eyes filled.

"It's okay, Eddy's our friend, too," I comforted her. "We're on your side. We won't say a thing."

"Thanks." She pasted on a smile. "Enjoy your burgers..." Her smile wobbled. "If... if you still want them..."

"Hell yeah!" Hellhound took a giant bite. "Kickass," he mumbled through his mouthful. "Just like always."

My stomach let out a growl loud enough to be heard over the music. "Nobody's taking this beauty away from me," I told Darlene, pulling my plate closer. "Don't worry, it's probably just a screwup at AHS."

She squared her shoulders. "You're right. Of course." She put on another smile and scurried off to attend to the rest of the patrons.

We ate in silence for a while, concentrating on the delicious burgers and our own thoughts.

What if they closed Eddy down? This was my home away from home. My haven of good food, good music, good company...

"Fuck," Hellhound said, glowering at his plate.

My gut clenched. "What's wrong? Is there something

wrong with your food?"

"Huh?" He looked up, his scowl clearing. "Oh. Fuck no, nothin' like that. Sorry. Just thinkin'." He absently stuffed a few fries in his mouth and chewed, frowning into middle distance.

I waited.

After a moment he blinked and returned his attention to me just as Eddy hurried over.

"I smell a rat," Hellhound began.

"Well, don't say anything to the other customers," Eddy joked as he slid into one of the chairs across from us, but the usual twinkle was absent from his eyes. "Sorry about that... um... earlier. Everything's fine. Nothing to worry about."

I studied him. "Don't take this wrong, Eddy, but I think you're fibbing."

He gave me a hunted look, and I reached across the table to take his hand. "Talk to us, Eddy. We're your friends. Let us help."

His grip tightened. "I..." He hesitated, clearly torn. "Oh, heck; I'm not going to lie to you." He blew out a tense breath. "Somebody called the health department on us. Claimed they'd found a dead mouse in their salad."

"Gross!" I said at the same time as Hellhound snapped, "Somebody's harassin' ya, I knew it. That's what I meant earlier when I said I smelled a rat."

"That's what I told the inspector," Eddy agreed. "There's no way that really happened. Nobody's sent a salad back with a complaint in..." He gazed up at the ceiling as if counting back years.

"Ever," he finished, returning his attention to us. "Nobody *ever* sent a salad back, that I can remember. And they sure as heck didn't do it yesterday, when the complaint was filed with the AHS." He leaned forward, lowering his voice. "But this morning..."

He glanced from side to side and leaned in closer to whisper, "There was a dead mouse in the corner of the kitchen. But I *know* we don't have mice. They leave mouse dirt everywhere. We'd have known they were there long before one upped and died right out in plain sight."

"Somebody planted it," I said with certainty. "Somebody's trying to get you in..." I suddenly realized I was still holding his hand.

Just like I had yesterday.

I pulled my hand away. "...trouble," I finished, feeling ill.

"What, Aydan?" Hellhound demanded. "What's wrong?"

They know how to get to Kelly.

"Eddy," I said in a small voice. "I'm sorry, but I think this might be my fault."

"What?" Eddy let out an incredulous laugh. "Not unless you sleep-drove to town carrying a dead mouse, let yourself in, dumped the corpse, locked everything up again, and drove home again without ever waking up. Because I can't imagine you intentionally doing anything like this."

"No, I didn't mean I did it," I said, my stomach churning. "I mean it's my fault. I think somebody has been trying to get to me through my friends. Everybody knows I eat here all the time and you're my bookkeeping client. And you said the complaint came in yesterday afternoon, after we talked at lunchtime. Did you notice any strangers in the bar yesterday?"

"I think you're reachin' a bit, darlin'," Hellhound objected.

"I think so, too." Eddy frowned. "Unless... is your ex-husband out of jail yet? He might have a score to settle with me, since I'm the one who called the police when he abducted you. What does he look like? When he's not in drag, I mean."

Shit, I had known that cover story would come back to bite me in the ass sooner or later. Hellhound and I exchanged a glance.

"He's got an eye patch and a peg leg," I said lightly. "You can't miss him."

Eddy gave me a mock glare. "Very funny. Seriously, what does he look like? With that wig and makeup on, all I could tell was that he was about average height and build. He could have been hanging around here and I'd never know."

"I'm sorry, Eddy, I didn't mean to make fun. He's still in jail," I lied. "It can't be him."

"Well, I can't imagine anybody else having a problem with you," Eddy said. "And even if they did, calling the health department on me is a pretty obscure way to show it." He patted my hand and rose. "Don't worry, it's not your fault. Probably just some small-town politics." Glancing at the entrance, he smiled. "Maybe I'll hire CRAPS to look into it."

Following the direction of his gaze, I spotted Lola and two of her elderly cronies coming in the door. She gave us a cheery wave and headed for the tables that Darlene had pushed together to form a group of ten.

"I have to get back to work," Eddy said. "Thanks for understanding about..." He gestured toward the kitchen, his lips twisting. "...that. Your food and drinks are on the house today."

"Eddy, you can't do that," I protested. "You're always giving me free meals. You need to make a living, too."

He waved a dismissive hand. "I do well enough. See you later."

He strode away before I could point out that I did his books, so I knew damn well that the bar's finances were barely in the black.

CHAPTER 26

Lola dumped her tote bag on a vacant chair at the gang of tables before hurrying over to where Hellhound and I sat.

"Hi, honey," she greeted me. "And..." Her warm smile flashed and she stuck out her hand to Hellhound. "Hi, I'm Lola. I've seen you around, but we've never been properly introduced."

Hellhound rose, making Lola step back a pace as her diminutive stature placed her approximately at eye level with his belly button. "Pleased to meet ya, Miz Lola." He bent to carefully enclose her tiny hand in his. "I'm Arnie Helmand."

"I'm sorry, I didn't realize I hadn't introduced you at Spider and Linda's wedding," I apologized. "Arnie's a very good friend of mine." I grinned up at him. "And Lola is one of my favourite clients. She runs a sex shop here in town."

Hellhound's eyebrows rose as a smile spread across his face. "Well, hell, darlin', ya been holdin' out on me. Sounds like we gotta go shoppin'."

Delight lit Lola's face. "Oh, yes! Come by the shop! We have all kinds of goodies. Something for everyone, no matter whether you're plain vanilla or spicy salsa." She gave Hellhound a flirtatious wink. "But something tells me you're not just plain vanilla."

Hellhound's guffaw boomed out, turning heads across the bar. "Sometimes I am. An' sometimes..." He bounced his eyebrows, grinning. "I ain't."

Lola's smile widened as she nudged me with a lascivious elbow. "Ooh, I like him!" She straightened as if struck by an idea. "Hey, why don't you two join our CRAPS meeting?" She nodded in the direction of their tables. "We're down a couple of members..." A momentary shadow crossed her face before she regained her usual perky smile. "...and we could use some younger people. We've gotten some support lately from some of the other Chamber of Commerce members; but the more the merrier."

Worry niggled at me. "You're down a couple of members? What happened?"

Lola's face fell. "Poor Bud Weems has pneumonia again. He just keeps getting it over and over, and each time he gets frailer." She sighed. "And Pearl slipped and fell on a patch of ice a couple of days ago and broke her ankle."

"Oh, no!" I turned to Arnie. "Pearl is ninety-three."

"But she's tough as nails," Lola countered. "They did surgery yesterday, and she's already up and hobbling around." She shook her head. "I keep telling her she should hire somebody to shovel her snow, but she insists on doing it herself. Says nobody else gets the sidewalk clean enough. But it's been so icy lately, I nearly fell outside the shop a couple of days ago, too." Her smile came back. "Well, I'd better get back to setting up our meeting. We start in twenty minutes. Will you join us?"

"Sorry, I can't," I said. "I'm booked solid this afternoon."

"What about you, Arnie?" Lola turned her smile up to him, doing her very best sweet-little-old-lady imitation despite her purple spiked hair and dominatrix-style stiletto-heeled boots.

He grinned, clearly not fooled by her act but enjoying her attempt. "Sorry, I got some stuff on this afternoon, too. Maybe next time I'm in town."

"Are you staying for long?" she inquired.

"You don't have to answer that," I told Hellhound. "She's just snooping."

He chuckled. "I'll prob'ly be here for a day or two."

"Well, be sure to come by Up & Coming for our Christmas sale!" Lola turned back to me. "See you tomorrow, honey. Bring Arnie along." She gave me a hug, then smiled up at Hellhound. "It was great to meet you. I need to give you a hug, too." She put her arms around him, looking like a pixie embracing a giant redwood.

He stooped, his powerful arms closing carefully around her in return. "Great to meet ya, too, Miz Lola."

As she walked away, Hellhound lowered his voice for my ears only. "I like her. Reminds me a bit of Miz Moonbeam. But what the hell is CRAPS?"

"That's Lola's other business: Citizens' Reconnaissance And Protection Services. She started it last summer when that crazy bridesmaid was trying to sabotage Spider and Linda's wedding. They're basically a bunch of geriatric snoops, but I guess there's enough illicit activity here to give them an occasional bit of excitement. Lost dogs, kids playing hooky from school, that kind of thing. I don't know if they actually charge for their services, but they have a great time digging for dirt."

"Maybe I oughta hire 'em for my P.I. business," Hellhound joked. "I'm always lookin' for good sources."

When we stepped out of Eddy's into the ice-glittering wind, I came face to face with Tom. We both pulled up short, and I did an awkward step-right-step-left at the same time he did.

I laughed. "Sorry. I'll just stand still and let you go by."

"No problem." Tom gave me a smile. "Maybe Eddy should install a revolving door." He shot a level look at Hellhound beside me. "Helmand. How've you been?" Not exactly a warm greeting, but at least he didn't sound hostile.

"Good," Hellhound said, matching Tom's noncommittal tone. "You?"

"Fine. Busy."

"I hear ya."

They did one of those silent male nods that indicated the conversational niceties were complete, and Tom turned back to me. "I'm glad I ran into you." He grinned. "Almost literally." His smile faded as he went on, "I left a message on your machine at home. Somebody shot up the Charolais sign at my front gate this morning."

My heart lurched. "This morning? You mean, after you dropped me off? So it was in broad daylight?"

He nodded. "I was in the barn when I heard the shots around ten this morning, and I figured it was just some overexcited newbie hunter back of the creek. But when I was leaving a few minutes ago, I realized they'd been shooting my sign." He shrugged. "No big deal, but I reported it to the police in case it was related to that trap. I swung by your place and didn't see any damage, but I was in a bit of a hurry so you should probably check things when you get home."

Hiding a shiver that had nothing to do with the temperature, I nodded. "Thanks, I will. And Tom..." I wanted to reach for his hand, but I didn't dare in case someone was watching. "Be careful, okay?"

He took my hand and squeezed it, negating my attempt to keep him safe. "You worry too much, Aydan. Signs get shot up all the time in the country." He lowered his voice conspiratorially, mischief twinkling in his eyes. "I might have shot up a sign or two myself when I was young and stupid; but you didn't hear it from me." Releasing my hand, he added, "I'm late, so I'd better get going. I hope everything's okay at your place. Call me if you need anything."

"Thanks, I will."

He went into Eddy's, and I stood frowning into space until Hellhound hooked a hand around my elbow and tugged me gently away. "Come on, darlin', no point standin' here waitin' to get hit by the door."

"Right..." Still deep in thought, I trailed after him to the Forester.

As we buckled up, Hellhound said, "What was that about a trap at Rossburn's place?"

"Somebody left a leghold trap outside his door. And now they're shooting at his sign. It's a threat."

Arnie frowned. "An' you're thinkin' it's 'cause a' you. Like the mouse at Eddy's."

"Yeah." I blew out a breath. "When Holt was questioning Grandin, Grandin told him 'They know how to get to Kelly'. I think somebody's letting me know that they could take out my friends anytime. The trap was welded open and they didn't take potshots at Tom's house, so they weren't actually trying to hurt him; and the mouse at Eddy's is the same sort of thing. There's no actual danger, but it's definitely a message that it could be serious if somebody wanted to take it to the next level."

"I dunno," Hellhound objected. "Like Rossburn said, there's lotsa dumbfucks out there that think it's funny to shoot up a sign. An' a dead mouse an' a busted trap ain't much of a threat."

"I know; I just..." I made a futile gesture, letting my hand drop back into my lap. "Hell, I don't know. Maybe I'm just a paranoid freak." At his humorously cocked eyebrow, I laughed. "Okay, fine, I'm definitely a paranoid freak; but maybe I'm reading too much into this, too."

Arnie sobered. "But your gut says ya ain't."

"Yeah. And I trust my gut."

"We'll keep our eyes open, then." He put the car into gear. "Where to?"

I affected a posh British accent and waved my fingers in a prissy 'move along' gesture. "To the office, my good man."

"Thought ya wanted to go to the hospital," he said as we pulled away.

"I do, but now that I've had some food and my brain's working again, I've realized I need to talk to Reggie before I talk to Ian. I don't think I'll be long, but if you want to drop me off at Sirius and do your own thing, that's fine."

"Nah, I wanna see Kane at the hospital, too, so we might as well stick together. I'll wait for ya at Sirius."

When Reggie's office door swung shut behind me a few minutes later, I asked, "Were you the Weapons Director when Kane killed my second husband with that classified heart-attack drug?"

Reggie blinked. "Uh... yes..." He gave me a wary look as he lowered himself into his chair.

"Don't worry," I assured him. "I'm over it."

I realized with mild shock that it was actually true. Mostly, anyway. I would never know whether Robert had truly loved me or only faked it convincingly; and my memories of our time together were so tainted by the ugly baggage from my first marriage that I still hadn't unravelled whether Robert had treated me well or fucked me up more. Maybe I'd never know that, either...

"Kelly?" Reggie inquired worriedly.

"Um. Sorry. I zoned out for a second there. I'm really tired." I flopped into the chair across from him. "So John said he got the drug from the Weapons lab. As the director, did you give it to him personally?"

"Yes. And I had an observer as per regs." Reggie still looked cautious.

"What's your protocol for that?" I asked.

"I get a requisition signed by the Director of Clandestine Ops and at least one other person higher than the DCO in the chain of command. While I'm issuing the dose to the agent I'm observed by one other staff member who's selected by random lottery; and the agent had damn well better have a dead body to show for each issued dose or there's an investigation that makes a body-cavity search look tame."

"Hm." I frowned into space, mentally flipping through the data I'd stolen from MI5. "So there's theoretically no way a dose could ever go missing?"

"No. Our stock has always been accounted for. I've only issued two doses the whole time I've been Director, and both times there was a kill right on schedule..." His gaze wavered. "Sorry."

Waving off his discomfort, I said, "It's okay. So what happens when the drug expires?"

"It doesn't really expire. The old doses would probably

be fine for at least five years, but we replace them every year just to be on the safe side. The disposal process-"

I jerked forward in my chair, pulse pounding. "Wait, it's good for *five years?*"

"Yeah, probably a lot more. That's what the initial tests indicated, anyway." Reggie frowned. "Is that significant?"

"Oh, shit, yes," I whispered, my throat suddenly dry. "Yes, it is."

CHAPTER 27

"Talk to me," Reggie demanded.

"I, um... I can't," I mumbled. "Sorry. So how are the new doses made and stored?"

Reggie leaned back, frowning. "Are you conducting an internal investigation?"

"No..." Belatedly, I peeked into my waist pouch and activated my bug detector. We both relaxed when it flashed green, and I lowered my voice. "I'm not investigating our Department."

His gaze sharpened. "So one of our allies is getting careless."

"Maybe. Walk me through the whole process, from making the drug to storing it to disposing of the old doses."

"Okay..." He took a swig from the water bottle on his desk. "There's a huge paper trail to make new doses. Once everything's all signed and sealed, one of the chemists and another staff member get picked by random lottery. The observer checks the raw materials to be sure the chemist isn't making more than the required number of doses, and the whole process is recorded on video from multiple angles."

"What's the required number of doses?" I asked.

"Unless we're told otherwise, two per year. When they're

finished, they get locked away and the chemist and observer sign off the chain-of-custody documents."

"And do all our allies do it that way, too?"

"They're supposed to."

"How do you get rid of the old doses?" I asked.

"That's another process of paperwork and random draws. Then the whole vial is incinerated without ever being opened, with observers and video recording from all angles." He eyed me with interest. "Why? Did a dose go missing? Tell me what's going on. Maybe I can help."

I hesitated.

Hell, I trusted Reggie. And as long as he didn't know how I'd gotten the information in the first place, I wouldn't be revealing anything above his security clearance.

"An agent was issued a dose, he used it, and it didn't work," I said. "And a few months later, somebody totally unrelated died of a sudden heart attack."

"So you think somebody stole a dose and replaced it with a fake." He frowned. "This is part of your investigation of Nora, isn't it?"

"Yeah. Ian thinks she might have stolen the drug and killed her predecessor."

Reggie bolted upright in his chair. "What? Howie's *dead*? When? How? I thought he'd retired!"

I grimaced. "He retired permanently, of an unexplained heart attack in September. There's no evidence, but Ian says he suspects Nora killed him with a stolen dose of the drug."

Reggie fell back in his chair. "That bitch," he muttered. "Tell me exactly what happened."

"You never heard what I'm about to tell you. Their paperwork was done just like you described, and there was no record of a dose ever going missing, but a dose failed.

Their Weapons department investigated and said it must have lost its effectiveness because it was near its one-year expiry date."

"Bullshit," Reggie said flatly. "Even if the dose had lost fifty percent of its potency it'd still be more than enough to kill; and the development research showed ninety-three percent potency at the five-year mark. I bet the agent pretended to give the drug to the subject but pocketed it instead, and then handed it over to Nora so she could kill Howie and cover the whole thing up. Who was the agent?"

My stomach plummeted. "Um... Ian." My voice came out very small.

"That fucking crooked bastard," Reggie snapped.

"But they investigated him up, down, and sideways, just like you said," I argued. "And Ian's not stupid enough to set himself up for a massive investigation. If he was going to steal a dose, he'd just quietly kill his guy and pretend the drug had worked. Since the drug is undetectable in an autopsy, nobody would ever know he hadn't administered it." I straightened. "And anyway, he was out of the country when he used the drug in June, and he hadn't gotten back yet when Coleman died in September. So he wouldn't have had a chance to give the drug to Nora."

"Oh." Reggie deflated slightly, then regrouped. "So don't tell me, let me guess: Nora was the observer for the previous drug changeover. She somehow managed to slip a dose out."

I sighed. "No, she didn't observe the destruction or the remaking. And it was Howard Coleman who handed the dose to Ian, with a different observer. Nora was nowhere near any of it."

"Shit. Then why does Ian suspect her?"

"I don't know. I guess she was the only one with anything to gain by Howard Coleman's death. But his death was ruled natural causes, so Ian's probably just making shit up." I grimaced. "As usual."

"Maybe." Reggie stared into space, drumming the fingertips of his good hand on his knee. "Or maybe Nora convinced the chemist to put fake doses in the safe and give her the real thing when they were creating the replacements..." His frown deepened. "Most years the doses don't even get used, so they were probably hoping it would never come to light. What do we know about the chemist? Did the same person make the drug and then rule that it was ineffective?"

"I didn't have time to find out. I'll keep digging." I studied Reggie's unhappy scowl. "Why are you buying into Ian's story? He was probably just playing me."

Reggie's chin sank. "Maybe, but I can't believe Howie died of natural causes. He was so fit." His voice softened, as though he were talking more to himself than to me. "Last time I saw him, he tried to convince me to come over and run the London Marathon with him..." He sat up. "Rand's a shithead; but if he says Howie was murdered, I believe him. And if I find out Rand had something to do with it..."

I shivered at his tone.

Rising, I rolled my shoulders in a futile attempt to ease my tension. "Okay. We never had this conversation. Our story is that Ian told me Nora might have stolen the drug and killed Howard Coleman, and I questioned you about the drug and our procedures around it."

Reggie held up a restraining hand. "Got it. Nobody has a high enough security clearance to ask me about it anyway, so don't worry." He hesitated. "Except Stemp."

"You can tell him if he needs to know."

"Okay." Reggie gave me his fearsome scowl. "Go nail Nora. That murdering bitch."

When I emerged from the secured area, Hellhound rose from one of the lobby chairs. "Hospital next?"

"Yeah." I dropped my security fob into the turntable and scrawled my signature on the control sheet. Glancing at my watch, I sighed. "I'm sorry, that took longer than I expected."

"No problem." Hellhound grinned. "I was workin' on a new song while I waited for ya."

"Without your guitar?"

"It's in the truck. I was just writin' it in my head, but I'll try it out later."

I snuggled closer as we headed for the door. "You're amazing."

He winked. "Hell, yeah. An' I'm good in bed, too."

"That you are." I pulled away and feigned a doubtful expression. "I think. My memory's fading. I'll have to do some more testing to be certain."

He nodded virtuously. "Anythin' for science."

When we arrived at the hospital, the receptionist informed us that Daniel had been treated and released.

I turned to Hellhound. "You might as well go over to John's and see them, then."

"Nah, I'll wait for ya an' then we can both go to Kane's."

"I might be a while," I warned. "Last time Ian bullshitted me for twenty minutes before he got to the point."

Hellhound shrugged. "No problem. I'll be workin' on my new song, so take as long as ya want."

"Okay, thanks." I kissed him and headed for the secured wing.

Striding down the corridor, my mind churned. If I mentioned some detail Ian hadn't told me, he'd think MI6 had a leak and the shit would hit the fan when I refused to tell them where I'd gotten my intel.

And I sure as hell wouldn't let him snuggle up and monitor my pulse again. Sneaky bastard.

My lips curved up in spite of my annoyance. Ian might be irritating, but he was also an excellent agent. I could learn a lot from him.

Just as long as he didn't learn anything else from me.

I sighed and bent for the retinal scan.

When I poked my head into Ian's room, he startled awake from an uncomfortable-looking slump in the reclining chair beside the bed. "Storm! Finally! What have you found out?"

"I'm fine, thanks," I teased. "And how are you today?"

"Tired. In pain." He scowled. "Sick of being locked up."

"The security guard is here to protect you, not keep you inside," I pointed out. "Why didn't you get him to go for a walk with you?"

"I don't trust him. I don't trust anybody." A smile softened his face and he widened those gorgeous green eyes at me. "Except you."

"Yeah, cut the crap." I pulled the uncomfortable guest chair over beside him and dropped into it. "So I've been trying to investigate..." Lowering my voice to a whisper, I leaned close to his ear and went on, "...but short of slapping the lie detector on Nora and asking her point-blank if she murdered Howard Coleman, there's not much I can do. I need more information."

"I wish I could help, but I've already told you everything I know," he said smoothly.

Bastard.

Even when I was investigating a murder for him, he still had to play his stupid fucking mind games.

My temper boiled up and over. "No, you fucking haven't," I hissed. "And I don't need to take your pulse to know it. Now, either you give me *all* your related intel, or I'll call off the guard, get the hospital to release you, and you can fly away home with your dirty little secrets. I don't really give a shit whether Nora murdered Coleman, or whether she's coming after you next. If you won't tell me what you know, she's your problem, not mine."

"Storm..." Ian pulled away to give me a heartwrenching look of pure hurt. "How can you be so cold after all we've been through together?"

I stared at him in silence for a long moment, fighting down the urge to yell, or possibly strangle him.

But it wouldn't help. Until he decided that my assistance was more important to him than his own entertainment, he'd just keep playing me.

"Last chance," I said quietly.

He widened those stunning green eyes at me. "Honestly, Storm, I've told you everything I know. But come closer and we can..."

Before he finished the sentence I was on my feet and walking away. "Good talk. I'll let the hospital know you're leaving."

Ian had balls of steel. He didn't say a word while I went out the door. Using every ounce of my fortitude, I didn't glance back at him.

As the door closed behind me, I glanced at the security guard's nametag and raised my voice a touch louder than necessary. "Thanks, Nolan. I'm lifting the security restriction, so you can go now."

He nodded and strode off down the hall, and I made for the nursing station. I didn't recognize the nurse on duty, so I held up my security fob as identification and said, "Agent Rand can be released now."

Her eyes widened. "Uh... we need the doctor's signature to release him..."

"Okay." I shrugged, hoping she couldn't hear my heart pounding.

Dammit, Ian, call me back into your room, you stubborn asshole...

"I'm done with him," I added. "So whenever the doctor wants to release him it's fine with me."

She made a note on the file and gave me a smile and a nod, and I turned and set a brisk pace down the hallway.

Shit, shit, shit.

The bastard had out-bluffed me. Now that I'd thrown down the gauntlet I couldn't go crawling back to him.

And what if Nora really was trying to murder him? What if she killed him while he was alone and helpless here in the hospital? I'd never forgive myself.

An announcement over the public address system coincided with a flurry of activity behind me. They were calling a code...

I spun in time to see a nurse hurtling down the hallway with a crash cart.

Toward Ian's room.

"FUCK!" I launched myself down the corridor, my heart

trying to rip from my chest and outpace me to Ian's room.

The few seconds it took to get to his door felt like eternity. As I lunged into the room a nurse barked, "Stay back!", then recoiled at the sight of my face.

Or maybe she was reacting to the Glock I hadn't realized I'd drawn.

"*What's happening?*" My voice was a raw shout. Surrounded by nurses, Ian's body arched grotesquely off the bed as though his midsection had been yanked skyward by brutal unseen hands.

"We don't know yet, please stay back!" The nurse dove back into the fray. The frenzied beeping of monitors overlaid the rapid-fire commands of the staff.

Ian was still convulsing.

Bright blood stained his pillow, oh God no...

He let out a cry that sounded as if it had been torn from his very soul and the agonized arch of his spine reversed into a fetal curl as he vomited. Over and over the spasms racked his body, wrenching animal-like sobs from him.

Helpless, I clutched my Glock until my knuckles cracked and pain lanced up my arm.

Ian's cries lashed me like red-hot whips.

My fault. All my fault.

His cries weakened and his spasms grew feebler.

Don't you dare die on me, you bastard...

He drew a single shuddering breath.

His body went limp.

My chest heaved as though I could force air into his empty lungs by proxy.

No-no-no...

He gasped.

Sucked in another breath.

Then he was panting. Ragged glorious breaths.

Small hysterical whimpers rose above the slowing cadence of the monitors, and I realized they were coming from me. Clamping my teeth on my tongue, I focused on the pain.

Keep it together.

"What... h-happened?" I repeated. My voice came out as ragged as Ian's panting.

The nurse who had stopped me earlier turned away from the bed. "We're not sure. His monitor alarmed, indicating a cardiac arrest, but when we got here his vital signs were strong. Then the convulsions started. Sometimes a concussion can cause convulsions, but usually not forty-eight hours after the original injury. We won't know until the doctor examines him."

"What about the blood?" I pointed a shaking finger at the crimson on his pillow. "Why is he bleeding?"

"That's not serious," she assured me. "The convulsions forced the back of his head into the pillow and tore some of his stitches."

"Storm?" Ian's voice was a pathetic wisp. "Are you there?"

"I'm here." I pushed past the medical staff, my stomach lurching as I navigated through the patchwork of vomit on the floor. "What happened?"

"I... I don't know." He gazed up at me from the blood-drenched pillow. "I was... feeling... odd, while you were here. I decided to lie down... and... then... I don't remember."

"But nobody else came in here, did they?" I asked.

"I... don't remember."

"Did anyone else come in here after I left?" I demanded of the nursing staff. "Did anybody see anything?"

Blank expressions and headshakes were my only reply.

Dammit, I hadn't even turned my back on his door until I'd started down the hall. Nobody could have sneaked in and attacked him in the few seconds I'd left him unguarded.

"Ian, what-" I began, but a large hand closed around my upper arm.

"Agent Kelly, please come with me." Nolan the security guard was back, and he didn't look as friendly as before.

"No, I need to-"

"You told the nurse in charge that you were done with Agent Rand, and you dismissed me," he said sternly. "And you were the last person to be alone with Agent Rand before his attack. I'm taking you into custody for attempted murder."

CHAPTER 28

"For fucksakes, I didn't do anything to Agent Rand!" I snapped, fighting sheer terror while trying to sound calm and in charge. If they dragged me away now, anybody could get to Ian.

And he might not survive the next attack.

Ian was alert now, his wide-eyed gaze bouncing between me and the grim-faced guard.

"Wait," he croaked. "Agent Kelly didn't attack me."

"You said you don't remember," the guard replied implacably. "And I won't take the chance. Agent Kelly, let's go."

"Wait!" Ian barked, his forcefulness a startling contrast to the feeble voice of a moment ago. When we all gaped at him, he stared back at us for a moment in silence. Then he blew out a sigh. "Oh, bollocks. All right, then. I faked the whole thing." He propped himself up on one elbow and extended a rock-steady hand to pour a cup of water from a pitcher on the side table that had miraculously survived the upheaval.

While we all stood frozen, he rinsed his mouth and spat into the cup, then lay back with another sigh. "Come on, you lot, get with the program. Agent Kelly didn't attack me. We were negotiating, she was winning, and I didn't want to lose face by giving in. So I staged a medical crisis. Now, may I please have some clean linens?" He plucked distastefully at his vomit-stained gown.

"Stand back, everybody," I said faintly. "Because now I really am going to kill him."

"I'll help," the nurse growled, looking remarkably dangerous for a woman wearing pink dancing-kitten scrubs.

"You can't," Ian said cheerfully. "You both took oaths."

"I'll give you an oath right up your ass, you-" I lunged forward, only to be restrained by Nolan.

"Sorry, Agent Kelly," he said, sounding regretful. "I can't let you kill him."

"How about if I just maim him a little?" I grated.

"I'm already maimed," Ian said plaintively, indicating his crimson-smeared pillow.

"Not as much as you deserve to be!" I pulled half-heartedly against the guard's grip, but he didn't let go.

Probably a good thing.

Sucking in a deep trembling breath, I drew myself up and summoned an authoritative voice. "Okay, this show's over." I turned to the nursing staff. "Thanks. You can all go back to work now. Just leave clean linens and a mop and bucket outside the door. Agent Rand will be cleaning this mess up and remaking his own bed."

"I'm in no shape to-" he began, but I gave him a death-glare and kept talking as everyone filed out except the guard and the pink-clad nurse. "He'll change his gown and we'll finish our interview in another room-"

"The vomiting was completely unintentional, I assure you," Ian said earnestly. "I'm still very nauseated-"

"And then he'll come back and clean everything up," I

ground out, glaring.

"He'll have to have his wounds re-stitched, too," the nurse said grudgingly.

"After I'm done with him. And not until he finishes cleaning the room." I jerked my chin at Ian. "Get in the bathroom and change. And you'd better do a good job cleaning this room, or I'll make you lick this fucking floor from wall to wall."

He opened his mouth as if to retort, then took a good look at my expression and pressed his lips shut again. Easing cautiously out of bed, he shuffled toward the bathroom.

My stomach twisted at the blood-caked mess on the back of his head.

"We'll have to re-stitch that and dress it," the nurse said quietly as the bathroom door closed behind him. "And he'll need more antibiotics to prevent infection. The idiot. And he definitely wasn't faking the vomiting. He's still in the early stages of recovering from his concussion, and strenuous activity like faking convulsions ..." She blew out her breath in an angry hiss.

"God, I could kill him right now," I growled.

"I understand." She handed me a box of tissues. "The room beside this is vacant. You can use the bathroom to clean up."

After a moment of incomprehension I touched my cheek, where the sticky residue of tears was beginning to itch.

"I'm really going to kill him," I muttered. Turning to Nolan, I added, "Stay with Rand. Bring him next door when he's cleaned up."

A few minutes later Nolan and the nurse ushered Ian into the room and the nurse pointed him to the reclining chair. "Be careful of your head," she said. "That's only a temporary dressing."

He sank into the chair with a sigh and turned a penitent expression up at her. "Thank you. You're such a love, and I am terribly sorry about all this." He batted those thick dark lashes, looking grave and heroic with his pale face and bloodstained dressing. "But it was a matter of national security. You understand, don't you?"

She flushed and patted his arm. "Of course." As she straightened she caught my outraged glare. Her blush deepened and she hurried out.

"You can wait outside, too," I said to the guard. "Close the door behind you."

He gave me a doubtful look.

"I won't kill him," I promised.

Nolan nodded, squared his shoulders as though this was against his better judgement, and left.

When the door closed behind him, Ian gave me a brave, wan smile. "You understand why I had to do what I did, don't you, Storm? We're both top agents-"

"Can it," I snarled. "If you don't want to tell me anything more, just say so. I'm okay with that. But if you jerk me around just one... more... time..." I had to stop for a calming breath.

"But... I thought..." He looked genuinely lost. "It's all about the game. The lies; the half-truths; the elaborate deceptions. The thrill of the chase; the glorious adrenaline high of almost getting caught. I love the game. I thought you did, too."

"No. I fucking *hate* the game."

"Oh." His face fell. "Then I sincerely apologize," he said to his lap.

And damn him, my heart twisted at the dejected sag of his shoulders.

No, damn *me*.

Me and the fucked-up programming that urged me to hug him and tell him everything was all right and I was sorry for being such a bitch...

"Apology accepted," I snapped. "So are you going to tell me anything more, or are we done here?"

Ian gave me the penitent look that had melted the nurse, and I braced myself.

"To be completely honest..." he said slowly, "...and believe me when I say that complete honesty is very uncomfortable for me... I..." He hesitated, then his words came out in a rush. "I made up the accusation against Nora on the spur of the moment because I'm terribly afraid of hospitals and I was hoping you'd stay with me if you thought I was in danger."

The vulnerability in his eyes punched my heart so hard it left me breathless.

I swallowed.

"Oh." My word came out faint, and my mind refused to supply anything more useful.

"I'm very sorry," Ian went on hurriedly. "I understand that you're furious with me, but in my defense, I knew you were investigating Nora anyway so I wasn't completely wasting your time..."

His voice faded into the background as my brain rebooted and spun up to speed again.

"Hang on," I said. "So you completely made up your suspicions about Nora? There was no basis at all?"

Ian paled and fell silent. Then his eyes narrowed as if in thought. "Actually, now that you mention it..." He straightened. "Will you please come closer-" He flung up both hands at the sight of my expression. "Please, Storm, I promise I'm not playing you. No matter how much I might trust your assurances that this site is secure, I am still an MI6 agent in a foreign country, in a situation where I can neither verify nor control the security of our communication. It's my duty to do whatever I can."

I sighed. He was right, of course.

Sliding my chair over beside his, I leaned in. "Okay, talk to me."

"Thank you, Storm," he whispered, his lips skimming my hair. "You're right; my accusation wasn't completely groundless, but I only just realized it. I must have subconsciously put the pieces together, and now it makes sense. Three months before Howard Coleman died, I was on a mission where I used a dose of Substance X, which is our classified designation for the drug..."

My heart slowly warming, I listened while he laid out the events I already knew. Finally, he was telling me the whole truth.

"...so Coleman's death seems too coincidental," Ian finished. "And I've simply never felt comfortable with Nora. You know how it is when your gut tells you that a suspect is hiding something..." He trailed off, then finished wryly, "Well, obviously you have the same instinct. You called me out; and I'm a professional liar."

"True; but Nora actually was hiding something," I pointed out. "An entirely fake identity."

"Yes, and maybe that's the only reason for my uneasiness," he agreed. "I really have nothing but circumstantial-"

"Maybe not," I interrupted. "Thanks to your fake

suspicions I talked to Reggie about the drug, and I found out something interesting." I turned to face him. "The drug doesn't expire. You say your chemist reported that it failed because it was an old dose, but that wouldn't happen after only a year. It's good for at least five, probably a lot more." Ian's eyes widened as I went on, "So somebody..."

"...is lying," Ian finished. "Bugger! I need to contact my superiors immediately."

"How can I help?"

"I have a secure communication device in the other room." He grimaced. "Which I have yet to clean." He rose cautiously, bracing himself on the arms of the chair. "Oh, damn," he murmured. "May I borrow your arm?"

One glance at his pasty face and sweaty forehead told the story.

"Sit." I pressed him gently back into the chair. "Relax. Close your eyes and breathe."

"Thank you," he whispered, and obeyed.

"I'll bring your communication device if you'll tell me where to look."

"You won't find it." He eased his head back onto the headrest, wincing. "I'll just rest here a moment and then-"

A tap on the door interrupted him. I rose, Glock in hand, and opened the door a crack.

Dr. Roth's frown greeted me. "Are you finished interrogating him? If he was convulsing and vomiting, we need to get him into the MRI as soon as possible."

"The convulsions were fake," I told her, and holstered my Glock before opening the door.

"Sadly, the vomiting was real," Ian said, his eyes still closed. "As was the bleeding."

"Which was your own stupid fault," I replied without

heat. I turned to the doctor. "He's all yours."

"May I have the guard again, please?" Ian asked humbly.

"Yes. I'll make sure you're safe." I stepped over to squeeze his shoulder. "And I'll be back to visit you as soon as I can."

"Thank you, Storm." He took my hand and turned that heart-wrenching vulnerable gaze up to me. "That means a lot."

Playing me again. It was as natural as breathing to him.

I gave him a fake smile and left.

By the time I plodded back to the main reception area, the last of my adrenaline had trickled away. Hellhound rose as I approached, his forehead creasing in a frown.

"Jesus, darlin'," he greeted me. "Ya look like ya just went ten rounds an' barely made it outta the ring."

"That's how I feel." I leaned into him. "I want to sleep for a week, but I've only got an hour before my next thing and I still have to go and see John."

"Nah, skip it. I called him. He's sick as a dog an' doesn't want us to come over."

Suddenly and unpleasantly alert, I jerked out of my exhausted slouch. "What is he hiding?" I demanded.

Hellhound eyed me worriedly. "What d'ya mean?"

"He told me that yesterday, too! This morning the hospital said he was here, but what if he bribed them to say that? He could be halfway across the country by now, stringing everybody along by forwarding his calls to his cell phone until he vanishes for good!"

"Whoa!" Hellhound tapped my temple with a gentle fingertip. "Give your head a shake, darlin'. This's Kane we're talkin' about."

"Yeah, he's a fucking spook!" I snapped. "You think you

can trust them, but they're all players and they'll screw you over the instant it suits them."

"Not Kane," Hellhound said with certainty.

Arguing would be futile. He'd never believe anything bad about his best friend.

I sighed. "Maybe, maybe not, but I'll never know. There just are too many things he can't tell me."

"Hell, there's tons a' things ya can't tell him, too." Hellhound shrugged. "Just like there's tons a' things I ain't told ya. Everybody's got shit like that."

Alarm flickered cold in my belly. "Wh-What haven't you told me?"

He folded me into a hug. "Stop freakin' out," he said gently. "If I told ya every little thing about me you'd die of fuckin' boredom."

I pulled back, frowning. "I don't need to know every little thing, but I need to know the big things."

"None a' those left. Don't worry, darlin', ya already know all the bad stuff about me." Mischief glinted in his eyes. "Unless ya find out about my thirty-fifth birthday party, where I got shit-faced an' passed out; an' when I woke up I was naked in bed with another guy, two chicks, an' a goat."

I snickered. "That doesn't even surprise me."

"The bed was in a department store window," he added, straight-faced. "At noon."

Helpless giggles seized me. "Ohmigod! Seriously?"

"God's honest truth, darlin'. That was the last time the Forces busted me back to Private. Lucky I'd lost my uniform somewhere along the way, or I'd'a prob'ly ended up with a dishonourable discharge. I laid off the booze a bit after that."

I fell into the nearest chair and laughed until my stomach ached. When I finally recovered, I said, "Thanks.

I'm sorry for being such a paranoid freak again, but Ian just messed with my head. The guy's such a liar! Just a few minutes with him can make me lose faith in everybody."

"It's okay, darlin'." Arnie offered me a hand up. "So what's the plan now?"

I sighed and let him haul me to my feet. "Back to Sirius to update my reports, and then I have to go for dinner at Stemp's. And probably see Nora again, too."

He winced. "Christ. Your day just keeps gettin' worse. Since when are ya buddies with Stemp?"

"I'm not. Moonbeam invited me."

Hellhound's eyes softened. "Guess ya can't turn her down."

"Nope." A thought struck me. "Hey, she'd love to see you..."

His eyes widened and he backed away. "Shit, darlin', I forgot to tell ya, I got somethin' real important planned for tonight..."

I laughed. "It's okay. I know how you feel about Stemp, and I wouldn't do that to you. Do you have enough time before your 'important thing' to give me a ride back to Sirius?"

"Sure." He settled his arm across my shoulders as we turned for the door. "I was only kiddin'. If ya want me to come, I will."

"No, it's okay. No need for both of us to suffer. I'll see you at home tonight."

"Ya gonna be late?"

I sighed. "No idea."

CHAPTER 29

Promptly at five, I was mounting Stemp's front steps when the door swung open. Moonbeam's luminous smile greeted me, along with a warm rush of richly-spiced scents that made my taste buds flood with eagerness.

"Welcome," she said. "Please come in."

I stepped inside, stamping the snow off my boots and shedding my parka. Moonbeam appropriated the garment and hung it in the closet before giving me a warm hug.

When she led me into the living room, Skidmark rose from one of the chairs and claimed a brief hug, too. He was as scruffy and marijuana-scented as usual, but at least his clothes were clean and he was otherwise odour-free.

Karma and Stemp emerged from the kitchen, and a moment later I was engulfed in Karma's hug.

Stemp offered me a polite incline of his chin from safely beyond hugging distance. "Welcome. May I offer you a drink? I have beer or non-alcoholic hot spiced cider."

Beer? He had beer?

I wavered.

No, I'd better not.

"The spiced cider sounds delicious," I said, somehow managing not to sound regretful. "Thank you."

After the drinks had been delivered, Stemp gave me another polite nod. "If you will excuse me, there are a few remaining kitchen duties before our meal is ready. Karma, if you will assist me...?"

Karma grinned, joy glowing in his broad seamed face as he turned for the kitchen. "Just like old times, eh, son?"

Stemp smiled; a real smile that lifted both corners of his mouth and warmed his eyes. "Just like old times; only without the friction, and with meat on the menu."

Karma chuckled and threw an arm around Stemp's shoulders as they vanished into the kitchen, and my heart warmed at the sight of Stemp's arm encircling his surrogate father in turn.

Skidmark snorted. "I'm getting diabetes from all the goddamn sweetness around here." He took a swig of his beer, but he was hiding a smile in his beard.

Moonbeam perched on the arm of his chair and leaned down to hug him and drop a kiss on his lips. "Maybe now you'll be able to develop some traditions with your son, too."

Skidmark shrugged. "Not unless he learns to drink beer and work on cars. Cooking was always his and Karma's thing." His indifferent façade didn't quite hide the regret in his eyes.

I leaned forward and touched his hand. "Try," I said quietly. "He'll meet you halfway. He's proud of you, you know. He told me how impressed he was that you'd fooled him with your act all these years."

Skidmark's chin came up in his usual stiff-necked rejection of sympathy, but his eyes looked suspiciously soft. "Fine, I'll try," he growled. He took another gulp of beer and looked away.

"So, Storm Cloud Dancer..." Moonbeam tactfully

diverted the conversation. "I do hope you like spicy food."

"Love it!" I assured her.

We made small talk until Stemp called us to the table. After we had taken our seats, Stemp and I urged his parents to reminisce about their past missions; and narrow escapes that had been terrifying at the time became entertaining under the influence of luxurious butter chicken, soft fresh naan bread, and fiery beef vindaloo. Moonbeam and Karma adhered to the vegetarian side of the menu, and the rest of us devoured the vegetable curry and pakoras and samosas with as much relish as the meat dishes.

By the end of the meal I was certain that someone had slipped some hallucinogen into the food, or else I was asleep and having a highly improbable dream. Nobody fought, or even disagreed. Stemp smiled. Skidmark didn't insult anybody. Moonbeam and Karma presided like the benevolent pseudo-spiritual leaders they impersonated at their commune.

By the time I finished the last mouthful of creamy rice pudding, I was vibrating with nerves. This was too easy. Too nice. Something was about to go catastrophically wrong, I knew it.

When Stemp rose with a regretful expression, I tensed.

"Please carry on with coffee," he said to his parents. "Aydan, I apologize, but I have some matters to discuss that can't wait for tomorrow. Will you accompany me to my study, please?"

My overfull stomach sank.

I *knew* it had been too much to ask to have just one pleasant evening...

I followed Stemp down the hall and sat in the chair he indicated. Swinging the study door closed, he took a seat behind his desk and activated a bug detector. I eyed the green light gloomily.

Here we go...

"I am on vacation as of now," Stemp said without preamble. "Dermott has taken over for me."

I had a memory-flash of Dermott's murderous look when I had unintentionally revealed his sloppy management to a roomful of his commanders, peers, and subordinates two days ago.

"Oh, God." The words fell from my lips before I could stop them, and I clapped a hand over my mouth until I was certain nothing else was going to pop out. Removing my hand cautiously, I amended, "I mean, 'Okay'."

"My parents and I will be flying overseas tomorrow morning," Stemp went on as though I hadn't spoken.

Despite my dismay about Dermott, happiness washed over me. "You're going... visiting?"

Stemp met my smile with one of his own. "Yes. My parents will meet their granddaughter and daughter-in-law for the first time. And I will be with my *whole* family for Christmas." He emphasized the word with satisfaction, and my smile widened until it threatened to split my face.

"That's wonderful! I can't tell you how happy I am for all of you!"

"Thank you." Stemp sobered. "We will be taking a direct flight from Calgary to Heathrow, arriving Wednesday around zero three thirty London time. This morning I deployed an Interpol operative to infiltrate the Sirius Dynamics office in London and acquire the network generator and Ms. Stile's network key. To the best of his knowledge, he was successful."

"To the best of *his* knowledge? Did he get them, or

didn't he?"

Stemp clarified, "He acquired a USB thumb drive and twenty-four small pieces of circuitry. I did not divulge their purpose to the agent; and even if I had, he would have no way of testing them."

"*Twenty-four?* Shit! Sam had duplicate network keys!" I did the mental math and sucked in a breath. "One set for each of the original eight Knight/mage pairs and two pairs for Rebecca, but... that leaves two pairs left over."

"Yes."

I clenched my fists in my hair. "So there might be *another* damn mage!"

"So it appears." Stemp leaned tiredly back in his chair. "But at least we have all the keys. The agent will safeguard them until we arrive. I will rendezvous with him to acquire them, and coordinate with Dermott to select a time when you can guide Ms. Stile to the network portal and allow her consciousness to exit into her body. Although I have divulged no details to my parents, they are prepared to work with me to provide whatever distraction may be necessary to achieve our contact with Ms. Stile at the hospital."

"Okay..." I said slowly.

Stemp frowned. "You have a concern?"

"I'm just... thinking..." I massaged my forehead with the heel of my hand. "You'll have to turn off the network generator the instant she comes through, because otherwise she could bounce back in again without realizing she was doing it. But that's... there's something else. Come on, brain..."

Realization struck.

"Shit." Hot on its heels, a second revelation rocked me, sending a flood of adrenaline into my veins. "Oh, *shit!*"

"Do you intend to enlighten me about your concerns at any point, or merely gibber uselessly?" Stemp inquired.

"Um. Sorry. The first thing that hit me was that I can't actually look through a portal and see where Rebecca's going. If I go through any portal in the network, my consciousness always ends up in the place I came from."

His frown deepened. "So you're saying you can't usher Ms. Stile through a portal."

"No. Well, maybe." I pondered. "If we both went through the same portal at the same time... we'd probably each end up where we came from. I don't know. I've only looked through other portals, I've never tried to go through one."

"A possible complication," Stemp agreed. "But not your main concern?"

"No... well... one of them; but..." I drew a deep breath. "I just thought of something for the first time. We've accepted the idea that Rebecca got separated from her network key and ended up trapped in the internet, but..." I had to stop and swallow to moisten my dry throat. "...that means that I could get stuck in there, too, if somebody walked off with my network key while I was in there. We... we never tested it. We always assumed that if I got separated from my network key I'd crash out of the network in horrible pain, so we just... *we never tried it.*" I clenched my fists so he wouldn't see my hands shaking.

Stemp was still frowning. I leaned forward, willing him to understand how close I'd come to living my worst nightmare. How I could still end up trapped in an eternal hell.

"That could..." Suddenly realizing I was about to reveal the breadth and depth of my claustrophobia, I bit off the words 'that could have been me'. I forced my voice steady. "That could mean there are a lot of other things we haven't found out about the network keys just because of our own assumptions."

"True." Stemp eyed me quizzically. "But hardly a revelation. This has been uncharted territory from the beginning."

I leaned back in my chair, faking calm for all I was worth. "Yeah, I guess you're right."

"But you haven't stated your main concern," he said. It wasn't a question.

For a moment I considered denying it, but he'd know I was lying.

Heaving a sigh, I met his gaze with the best honesty I could fake. "You're right. I'm worried about Rebecca. When I get stuck in the internet for a long time, I can feel myself kind of... I don't know how to describe it. Thinning, I guess. It gets harder and harder to hold my consciousness together. I'm afraid that by the time I get to Rebecca, she won't have enough consciousness left to salvage. Or else she'll be so messed up from being stuck in the internet for days that she'll be completely nuts even after we get her back into her body."

"In that case..." Stemp said slowly, "...our duty is clear."

Staring at his emotionless façade, my blood chilled. I wasn't going to like this...

"I will kill Ms. Stile's physical body," he said with brutal precision. "And you will kill whatever remains of her consciousness in the internet."

CHAPTER 30

"No!"

The fierceness of my refusal left Stemp and me staring at each other across his desk, only a few feet away but light-years apart.

I lunged to my feet. "I won't murder an innocent woman in cold blood!"

Stemp pinched the bridge of his nose as though battling a crushing headache. "That would be a last resort. As always, I look to you for an alternative that will allow us both to sleep at night."

His lack of resistance cooled my fury. Whooshing out a long breath, I sank back into the chair.

"But I must emphasize..." Stemp went on, his hard amber gaze drilling into mine. "...our top priority is national security. I share your reluctance to follow such an extreme course of action, but the good of the many..." He made a weary gesture and didn't complete the quote.

"I'll figure out something," I vowed.

"I know you will do your best. But remember that your duty prevents you from sacrificing your own life to save Ms. Stile's."

"How the hell do you figure that?" I demanded. "Aren't

we supposed to be protecting innocent civilians, not murdering them for our own convenience? Rebecca hasn't done anything wrong! She doesn't deserve to die!"

Stemp sighed. "It is our duty to protect as many innocent civilians as possible. Sometimes that causes collateral damage. Ms. Stile's death, however tragic, would affect only a handful of people. Yours could impact nations." He held up a restraining hand as I opened my mouth. "Please allow me to finish."

Poised on the edge of my chair, I fought the need to spring to my feet and yell.

Stemp waited, as if doubting my ability to contain myself.

When I gave him a sharp nod, he went on, "Consider the alternatives. If Ms. Stile's consciousness is as... frayed... as you postulate, then even if you succeed in returning the remains of it to her body, she will suffer for the rest of her potentially long life with significant cognitive, physical, and/or psychological deficits."

Fixing me with his reptilian gaze, he moved to his next point. "If her consciousness is intact but psychologically damaged, then returning it to her physical body would allow her to undertake actions that could cause significant harm to herself, or to thousands if not millions of other innocent citizens if she also retains classified knowledge and uses it inappropriately."

"But-"

He silenced me with an upraised palm. "Even in a best-case scenario where Ms. Stile's consciousness remains intact and you are capable of returning it to her body, she will have to be incarcerated in a high-security facility, possibly for the rest of her life, to protect the classified knowledge she may have acquired. Do any of these scenarios seem preferable to a quick and merciful death?"

I hid my instinctive shudder. Dammit, he knew me too well.

"I don't know," I said, holding onto control with all my might. "I can't make that decision for Rebecca."

"I can." Cold dispassionate Stemp was back. "Unless you find her consciousness intact and edit her memories to remove all traces of classified information, Ms. Stile will be terminated."

"That's BULLSHIT!" I launched to my feet, my frustration escaping in a full-throated bellow. "WHO THE HELL DO YOU THINK YOU ARE? GOD HIM-FUCKING-SELF?"

Stemp eyed my quivering fists for a long moment before replying, "No; and if such a deity or deities actually exist, I do not envy him, her, it, or them. I am merely stating our duty." The hard line of his mouth eased. "Despite your..." He allowed himself a small sigh. "...forceful opinions... I am nevertheless grateful for your input. I have been doing this job for too long; and you remind me of what it was like when I still retained my humanity."

I sank into the chair again and buried my head in my hands. "There's nothing wrong with your humanity. Like you said, you're just stating the facts." I rubbed my aching eyes. "I don't see any alternatives, either. I was just... shooting the messenger. Sorry."

"No apology necessary."

Letting out a sigh, I slumped back in the chair. "But even if I put aside for a minute that killing Rebecca is just immoral, your plan has a serious flaw. I don't have a clue how to kill her consciousness in the internet. I don't think it's even possible."

His gaze pinned me to the chair. "Are you lying to me?"

I took no offense. "No. We can go over to the office and I'll say it again under the lie detector if you want."

A tense silence settled between us.

After a long moment, Stemp sighed. "I will be forced to verify your statement under the lie detector. The stakes are simply too high, and the chain of command will require it."

"Okay."

He rose tiredly. "Let's go."

When we emerged from the hallway, three anxious faces turned toward us. Moonbeam inquired, "Is everything all right?"

"Fine," I assured her. "We just have to go to the office for a few minutes."

"With all due respect to you and our son," Moonbeam replied, "We don't believe that this is as inconsequential as you say. We could hear you shouting."

"Mother," Stemp said with fond patience. "I merely have to verify one of Agent Kelly's statements under the lie detector to satisfy the chain of command. If she is not lying to me, and she assures me that she is not..." He gave me a 'you'd-*better*-not-be-lying' glance. "...then we will literally be only minutes."

"And what if she's lying?" Skidmark inquired.

"Then... we will be considerably longer."

"Then we will come, too," Moonbeam said matter-of-factly.

"Mother!" This time Stemp's tone was pure exasperation, but a moment later his shoulders relaxed and he gave her a shrug and a wry smile. "Very well, then; let us complete our social evening at Sirius Dynamics."

"Nah, I'm good," Skidmark demurred. "It's cold out, and I don't feel like traipsing across town when there's nothing I can do to change the outcome anyway. See you, Storm. I hope you're not in shit."

"I'm not." I hugged him. "Have a good trip."

"Thanks, girlie. Stay safe."

"I think everyone's interests will be suitably protected," Karma rumbled, eyeing Moonbeam with a smile. "So I will say my farewells now, too." He came over to place his hands on my shoulders. "Remember, should you ever need our assistance, you have only to ask. May the Earth Spirit guide and protect you." He drew me into a warm hug.

"You, too," I mumbled into his shoulder. "Thanks. Enjoy your trip."

He released me, smiling. "I'm sure I shall." He turned to Moonbeam. "Stay warm, my love." They shared a kiss, parting unhurriedly. Moonbeam kissed Skidmark with equal tenderness while Stemp looked on with a fond expression that told me he'd finally accepted his three parents; and despite the nervousness prickling the back of my mind, I was smiling when we departed.

A short time later, Stemp faced me across the table in the interrogation area while the crown of electrodes sat heavily on my head.

Dispensing with his usual warmup questions, he asked, "Do you know if it is possible for you to kill or destroy Rebecca Stile's consciousness in the internet?"

"No."

The green light indicated that I'd told the truth, and he rephrased the question. "Can you think of any way that it might be possible for you to destroy or kill Rebecca Stile's consciousness in the internet?"

"No."

The green light shone again. Stemp eyed me frowning. "Do you think it would be possible for you to come up with a way to destroy or kill Rebecca Stile's consciousness in the internet?"

I frowned back at him. "I don't know. I might, if I thought about it long enough, but I can't imagine how. Rebecca and I are both just a bunch of data bits, floating along in a bigger stream of data bits. If you think of it like a stream of water, how would one part of the water be able to attack another part of the water? It's all just a bunch of identical molecules tumbling along."

"I see the conundrum," Stemp agreed. "However, the lie detector requires a yes or no answer."

I sighed. "Ask the question again."

"Do you think it would be possible for you to come up with a way to destroy or kill Rebecca Stile's consciousness in the internet?"

"No."

The yellow 'inconclusive' light flashed.

I shrugged and said, "Yes", and the yellow light flashed again. "See, I really don't know."

Stemp smiled and rose. "Thank you for your patience. I will be pleased to return you safely to your protector now."

Slipping off the headdress, I stood, too. "Your mom wasn't taking sides against you, you know. She didn't believe either of us."

"I realize that." He held the door for me, and we walked down the hall together. "It is not your responsibility to broker peace between us," he added. A smile warmed his voice. "Though we appreciate your tireless efforts."

"I didn't mean to overstep," I said hurriedly.

"I know."

When we emerged from the secured area, Moonbeam stood up, her gaze searching the air around us. Her face relaxed into a smile. "I see from your auras that all is well."

"Yes, Mother." Stemp gave her an answering smile. "As I assured you earlier."

"So you did," she agreed. "But despite your assurances to me, you were unsure yourself. Now your worries have been resolved."

Stemp's smile faded. "My questions have been resolved. My worries remain."

Moonbeam caressed his cheek. "My dear son. Yours is a difficult job."

Her tender pride sent a stab of pain through my chest. Why couldn't my mother be like Moonbeam?

I was turning away to hide my expression when my phone vibrated.

Uh-oh.

Thumbing the 'Answer' button, I snapped, "Kelly."

"It's Security calling from the hospital. There's a woman here who claims to be Nora Taylor, Weapons Director from the UK. Her credentials and biometrics check out. She's asking to see Agent Rand. A man came in with her and he's waiting in the lobby. Didn't ask to see Rand, but he hasn't left, either. No hits on him in any of the facial-recognition databases."

My heart lurched into rapid drumming. "Don't let them anywhere near the secured area. Tell them Agent Rand can't have visitors, and put Rand's guard on high alert. Put a tail on Taylor and her friend when they leave. I want to know where they go, what they do, and who the hell that guy is."

"On it. I'm uploading his biometrics to the analysis team and your desktop now."

"Thanks," I said, but the connection had already closed.

When I turned, the other two were eyeing me worriedly.

"Problem?" Stemp inquired.

"No, just a development." Hiding my anxiety, I summoned a smile. "Have a good trip, both of you. I'm going to hit my desk for a while..."

"And then go home and sleep for at least eight hours," Stemp prompted. "Dermott has been apprised of your status."

His warning came through loud and clear, and I sighed. "Yes, I'm definitely going home to sleep after I finish. I don't think this will take too long."

"Very well, then." Stemp gave me a nod. "I will be in touch."

"Good luck, dear." Moonbeam enfolded me in her soft embrace. "May the Earth Spirit guide and protect you."

"Thanks." I hugged her in return. "You, too."

A few minutes later I was slumped in my desk chair scowling at the biometrics the analyst had sent.

Who was this guy, and how did he know Nora?

He was the same man Nora had greeted at the hotel, but I was pretty sure I'd never seen him before that. I'd just have to wait for the analysts to finish checking the databases. Dammit.

Sighing, I brought up the surveillance logs from Nora's day.

Half an hour later I still had nothing. She'd had a couple of conversations with her lawyer about regaining ownership of Sirius Canada, and she'd called the management company to request their financial records pertaining to Sirius. Other than that, the bug in her hotel room had only picked up a few hours of quiet page-turning followed by bathroom noises, and then the sound of the hotel room door closing behind her when she left. She hadn't even used her credit cards to buy dinner.

Dammit!

I should have slipped a bug into her purse when I'd met her for coffee. Instead, she had left her room, gone who-knew-where with who-knew-whom, and I'd missed the whole fucking thing.

CHAPTER 31

Grabbing the phone, I punched the analyst-on-call extension. When a wide-awake female voice replied, I asked if they were working on the data that had just come in from the hospital.

"Yes," the woman replied crisply. "I ran it through the espionage and police databases and came up empty; and I'm waiting on the results from our worldwide biometric search now. It'll likely take a while, but I'll upload any hits directly to your desktop."

"Thanks. Ping my cell phone, too, would you, please?"

"Will do."

My next call went to the Security desk. Leo had clocked out for the day, but his replacement assured me that Nora and her companion were under surveillance.

"They left the hospital and went straight to the hotel bar," he reported. "They look pretty chummy. Not sexy; but relaxed and friendly. We've been trying to lipread them but it's dark in there. We've only caught part of the conversation, and it seems like they're talking about their families. I'm uplinking the video feed to your desktop now."

"Their families?" My fingers quivered as I brought up the surveillance screen. "Has Nora mentioned me?"

"We only caught the guy talking about his. Any keywords we should watch for?"

I hesitated, studying Nora's grainy image as she chatted with her companion. "Just the usual ones, I guess..."

Nora threw back her head and laughed, then reached over to lightly clink her glass against the man's. They downed the last of their drinks and rose.

"Looks like they're calling it a night," the security guard said as they left the bar and turned toward the hallway that led to the rooms. "Which one do you want our guy to follow?"

As he spoke, the camera view jiggled and shifted, then moved toward the door of the bar. A moment later it rounded the corner in time to catch Nora raising a hand in farewell to her companion. He returned the salute and disappeared into one of the rooms.

"Get that room number and then follow Nora," I snapped. "Find out who's renting that room, put a camera on it in the hallway, and put another camera outside Nora's room. When you get the guy's name, shoot it up to the analysts. Um, thanks," I added belatedly.

"No problem." The clicking of computer keys drifted faintly over the line.

We watched while our covert camera followed Nora to her room. When she went inside, I fell back in my chair with a long sigh and checked my watch. Only nine-thirty, but it felt like the middle of the night.

Instead of the groan I wanted to emit, I said, "Nora's probably in for the night. I don't want to waste resources by keeping our guy at the hotel, but send video feeds from the hallway cameras to the analysts. If that guy or Nora comes out of their room any time tonight, I want them followed."

"Done."

"Thanks," I repeated, and hung up.

I eased the kinks out of my shoulders and knuckled my gritty eyes. At least we'd get a name off the hotel register for Nora's new friend, even if it wasn't his real name.

But I might have a better source.

Grabbing the phone again, I dialled Nora's number.

"Dani-dear!" she exclaimed when I identified myself. "It's been such a long day without you! This hotel room is so lonely."

Dutiful-Daughter-Me swallowed burning guilt. My own mother, visiting from an ocean away after all these years, stuck alone in a hotel room while I had an unused guestroom in my three-bedroom house.

Secret-Agent-Me kicked Dutiful-Daughter in the ass and took over the conversation. "I'm sorry it's been such a long day for you. Didn't you go out at all?"

"Oh..." Nora hesitated. "Only for a little while."

More like a few hours, you liar.

"I went over to the hospital to visit Ian, but they said he couldn't have visitors," she added. "I didn't realize he'd been so badly injured."

"Yes, he's in bad shape. He was having convulsions today, and they were doing more diagnostics to check for brain damage."

"Oh, my heavens, how awful!" Nora's voice vibrated with concern. "They wouldn't tell me anything at the hospital. If you see him and if... he's... able to understand..." She swallowed audibly. "Please give him my best wishes for a speedy recovery." She hesitated. "Do you think... how serious...?"

Dammit, if only I could see her expression. Was she

secretly hoping Ian would die and save her the trouble of murdering him? Or was she honestly concerned?

"It's hard to tell with brain injuries," I said solemnly. "He was just going into the MRI when I was there today, so I hope we'll have some news tomorrow." Shifting into my best concerned-daughter voice, I added, "It's too bad you walked all the way over to the hospital for nothing. I hope you were warm enough for such a long walk in the snow."

"Oh, I didn't walk. I've met a nice man here at the hotel and he drove me over."

Gotcha.

Hiding my surge of predatory glee in an offhand tone, I said, "Oh, that's nice. What's his name? Maybe I know him."

"You likely do," she replied. "He's a local man, Bob Armstrong. He's having some marital difficulties, so he's temporarily moved into the hotel."

"Nope, the name doesn't ring a bell. But I haven't lived here long enough to know everybody yet."

Nora sniffed. "Well, you must be the only person in town who doesn't know him, then. I loathe small towns. The gossip is simply intolerable."

"Oh, really?" I didn't have to fake my avid interest. "What's the gossip?"

"Honestly, Aydan, don't be so petty."

I waited.

"I'm sure it's completely unfounded..." she began.

"How sure?" I inquired cynically.

"Well, not 'unfounded', exactly, but unjustified. He was caught in flagrante delicto with another woman; but it was completely excusable. His wife is very cold and indifferent."

"And you know this because...?"

"He told me all about her. He's a very warm passionate man."

"That's a nice euphemism for 'he can't keep it in his pants'," I drawled. "So he was screwing around on his wife. Why didn't he just divorce her if he was so unhappy in his marriage? Don't tell me; let me guess. He didn't want to *hurt* her by letting the neighbours find out that she couldn't satisfy him."

"I believe this conversation is over," Nora said stiffly.

Click.

"Goodnight, *Mom*," I said to the dead air on the line. "You slimy piece of shit." I slammed the receiver onto the cradle and dropped my head into my hands.

Stupid.

I'd let my emotions get in the way of my mission again.

Hissing out a breath between my teeth, I picked up the phone and dialled Nora back.

"Yes?" The chill in her tone jabbed an icicle straight through my heart.

"I'm sorry," I said quietly. "That was childish of me. I don't want to fight with you; I just... I'm having a really hard time..." My voice wavered right on cue, but unfortunately I wasn't faking it. Dammit, get a grip. "I'm sorry," I whispered.

"Oh, Dani-dear." Emotion choked her voice, too. "I knew this wasn't going to be easy for either of us. I wish we could just let go of the last thirty years. Remember how we used to celebrate the days when school was closed for a blizzard? Cuddling together under the covers and reading in our pajamas all day, and eating cookies and ice cream in bed? I wish we could do that now."

A wave of memory crashed through my defenses,

flooding my heart with bitter warmth and tightening my throat.

"I... I'd forgotten that..." I swallowed hard, trying to steady my voice.

"But you must remember our shopping sprees in Saskatoon," she pleaded. "When we used to catch the Greyhound bus in town and ride to Saskatoon; shop all day and then ride the bus home in the evening?"

"N-no... I remember when I was seventeen, I used to drive to town and ride the Greyhound to Saskatoon by myself."

"Oh, Dani-dear, how do you think you knew how to ride the bus and where to go in the big city? We did it together time after time, when you were younger."

"I... I can't remember that," I stammered.

But I remembered her cold silences when I'd done something that displeased her. I remembered the time I'd given her backtalk and she'd slapped me across the face, the shock and pain still reverberating in my memory.

I shook myself free of the past.

Get it together. You're an agent with a job to do.

"It's been so long. I'd like to revisit those good times with you," I said. "Can we get together tomorrow?"

"Of course, darling. I'll be waiting for your call." She hesitated. "Good night, Dani-dear. I love you."

"I love you, too." The words were out of my mouth before I could stop them. "Goodnight," I croaked, and hung up.

Collapsing forward, I let my forehead thump onto my desk. If the analysts, or worse, Stemp, listened to the recording of that call, I hoped to hell they thought I was just the world's best actor. Because if they thought I couldn't handle a mission without getting personal, there was a nice cozy cell waiting to hold me for the rest of my life.

I called the analysts and gave them Bob Armstrong's name, then updated my reports with all the facts and none of the emotion. At last I headed for the door.

The fifteen-minute drive home felt like hours. Fighting sleep all the way, I opened my car windows to the frigid winter air and sang along with the radio at the top of my lungs.

When the bright warmth of my garage embraced me at last, I turned off the ignition and hit the button to roll the door down behind me.

Home. Safe.

I let out a long breath and relaxed.

My car door wrenched open.

Big dark figure reaching in...

I shrieked, my left fist pistoning out at the threatening figure. My right hand scrabbled uselessly at my parka where my holster should have been, dammit-*dammit*...

CHAPTER 32

"It's okay! Aydan, you're okay!" Hellhound's urgent voice penetrated my panic. "It's just me. You're okay. You're home an' you're safe."

Realization dawned and I fell back in the driver's seat of my car, gasping. "Oh, fuck, you scared the shit out of me!"

"Sorry, darlin'." He leaned down to study me worriedly. "I guess ya musta fallen asleep."

"No, I just drove in."

His frown deepened. "No, ya drove in twenty minutes ago. I saw the garage door roll down but ya didn't come in the house. I figured ya were just doin' somethin' out here, but after a while I started wonderin'."

"Oh." I rubbed my forehead, which bore an aching indentation where it had rested on the steering wheel. "You're right, I must have fallen asleep. Thanks for coming to get me."

"No problem, darlin'." He reached down to me. "Come on, let's get ya to bed."

"Heaven," I sighed, and gave him my hand so he could hoist me out of the car.

The ring of the phone jerked me out of warm and wonderful oblivion. Eyes still glued shut, I hit the 'Talk' button and croaked, "H'lo?"

"Good morning, Dani-dear..." Nora hesitated. "Did I wake you?"

"Uh... yeah..." I dragged my eyelids open. From the other pillow, Arnie gave me a sleepy smile before closing his eyes again. Eyeing the slow rise and fall of his muscular tattooed chest, I banished my momentary envy at the fact that he'd fallen instantly back to sleep.

Nora was still talking, and I interrupted gently. "I'm sorry, I'm not quite awake yet. What did you say?"

"Should I call back later?"

"Um... no, that's okay. I'm awake now." I gave my head a shake, trying to kickstart my brain.

"I was calling to see when we could get together today," she said.

"Um... what day is it...? Right, Tuesday..."

Shit, I wasn't cleared for active duty yet.

Or maybe I was. I glanced at the clock radio. Nine AM. Holy shit, I was late for work. Stemp was going to...

No, Stemp was on his way to England. Dermott was going to kick my ass.

But I'd slept for nearly eleven hours. I could tell him I was just making *really* sure I qualified for active duty again...

"Aydan, are you still there?" Nora inquired.

"Um, yeah. Sorry. Tuesdays are really busy for me. I overslept, so I have to get to the office as soon as I can. And I have two-hour meetings back to back at eleven and one, so I won't finish until three..."

"Oh." Her voice was distinctly cooler. "Well, I certainly wouldn't expect you to put your mother ahead of any of those... responsibilities. I must have misunderstood when you said you wanted to spend more time with me. Why don't you give me a call when you have a few spare minutes?"

I knotted my fist in my hair. "Shit, I didn't mean it like that. I could probably make it around ten-thirty, but only for half an hour..."

"Watch your language," Nora said stiffly. "And you needn't throw me any crumbs. I'll be too busy to see you this morning anyway."

The unspoken 'I'm terribly disappointed in you' pushed every one of my dysfunctional buttons.

"I'm sorry, of course you're important to me..." I began, then caught myself. Stop apologizing. "Let's make plans for this afternoon. Is it okay if I pick you up around three fifteen?"

"I don't know if I'll be ready to see you then."

I jerked up to sitting position, my frustration and guilt bursting out. "Can we *please* not do this? Look, I'm sorry you're disappointed. I didn't mean to hurt you and I really want to see you. Can we please just get together this afternoon?"

Nora heaved a long-suffering sigh. "All right, Aydan. I forgive you, of course. I'll be ready at three-fifteen."

"Thanks. I'll see you then."

I punched the disconnect button and fell back on the pillow, pressing my hands over my face and fighting the urge to scream, swear, and beat the hell out of something. Not necessarily in that order.

"Okay, darlin'?" Hellhound rasped softly.

Dropping my hands, I looked over to see him studying me. Guess he hadn't gone back to sleep after all.

"Fine." I slapped the handset back onto its charging

cradle and sat up, swinging my legs over the edge of the bed. "I have to get to work. I'm late."

I made for the bathroom, hoping he wouldn't follow me into the shower.

He didn't.

Rinsing the conditioner out of my hair under the hot spray a few minutes later, my heart sank as I processed his absence.

I didn't even remember saying goodnight to him last night. We had exchanged some promising kisses while we undressed, and then...

Shit, I'd collapsed into bed and fallen instantly asleep. I vaguely remembered nightmares soothed by his soft reassurances and gentle hands, but I hadn't woken enough to even thank him.

And this morning I hadn't kissed him, or even wished him good morning.

He was hurt. And rightfully so.

Tension wound up in my shoulders while I towelled off at warp speed. I'd have to make it up to him before I left. Maybe a quickie would do it.

Pasting a smile on my face, I hurried out of the bathroom, my wet hair still dripping down my back.

Arnie was reclining against the pillows with his arms tucked behind his head, smiling at me. But the smile didn't reach his eyes.

"Hey, who's this hot guy in my bed?" I teased as I snuggled in beside him. Trailing kisses along his neck, I finger-walked down the hard muscle of his stomach to the coarse hair that surrounded my goal.

His arm came around me, but his free hand stopped mine before I could fondle him. "Ya don't really have time for this, do ya?"

My stomach clenched.

He *was* hurt. Now he'd go cold and silent...

Arnie frowned. "Aydan..."

Oh God, he was angry, too.

He hesitated. "So... ya know how I said I was comin' up here to give ya a reality check if the mother-bitch started mind-fuckin' ya?"

The air vanished from my lungs.

He'd lied to me.

He had some other agenda, and he'd lied to me.

I turned away so he couldn't see my heart ripping in two. "Yes...?"

"She's mind-fuckin' ya," Arnie said softly.

"Okay," I said without meeting his gaze. "But why are you really here?"

"Aw, darlin'." He folded me into his arms. "That's why I'm here."

"B-but you just said..."

"That's what I mean. She's twistin' ya up so ya don't trust anybody anymore, not even me." The pain in his voice stabbed my heart.

"I'm sorry!" I hugged him tightly. "I didn't mean to hurt you."

"Christ, Aydan, ya ain't hurtin' me. I'm hurtin' *for* ya. Just... look at me, okay?"

When I pulled back a few inches, he tipped my chin up and held my gaze with his. "We're friends, an' I'm never gonna lie to ya. Ya still believe that?" When I nodded uncertainly, he went on, his gaze holding mine. "So believe me when I tell ya that you're a good person an' a good friend an' a good agent. An' anybody that makes ya stop believin' that, they ain't worth your time."

Hope stirred cautiously in my heart.

"So... you're..." I studied his face, alert for the tiniest cue. "...not upset?"

"No, darlin'," he said gently. "Why would I be upset?"

"I didn't give you any dinner, I fell asleep on you last night, I didn't even say good morning; and now I'm leaving you with blue balls. I've been treating you like shit, and I feel awful about it."

He went still. "You're treatin' me just fine. I'm here to make sure you're okay, not to get fed or fucked."

I pulled away with an incredulous laugh. "Um, hello, Mr. Condom?" I pointed at the large unopened box on the bedside table.

Arnie grinned. "Okay, ya got me there; but just listen for a sec." He sobered and took my hand. "Anytime ya wanna get horizontal, I'll be hot an' ready; but it wouldn't matter if we never did the tube snake boogie again. I can always find some chick to get my rocks off, but..." He planted a gentle whiskery kiss on my forehead. "...I'll never find another friend like you. So if ya don't have time or ya ain't in the mood, it just ain't a big deal. Ya don't hafta pretend."

"I've never pretended," I assured him. "Trust me, you're so good in bed you could give an orgasm to a marble statue of the Virgin Mary."

He stared at me open-mouthed for an instant before his laugh burst out. "Hell, darlin', I dunno whether to be flattered or weirded out."

I snickered. "Okay, that mental image was a little disturbing. But you get my point."

"Yeah," Arnie said quietly. "But here's my point: You're worthwhile for who ya are. Ya don't hafta be a servant or a sexpot."

His words hit me like lightning bolts. I opened my mouth but nothing came out. After a moment, I closed it again.

"Aydan?" Arnie's brow furrowed. "Talk to me, darlin'."

"I, um..." My voice came out in a croak. I swallowed. "I... wow. You just... completely upended my worldview. And I never thought I'd be happy to hear a guy say 'if you don't put out, I'll find a woman who will'."

"Shit, I didn't mean-" he began anxiously, but I flung my arms around him.

"You're perfect." I kissed him, long and slow. "You." I kissed him again. "Are." Kiss. "Perfect." Another kiss. "Abso-fucking-lutely perfect. How did I ever get lucky enough to find you?"

He flushed. "Shit, I ain't anythin' special. Anybody'd look good compared to the fuckin' losers you've had so far."

"No." Cupping his chin in both hands and enjoying the roughness of his beard against my palms, I smiled into his eyes. "You make *all* other guys look like losers."

"Stop," he grumbled. "You're gonna give me a swelled head."

Cuddling closer, I coasted my hand downward. "Turns out I like swelled heads."

"Mmm." His voice deepened as I stroked him. "Is that a fact, now?"

"Mmhmm..." My response was muffled by his mouth, and I melted against him.

Lord, the man could kiss. Lips, tongue, and whiskers in perfect nerve-tingling harmony-

The phone rang.

CHAPTER 33

Reluctantly pulling away from the hot temptation of Arnie's kiss, I checked the call display.

"It's Dermott." I grimaced. "Sorry, I have to answer this." Bracing myself for a flood of invective, I pressed the Talk button and said, "Hello?"

"What the hell are you doing still at home?" Dermott snapped. "It's a quarter to ten! We need you here for a briefing, pronto!"

"Dr. Rawling said I had to get eight hours of sleep before I could go back on active duty," I replied, unhesitatingly shoving Rawling under the bus to save myself.

"Fuck Rawling and his pansy-ass psych shit! You're reinstated because I'm the DCO and I say so. Now get your ass in here!"

'Fuck you' hovered at the tip of my tongue, but I managed to bite it back. "On my way," I said instead, and hung up.

Arnie frowned. "Ya ain't cleared for active duty?"

"I am now, according to His Royal Highness Brent Shirley Dermott."

Hellhound's frown deepened. "Fuck him. Call Doc Rawlin'. If he says ya ain't ready..."

"I'm ready. It was just a technicality. And thanks to you..." I dropped a kiss on his lips. "...I got 'way more than the eight hours of sleep I was supposed to get."

Sitting up with every intention of getting up and dressed, I stole just one more appreciative glance at the tattooed muscular body displayed so temptingly on my sheets.

Damn, he looked good.

Arnie's lips curved up in a slow smile as he regarded me with heavy-lidded eyes that promised sinful pleasure to come. "Like what ya see, darlin'?"

"Oh, hell yeah."

I succumbed, leaning down to run a hungry hand over his chest and steal another kiss.

Mmm.

Just one more kiss...

Maybe Dermott would get pissed off enough to have a stroke. If he was in the hospital his briefing would be called off...

The phone rang again.

"For chrissake!" I rolled off Arnie and grabbed the handset. "I'm on my way, okay?" I barked. "Just take a pill!"

Kane's amused baritone warmed my ear. "Well, all right; as long as you're on your way."

"Oh." I flopped back on the bed. "Hi, John. Sorry; I thought it was Dermott getting up my ass again."

Kane hesitated. "Oh. Well... I was calling to see if you and Arnie could come over around three this afternoon. Daniel and I are feeling much better, so we'll be leaving for Calgary around three-thirty. But it sounds as though you have enough on your plate today."

Something in his voice told me this was more important than he was admitting.

Shit.

I thumped my head against the pillow a couple of times. "You're right, it's shaping up to be one of those days. But I should be able to make it..." I did some rapid mental calculations. "I'll be at Lola's this afternoon and I could leave there a few minutes early to get to your place at three; and I can probably push my three-fifteen meeting a bit..." Wincing, I imagined Nora's reaction if I was late.

Screw it. I'd call her at three-fifteen and tell her I was on my way.

"Don't worry if you can't make it. It's not urgent," Kane said, but there was still that odd intonation in his voice. "I'll give you a call later if we don't connect today."

Maybe I was imagining things. Maybe everything was fine.

Maybe he wanted to discuss returning to the Department. My hopes rose, only to seesaw back into anxiety.

Or maybe he wanted to tell me he wasn't coming back. He'd want to have either of those conversations in person...

Keeping my tone light, I said, "Okay, thanks. I'll try to make it, but if I don't see you before you leave, have a safe trip." I disconnected and turned to Arnie. "That was John. He wants us to go over to his place around three. He and Daniel are leaving for Calgary at three-thirty."

"Okay. I'll come to Lola's shop around two-thirty, an' we can go from there as soon's you're done."

"Do you know where Up and Coming is?"

Hellhound grinned. "It's a small town, darlin'. If there's more than one sex shop, I'll just keep checkin' 'em out 'til I find the right one." He rolled off the bed, pulling me up along with him. "Ya better get goin' before Dermott blows a blood vessel."

"Ha. I wish."

When I tapped on the open door to Dermott's office, he looked up from his computer with a scowl. "It's ten-fucking-thirty! What took you?"

"Sorry," I said perfunctorily. "I had a call from Kane that delayed me a bit. I got here as soon as I could."

Dermott leaned back in his chair, his ruddy complexion darkening in a scowl. "Well, while you were lying around gabbing with your *boyfriend*, I was handling your real mission and walking your *mommy* around Sirius Dynamics. Maybe Stemp lets you stroll in here whenever you damn well feel like it, but don't expect any fucking special treatment from me. If you don't show some results pronto, I'll personally file the dereliction of duty charges against you and chuck your special little ass in a special little prison cell for the rest of your special little life."

My guts liquefied. He was out for revenge.

An instant later my fear flashed into rage as usual, propelling me a threatening step forward. "Listen, asshole," I ground out. "Talking to Kane *is* my mission. And the day you show me your service record as an agent is the day you get to tell me how to run my ops." My fear and anger surged higher, my mouth still running off. "If you want to look good with the chain of command, you'll stay the fuck out of my way and let me get the job done. But if you want to look like a whiny civilian crybaby, you just run and tell them how you think I'm not doing my job right; and one of them with *actual field experience* will explain to you how missions like these can take weeks or even months to get results."

Dermott turned crimson. As he opened his mouth, Holt breezed into the office, swinging the door shut behind him.

"Hey, Kelly," he greeted me, then turned to Dermott. "We still on for beers and the hockey game tonight?"

Dermott relaxed and grinned. "Sure. Good thing you don't have a *bedtime* like Kelly here."

"What's that supposed to mean?" Holt asked.

Dermott's mocking grin widened. "Stemp pulled her from active because she didn't get her beauty sleep."

Holt frowned. "Yeah... I'm assigned to her project, remember?" He turned to me. "Are you ready to tackle Stiles in the network now?"

Whew. This was Holt The Okay Guy. I wouldn't have to strangle anybody in the next five minutes.

Not Holt, anyway. Dermott was still a distinct possibility.

With an effort, I let go of my irritation. "As ready as I ever am. Is that what this briefing is about? Do we have a timeframe for getting Rebecca out?"

"Late tonight or early tomorrow morning," Dermott said. "Stemp's barely in the air so we won't know until after he gets to the hospital in London. This briefing is about the sting op."

He was acting professional in front of Holt, but his eyes still glittered with suppressed anger. The gloves were definitely off.

"Marvelous," I muttered.

Holt either failed to register my sarcasm or chose to ignore it. "Yeah, it'll be great," he agreed. "I'm betting Grandin's contact is the key to everything. The rest of Five Eyes is pretty interested in finding out who in the U.S. government gave the order to screw us all over, too." He grinned, his chest expanding. "And yours truly is going to deliver the whole thing all wrapped up in a pretty bow."

Shit, Holt The Magnificent was back.

"Today I'll get Grandin to call his contact and say he has you," Holt went on. "The drop location is a nursing home in Calgary, so he'll set up the exchange for ten-thirty tomorrow morning. We'll tie you up and…"

A wave of claustrophobia drowned out his words.

"Hang on," I snapped. "Nobody's tying me up!"

"Well, of course not." Holt gave me an 'are-you-stupid?' look. "We'll put cuffs on you but they won't be fastened, and you're going to pretend to be unconscious. That's why we're doing it at a nursing home. Nobody will look twice at a limp body in a wheelchair. And don't worry, we'll have the site locked down tighter than a nun's cu-" He bit off the c-word at the last instant and substituted, "…chastity belt."

"Okay…" I drew a breath that was supposed to be calming. It didn't work. I went on, "…but this person must be really high up in the U.S. government to send down orders like that. I can't see us catching the big boss at the drop. They're going to send a flunky to pick me up."

Holt flushed. "Of course we're not going to catch the big cheese at the drop! We want to let them take you and see who's at the end of this chain-"

"Oh, that's just fucking marvelous!" I sprang to my feet and unconsciously backed away a couple of paces before I caught myself. Planting my fists on my hips, I scowled at Holt. "Because, hey, what could possibly go wrong while I'm lying there alone and helpless in their car? These people aren't idiots! They're going to check the cuffs, find out they're unlocked, and tie me up so tight I won't even be able to…"

My mind went momentarily blank with fear at the thought but I forced it back on track and stayed loud, hoping Holt and Dermott would hear outrage instead of terror. "And they'll know they've been set up. They won't lead you anywhere, except to the edge of the cliff they drop me off!"

"They wouldn't kill you, idiot," Holt snapped. "They've gone to huge trouble and risk to acquire you. I guarantee that whoever picked you up from Grandin wouldn't harm a hair on your head until the big boss got everything he wanted from you."

"Oh, that's a nice guarantee," I snarled. "Remind me to collect on that after I'm fucking *dead*!"

Dermott's palm hit the desk with a nerve-jolting smack. "For chrissake, Kelly, grow a pair! We wanted to let them take you, but the chain of command nixed it because you're so fucking special. You'll only be there to lure the buyer into the open, and the team will take him down as soon as he shows. So stop being a fucking *whiny crybaby*..." He spat my earlier insult back at me. "...and get the hell out of my office." He turned pointedly back to his computer and began to type.

Somehow I managed not to lunge over the desk and wrap my hands around his throat.

"Let me know when you hear from Stemp," I said instead, and marched out.

Holt followed. As I turned away, he caught my elbow. "You okay with this?"

"Do I have a choice?"

"Well, if you're so shit-scared you're going to fuck it up..."

"Bite me," I snapped, and stomped down the hallway.

CHAPTER 34

Spider hailed me as I passed his office, and I U-turned and went in.

"Good morning," he greeted me cheerfully. "I see we've got an espionage kingpin in town."

My guts clenched. "Where? Who?"

His smile vanished. "Sorry, I guess I shouldn't joke about stuff like that. I was talking about Bob Armstrong."

"What about him? What do you mean, you were joking?"

"I mean he's lived in Silverside all his life and he doesn't have any shady connections at all." Spider grimaced. "Not in espionage, anyway. He cheats on his wife, gets into bar fights every now and then, and rips people off in his renovation business whenever he can get away with it, but that's it. His wife kicked him out after his latest fling, so it looks as though he and Nora are only casual acquaintances because they're both stuck at the hotel."

"Are you sure there's no connection between him and Nora?" I demanded.

"Ninety-nine percent. He's probably just buttering her up, hoping to get some free meals. He can be charming when he wants to be."

"Well, shit. I was hoping this would be my big break in the case." I sighed. "At least he's met his match in con artists. *Somebody* bought Nora's dinner and drinks last night. Speaking of Nora... Dermott said something about walking her around here this morning. Do you know anything about that?"

"He gave her a tour and she's in the boardroom down the hall right now, meeting with the management company. It looks as though she's trying to learn as much as she can about Sirius Canada."

"But she doesn't own the company," I protested. "She's trying to get it back from the government, but I'm surprised Dermott would let her walk in here and poke into everything."

"He didn't." Spider grinned. "He showed her the offices, just like any other civilian. And she won't get anything from the management company. They don't know anything."

I let out a breath. "That's a relief. I don't trust her any farther than I could throw her."

Spider gave me a sympathetic twist of his lips. "This must be really tough for you. Are you..." He hesitated. "...doing okay?"

My last angst-laden conversation with Nora replayed in my mind, and I winced. "You listened to the audio recording?"

His eyes widened. "Um, no... should I have? I can do it right now..." He reached for his keyboard.

I flung out a restraining hand. "No, it's okay. I just... had an, um... emotional talk with Nora last night, and I was hoping nobody would listen to it and get the wrong idea."

Spider's brow furrowed. "What do you mean?"

"Well..." Shit, why had I opened my big mouth in the

first place? "...I just meant I wouldn't want anybody to think I was so emotionally involved in the case that I couldn't do my job."

His frown deepened. "But... that's kind of the whole point, isn't it? You're supposed to be convincing her that you're emotionally involved."

Bless Spider and his innocent faith in me.

I gave him a smile and a shrug. "Yeah. Forget it. Dermott was just... poking at me this morning, so I guess I'm feeling a little defensive."

"Don't worry, Aydan." Spider gave me his sunny smile. "Everybody knows you're a top agent. You don't have to prove anything to anybody."

If only that were true.

"Thanks, Spider." I gave him the best smile I could fake, and left before my mouth could get me in any more trouble.

Still replaying the cringe-worthy conversation with Nora in my mind, I slowed as I approached my office.

Hmmm...

Moments later, I was dialling the number Dr. Rawling had given me.

"Hi, it's Aydan," I said after his 'hello'. "I'm sorry to bother you on your vacation."

"It's quite all right. As I told you earlier, you're not intruding." His mild voice exuded comfort and reassurance, and I tried to feel comforted and reassured instead of twitchy and creeped out. "How can I help you?" he asked.

"I have a question about repressed memories."

"What would you like to discuss?" The kind interest in his voice made me shudder.

I summoned my best professional tone. "I've been talking to Nora, and I can't remember a lot of the things she said we used to do together. Is that normal? Or could she be messing with me?"

Rawling hesitated, and I imagined him wearing his pleasant neutral expression. And salivating while he eagerly poised a spoon above my open skull. I shook the image out of my head as he began, "Well, Aydan, 'normal' is a bit of a misnomer. All behaviours fall along a continuum-"

"Right," I interrupted. "Sorry, let me put that another way. Is it possible that I could have forgotten a lot of the things she's telling me we did?"

"It's possible. Family members often remember episodes of shared history differently; or one family member may recall an episode that another family member has completely forgotten."

"Okay, so... I've heard about people repressing memories, usually of traumatic experiences. Does that really happen?"

"It can."

I leaned my elbows on my desk, lowering my voice. "But these things with Nora should be good memories. Does that mean those activities were just more meaningful to her than to me, so I've forgotten them? Or could she be lying?"

"She could be lying; or she could simply be interpreting shared experiences through a different lens. Or, as you say, the experience may have been more meaningful for her than for you at the time."

"But why can't I remember all the good times she said we had?" I burst out. "All I remember is the crappy times when we fought and she made me feel-"

Shit, don't let him in your head!

"I'm sure we must have had *some* good times together," I went on as smoothly as I could. "For the last thirty years I've thought she was a great mom. Could that have been programming planted in my mind? Because even though I feel like I had a happy childhood, I can't remember *specific* times when I was happy. Doesn't that sound suspicious to you?"

Rawling's voice softened. "Aydan, you were a teen on the cusp of adulthood when your mother left and you believed her to be dead. Did you have any psychological support at the time?"

"No."

"And do you feel that you adequately grieved your mother's loss then?" His gentle voice made me squirm.

None of your damn business.

"I don't know," I said flatly. "I'm more interested in the memory question right now."

In the momentary silence I imagined him scribbling a note on his ever-present pad: "Avoidance. Repressed anger."

"Your grieving, or lack thereof, is relevant to your questions about memory," Rawling said in his usual mild tone. "Any memory can be repressed, if remembering it is too painful." His voice softened. "Such as in the case of a child repressing happy memories of a mother who is gone forever."

Grief gut-punched me.

Breathless, I folded over the aching chasm inside my chest.

I want my mom back...

"Thanks," I croaked. "That's a big help." Bracing my palm against my desk, I pushed myself upright and stiffened my spine. "That's all I needed to know, so I'll let you get back to your vacation now."

"Would you like to talk about this more? I could meet with you any time today-"

"No." The word came out too fast, and I forced my 'professional' voice again. "I'm booked up solid for the rest of the day, but thanks. I really appreciate you making the time to answer my questions. Have a nice vacation. 'Bye."

I dropped the handset back into its cradle as if ridding myself of a snake, and wrapped both arms around myself.

Holding myself together through sheer physical effort.

Spider strolled by in the hallway, glancing in only to stop short. A concerned frown replaced his smile. "Are you okay?"

With an effort, I relaxed my arms and managed a stiff smile. "F-Fine. Just cold."

"I hope you're not coming down with that flu." He studied me worriedly.

Yanking myself under control, I pushed to my feet. "No, I'm just chilly." I glanced at my watch. "I'd better get going. I have to grab a bug to plant on Nora, and then I'm due over at Eddy's to do his books."

I left Blue Eddy's slightly before one PM, soothed by a full belly and the knowledge that Eddy hadn't received any more threats.

When I arrived at Up and Coming, a smile tugged at my lips. Lola's twisted sense of humour had manifested itself in the window display, as usual.

The lower part of the display window was obscured to block the view of young eyes, and the visible part displayed only mannequins in tasteful lingerie. But lurking at the bottom of the display was the big black silicone dildo Lola had nicknamed Big John after her memorable glimpse of Kane in his leather motorcycle chaps. A fur-trimmed red Santa hat perched at a jaunty angle on Big John's bulbous head.

Dipping my knees to check the sightlines, my smile widened. Anyone shorter than me would never know Big John was there, so clearly Lola had calculated the angles with enthusiastic precision.

Grinning, I strode into the shop to confront the perpetrator.

"Hi, honey!" Lola hurried over for a hug.

As I straightened, I sniffed the air. "Is that you, or is there a Purple Jesus party going on?"

Lola grimaced and smoothed the front of her low-cut magenta leather mini-dress. "It's me. This is the newest sample from that scented-leather company. It's supposed to be 'acai berry', but it really does smell like grape Kool-Aid, doesn't it?"

"It really does." I leaned closer and sniffed again. "Talk about a blast from the past. I haven't had grape Kool-Aid in years."

Lola's smile came back. "Well, that's okay. Most guys wouldn't know an acai berry if it jumped up and bit them; but they probably have happy memories of grape Kool-Aid."

"Or horrible memories of vomiting it up laced with vodka," I pointed out.

She laughed. "Well, maybe I won't order much stock. The chocolate-scented leather is still my top seller anyway." Giving me a wink, she added, "I'm sure Arnie would like it. You never told me you had a boyfriend. All this time I've been thinking you had the hots for Big John. Did that fizzle out?"

"Um... not exactly." Rapidly changing the subject, I added, "Hey, I shouldn't be standing here wasting time. I'll get to work."

I turned toward the office but Lola planted herself in my path, frowning. "Aydan, you're not sneaking around on Big John, are you?"

"No." I attempted to detour around her. "He's known about my thing with Arnie right from the start."

She sidestepped in front of me again, her eyebrows going up. "You mean you've got both of them on a string?"

"Neither of them is on a string," I explained with all the patience I could muster. "We each just do whatever or whoever we want. 'Scuse me."

I managed to slip by her, but she followed me into the office and perched on the corner of the desk while I fired up the bookkeeping program.

"I don't mean to pry, honey," she said, then hesitated. "Well, that's silly; of course I mean to pry," she amended, giving me an unabashed grin that lit her wrinkled face. "Have you tried ménage à trois with them?"

"Lola!"

"This is important market research," she added earnestly. "I've read all about it, but I've never known anybody personally who tried it. I promise that anything you tell me will be strictly confidential."

"No! Jeez!"

"Why not?" Her question was matter-of-fact.

I sighed. She wasn't going to let it go. "Because they're both amazing lovers and I can barely keep up to either of them, never mind both at the same time. And anyway, they're both huge..."

Lola's eyes widened.

"Broad-shouldered!" I clarified hurriedly. "Big guys. Just sleeping between them made me claustrophobic..." Her delighted expression made me backtrack again. "Once! It was only once, and nothing happened-"

The sound of a male throat clearing made me snap my mouth shut. Shit, I'd been so focused on evading Lola's questions that I'd missed the jingle of the bell over the front door.

A moment later a far-too-familiar voice called from around the corner. "Lola? Are you here?"

Shit.

"We're in the office, Tom!" Lola called. "Come on back."

My face flamed as Tom rounded the corner. "Ready to go?" he asked Lola, then gave a start that looked just a little too contrived. "Oh, hi, Aydan. I didn't realize you were here."

Fuck. He'd heard everything.

"Hi, Tom." I faked a casual tone. "I didn't know you were one of Lola's customers."

Too late, I realized how that sounded. Oh, Lord, could I just shrink to nothing and disappear under the desk?

Hooking his thumbs in his belt loops, Tom gave me a slow smile. "Well, I'm not buying today, but I'm not saying I never will." He turned to Lola. "Ready to go?"

"Sure." She jumped up, teetering a little in her stiletto boots.

"Where are you off to?" I inquired jovially, hoping to hide my embarrassment.

"Just to the bank to make my deposits," Lola replied. "We'll be back in a few minutes."

My oh-shit-ometer redlined. Lola had never needed an escort to the bank before.

"Tom, why are you here?" I demanded.

He frowned. "Didn't Lola tell you?"

I shot her a 'you're in deep shit' glower. "Lola? What would you like to tell me... right... *now?*"

"Oh, honey, it's nothing to worry about. Tom is just overprotective." She patted his denim-clad arm fondly. "It's that cowboy thing, you know. They're so used to taking care of their livestock, they try to take care of everybody."

That was true. Tom was always trying to take care of me; along with anybody else who needed help. Volunteer firefighter, trained as a first responder... maybe it *was* just a cowboy thing.

Which brought me back to my original question.

"And why has he suddenly decided that you need taking care of?" I growled.

"She had threatening phone calls," Tom said. "And she asked at the Chamber of Commerce meeting if any of us were receiving them. We weren't. It was only her."

"Not really threatening..." Lola began.

"The caller said 'you'd better watch out'," Tom said. "That's threatening."

"Maybe it was just a concerned citizen reminding me to be careful on the ice..." Lola began lightly, but I overrode her, my guts twisting into a cold lump.

"When did you get the call? Was it a man or a woman? Have you had any more? Have you seen anybody hanging around that you don't recognize?"

"Aydan!" Lola threw up her hands. "Heavens, relax! There was only one call, and it's been so icy outside the back door of the shop. It was probably just a delivery man who slipped and wanted to warn me..."

She chattered on, but I barely heard her.

Lola had been one of my first clients. Everybody knew we were friends. And I had hugged her in the Melted Spoon.

They know how to get to Kelly...

"You said 'delivery man'. So it was a man? When was the call?" I demanded.

"Yes, it was a man, but I didn't recognize his voice. And it was Monday morning," she confessed. "But-"

"And you didn't *tell me?*"

Her brow furrowed. "Honey, I own a sex shop. I get all kinds of weird calls." She grinned. "And that's not counting the ones that come through the 900 number."

I pressed my fingertips to my suddenly-aching forehead. "Thanks for looking out for her, Tom. Somebody obviously needs to."

"Hey," Lola said indignantly. "I'm still here in the room, you know. And I'm a tough old bird. It takes more than a phone call to scare me."

Eyeing her diminutive figure, I suppressed a shudder. Tough, my ass. Those tiny delicate bones could snap like twigs...

"Shit!" I bolted upright. "Lola, the ice! Somebody's been trying to hurt you!"

CHAPTER 35

Lola frowned. "Honey, you do know it's wintertime, right? That time of the year when it snows and there's ice on the sidewalks..."

"No, there isn't," I snapped. "It's been really cold lately. Cold snow doesn't freeze to the sidewalks; you can just sweep it off. You said you've had ice outside your back door, but there's no ice anywhere else."

"There's ice all over the front step at my house, too," she protested. "It's just normal winter conditions."

All my instincts went on red alert. "Your house, too? Near the door? But not on the main sidewalk where everybody else walks?"

"It's probably just some water dripping off the eaves..." she began uncertainly.

"At twenty below? I don't think so." I lunged to my feet. "Show me."

"There's nothing to see," Lola explained patiently. "There was ice, I put salt on it, and now it's gone."

"How many times have you put salt on it during the day and then found ice again the next morning?" I demanded as I hurried to the back door and flung it open.

"I don't know; I didn't really think about it. A few days.

And it wasn't just at the back door, there were patches of ice here and there at the front and back, so I'm sure it's just natural." She joined me at the door. "See? There's no ice, and you can see where the salt was." She indicated the white crystalline residue.

"Yeah, and there's no way ice would form there again," I growled. "Not unless somebody rinsed the salt away first."

"Aydan's right, Lola," Tom agreed from over my shoulder. "You should take this seriously." He regarded her stiletto heels. "And you should wear some boots with better traction."

"Well, I'm not going to call the police just because I have ice on my sidewalk," Lola said firmly. "Thank you both for your concern, but I really think you're blowing this out of proportion."

Tom and I exchanged a glance. "Okay," he agreed with a sigh. "But be careful. And I'll be here every Tuesday to escort you to the bank, just in case."

"You're a sweetheart," Lola assured him.

I gave Lola my best 'don't mess with me' look. "And I want you to promise that if you get any more phone calls, or any more ice, or anything at all that just seems out of the ordinary, you'll call me right away."

"Honestly, Aydan, there's nothing you can do," she argued. "You can't keep my phone from ringing or the sky from snowing."

"No, but I still want to know what's going on. I might not be able to stop it, but at least I'll know what to tell the police if something happens." When she hesitated, I gave her a meaningful glare. "You do still remember the time you got kidnapped by that weird religious cult, right?"

Lola sighed. "Okay, I promise I'll let you know if

anything else happens."

"Let me know, too," Tom put in.

"Okay," she agreed meekly. Turning back to me, she added, "Aydan, do you mind manning the counter while we're at the bank?"

"Sure. If anybody asks me questions about the merchandise I'll tell them you'll be back in a few minutes."

"Thanks, honey."

"No problem. And thanks, Tom," I added quietly as they turned to go. He gave me a nod and a look that said we'd be talking later, and they left.

I accomplished very little bookkeeping in the twenty minutes they were gone. My mind whirled with anger and fear. Who was next? Spider? Linda and her precious unborn baby? They were the only close friends I had left in Silverside who hadn't been targeted. Yet.

And what if my unknown enemy decided to work his way down my list of co-workers? Like Jack and her two young children?

Or what about my other clients? Like Jeff and Donna Latchford, the young couple who ran the Greenhorn Café? They were hard workers, but neither of them could defend themselves against anything more than a strong wind.

My mind ticked over my other clients, all vulnerable.

I had to stop this maniac before the threats turned into something more deadly. And they would. My unknown enemy was just taking his time to make a point; and soon I'd get a demand.

God, please don't let it be accompanied by a friend's severed finger. Or worse.

I shuddered. No, dammit, I wouldn't let that happen.

The jingle of the bell over the shop door brought me to

my feet, but Lola's cheerful call had me sinking back into my chair. "It's just me. Thanks for holding the fort, Aydan!"

"No problem," I mumbled, returning to my train of thought.

This asshole had made a big mistake by targeting Lola regularly. Tonight I'd be here waiting for him. And when I caught him...

"Honey, if I were that computer, I'd be shaking in my boots," Lola teased from the doorway. "What's wrong? Are you having problems with the program?"

"Um. No." I rubbed the frown wrinkles out of my forehead with the heel of my hand. "Just concentrating."

She didn't need to know about my plans. She had already suffered an attack once because of me, but this time I'd eliminate the threat before...

"Aydan." Lola let out a nervous laugh. "Now you're scowling at me. And seriously, if I didn't know you, I'd run the other way."

I yanked myself back to the present and forced a laugh. "Sorry. Dark thoughts about your point-of-sale program."

She relaxed into a smile. "That's the only kind I ever have about it. It's been so much better since you overhauled it, but it still drives me crazy."

"I'll have another go at it," I promised. "But I'd better get back to your bookkeeping. Arnie's going to be here in about an hour, and then I won't get anything else done."

Lola's larger-than-life laugh rolled out. "Well, honey, as long as you get him done, that's what's important."

"You're incorrigible." Grinning in spite of myself, I went back to work.

Promptly at two-thirty the bell over the door jingled wildly and Hellhound's voice said, "Ow. Shit."

I poked my head around the corner in time to catch him rubbing his forehead while Lola fluttered around him in concern.

"No offense, Miz Lola," he said. "But that bell's only safe for midgets."

"Oh, I don't know," she deadpanned. "I've never had a problem with it." He chuckled, and she tugged his sleeve, serious again. "I hope you didn't hurt yourself badly. Bend down so I can see."

"I'm fine. Just buggin' ya." He looked up with a smile. "Hey, darlin'."

"Hi." I hurried over to collect a hug and kiss. Then I inspected his forehead. "Well, Lola, I don't think you need to worry about a lawsuit."

"Whew, that's a relief." She gave Hellhound her flirtatious grin. "How about a discount to make up for your pain and suffering?"

"Now you're talkin'." He dropped another kiss on my lips before turning me around and nudging me back toward the office. "Get back to work, darlin', an' no peekin'. Christmas is comin', an' I got shoppin' to do."

"Oooh! See, I told you I liked him," Lola purred. "Come on, Arnie, let me give you the grand tour."

I resumed my seat at the computer, half embarrassed by Lola's prurient interest and half turned on by the thought of the gifts to come. Or more to the point, the gifts that would make me come.

Damn, Arnie was mind-blowing in bed without any external aid. Toys couldn't possibly make sex with him any better.

Could they?

A hot shiver hurried down my spine and my breath

shortened.

Even straining my ears, I couldn't quite make out the words in Arnie's teasing rumble and Lola's giggles. I tried to map the store in my mind and figure out what they might be discussing, but that only sent me on a fantasy tour that resulted in three wrong bookkeeping entries in a row.

Squirming in my suddenly-hot chair, I corrected them only to make more.

Dammit, I was horny as hell.

Twenty long minutes later, Hellhound's sexy rasp raised the small hairs on the back of my neck. "Hey, darlin'. Ya gonna pack up pretty soon? We oughta head out if we're gonna make it to Kane's for three."

"Yep, I'm ready to go." I shut down the computer and emerged from the office, glancing innocently at the bag in his hand.

He sang softly, "Santa's comin'..." Then he winked at Lola and added, "But I'm glad I ain't Santa."

"Why?" she asked. "You'd make a great Santa. You could powder your beard white..."

He grinned and delivered the old joke. "'Cause Santa only gets to come once a year."

"Oooh, Lordy!" Lola threw up her hands, laughing. "I can't believe I fell for that!"

A few minutes later, I followed Hellhound's Forester around the corner and parked in front of Kane's house. As I trudged to the door, my mind ticked over the possibilities. This wasn't just a social invitation, I was sure of it.

Was Kane hoping Daniel and I would bond? I suppressed a shudder.

Or maybe...

The door swung open, interrupting my guessing game.

"Come in," Kane said with a smile. As we stepped onto the mat he swung the door shut behind us and retreated, adding, "I'm reasonably certain we're past the contagious stage, but I won't get too close just in case. I wouldn't wish that experience on my worst enemy."

Kicking off my boots, I surveyed the cozy domestic scene. A box of toys peeked around the corner of the sofa and Daniel sat on the rug by the coffee table, murmuring to himself while he manipulated a small army of toy soldiers.

Kane waved us in, and Hellhound and I crossed the room to sit together on the sofa.

Shit, this was awkward.

Pasting on a bright smile, I said, "Well, this is a much happier scene than Sunday."

Kane smiled and sank into the armchair across from us. "It certainly is. We got through it together, didn't we, Daniel?" He ruffled Daniel's hair.

"Uh-huh!" Daniel leaned back against Kane's legs, beaming up adoringly. "Like soldiers!"

"Well, that's great," I said too heartily. "I'm glad you're both feeling better."

What were we doing here? What did he want?

"Would you like a drink?" Kane inquired.

"No, thanks, I'm driving." I shifted uncomfortably, wondering how soon I could leave without looking rude. "And I'm actually supposed to be picking up Nora in a few minutes," I added. "It won't be a big deal if I'm a bit late, but I can't stay too long. Sorry."

"That's all right; I know how busy you are, and I'm glad you could drop in even for a few minutes." Kane smiled, but he looked uncomfortable, too. "Actually..." He hesitated. "I have something to tell you."

Uh-oh.

Leaning forward, I faked a smile. "Well, don't keep us in suspense. What's up?"

"I've made..." Kane hesitated again. "...a major decision."

My belly went cold. If it was good news, he'd have just said it.

Shit, shit, shit...

"I'm going to sell this house," Kane said. "And give up the office space I've been sharing with Webb here in Silverside. I've been watching the housing market in Calgary for a couple of months, and this latest episode with Alicia has made up my mind. My realtor called me yesterday about a house that came up for sale on the same block as Alicia's." He squared his shoulders. "I put in an offer this morning, and the seller has to respond by six o'clock. I'm hoping to close the deal tonight."

My throat froze shut.

Fortunately Hellhound spoke. "That's a helluva big decision, Cap. What's the story?"

"I've done a lot of soul-searching in the past four months." Kane smiled down at Daniel, who leaned his head against Kane's knee. Kane's hand drifted down to caress the boy's hair as he went on, "Alicia and I both agree that Daniel is the most important thing in the world to us, but we also agree that we can't live together. And I'm not willing to be a part-time dad. I've missed nearly seven years of Daniel's life, and I refuse to miss any more."

"I wish you could keep living with us, Daddy," Daniel said, his lip quivering.

"I wish I could live with you fulltime, too," Kane said. "But your Mommy and I both have our own lives; and you remember that when I moved in a few months ago, I told you it wouldn't be forever. I'll live a few houses away, and we can see each other anytime we want. Sometimes you'll live with me, and sometimes you'll live with Mommy."

Daniel buried his face in Kane's pant leg, but didn't raise an outcry. Which was good, because I was freaking out enough for both of us.

With a supreme effort I kept my expression neutral. "So I guess that job offer we discussed is a no-go."

"I'm afraid so." Kane gave me a bittersweet smile. "At least I know that's no surprise to you."

"No, it's not." I was proud that my voice came out dead level.

No surprise. No good news, either. His choice might cost my freedom.

"I'm sorry for the timing," he added. "If the house in Calgary had come up for sale just a few days sooner, the whole thing could have been a non-issue. As it is, you'll just have to tell Stemp that I had already made this decision before you had a chance to talk to me about the Department's offer."

"It's no big deal," I lied. "If it's the right decision for you and Daniel, that's all that matters. Will you be selling your condo in Calgary, too?"

"I never owned it in the first place. The Department has given me three months' notice to vacate, so the timing for this move is good all around."

"Well, that's great, then." Somehow I managed to keep my voice from cracking. "Congratulations on your decision. It's a big step, but I'm sure it's the right choice for you."

God, I had to get out of here.

I stood, forcing a smile onto my face. "I'm sorry I can't stay any longer. I'll keep my fingers crossed for your house deal. Let me know if you get it, okay?"

"I will." Kane rose, too, and trailed me to the door. "You'll be invited to the housewarming party."

Somehow my chuckle came out sounding normal. "I'd better be! Have a safe trip home."

"Thank you. Oh, and before you go... will you be near Calgary in the next few days? Dad is flying in tonight and I know he'll want to see you. You're welcome to stay at my condo, and we'd all..." He included Arnie in his gesture of inclusion. "...be delighted if you could join us for Christmas dinner."

"Um... I... don't have a clue what's going to happen in the next few days..."

Except potential death in Holt's sting and incarceration if Dermott found out I'd failed here.

"...so I'll have to give you a call," I finished, keeping my tone carefully casual. "I hope I'll be able to get down to Calgary for a short visit at least."

"Don't stress over it," Kane said. "We all understand that you can't control your schedule." He gave me an uncertain look and held out his arms. "Do you dare risk a hug with a former germ factory?"

"Sure." I stepped in and hugged him, but I kept my face from touching his T-shirt just in case. The stomach flu would be the final shitty touch to this thoroughly craptastic week.

And it was only Tuesday. The worst part of my week was still to come.

Fuck.

CHAPTER 36

When I pulled up in front of the Silverside Hotel, there was no sign of Nora. After waiting a few minutes, I blew out a breath and drove around to park in their lot.

She wasn't waiting in the lobby, either. Poking my head into the restaurant and sports bar awarded me nothing more than an instant headache as the too-loud commentator bellowed hockey play-by-plays from the big screen.

Irritation and anxiety nibbled at the edges of my mind. Was she playing head games, punishing me for being ten minutes late? Or had something happened to her?

I'd been seen with her frequently. What if my unknown enemy had decided to abduct her? What if this was the culmination of his threats?

My heart thudded faster than necessary as I hurried down the hall toward Room 106. Shit, even though she'd tied my emotions in a knot, she was still my mother.

And double-shit, she was still MI5's Weapons Director. And Ian was stuck in the hospital. If she was harmed on my watch, I'd be in deep shit.

My knock on her door was more like urgent pounding.

"Just wait a moment!"

Her testy response relieved one set of my worries only to

supplant them with another. She was angry because I was late, and now I'd have to suffer through her punishment.

I sighed. I had been hoping we could just have a normal pleasant conversation.

Hell, I'd settle for a weird stilted conversation as long as it was non-confrontational...

The door jerked open and Nora frowned at me, her phone held to her ear. "Come in," she snapped, and turned her back on me to hurry over to the small writing desk near the window.

Mentally bracing myself, I came in and sat down.

"And that's the best you can do?" Nora said to her caller. "There's absolutely nothing else?" She listened for a moment, then hissed out a breath. "That's simply too much. Surely under the circumstances you can find it in your heart to reduce the price. She's my *daughter*, for heaven's sake!"

What the hell?

Nora's chin came up, her jaw clenching in the familiar posture that said she'd had enough. "As I explained to you earlier," she said icily, "That is not possible. I have-"

Apparently the person on the other end of the call had had enough, too. Nora listened for a few more moments, an angry flush rising on her cheeks.

"Oh, fine, then!" she snapped. "I'll take the flight that leaves at two PM. You have my information." She slapped the receiver back into the cradle and glared out the window for a moment, her shoulders rigid.

I was pretty sure I wouldn't like the answer, but...

"What was that about?" I asked cautiously.

Nora blew an angry breath through her nose and turned to face me, arms crossed. "I'm going home tomorrow. My flight leaves at two PM so I'll need to be at the Calgary airport by eleven. I suppose you'll be too busy to drive me, so tell your Director to arrange my transportation."

I had thought I'd prepared myself for anything, but her words hit me like that long-ago slap in the face. For a frozen second I could only blink at her through the shock of pain.

I'm ten lousy minutes late, and she stomps out of my life like a toddler in a tantrum.

The fear struck a moment later. If she left now, Dermott would bury me.

She'd shattered my life thirty years ago, and now she was destroying the rest of it.

I lunged to my feet. Too enraged to form words, my mouth opened, closed, then opened again soundlessly.

Nora's eyes widened. "Oh, Dani-dear, I'm sorry! I didn't mean that the way it came out. It's just that I've had some terrible news from home and I wasn't..." She laid a gentle hand on my fist. "I'm sorry."

I dropped back into the chair. "Wh- What happened?" I croaked.

Nora sat on the bed across from me. "I've just found out that a young woman who works for Sirius UK has fallen into a coma."

"Your *daughter*?" I demanded. "Do I have a half-sister? When were you planning to drop that on me?"

"What? Oh. No, of course not." Nora waved that away with an impatient hand. "She's not really my daughter. I was only trying to get them to reduce the price of the ticket. They want a thousand dollars more than what I'd already paid for my return ticket, can you imagine it? But they wouldn't give me the compassionate fare reduction unless I could produce a birth certificate..." She frowned into space for a moment. "...well, that should be easy enough. I'll make up some documents and apply for the discount after I get home."

"You're going to forge a birth certificate?" I eyed her with disgust.

"Oh, don't be so self-righteous. I'm sure you have several fake IDs."

I couldn't argue with that. I changed the subject. "So if she's just somebody who works for Sirius, why are you rushing home? If she's in a coma there's nothing you can do anyway."

Her face softened. "Dani-dear, are you jealous?"

I bit off my instinctive denial. This could work for me.

Letting my gaze waver, I mumbled, "A bit, I guess. You've been telling me how much you love me and how important I am to you, and then you rush off to be with some stranger instead."

"Oh, my dearest. I do love you and you are important to me. But she's not a stranger. She's..." Nora hesitated. "I don't want to hurt your feelings, but she's... Rebecca was a surrogate daughter to me at a time when I was missing you so terribly. She's a wonderful girl... well, a grown woman, of course; she's the same age as you..."

She fell silent, her eyes going distant as though gazing back in time. Then she smiled and leaned forward to touch my hand. "She was never a substitute for you, of course; but she was far away from her parents for the first time in her life, and I was missing you so much. We eased each other's loneliness, and we've grown quite close over the years."

"Nearly thirty years," I pointed out, my heart aching despite my effort to stay detached. "Almost twice as long as you were my mother."

"Oh, Dani-dear, I've always been your mother. I always

will be."

And that wasn't necessarily a blessing.

I didn't say that out loud.

"So you said she's in a coma," I prompted. "What happened? Was she in an accident?"

"No, that's what makes it so awful. She seemed perfectly well, and then she collapsed. I only found out today because I had asked her to send me some financial archives to prove to the courts that all of the income from Sirius Canada was legitimate. Rebecca is usually so prompt, so when I hadn't heard from her I called the office and found out..." Her voice choked off. "This is terrible. I must get back."

I hesitated. Had Sam told Nora that I sometimes lapsed into a coma when I was spying in the internet? Had Nora's momentary gaze into space been a memory of good times with Rebecca, or a realization that Rebecca was actually a mage like me?

If Nora was only cultivating me in the hope of profiting from my abilities, right about now she'd be realizing that her sweet pseudo-daughter Rebecca would be a whole lot easier to manipulate than stubborn, bitter me.

Shit, I had less than a day to make her talk. If she went back to the UK, I was doomed.

"I'm sorry about Rebecca," I said with more sincerity than she'd ever know. "You said she worked for Sirius. Is she a scientist?"

"No, she was Sam's personal assistant. He hired her when she was only eighteen on a very generous contract..." Another hesitation.

Right there. If Nora hadn't known the truth before, she realized it now.

She gave me a small self-deprecating smile. "Of course,

you can imagine what I thought at first. I had moved to the UK while Sam stayed here; and I waited and waited, wondering whether I'd made a terrible mistake in trusting him. And then he finally arrived months later, bringing this beautiful young protégé with him. It took a long time before I truly believed that there was nothing between them but a business relationship." She sighed. "But that's all it was. Sam was an honourable man."

Except when he was trading international secrets or seducing another man's wife.

I didn't say that out loud, either.

"That must have been a terrible time for you," I said instead. "Stuck out in the sticks, alone in a strange country. Is that when you decided to start your own career?"

"Yes. And when Sam finally arrived, he encouraged me." Nora's smile was fond. "He could have insisted that I work with Sirius, but he wanted me to fly as high as my heart desired. He's the one who suggested that I apply to MI5."

That made sense. Having Nora planted in MI5 would have provided him with another source of secrets. But had she known his intentions at the time?

"I still can't believe you made it all the way to the top," I said admiringly. "What an achievement! You were only a few years younger than I am now when you started. To me, the thought of starting a whole new career at my age is just... revolting."

"But yet, that's what you've done," Nora countered. "You only became an agent last year."

I didn't bother to point out that it hadn't been my choice.

"I guess you're right," I agreed. "But I'm hoping I won't have to do it for long. You must really love your work to stick with it past the usual retirement age."

"I do love it, but I would have liked to have retired by now." Nora sighed. "Just a couple more years, and I can finally get my pension and quit."

Aha.

"Why do you have to keep working?" I asked innocently. "I thought there was some kind of magic number for pensions; your years of service plus your age or something. If you've been working for MI5 for nearly thirty years, surely you must qualify for a pension by now."

"Yes, I qualified years ago; but the benefit calculation considers your salary at the time of retirement. And you have to be employed at that salary level for at least two years." She grimaced. "It's to prevent people from getting a promotion and then quitting immediately. In order to get the pension amount I need, I have to keep working. Damn Howard Coleman! Without him, I could have retired years ago."

Play dumb. Keep her talking.

"Who's Howard Coleman?"

Nora scowled. "The former Weapons Director. He was only six years older than I, and if he'd retired at sixty-five like a normal person, I could have taken over the Directorship at age fifty-nine and retired at sixty-five myself. Instead, he stayed on, and on, and ON! Thank heaven he's dead." She recovered herself with a small headshake. "I know that's a terrible thing to say; but that old goat singlehandedly blocked my career for nearly *thirteen years!*"

"I'd have been ready to kill him myself," I said.

She gave a short laugh but didn't fall into my trap. "With your temper? You would have done him in after thirteen months."

I had heard Coleman described as a curmudgeon, but

Reggie had liked him. And he had been a dedicated man who hadn't deserved to be murdered.

Especially not by a self-centred bitch like my mother.

"So how did you do it?" I asked flatly.

Nora gave me a blank look. "Do what?"

"Kill Howard Coleman."

Her back stiffened. "Young lady, did you just accuse me of murder?"

I let out an incredulous laugh. "Jeez, I was only joking! Now that I'm an agent, everybody else seems to have lost their sense of humour." I sighed. "Remember the days when you could say, 'I could just kill him' and nobody thought twice about it?"

Nora's laughter sounded forced. "I suppose you're right. But things were different then."

I *was* right. If she didn't have a guilty conscience, why had she taken me so seriously? Wouldn't an innocent person just laugh it off?

Nora stood decisively. "Let's go to the Melted Spoon. I need caffeine, and I've had enough of this hotel room."

Enough of our conversation, more likely.

"Okay." I was rising from the chair when my cell phone rang. "Sorry, I have to take this," I added, and accepted the call.

Lola's hesitant voice made my stomach plunge. "Hi, Aydan. I got another phone call. It wasn't really threatening, but you said you wanted to know."

"The same guy? What did he say?" I demanded.

"I don't know if it was the same man. He just said to be careful."

"What were his exact words?"

"He said 'Be careful. We wouldn't want anything to

happen to you.' I'm still not convinced he's threatening me-"

"Stay in the shop," I snapped. "Put up the 'closed' sign, lock the doors, and draw the blinds. I'll be there in a few minutes. And call Tom."

"But, Aydan..."

"Do it now, Lola!" My voice snapped out like a whip.

"O-Okay..."

"See you in few minutes. Don't open the door for anybody but me. Call Tom," I repeated, and disconnected.

"What...?" Nora began.

"I have to go. Somebody's threatening Lola."

"But I'm your mother..."

I let the door slam on her words.

CHAPTER 37

Sprinting down the corridor of the Silverside Hotel, I punched the speed dial for Hellhound's cell.

"Hey, darlin'," he began. "How ya-"

"Get to Lola's shop, now!" My words came out jerky from running. "Secure the perimeter!"

"On my way."

No questions, no arguments. He was worth his weight in gold.

I rocketed through the lobby and stiff-armed the door open, nearly bowling over a couple who were approaching the hotel.

Less than five minutes later I slammed on the brakes at Lola's shop. As soon as my car slid to halt at the curb I punched Hellhound's speed dial, sprang out, and raced for the front door.

"Status?" I barked when he picked up on the first ring.

"Secure. Rossburn's got the front; I've got the back."

I spotted Tom as Hellhound spoke, and I slowed and let out a breath. "Okay, thanks. Stay in place. I'm going in the front." I disconnected as Tom strode up.

"What's happening?" he demanded. "Helmand met me here and told me to watch the front door but not to go near the building. He made it sound like some kind of military operation. Is he..." He hesitated and made a tentative rotation of his finger at his temple. "...okay?"

I forced a chuckle. "He's fine. He spent a lot of years in the army, so it's just reflex for him to secure a building like that. So Lola called you?"

Tom's shoulders relaxed. "Oh, I didn't realize he'd had military training. Yes, Lola called me and said she'd had another threatening phone call and that you'd told her to lock the doors and stay inside, and not to open up to anyone but you. I was down at the fire hall, so I was able to get here fast."

"Good. Thanks for coming." I took a deep breath, trying to slow my pulse. "I'm just going to call and make sure she's okay in there and then I want to talk to you."

He nodded, and I dialled Lola's number.

When she answered, I said, "It's Aydan. Are you okay?"

Her deep chuckle rolled out. "Of course I'm okay, honey; I have a bathroom, a lunchroom with food in the fridge, and all the mechanical boyfriends I could ask for. The worst thing that could happen to me in here would be running out of lube."

I laughed. "That's 'way too much information, but I'm glad you're okay. Just hang tight. I'll be there to get you in a few minutes."

When I hung up, Tom asked, "You really think she's in danger, don't you?"

"I don't know, but I don't want to take a chance."

"Do you think it's those religious extremists again?" Tom's frown deepened. "We should call the police. The last time those freaks came after her, they were serious enough to kidnap her and tie her to a bomb."

"You're right," I agreed, grateful that the cover story for Lola's abduction was still intact. "I know the police can't do anything unless a crime has actually been committed, but at least if we file a report about the phone calls we'll be justified if we have to take desperate measures."

"Not so fast." Tom shook his head. "There's no 'we'. I don't want you in any danger, and I'm sure Helmand doesn't, either. You and Lola lie low, and let us take care of this."

Biting back the urge to tell him exactly how misguided he was, I said, "You're forgetting that you've been targeted, too. I haven't." He shook his head again and began to speak, but I kept talking over him. "And I have to go out of town on business, so I can't stay with Lola. She doesn't know Arnie very well so I think she'd be more comfortable with you guarding her."

Putting two potential victims in one place might not be ideal, but at least if Tom took the threats against Lola seriously, he'd be better equipped to handle anything that came his way, too.

I gave him my best imploring look. "Could you please stay with her tonight? Or could she stay at your place?"

"I need to get home and see to my livestock, but she'd be welcome to stay out at the farm..."

"That would be great," I said before he could add any conditions. "Arnie will watch her house and the store, and you can call him for backup if you need it."

Tom laughed. "I have a shotgun. I won't need backup."

If only I could believe that.

I fluttered my helpless bookkeeper's eyelashes up at him and cooed, "Thanks, that makes me feel so much better! I'm going to go and get Lola now."

Hurrying away before he could object, I gave thanks for

his stubborn cowboy chivalry. Lola would be as safe as I could make her without actually blowing my cover.

After considerable arguing, the three of us finally convinced Lola to cooperate with our plan, and Tom's big half-ton carried her safely away.

"So, we're gonna stake out her house an' the store tonight?" Hellhound inquired.

"Yes. If anybody was hanging around the store earlier, they've probably been scared away by all this activity; but that's fine. It'll give me a chance to install a couple of cameras. We can monitor them remotely, nice and warm in our vehicles." I slid an arm around him. "Thanks for dropping everything again."

"No problem. I was just hangin' at Eddy's." Hellhound grinned. "Lucky I left my guitar behind so they'll know I didn't dine an' dash."

"Eddy and Darlene would know that anyway, but they're probably worrying because you ran out so fast." I reached up to kiss him. "I'll go and get the cameras and put them in place, and then I'll meet you at Eddy's and give you the monitor." I grimaced. "I ran out on Nora so she's probably pissed at me. I'll have to go back and suck up. Maybe I'll take her out for dinner."

"Fuck her," Hellhound growled.

I sighed. "I can't. She's my mother. And I'm going to be in deep shit with Dermott if I can't get her talking tonight..."

Fear shivered my bones. Don't think about that.

"Good thing she loves to talk about herself," I added. "At least I don't have to waste a bunch of effort deciding what to tell her about my life."

His arms came around me. "You'd think she'd at least pretend to give a shit."

Burrowing into the comfort of his embrace, I mumbled, "If she's trying to influence me, shouldn't she be all lovey-dovey? And if she's making it so obvious that she's not that interested in me, does that mean she *isn't* a criminal? Or does it just mean that she's smart enough to know that falling all over me won't work so she's trying to suck me in by making me work for her approval?"

"I dunno, darlin'." Arnie pressed a whiskery kiss to my forehead. "Far's I can see, it just means she's a shitty mother."

I kissed him again, feeling unaccountably better. "Thanks. I'll see you at Eddy's in a few minutes."

Driving back to Sirius Dynamics, I had time to consider the consequences of running out on Nora.

Dammit, if she'd called Sirius again, I'd be in even deeper shit. I had abandoned my mission for a personal matter that wasn't even a demonstrable emergency; and now Dermott would think it was my fault that Nora was leaving.

Hell, if he found out I'd fucked up both my missions, I'd be locked up for the rest of my life.

Sliding to a halt in the Sirius parking lot, I yanked out my cell phone. Maybe it wasn't too late. Maybe Nora hadn't called Dermott yet.

I punched in her number.

"Yes?" Her voice was cool.

"Hi, it's Aydan." I tried not to sound too ingratiating. "I'm sorry I had to run out on you like that. I have to go to the office for a while, but I'd like to take you to dinner afterward. I could pick you up around five-thirty."

"Don't bother," she snapped. "I wouldn't want to inconvenience you."

The last of my stale adrenaline combusted into fury. I tried to hold my tongue.

I really tried.

Fuck it, I was doomed anyway.

"Listen," I grated. "I'm sorry you don't like it, but this is my job. If you'd given me more than ten seconds warning before you showed up, maybe I could have arranged it so I had more time for you. As it is, I'm damn well doing the best I can. So you can quit the drama-queen head games and make the most of the time we have left together, or you can keep pissing and moaning and playing the martyr and I'll say goodbye right now; and good fucking riddance. Your choice. You have ten seconds to decide."

"Now you listen here, young lady," she began.

"Nine!" I barked.

"I am your mother and you can..."

"Eight!"

"...treat me with respect!"

"Seven!"

"You will not use that tone with me..."

"Six!"

"You owe me an apology!"

"Three!"

"*What?* You skipped five and four!"

"Two!"

Silence.

My pulse hammered in my ears. "One!"

"Let's go out for dinner," Nora said hurriedly.

"I'll pick you up at five-thirty." I disconnected and

collapsed in my seat, sucking in gusts of air and waiting for my heart rate to stabilize.

Score one for me. So either she wanted something from me; or she loved me. I was banking on the former, but my idiot heart gave a little skip of hope nonetheless.

"Don't get excited," I growled, and got out of the car.

A few minutes later I hurried past Dermott's open door with every nerve on alert, but he didn't stop me. Nora hadn't called him. Whew.

But I still had to tell him she was leaving tomorrow. That would go over like a fart in a spacesuit.

I'd tell him later.

Scooting into my office, I filed a quick report outlining the events to date and my worries that someone was targeting my friends in an attempt to gain leverage over me; or possibly Arlene Widdenback. I kept a wary eye on the doorway, but Dermott didn't walk by. Hurrying out, I ducked into Stores, grabbed the camera gear, and fled.

When I walked into Blue Eddy's, the warmth and music wrapped around me like a hug and my stomach growled in a Pavlovian response.

Fighting off an almost-irresistible hunger for hot chicken wings, I made a beeline for my usual table where Hellhound and Eddy sat with their heads together. Hellhound's clever fingers danced over the strings of his guitar while Eddy nodded in time. Then Hellhound stopped playing and they conferred for a moment before repeating the process.

"Hi guys," I said as I slid into a chair across from them, acutely aware that my back was exposed to the rest of the bar.

"Hey, darlin'," Hellhound greeted me. "Ya ready to go?"

"What, no dinner?" Eddy gave me an incredulous look.

"Are you feeling okay?"

"I want hot wings so badly I'm nearly drooling on your table." I mimed wiping my chin. "But I can't have any," I added hurriedly as he jumped up. "I'm taking my mother out for dinner in less than an hour."

"I hope you're bringing her here." He smiled. "I'd love to meet her."

Shit. Nora would hate Eddy's. And I needed to talk to her without worrying about Eddy overhearing us as he came and went from our table with his usual attentiveness.

"I'm sorry, I didn't mean to pressure you," Eddy added quickly. "I'm sure you have plans already." He was still smiling his usual warm smile, but I saw a flash of hurt in his eyes.

Oh, God. I couldn't hurt big-hearted Eddy.

"I'd love to bring her here," I blurted. "I was just... I'm kind of... messed up about the whole thing. It's complicated."

Concern furrowed his forehead as he pulled up a chair beside me. "How can I help?"

I sighed. "I wish you could help, but I'm just going to have to muddle through on my own." I hesitated. I hadn't told him anything about Nora, but he *was* a bartender in a small town. "Have you heard any gossip about her?"

Eddy nodded. "I heard she'd faked her death and taken off with another man when you were only seventeen; and now she's back with some crazy story about being in witness protection for the last thirty years."

I winced. "That about covers it. And you still want to meet her?"

"I listen to gossip, but I never believe it." Eddy met my gaze squarely. "I form my own judgements of people when I meet them, and not before."

Relaxing in my chair, I looked into his clear honest eyes and smiled. "Well, in that case, your professional opinion of Nora would mean a lot to me. We'll be here around five-thirty."

"I'll reserve your table." He rose with a smile, patted me on the shoulder, and headed for the bar.

"Sure that's a good idea?" Hellhound asked when Eddy was out of earshot.

"Nope." I blew out a breath. "It could turn out to be the dumbest thing I've done in a long time; or it might help. Eddy's a great judge of character; and like you said earlier, Nora's got me so twisted up that I can't tell my ass from my elbow."

"She's a mind-fuckin' bitch," Hellhound growled. "Ya don't need Eddy to tell ya that."

"You haven't even met her." My voice came out sharper than I'd intended.

"An' I don't wanna." He scowled. "Eddy says he judges people when he meets 'em; well, I judge 'em by what they do. Last week that bitch lied to ya just 'cause she fuckin' felt like it. She didn't give a shit that it put ya through hell; an' she never fuckin' apologized for it, did she?"

I picked at a ragged cuticle, pretending absorption.

Hellhound's voice softened. "I know she's your mother an' ya wanna give her the benefit a' the doubt, but ya been programmed all your life to make excuses for people even when they treat ya like shit. I'm just sayin' ya need some perspective."

"I know, but..." I shook my head and tried again. "I..." Hissing out a breath, I knotted my fists in my hair. "Fuck it, I can't handle this right now. It doesn't matter anyway. It's my job to find out whether she's a criminal, and the only way I'm going to do that is by spending more time with her." I stood. "I'm going to go and install those cameras, and then pick up Nora."

Hellhound sighed and rose. "I'll come with ya an' set up for the stakeout."

CHAPTER 38

An hour later Nora stopped a few paces into Blue Eddy's, her lip curling. "This isn't my kind of place. Let's go somewhere else."

Eddy was already hurrying over, smiling.

"Tough," I muttered. "It's my kind of place, and we have a reservation. I'm staying. If you want to walk back to the hotel, feel free."

"That is so inconsiderate..." Nora began.

"This is my friend Eddy Carlson," I said firmly as he arrived. "And Eddy, this is my mother, Nora Taylor."

"Mrs. Taylor." Eddy gave her his friendly, open smile and a polite half-bow. "What a pleasure to meet you. I can see where Aydan gets her beauty."

My face went hot.

Nora flushed, too. "Oh, my!" She smiled and leaned confidentially toward Eddy. "Flattery will get you everywhere."

He gave her a wink. "So I'm told. But it's not flattery if it's true."

"Ooh..." Nora fluttered a coquettish hand. "You're such a charming liar."

"Not at all, Mrs. Taylor. May I show you to your table?"

"Oh, yes, please." She took his proffered elbow. "And please call me Nora."

"Thank you, Nora. And I hope you'll call me Eddy." He ushered her to our table as though escorting a queen to a state dinner.

I followed, trying not to let my jaw dangle. Somehow my down-to-earth friend had transformed into a suave lady-killer.

Good God, he even pulled out Nora's chair and seated her. When he pulled out my usual chair for me and waited politely behind it, I nearly choked. Somehow I managed to keep a straight face while he seated me, too.

"Now, what can I get you ladies to drink?" he inquired. "Mrs. Taylor, do you have a favourite?"

"Oh..." She batted her eyelashes at him. "It's just Nora, please! And... I rarely imbibe, but... maybe you have a specialty...?"

"Mixing drinks is my passion," Eddy confided, his voice dropping meaningfully on the word 'passion'. "Do you like your drinks sweet or tart? Or... spicy?" He gave her a slow smile.

Oh. My. God.

Eddy. Flirting.

He was devastating.

"Oh..." Nora flushed again. "I'm afraid I don't dare try anything spicy." She batted her eyelashes some more. "Can you do something sweet, with a little tart?"

I clamped my hand over my mouth but a snicker exploded in spite of my efforts.

They both turned to me, Nora with a frown and Eddy with a devilish twinkle in his eyes.

"Aydan!" Nora said in a tone of rebuke.

I opened my mouth to apologize but laughter burst out instead. "Sorry," I gasped. "You just... You asked if he could do something sweet with a little tart. Who's the little tart?"

Eddy spun to face the bar, his shoulders shaking with suppressed laughter. Fortunately Nora was too busy glaring at me to notice.

"I'm humiliated that any daughter of mine would have such a low mind," she snapped.

Suddenly I just didn't give a shit anymore.

"Sucks to be you, then." I slouched in my chair and stretched out my legs, crossing my ankles. "Eddy, would you bring me a beer, please?"

"Of course." Somehow he managed a grave expression as he turned back to Nora. "And Mrs. Taylor..." He gave her that deferential half-bow again. "If you will honour me with your trust, I would like to create a special cocktail just for you."

Good Lord, if he didn't stop soon I was going to either gag or fall on the floor laughing. Maybe both.

"Oh, that would be lovely." Nora smiled up at him. "Please excuse Aydan's rudeness. Obviously her upbringing suffered from my absence."

Eddy gave her a serious look and leaned in. "Mrs. Taylor, Aydan is a wonderful woman with a great sense of humour. She has nothing to apologize for, and neither do you. I'm sure that when you get to know her better, you'll be proud of her."

A lump rose in my throat. "Thanks," I mumbled.

Nora gazed up at Eddy. "That's very kind of you," she said. "Thank you."

He gave her a nod and a smile and withdrew.

"What a lovely man," Nora said. "Are you dating him?"

"No."

"You should.   He's not married; I checked his ring finger."

"I'm pretty sure he has a girlfriend," I muttered.   "And anyway, I'm seeing somebody else."   Two 'somebody else's, but she didn't need to know that.

"Oh, yes, that ugly man.   Artie, was it...?"

"*Arnie*," I gritted.

She waved my reply away.   "Eddy is much better looking. And I'm sure he's nicer and more educated, too.   And a successful businessman."   She eyed our surroundings as though calculating resale values.   "He's obviously-"

Fortunately my phone rang before I could respond. "'Scuse me," I snapped.   "I have to get this."

Nora's nose lifted, but she said nothing as I punched the Talk button.

"Hi, Aydan," Eddy's familiar voice said.

As I glanced over, he gave me a wink from behind the bar and casually turned his back, his phone to his ear.

"Are you driving?" he asked.   "I could bring you a non-alcoholic beer if you'd like."

Thank goodness Eddy was watching out for me.   Getting drunk out of sheer irritation wouldn't do anything for my mission or my credibility as an agent.

I let out a breath of gratitude.   "That would be great. Thanks."

"And your mother's cocktail..."   He hesitated.   "How alcoholic should it be?"

"Very," I said fervently.

I could hear the smile in his voice.   "One very special drink, coming up!"

Stowing my phone back in my waist pouch, I faced Nora

again.

"Good news?" she asked, and I realized I'd been smiling.

"I hope so." Leaning back in my chair, I gave myself yet another attitude adjustment. Be nice. Suck up.

"So..." I began at the same time as Nora said, "Dani-dear, I'm afraid I owe you an apology."

I stared at her. "Um... okay...?"

"I've just realized that I've been terribly critical of you, and I'm sorry." She attempted a smile, but her lips wobbled. "The last time I saw you, you were only seventeen; and somehow, I... forgot that time doesn't stand still. In my heart, you're still seventeen and I've only just left you..." She stopped to compose herself, touching a delicate fingertip to the corners of her eyes. "I've dreamed of reuniting with you for so long, I built up this rose-tinted fantasy where we fell into each other's arms and picked up where we'd left off."

She sighed. "It was foolish of me; and it was even more foolish to take out my disappointment on you." Reaching toward me, she said, "I'm sorry, Aydan. Can you forgive me?"

My guts clenched. "Of course." The words were out of my mouth before I could stop them. I took her hand. "And I'm sorry I've been such a disappointment. I just... don't trust people very easily."

"And I'm sure the events of the past week haven't improved that," Nora said regretfully. "I am so sorry, Dani-dear. Can we start over?"

"I'd like that."

We were smiling at each other when Eddy arrived at the table bearing a tray. "Your beer," he said, placing the mug in front of me. "And..." With a flourish, he placed a tall frosted glass containing pink-tinged liquid in front of Nora. "A unique creation for a unique woman. I hope you'll enjoy it."

"Oh, thank you!" Nora sipped, her eyes widening in pleasure. "Oh, my, this is lovely! It tastes like..." She sipped again, closing her eyes. "...cherries and lemonade." She opened her eyes to gaze up at Eddy with admiration. "You are an artist."

Eddy smiled. "I'm glad you approve. Now, here's a menu for you, and today's special is..."

I tuned him out, studying Nora's rapt face while she listened to him.

Had her apology been sincere? Or was this just another attempt to manipulate me? Dammit, this would be so much easier if I could just hook her up to the lie detector...

"Aydan?"

Blinking back to the present, I found Eddy eyeing me inquiringly.

"Um, sorry... what did you say?" I asked.

He chuckled. "I asked if you needed a minute with the menu. I'll take that as a 'yes'."

"Oh. No, I'll have the special. It sounded great." I gave him a smile, hoping to hide the fact that I hadn't been listening.

When he hurried off to place our food order, Nora and I regarded each other over our beverages for a moment.

How could I ask her about Sam's secrets? If she didn't know anything about the darker side of the VR network, telling her about it would be a massive security breach.

Another reason to be jailed for life. How fucking many did I need?

But this was my last chance. I'd have to give away something to get something.

God, I hope I get something...

I leaned forward, lowering my voice. "Can I ask you about Sam's other mages?"

Nora took a gulp of her drink, then let out a delicate cough. Eddy must have taken my request for high alcohol content seriously.

Or was she hiding her reaction to my question?

"I'm afraid I don't know much about them," she replied, matching my quiet tone. "But I'll answer your question if I can."

Thank God. She knew about the other mages. I hadn't committed treason yet.

Hiding my relief behind a serious expression, I asked, "How much do you know about the way we get into the network?"

She hesitated. Took another drink.

Stalling.

"Is this place... secure?" she asked.

Opening my waist pouch, I activated my bug detector and tipped the pouch in her direction so she could see the green light.

"Ah." Shoulders easing, she drank again before leaning forward and speaking so quietly I could barely hear her over the music. "I know that you use tiny electronic devices. Sam called them keys. But I don't know how they work."

Truth or lie?

"Okay, good," I said. "So do you know if any of the other mages had a... reaction... to going in and out of the network?"

"What do you mean?"

"I can go in without a problem, but every time I come out I get this hellacious headache that lasts for about five minutes. It feels like my head's going to explode."

Nora's brows snapped together.

"And if I go in and out a lot..." I faltered as her knuckles whitened on her glass. "...um... is something wrong?"

"Go on," she said in a steely voice. "What happens if you go in and out a lot?"

"Um... the headaches get worse. And last longer. The more I do it, the more they run together until I have a permanent headache."

Her voice came out in a venomous hiss. "Damn him! He promised he wasn't hurting you!"

"Um... you mean Sam?" At the vicious jerk of her chin, I added, "Well, *he* wasn't hurting me; it's just the way the system works for me. So did that happen to any of the other women?"

I already knew the answer, but what would she tell me?

Sweet motherly Nora was gone, replaced by a woman who looked perfectly capable of murder. "That... *liar!* If he wasn't dead already, I'd kill him!"

CHAPTER 39

Nora took a gulp of her drink, and an instant later the dangerous light was gone from her eyes, replaced by a regretful frown.

"Oh, Dani-dear, I'm so sorry!" She reached over to squeeze my hand. "If only I had known, I would have left my job and come here to stop him!" Her voice trembled with sincerity.

Doubt seized me.

Why did this feel like the truth? Had she messed me up so much that I was actually starting to believe her lies? Or was my pain and anger finally subsiding enough for me to hear her side of the story?

Shit, what if I'd been wrong about her all this time?

"It's okay," I said cautiously. "So are you saying all the mages have headaches when they come out of the network?"

"I don't know. Sam didn't tell me much, but I know of at least one other woman who had terrible nausea. She vomited every time she came out."

I winced. "That would suck. I'll take the five minutes of pain."

"I'd rather you didn't suffer at all!" Nora snapped. "Who knows what it's doing to you? It might be damaging your brain! Damn Sam and his obsession!"

A 'ding' came from the kitchen and I spotted Eddy hurrying over to its swinging door. That was probably our food order. Nora was only half-finished her drink, but the booze should be hard at work in her empty stomach. I wouldn't get a better chance.

"Was the other mage's reaction any different if she went in with her Knight?" I asked.

Nora hiccupped, but the sound seemed delayed. As though she'd twitched first and then hiccupped to hide it.

Or had I imagined that?

"Oh, excuse me!" she exclaimed. "This drink is delicious but very strong. I'm sorry, Dani-dear, I don't understand what you're asking. Why would it matter whether it was night or day when she went in?"

Shit, she wasn't drunk enough to admit she knew about the Knights. But I hadn't really expected her to blurt out the truth. She was tipsy, not stupid.

Glancing over at Eddy emerging from the kitchen, Nora added, "Oh, look, here comes our food," and sat back with a smile that could easily be interpreted as relief by someone as suspicious as me.

As Eddy placed a gloriously sauerkraut-laden Reuben sandwich in front of me, my cell phone vibrated.

Tom's number. Shit.

"Sorry, I have to get this." I sprang up and hurried to the lobby before accepting the call.

"Hello?"

"Hi, it's Tom. Are you working late today?"

"Yes." I gripped the phone a little tighter. "Why? Is everything okay at your place?"

"Everything's fine. I was just calling because I hadn't

seen your car go by yet, and Lola made enough of her famous spaghetti and garlic bread to feed half the town. We were wondering if you'd like to come for supper."

"I wish I could, but I'm actually having dinner with..." I hesitated. He hadn't met Nora, so her name wouldn't mean anything to him. "...my, um... mom. So thanks anyway. Maybe next time."

It was his turn to hesitate. "Your mom? I thought you said..."

Forestalling the question, I broke in, "I thought she died when I was seventeen but I was wrong. Lola will explain it to you." His 'okay' sounded dubious, but before he could ask anything else I went on, "Thanks again for the invitation, and call me if anything out of the ordinary happens."

"Don't worry, everything will be fine," he reassured me with far too much confidence. "Take care, and I'll talk to you soon."

When I returned to our table Nora was looking miffed, but she gave me a smile as I sat down again. "More important business?" she inquired with a slight edge.

"Just a check-in to make sure Lola's safe." I turned my attention to my Reuben sandwich, my mouth watering.

"You said someone was threatening her?" Nora made it into a question.

"She had some worrisome phone calls, and I don't dare take a chance." I bit off a big juicy mouthful.

I had barely swallowed it when my phone vibrated again. "Sorry..." I began.

Nora gave me a look. "I know. You have to take it."

I nodded and hurried back to the lobby.

"Hey, darlin'," Hellhound's sexy rasp greeted me. "How's your dinner goin'?"

"Not bad, actually. I haven't even lost my temper yet."

He chuckled. "Good. Just wanted to let ya know I moved over to the bowlin' alley parkin' lot. Now that the stores are closed I was too easy to spot parked on the street."

"Okay, thanks. So no action on the cameras yet?"

"Nah. I figure this asshole'll wait 'til the middle a' the night before he does anythin', but I'll keep watchin' anyway. If I ain't in the Forester when ya show up, I'll be in the bowlin' alley takin' a leak. That phone app ya gave me beats the hell outta doin' stakeouts the old-fashioned way."

We said a quick goodbye and I hurried back to the table, hoping my sandwich was still warm.

As I slid into my chair again, Nora set down her almost-empty glass. "How nice of you to join me."

"Sorry. Another check-in."

Nora rolled her eyes. "Lola again? Honestly, how much danger do you really think she's in?"

"I don't know. That's why I'm not taking any chances." I wolfed down several bites of sandwich and a few cooling fries in the ensuing silence.

When I looked up, Nora was frowning.

Shit. I knew that look.

I was bracing myself for a cutting remark when Eddy hurried over.

"May I get you another drink, Mrs. Taylor?" he inquired.

"Oh, thank you, no. It was delicious but very strong." She giggled. "I feel quite... bubbly."

That wasn't the word I would have used to describe her a moment ago, but her mood seemed miraculously improved by Eddy's presence. Seizing the opportunity, I gobbled more of my meal while they bantered.

When Eddy left, I tried again. "So, when you-"

"Oh, enough about me." Nora gave me a smile, and I braced myself in half-hopeful defensiveness. Maybe she did care enough to ask about my life...

"How is Agent Rand?" she asked. "Did they get the results from his tests yet?"

Disappointment soured my stomach, intensified by guilt. I hadn't kept my promise to visit Ian. Hadn't even called the hospital to see how he was doing.

A moment later my suspicions sprang to attention. Why was she so interested in Ian's condition?

"I don't know." I gulped another mouthful of my sandwich without tasting it. "I haven't had time to check in at the hospital yet today."

"Oh." Nora finished the last bite of her meal, her unspoken disapproval hovering between us. "Maybe we can go and see him after we finish here."

"They probably aren't allowing him visitors yet."

Her eyes narrowed. "You imposed a 'no visitors' order, didn't you?"

Dammit.

I gave her my best fake honesty. "Yes, it's standard policy whenever someone with diplomatic immunity or a security clearance is hospitalized."

"Hmph." She crossed her arms. "You could have told me that yesterday."

"Sorry, but I didn't know you were going to try to visit him."

"You could have told me when we talked about it afterward."

I sighed. "You know how security regulations are. Never give out any more information than necessary."

"I suppose." Nora frowned. "So were you lying about his

condition, too?"

"No, that was true," I half-lied, and took another bite to give myself more time to think if she hit me with another question. He *had* been vomiting and he *had* been scheduled for more tests. She didn't need to know that it wasn't directly due to the severity of his injuries.

"Well, I would have thought you'd be more concerned about him, considering how close the two of you are."

"Close?" I nearly gaped at her, but at the last moment I remembered my mouthful of half-chewed sandwich. I swallowed it and went on, "Hell, no. I barely know the guy. We only met last week." I chased that lie with a mouthful of lukewarm fries.

"Oh, please, Aydan; you don't expect me to believe that, do you?" Nora gave me an affronted look. "Any fool could see the way he was looking at you."

I snorted. "Rand looks at all women that way. Some men, too, from what I've heard. If you've been around him at all, you must know that."

"I wouldn't know," she said stiffly. "We only met a few days before we left the UK, when I found out he was the agent in charge of our trip."

"And you asked him to set up a meeting with me," I prompted. "Why did you bother? If you've been keeping track of our family like you said, you must have known where I was. You could have just introduced yourself like a normal person instead of doing all the cloak-and-dagger stuff."

Her chin rose. "And that was my intention. But then I found out you were an agent..."

Had I imagined a fractional hesitation?

She went on smoothly, "...and that *fiasco* happened during the Weapons presentation, so I wasn't sure whether to trust you."

"But you-" I began, then subsided as Eddy arrived to collect Nora's empty plate and offer her coffee. When he departed, I had just opened my mouth to try again when my phone vibrated.

A glance at the call display showed a two-word text: 'Call home'. Dermott's summons.

Shit, now what?

CHAPTER 40

As I looked up from Dermott's text, Nora snapped, "Oh, don't bother apologizing. Just talk to your precious Lola."

"It's not-" I began.

"Just go." She made a shooing gesture.

"Fine." I jumped up and hurried back to the lobby.

Pulling out a secured phone, I punched the speed dial. An unfamiliar voice answered on the first ring, and I let out a breath of relief. Dermott had delegated the secured line to an analyst. Thank God. At least some good had come out of humiliating him in front of everybody.

"It's Aydan," I said. "Somebody called me?"

"Yes, the DCO wants you to come in for a briefing at twenty-one hundred."

"I'm in the middle of a mission and I don't know if I'll be able to get away then. Did he say what it's about?"

"Yes, it's a conference-call briefing with Director Stemp from overseas."

I sighed. "I'll be there." I disconnected, pitched the phone into the garbage, and headed back to the table to face Nora's wrath.

When I slid into the chair wearing my best apologetic expression, Nora looked down her nose at me. "Really,

Aydan, this is getting tiresome." She sighed. "You're right; it was unreasonable of me to think you'd be able to make time for me on such short notice." She rose and put on her coat. "I think it would be best if you took me back to my hotel room now; and you can get on with your important business."

Trying to hide the red fury searing my veins, I said, "I thought we talked about that martyr thing."

My voice came out too sharp.

"You have such a quick temper!" Her face softened. "I'm sorry, I didn't mean to sound that way. It's just that my drink was very strong and I'm feeling sleepy and a bit headachey. I want to go back to my room and lie down for a while. Why don't I call you later, after I've had a rest? Maybe that will give you an opportunity to clear your schedule."

Shit.

This was my last chance. When Dermott found out she was leaving, he'd fly off the handle. And I'd damn well better have some progress to report, or the chain of command would side with him. Fear shortened my breath. I could be in prison by tomorrow afternoon.

"I have a briefing at nine tonight and I don't know how long it'll take," I argued. "Are you sure you can't stay a little longer now?"

"Really, Dani-dear, I feel quite..." She touched her forehead delicately. "...out of sorts. But please call me when you finish your briefing, no matter how late it is. I'll be jet-lagged after my trip home tomorrow anyway, so I'm not worried about throwing off my body clock tonight. And I do very much want to spend more time with you while I can." She bent to kiss my temple. "I need some fresh air. I'll wait for you outside."

As she made her unsteady way to the exit, Eddy hurried over. "Is everything okay?"

"Fine." I sadly eyed the congealed remains of what had once been a juicy and delicious sandwich. "Could you please box this up for me? I have to take Nora back to her hotel."

"Okay..." He hesitated. "You asked for my professional opinion earlier..." He trailed off, looking troubled.

"It would mean a lot to me."

"Well..." He stared at his toes. "I don't know... I mean, I'm only a bartender. It's not like I have any training or anything, and I've been wrong before."

"Not often, I bet."

He sighed. "Often enough."

"It's okay, Eddy. I won't be upset if you're wrong." I gave him a wry smile. "Or if you're right."

He straightened, meeting my gaze. "I'm sorry, but... her body language is all over the place when she's with you. One minute she's affectionate and the next minute she's completely detached. Maybe she's just really conflicted about reuniting with you..." His voice turned thoughtful. "That would make sense if she's feeling guilty about running out on you." He squared his shoulders. "That's probably all it is. After all, you two have a lot to work through."

But he didn't sound convinced.

"Thanks, Eddy. I don't trust her, either."

"Sorry." He patted my shoulder awkwardly. "I'll go and get a box for your sandwich. Be right back."

As he strode away, realization struck me. Nora had out-manoeuvred me again. She'd stuck me with the bill.

Conniving old bag.

Our trip back to the hotel was quiet. Nora closed her

eyes, and I had more than enough worries to occupy my mind. What if she wouldn't talk to me again after my briefing tonight? That would be my last chance to get any information out of her. Tomorrow morning I'd be on my way to Calgary by eight-thirty.

As I parked at the hotel, inspiration struck.

"We're here," I said quietly. When Nora opened her eyes, I added, "By the way, I'll be taking you to Calgary tomorrow. I'll pick you up at eight, so that will get you to the airport around ten. I'm sorry it's a little earlier than you need to be there, but I have a meeting in Calgary at ten-thirty. At least we'll have a couple of extra hours together during our drive. I hope that's okay."

I held my breath. Would she go for it?

She smiled wanly. "Thank you, Dani-dear. I'm glad we'll have a bit more time together."

Somehow I managed not to release my sigh of relief. "I'll walk you to your room," I volunteered. "You didn't look too steady on your feet earlier."

"Oh, no, I'm fine." As though realizing she'd just contradicted herself, she put a hand to her temple. "Oh, my. I just had a bout of dizziness. Maybe you're right."

We both got out, and I escorted her into the hotel. As we passed the sports bar Bob Armstrong waved from within, but Nora merely waved back and made no attempt to detour inside. Not that she could have plausibly done that anyway, having just pled an alcohol-induced headache.

I made a mental note to tell the analysts to notify me immediately if she left her room...

Shit!

Analysts. Surveillance. I barely prevented myself from smacking my own forehead. I had completely forgotten about the bug I had intended to plant on Nora.

Dammit, I had let my feelings get in the way of the mission again.

But at least it wasn't too late to fix my mistake. I casually slid my hands into my pockets, peeling the backing off the tiny self-adhesive bug one-handed.

As we turned toward the corridor, I tucked my hand under Nora's elbow. "Watch your step here. There's a ripple in the carpet."

She glanced up at me, looking surprised. "Oh. Thank you. I saw it."

I nodded and let go of her elbow, but not before I'd pressed the bug into the seam of her purse.

At her door, I said, "I'll call you as soon as I can after my briefing. I hope it won't be too late."

Nora smiled and patted my cheek. "It will never be too late for you and me, Dani-dear."

Smiling back at her, I waited until she'd opened the door and stepped inside. "Have a good rest. I hope you feel better soon," I said, and turned away, listening for the sound of her door closing.

When I heard its soft click, I hurried down the corridor and out to my car, where I phoned the analyst on call and delivered my instructions to watch the surveillance camera outside Nora's door and to monitor my newly-located bug.

"Okay, we've got it," the analyst said, then added, "Hang on, she's leaving her room now."

"Already? That sneaky bitch," I muttered. "Give me the audio feed from that bug I just placed."

A moment later, rhythmic bursts of soft static accompanied the swing of Nora's purse as she walked. Then the unmistakable roar of the sports bar assaulted my ears.

She was going to see Bob Armstrong.

Heart thumping, I held my breath and waited.

"Good evening," Nora's cheerful voice said. A hell of a lot different from the wan quaver she'd affected earlier.

"Hi, Nora." Bob's hearty voice boomed through my speaker. "Pull up a chair and take a load off!"

"Oh, thank you, I'd love to; but I can't," she demurred. "I'm actually going back to my room to lie down for a bit. I had dinner with my daughter and my drink was terribly strong."

His laugh boomed out. "Gotta sleep it off, eh?"

"Yes, but I didn't want you to think I had been ignoring you when we passed."

Fuck, seriously? My big exciting lead had fizzled to my mother simply being polite?

"I hope to see my daughter again a little later," Nora went on. "It's been a difficult reconciliation, but I feel as though we're making progress."

"Glad to hear it." A chair scraped across the floor. "Well, maybe I'll see you later if you and your daughter aren't out too late. I'm going to turn in early tonight."

"Oh..." Nora hesitated. "In that case... I hate to impose, but..."

"Whatever it is, you're not imposing!" Bob let out another loud laugh. "I'm just killing time here until the Missus settles down and lets me move back home again. What can I do you for? You want a ride back to the hospital to visit your friend again?"

"Yes, but first I need to lie down for a while. But if you're going to bed early..."

"Hell, why don't you just take my car?" Keys jingled. "I'm in for the night. Just park it back in the lot when you're done, and leave the keys for me at the front desk."

"Oh, thank you! I promise to drive carefully."

Bob's big laugh boomed out again. "Can't get into too much trouble around Silverside! Just make sure all the booze is outta your system before you get behind the wheel."

"Oh, I will. Thank you, and good night."

"Cheers!"

The sound of the bar faded rapidly as Nora walked away. A couple of minutes later I heard a door close and the analyst said, "She just went back into her room."

Slumping in my seat, I muttered, "Thanks. Keep me posted."

Shit.

I was running out of time. I had nothing concrete on Nora except her one desperate lie to me last week; and as Dr. Rawling had pointed out, even the most well-meaning people could make bad decisions when the personal stakes were high.

What if she really had been trying to keep me from walking out of her life last week? What if her story was true and I was only pushing her away because of my own pain?

And if I didn't find anything incriminating, how would I ever get Dermott to believe I hadn't intentionally sidetracked the investigation?

The thought of being locked up in a tiny cell made my skin itch. Shuddering, I scratched at my arms through my parka sleeves.

I had to do something.

Anything.

Ian. Nora had said she was going to try to visit him again, even though she knew damn well that I'd imposed a no-visitors rule.

Why?

I fired up my car and headed for the hospital.

When I poked my head into Ian's hospital room, he was propped up in bed with his eyes closed, lashes dark against his cheeks.

At the whisper of my parka sleeve brushing the door frame, his eyes popped open. "Storm!" He sagged against the pillows. "Finally! I was afraid something had happened to you!"

"Sorry." I glanced at the guard beside the door. "I need a private conversation with Ian. Please keep everybody else out."

He nodded, and I swung the door shut and went over to pull up the chair beside Ian's bed.

"Sorry I couldn't come earlier," I said. "I've been trying to crack Nora, but I'm not getting anywhere."

"But you got my message, didn't you?" Ian demanded. "I might have the puzzle piece that pulls everything together."

My heart sank. "What message?"

His brows drew together. "The message I left with your Director. At noon today."

"*Noon?*" My voice rose dangerously, and I sucked in a breath and modulated my volume. "You left a message with Dermott at *noon?* That bastard never gave it to me!"

"What?" Ian stared at me. "I told him I needed to see you urgently."

"That..." I groped for a foul enough epithet to describe Dermott, failed to find one, and settled for, "...fucking *asshole!*" Yanking out my phone, I hit Dermott's speed dial and added, "I'm going to rip him a brand new-"

"Dermott."

Good Lord, he'd answered on the first ring. That *never*

happened. Well, fuck him and his first attempt at efficiency.

"You didn't give me Ian's message!" I barked.

"Kelly? What the hell?"

"Yeah, it's Kelly," I snarled. "Why the hell didn't you give me Ian's message?"

"Because your fucking *boyfriend* can wait to get his fucking rocks off, that's why! When the chain of command finds out you've been diddling him on the side instead of focusing on the mission-"

My last shred of patience evaporated. *"WHAT THE FUCKING HELL ARE YOU TALKING ABOUT?"*

Ian twitched at my sudden volume, then winced and gingerly eased his head on the pillow.

In the momentary silence that ensued, I realized I'd completely screwed myself. Antagonizing Dermott last week had been unavoidable, but pissing him off now had been fatally stupid. Now he wouldn't rest until I was rotting in prison.

When Dermott spoke again, the deadly ice in his voice chilled my whole body. "I'm talking about you, screwing Rand in his hospital bed when you're supposed to be on duty. You're going down hard, bitch."

CHAPTER 41

"I never screwed Rand!" I barked into the phone. "If you don't believe me, I'll come down there right fucking now and take a lie detector test. I needed his intel to do my job, and I needed *you* to do *your* job and pass the intel on to me when he offered it!"

"You were gone. Holt was here so I sent him instead," Dermott snapped, but I could hear the doubt seeping into his voice. "And Rand told Holt he could only talk to you."

"And from that you deduced that I was *sleeping with him?*" I unleashed a violent punch to Ian's mattress, making him twitch again. "*You-*"

Fortunately Dermott interrupted before I could get started on his irregular parentage, deviant sexual proclivities, and inadequate genitals.

"Rand didn't tell Holt anything, just joked around about getting in your pants. Didn't give him any valid intel at all..."

It wasn't difficult to imagine the conversation between Holt The Asshole and Rand The Liar. Rage momentarily short-circuited my hearing.

By the time I refocused, Dermott was saying, "...so Holt figured Rand was just bored and looking for a-"

"RAND!" Clenching Ian's hospital gown in my fist, I

came within a hair of shaking him until his brain dripped out his ears; but he clutched his head protectively and the fear in his face stilled my hand at the last moment.

I drew in a deep slow breath.

"Director," I said sweetly. "Rand has something he wants to say to you." Still clenching Ian's gown in my fist, I held my phone to his face.

"Rand here," Ian said faintly. "I'm afraid there's been a misunderstanding..."

A few minutes later, Ian concluded, "...Holt wasn't assigned to the mission, so protocol prevented me from disclosing anything to him. I assumed..." His accent took on the condescending tone that Brits do so well. "...that your man would do his duty and pass on my message. It certainly never occurred to me that he, and you, would take such a blatantly sexist stance against Agent Kelly. If she were male, there would have been none of this nonsense."

An ominous silence swelled from the phone.

Shit, Ian, you had to poke the bear, didn't you? You couldn't just give a straight-up report for once in your life...

When Dermott spoke again he sounded like he was strangling on his tongue. "I'm going to get to the bottom of this." The line went dead.

"That's him settled, then," Ian said cheerily.

Finger by finger, I released my hold on his gown, glowering at him the whole time. When I finally removed my hand, Ian smoothed the crumpled fabric and batted those gorgeous dark lashes at me.

"Smile, Storm," he coaxed. "You're so beautiful when you smile."

Glaring at him, I breathed through the urge to punch him. Then I breathed through the urge to shoot him. Then I breathed through the urge to take my razor-sharp jackknife to his balls...

"Penny for your thoughts?" he chirped.

I let out a slow breath.

He wasn't worth it.

"So what's your intel?" I asked.

When he beckoned me closer, I didn't bother to argue. He looked slightly disappointed when I stood up without comment and leaned down so my ear was next to his mouth.

"Make it quick," I said flatly. "I only have a few minutes."

To my shock, he obeyed. "I had my team pull the records on the chemist who created the last dose of Substance X, and also the chemist who ruled that the dose had expired. It was the same man."

My heart gave a hard thump. "Is he still-"

"He has also expired," Ian interrupted before I could finish the question. "Of a heart attack, a week after he filed his report on the doses."

"Fuck." I pulled away to stare at him. "Was there an autopsy?"

"Natural causes."

"Bullshit."

Ian spread his hands in a 'what can you do?' gesture. "He was middle-aged, overweight, sedentary, and was being treated for high blood pressure. Nobody thought to look beyond the standard toxicology screens, and his family cremated his body as soon as it was released. If there was any evidence in his bloodstream, it's long gone."

"For fucksakes!" I thumped a fist on the bed. "We can't catch a break here!"

"Or it's all coincidence," Ian said.

"You don't really believe that."

He sighed. "No. I've set my team digging for any possible relationship or contact between Nora and the chemist. They haven't found anything yet, but I know it's there. I *know* this is the connection we've been looking for."

My phone vibrated.

With a sense of foreboding, I slowly raised it to read the message.

"Call home."

Oh, hell.

"I have to go," I said.

"Is everything all right?"

If I hadn't just been jerked around repeatedly by Ian's lies, I might have been touched by the concern in his eyes.

"Probably not." I headed for the door.

"Will you come back?" The undisguised anxiety in his voice tugged at my heart even though I knew damn well that he was playing me.

I sighed. "If I'm not incarcerated or dead."

I closed the door on his plaintive, "Is that *likely?*"

"If Nora Taylor shows up here, don't let her anywhere near Ian," I said to the guard. "And I mean, *nowhere* near. Not even close to his room. And make sure he doesn't get any food or drink that didn't come directly from one of the nurses."

"Got it."

Striding down the corridor, I punched the speed dial on a secured phone and snapped, "It's Aydan."

The analyst's voice was devoid of expression. "Director Dermott would like you to come in for an immediate briefing."

What the hell, I was tired of living anyway.

"I'll be there in five minutes." There wasn't anything else to say, so I hung up.

The short drive to Sirius gave me far too much time to think. There was only one reason why Dermott would summon me right now, and it sure as hell wasn't to pat me on the back and apologize. He was probably revoking my clearances right now.

Would I even make it through the security sign-in before the guards seized my weapons and slapped on the handcuffs?

The fight-or-flight instinct hammered at me.

Run.

Run now!

A block away, my fears won out and I twisted the wheel to the right instead of the left.

The bowling alley parking lot was sparsely populated, and I spotted Hellhound's Forester without difficulty. Pulling up beside it, I parked and got out.

Hellhound swung out of the driver's seat and met me at the front bumper. "Hey, darlin'. How's it goin'?" He gave me a hug and a kiss.

Closing my eyes, I wrapped my arms around him and deepened the kiss.

He responded with enthusiasm, his hands winding into my hair while he teased me with exquisite little flicks of his tongue.

God, the man was a virtuoso. I pressed closer, running hungry hands down his back and up under his jacket to find the hot bulky muscles beneath.

He trailed whiskery kisses across my jaw and down the side of my neck as I let my head fall back, turning my mind off and absorbing every glorious tingle.

This kiss might have to last me for the rest of my life.

Pausing at my throat, Arnie nibbled his way up to my lips again, finishing with a light kiss as he drew away. When I opened my eyes, he was studying me. His battered features were almost grotesque in the harsh streetlights, but as always the gentle warmth of his eyes held me.

"What's wrong, darlin'?" he rasped softly.

Too much to say. I shook my head.

I wanted to say 'I love you', but when I opened my mouth all that came out was, "I have to go."

He stiffened. "Will I see ya again?"

Somehow I managed a smile. "I hope it's not going to be that drastic. Just a meeting with Dermott."

"Can I help?"

"No. But thanks. I just needed..." I sighed. "I just needed one good thing to remind me of why I keep trying."

Arnie smiled, the tension easing from his shoulders. "Ya keep tryin' 'cause you're a good person. Don't let that asshole get ya down."

"It's not just *that* asshole, it's *all* the assholes."

His lips twisted with wry humour. "I hear ya."

"I'd better go."

As I pulled away, he caught my hand and brushed a kiss across my knuckles. "I love ya," he said quietly. "Be safe."

"I love you, too." This time the words came easily, and I kissed him one last time before getting back in my car.

My heart pounded as I walked in the door of Sirius, but no guards swooped down to capture me. My clearances still worked when I signed in at the security desk, and my security fob let me into the office area.

My knees wobbled while I climbed the stairs. Back straight, chin high, I marched down the hall to Dermott's office. He might be able to bury me, but he couldn't make me crawl.

Rounding the corner, I halted in Dermott's doorway; mainly because my muscles had locked while my brain fought an internal battle between striding forward and fleeing pell-mell.

Holt and Dermott gave me matching hostile glares from inside the office. That was why Dermott hadn't called security. He hadn't needed to. Holt could take me with one hand tied behind his back.

"What are you waiting for?" Dermott barked. "Get in here. And shut the door."

Mechanically, I obeyed. My face felt frozen stiff. Somehow my legs walked to the only vacant chair and sat me down.

"I emailed you!" Holt burst out. "Don't you ever check your fucking email?"

My lips opened and a word fell out. "What?"

"Your fucking email, you idiot! I went to see Rand, he bullshitted me, and in the end all he said was to ask you to come over and see him. He didn't say it was urgent and he didn't give me any details. So I emailed you." Holt scowled. "I meant to call you, but I had to report to Dermott, and then I got sidetracked with Grandin and..."

"Wait," I croaked. "So you..." I turned to Dermott. "...sent Holt over to the hospital as soon as Rand called." Dermott nodded, glowering. "And you..." I turned to Holt. "...got a load of shit from Rand, came back here, and emailed me right away."

"Yes!" Holt leaned forward. "I wasn't trying to mess with you, I just..." His fists clenched. "Look, it wasn't because you're a woman..."

"Hold it." My muscles finally thawed and I held up a

hand to stop him. "Forget that part. In fact, forget the whole thing." A gush of anger heated my blood and strengthened my voice. "This is Rand's fault. That asshole!"

I gave Holt a look. "Actually, you're both assholes for talking about me like that; but I know you'd never jeopardize a mission." I turned to Dermott. "Rand is a twisty prick who gets his jollies from messing with people's heads. I'm pretty sure he doesn't mean any harm, but you can't trust him. This wasn't Holt's fault, and it turned out that Rand's intel wasn't time-sensitive anyway.   He's just jerking us all around."

Dermott flushed and opened his mouth.

I added, "And I'm sorry I yelled at you."

Dermott's mouth stayed open. After a moment he closed it and scowled. "Get the hell out of my office, both of you. Be back here in half an hour for our conference call with Stemp." He turned to his computer and started clicking keys.

Holt and I left in silence.

At the door to my office, Holt finally spoke. "Thanks."

"No problem. Rand's an asshole."

"So am I."

I shrugged. "Only part-time. You're 'way ahead of him."

Holt scowled. "I fucked up." Old demons haunted his eyes, roughening his voice and clenching his fists. "That could have been bad. Really fucking bad. I wouldn't tolerate that kind of incompetence from anybody I worked with."

"Yeah, I know," I said lightly. "But you're an asshole, remember? Normal people like me know that sometimes shit happens, even to the best agents."

For just an instant his steely eyes softened. Then he barked out a derisive laugh. "You? Normal? Nice try,

Kelly."

I grinned. "Hey, I almost slipped it by you."

An answering smile tugged unwillingly at his lips. "Not hardly." He hesitated, sobering. "Thanks."

"No problem."

He nodded and strode away, and I quivered into my office and collapsed on the small sofa.

When I was sure my legs would hold me, I trudged back down to the lobby and hit the speed dial for Hellhound.

He picked up on the first ring. "Aydan?"

"I'm here. Still in one piece."

The hiss of his exhalation tickled my ear. "Glad to hear it. Ya comin' back here?"

"Not yet. I have another meeting in a few minutes..."

I hesitated, calculating the time zones. At nine PM our time, it would only be four AM in London. Stemp wouldn't likely go to the hospital until later, when his presence would be less noticeable in the bustle of daytime hospital activities. So I shouldn't have to go into the network for a few hours at least...

"Aydan? Ya still there?"

"Yeah. Sorry, I was just thinking. My nine o'clock meeting shouldn't take long, so I'll meet you at the bowling alley afterward."

"Okay, darlin', see ya then. Love ya."

"I love you, too." Smiling, I disconnected. He was my one safe port in the shitstorm that surrounded me. What would I do without him?

All too soon, I was plodding down the hall toward Dermott's office again. My heart vibrated anxiously against my ribcage.

Would he have me arrested and jailed this time?

Surely not, when Stemp was expecting me to be present at the briefing. But he might lock me up immediately afterward.

No, he couldn't. They still needed me until Rebecca was back where she belonged. But after that...

Dermott was determined to take me down, and I had no defense. Nora was still leaving without any evidence against her; and Kane was still not coming back. Two failed missions plus a bad case of insubordination. That could only equal life imprisonment.

I clenched my teeth and kept walking.

Don't think about it.

Just don't think about it.

CHAPTER 42

The conference call with Stemp went exactly as I'd expected. Dermott glowered as though imagining his hands around my throat, Spider's pale face and trembling fingers mirrored my own anxiety, and Holt looked so smugly confident that I wanted to slap him from sheer envy.

The briefing was short. Stemp confirmed that he would arrive at the hospital to attempt Rebecca's extraction around ten AM in London, which would be three AM our time; and as soon as I got Rebecca out and came out of the network myself, I would call him to report on Rebecca's mental state. I left Sirius with Stemp's final admonition ringing in my ears.

'*Get some sleep. We need you functioning at optimum levels. This may be our only chance.*'

Sure, no pressure. I'd just go home and snooze as though I hadn't a care in the world.

Nerves strung tight, I drove back to the bowling alley parking lot. Only a few vehicles remained. Damn.

Hellhound met me with a kiss again. "They're closin' in half an hour. We're gonna hafta move on, but I ain't crazy about parkin' in the residential area. Small town like this there's always some nosy neighbour lookin' out the window."

"Yeah..." I considered. "I don't want to get too far away

from Lola's house or shop, though. How about the park? It's late enough that the dog walkers will be home already, and nobody else would go there in the dark and cold."

"Sounds like a plan. Lead the way, darlin'."

The single streetlight at the park cast a feeble glow that was swallowed by blackness after only a few yards. I parked in the shadows at the far edge of the lot, and Hellhound's Forester pulled in beside me.

When we reconvened at the front bumper, Hellhound gave me a hug. "Ya might as well go home an' grab some sleep. Ya know how stakeouts go. Prob'ly nothin'll happen at all; an' even if our guy does show up, it'll be in the middle a' the night. I'll take the first watch."

"Thanks, but I'd rather take the first one. I have to go back to Sirius at three AM, so I'll stay here until midnight and then you can take over while I go home and sleep for a couple of hours."

He pulled away, frowning down at me. "Three AM? That sucks. Why not head home an' catch some zees right now?"

I shivered with equal parts cold and nerves. "I'm too wide awake. Too much on my mind."

"Well, I'm wide awake, too, so let's just hang for a while an' maybe you'll get sleepy." He nudged me toward the passenger side of the Forester. "Get in, darlin'. It's too fuckin' cold to stand around out here, an' there's no point runnin' both engines to stay warm."

Settled in his passenger seat a few minutes later, I relaxed into the warmth of the vehicle with a sigh.

"Wanna talk about it?" Hellhound asked. "If ya got a lot on your mind, it might help."

I sighed. "Most of it you already know, and the rest I

can't tell you."

"Still got nothin' on Nora?"

"No. And she's leaving tomorrow."

"Tomorrow?" The glow of the dashboard lights revealed his frown. "Ya said she was stayin' for a coupla weeks."

"She was, but she found out her surrogate daughter in London is in a coma, so she's out of here on the first available flight."

"*Surrogate daughter*?"

"Yeah. She missed me so much she replaced me." I tried to hold my voice flat, but the bitterness seeped in anyway.

Hellhound's hand found mine in the darkness, squeezing gently. "Wish I could make this better for ya, darlin'."

"Thanks." I leaned over the console to lay my head on his shoulder, and his arm came around me.

After a few minutes of silence I sat up again with a sigh, rubbing the ache in my ribs where the centre console had ground into them. "I should have brought my truck. It has a bench seat."

"I can fix that." When I glanced over, Hellhound was smiling. "Just gimme a minute. Stay put."

He got out and opened the rear door, leaning in to fold the seats down flat. In minutes he had unpacked the large duffel bag that had occupied the cargo bay, laying out a foam pad and sleeping bag and affixing black fabric over the windows.

"All ready for ya now," he said proudly. "Move right in an' get comfortable."

Grinning, I got out of the front seat and let myself into the cozy nest in the back. "You've got a shaggin' wagon. I should have known."

He waggled his eyebrows. "That ain't all. Here we go..."

He tilted the front seats forward and installed a large blackout drape that partitioned the cargo bay off from the front seats entirely. "I actually set this up for stakeouts for my P.I. business, but..." He grinned and activated a couple of tiny LED candles, setting them at the sides of the bay. "...never hurts to be prepared." He took off his parka and bunched it up, tucking it behind his back so he could recline against the back of the driver's seat and stretch out his legs. He held out a welcoming arm. "Come here, darlin'."

I snuggled in, wrapping my arm over him and leaning my head on his shoulder. "You're brilliant."

"Yep." He dropped a kiss on my lips. "An' here's our surveillance." He propped his phone in the door's cupholder and toggled the displays through front and back views of Lola's house and store. "It's all quiet, so ya might as well have a nap. The ping'll wake ya up if anythin' moves; an' I ain't gonna be sleepin' anyway. It's too early for me."

"Okay, thanks." I grinned. "I was supposed to sleep before my meeting anyway, so look at me following orders." Letting out a sigh of contentment, I relaxed. His phone went into battery-saving mode, its display winking out to leave only the twinkling candles for illumination. I closed my eyes.

Safety. Darkness. The soothing sound of an idling engine. The soft steady hum of the heater keeping our hideout pleasantly warm.

Perfect for sleeping.

Ian's words replayed in my head. 'The puzzle piece that pulls everything together'. His team might be able to connect Nora with the chemist, but what good would it do? Nora was far too smart to leave a note saying 'Dear Chemist, please steal me a few doses of poison', so we'd only have circumstantial evidence at best. And even if they found concrete proof, that only solved Ian's case, not mine. I had to prove she was involved in selling classified intel, not poisoning people.

I shifted and blew out a breath.

And then there was my other mission. Kane. No hope there. Stemp's cold features hovered in my memory, his lips forming the words 'I recommend you don't fail'. He'd gone to bat for me before, but there wasn't much he could do if Dermott turned the chain of command against me.

Don't think about that.

Would I be able to locate Rebecca when I went into the network tonight? If I did, what would I find? A gibbering mass of insanity? Or worse, a woman who'd had time to figure out exactly what had happened to her? I had been able to overpower her and sift through our collective consciousness because she didn't know what was going on. What if she understood now? What if she fought me?

What if she won?

I blew out another hard breath and pressed the heel of my hand against my forehead, trying to drive away the fearful thoughts.

"Okay, darlin'?" Arnie asked softly.

"I can't settle." I sat up and scrubbed my knuckles through my hair. "Too much on my mind."

"Try lyin' down for a while. I've slept in here before an' I only hadta bend my knees a bit, so ya oughta be pretty comfortable."

"I'll try," I said doubtfully.

Stripping off my parka, I made a pillow-sized roll and lay down facing him, pulling the sleeping bag over me. His hand slid under the sleeping bag to make soothing circles on my back, and I sighed and cuddled closer, wrapping my arm over his legs and trying to relax into his gentle massage.

Still my mind wouldn't slow down. Replaying my conversations with Nora, I mentally catalogued all the tiny clues in her body language and behaviour. She had known about Sam's espionage all along; I knew it, goddammit, but I couldn't prove it. And tomorrow she'd be gone. I had to get the lie detector on her somehow. But how? If I asked her to take another test, she'd know I was investigating her and she'd simply invoke her diplomatic immunity and refuse.

Arnie kept rubbing my shoulders, but I couldn't relax.

And I still hadn't told Dermott that Nora was leaving.

Shit, shit, shit.

When should I tell him? Or should I just drive Nora to Calgary without saying anything to him?

But that would only postpone the inevitable...

Shut *up*, already! Just shut the fuck up!

Concentrate on sensations, not thoughts.

Jacket soft under my head. Foam pad comfortable beneath me. Arnie's hand caressing my back. His legs warm and firm under my arm. The faint scent of leather that always clung to him.

Yum.

My eyes cracked open. My forehead was tucked against his hip, and from that angle the tiny light silhouetted the bulge of his fly.

My body warmed at the thought of what lay beneath that worn denim. No underwear, as usual. Just warm naked skin, waiting for a caress to stiffen into hot temptation. All that pleasure, only inches away...

My mouth watered.

Sliding my hand over his thigh, I traced the seam of his jeans up to cup his crotch.

His hand stilled on my back.

"Well, hey there, darlin'," he rumbled. "Lookin' for somethin'?"

"Maybe." I made little circles with my fingertips. "Think I might find something interesting?"

"Guess you'll just hafta look an' see."

"Mmmm." Scraping my fingernail lightly up the length of his zipper, I found the button and worked it open. He exhaled and widened his legs as I slid the zipper slowly down, holding the tab away from his skin. Squirming closer, I propped myself against his thigh.

"Well, look who I found. I think he's glad to see me." I eased his rapidly-firming erection through the opening.

"He's always glad to see ya," Arnie rasped. "Really fuckin'... ahhh..." He groaned as I bestowed some soft flicks of my tongue on a particularly tasty spot. "...glad..." His voice deepened and roughened as I squirmed into a better angle and added some finger action. "...to... see... yahhhh... Jesus, darlin'..."

Savoring his pleasure, my excitement rose along with his. I slowly increased the pace and intensity.

"Ahhhh-yeah!" His hoarse moan kindled fierce heat between my legs. His hands came up to twine in my hair as his hips moved with my rhythm. "Fuck... me..." He tensed. "Shit. Stop, darlin'."

"What's wrong?" I popped up to eye him worriedly.

"Nothin' in the world." He blinked at me, heavy-eyed and smiling. "But I wasn't gonna last if ya kept doin' that."

"You don't have to last. That's the whole point." I dipped my head again.

He sat up, bringing me to my knees and gently diverting my lips up to his. "Yeah, but where's the fun in that?" He kissed me, then drew away with a smile. "If I'd wanted to blow my load in a coupla minutes, I'd'a jacked off in the shower this mornin'." Reaching for the button on my jeans, he added, "I got a better idea."

CHAPTER 43

"We can't." I stopped Arnie's hand before he could undo my pants. "We have to be ready to move in case we get a hit on the surveillance cameras."

He grinned. "Only one of us hasta be ready to move. I can get my pants up an' be drivin' in ten seconds, an' by the time I get us there, you'll be dressed an' ready to go. Besides..." His hand described an extremely persuasive arc across the curve of my hip and around my ass, trailing light fingertip-friction along the centre seam of my jeans. "It's only a quarter after ten. Nobody's gonna try anythin' 'til after midnight. Betcha an orgasm that I'm right."

I sucked in a breath of pure lust as he stroked me through my jeans. "Feels like somebody's trying something right now," I purred.

"Mmm-hmm." His lips claimed mine, his dexterous fingers still teasing me. "Is it workin'?" he mumbled against my lips before trailing kisses down my throat to that magic spot on my neck.

"Oh, *hell*, yes." Shivers arrowed down my spine as heat spread from his fingertips.

This was definitely a bad idea. Having sex in a public park, knowing we might be discovered at any moment...

Arnie was kissing me again, his tongue making sensuous promises. His hands...

Ohmigod, his *hands*...

My jeans loosened and eased down to my thighs. His hot fingers skimmed a mind-meltingly light touch over the front of my thong.

Right there.

Right... *there*...

"God, Arnie..." I moaned against his lips.

Unable to remember why this had seemed like a bad idea, I rocked from one knee to the other as he worked my jeans and underwear off one-handed.

"Come here," he growled, sliding down so he lay on his back, knees bent. "I got a moustache ride with your name on it."

A shock of arousal made me gasp even as I shook my head. "No. You'll drown."

He laughed. "But what a way to go." He urged me closer. "Come on, darlin'. Mount up."

"I..."

There was a valid objection here somewhere, but I couldn't remember it. His strong hands guided me into place.

Then his mouth went into action and all I could do was cling to the front seat, my only anchor in the storm of sensation.

Somehow the position seemed more intimate than anything we'd ever done, my thighs spread wide, my body fully open to his tongue as it licked and penetrated, flicked and circled.

Every nerve ending came alive. Waves of pleasure crashed through my body and my fingers dug into the headrest, whimpers choking me as I tried to hold back my cries.

Whiskers stimulating sensitized skin, lips sucking, teeth... nibbling... *tongue... oh...*

my...

GOD...

A cry ripped from my throat as the hurricane of orgasm flung me aloft. Blind and deaf, blazing with sensation, I soared until the spasms slowed at last and gravity claimed me again. Legs quivering uncontrollably, I got off him and collapsed to the mattress.

"Are..." I could only manage a breathless whisper. "You... still breathing?"

"Hell, yeah." Arnie's voice was deep with satisfaction.

I coasted a hand up his leg, discovering the hard evidence of his enjoyment. "Your turn now." I stroked him.

"Mmm." He stilled my hand. "*Our* turn, if you're up for it."

The tingles of my afterglow intensified to new desire. "God, yes!"

Arnie chuckled. "That's what I wanna hear." He pulled himself up to lean against the driver's seat again, delving down into the space below.

"Hurry." I straddled his legs and kissed him.

A plastic bag rustled and his lips turned up under mine. "How 'bout an early Christmas present, darlin'?" As I pulled away, he held up the bag from Lola's shop with a devilish grin. "Wanna play?"

"Yes!" I reached for the bag but he whisked it away, still grinning.

"Shut your eyes, then. I got a surprise for ya."

I obeyed with a shiver of anticipation.

"Keep 'em closed," he admonished over the crinkling sound of packaging. "I think you're gonna like this."

"I like it even without any extras," I assured him.

"Then you're really gonna like this." His hands worked momentarily between us. "No peekin'." As my hands slid down to explore his activities, he added, "No touchin', either." A kiss landed on my lips. "Just a couple more seconds, darlin'... there. Okay, no peekin'..."

His hands gripped my hips, urging me up onto my knees, then settling me on top of him. As he slid inside me I sucked in a breath that came out in a moan. "Oh God, you feel good!"

He pulsed gently under me, slowly filling me until I sat firmly in his lap. As he sat up straighter and pulled me to him, I felt an unaccustomed object between us.

"What's... that...?" I inquired breathlessly as I slid experimentally up and then down again. God, that extra bit of friction hit me in just the right place.

"Wait an' see..." He rocked his hips into an unhurried rhythm that intensified the friction, sparking electric sensation into nerves already sensitized.

"*Ohmigod!*" My hands fisted convulsively in his shirt and I ground against him, greedy for pleasure both internal and external.

He groaned and picked up the pace, driving deeper while the new device teased me into a frenzy.

It seemed like only moments before I was ascending the peak.

Just a...

few...

more...

strokes...

A sudden electric vibration hit me, sensation bright as a plasma arc.

My orgasm detonated like a bomb.

Too-much-too-fast-too-hard and I screamed for *more harder more*, my body bucking out of control, my mind shattering.

The world shifted and somehow Arnie was on his knees, holding my hips up and driving into me *more-harder-oh-god-fuck-me!*

He let out a wrenching groan and thrust hard once, twice...

The vibration stopped and he rocked me gently on his body, prolonging the glorious spasms.

Adrift in helpless ecstasy, I could only float down in shreds of myself, the last contractions still shaking me, flares of pleasure slowly ebbing.

When I could think again, I opened my eyes to see Arnie kneeling above me, his head and shoulders bent to avoid the roof of the Forester. His hands held my hips in place, our bodies still joined. He was panting almost as hard as I was.

"Christ, darlin'," he croaked.

Just the sound of his voice was enough to set off another mini-orgasm. As my body pulsed around him, he groaned and rocked back to sit on the floor again, his powerful arms keeping me in his lap.

Another orgasm ripped through me as my overstimulated nerves reacted to the movement. Arching my back, I let it take me. Shake me. Leave me drowning in pleasure, limp and pliant and utterly spent.

"Aydan?"

"Mm?"

"Ya okay?"

"Mmhm." Somehow I managed to drag my eyelids open. "If you even twitch," I mumbled, "I'm going to come again."

"Will ya live through it if I do?"

I let my eyes fall shut again, grinning. "Who cares?"

"Okay, then." I could hear the smile in his voice. His strong arms lifted me off and I collapsed to the mattress beside him, gasping and shuddering from the fresh explosion of sensation.

Eyes closed, I listened to the familiar sounds of condom disposal and cleanup, smiling.

A whiskery kiss brushed my cheek. "Okay, darlin'?"

I opened my eyes, smiling up at him. "So much better than okay. You?"

"Oh, *hell* yeah. But after all my talk about lastin', I sure as hell didn't last long." He squirmed down to lie on his back beside me, sharing my makeshift pillow.

"Any longer and my brain would have exploded." I cuddled in, resting my head on his chest as he tucked an arm around me. "What *was* that?"

"Vibratin' cock ring. With a remote." He held up a small device and pressed the button, and the shopping bag responded with a buzzing sound.

"Good Lord, it nearly killed me. That was amazing!"

He laughed. "Lucky we're out in the middle a' Bumfuck Nowhere so nobody heard us. The way ya were screamin', I wasn't sure whether to stop or go harder."

"'Go harder' is usually the right answer," I mumbled, sinking bonelessly into his warmth.

"Yeah, I figured; but I wouldn't'a wanted to explain all that screamin' to the cops if they showed up."

I snuffled a laugh into his chest. "Would you believe I was trying to be quiet?"

He guffawed. "Fuck me."

"I'm pretty sure I just did."

His chuckle rumbled up under my ear, and I sighed with pure contentment and let my world shrink to nothing but the strong steady beat of his heart.

Ping!

Earthquake.

The whole world was shaking...

My eyes flew open, my brain spinning up to speed as Arnie lunged out of our nest in the back of the Forester and flung himself into the driver's seat.

"We got action!" he rasped as he slammed the vehicle into reverse. "Get dressed, darlin'!"

I was already groping for my underwear and jeans, my gaze glued to the dark figure moving furtively toward the back entrance of Lola's shop.

"Park at the front," I barked. "We'll sneak around and box him in. I'll come up from the south and trank him, you stay behind the fence on the north side in case I miss or he takes off."

"Roger."

Giving up the effort to balance as the Forester swayed around corners, I flopped down and squirmed into my clothes. My Glock and trank pistol were still in place, and I smiled despite the urgency. How lucky was I to have a lover who didn't think twice about screwing a woman who kept weapons strapped to both ankles?

"He still there?" Hellhound snapped as the Forester slowed.

"Yeah, he's bent over doing something near the back

door." I yanked the blackout curtains off and tossed them to the back of the cargo bay, leaving myself a clear path to the door.

"Okay, I'm gonna cruise in slow an' easy. Don't want him spooked if he hears a car comin' up fast."

My nerves jangled as the Forester decelerated to what felt like an impossibly slow crawl, but it was probably just the speed limit. The dark figure straightened, then backed away from the shop door.

Had he set a trap?

Or a bomb?

We ghosted up to the front of the shop and glided to a halt.

"Go!" I hissed, and we both sprang out of the vehicle, leaving the doors hanging open.

No door slams to alert him.

Trank pistol clenched in my hand, I dashed for the back of the shop, trying to be silent. The snow crunched under my boots loudly enough to wake the dead.

Dammit, he'd hear us for sure!

I put on an extra burst of speed.

Christ, there'd better not be any ice here, or he'd get away clean when I fell and broke my fucking leg...

I hurtled around the corner, trank pistol at the ready.

He'd heard us. He was running.

I squeezed off a shot. Missed.

Don't run and shoot at the same time, idiot!

Skidding to a halt, I fired again, my lungs heaving for air. Missed.

Fuck, he was getting away!

I fired again, and again.

Hellhound sprang out from behind the fence just as the

figure wavered and fell.

I pounded forward, trank pistol at the ready.

Hellhound was already on his knees beside the fallen man. "He's out."

"Good, get the Forester."

Hellhound sprang up and sprinted for the front.

Reversing direction, I ran toward the back door of the shop, slowing as I approached. Fumbling my little LED flashlight out of my waist pouch left-handed, I shone its beam to where the intruder had been crouching.

No ice this time. But dammit, he'd been doing *something* down here. I crept closer, heart pounding.

The flashlight beam caught a quicksilver glint. A sliver of reflection, then nothing.

What...?

I crouched, easing closer. There it was again. This time I spotted its slim silvery path in the darkness. A tripwire.

"*Bastard!*"

No time. Already I could hear the Forester's engine approaching. Swallowing my rage, I studied the setup.

Was it a trigger device?

No, thank God. Only strong fishing line, stretched taut between two bushes, perfectly positioned to trip an elderly woman.

A violent kick was enough to snap the line. I hurried back to the fallen man and planted my foot on his shoulder to shove him onto his back, keeping the trank pistol trained on him just in case.

He flopped over limply, and as the Forester pulled up beside us its headlights flashed over his face.

Bob Armstrong.

"Fucking *asshole!*"

I kicked him in the head.

CHAPTER 44

Armstrong's head snapped over under the force of my kick, then rolled limply back.

Hellhound lunged out of the Forester. "Don't kill him!"

"I'm not." I glowered down at the unconscious face. "I barely touched him. Didn't even break his nose."

"Awright. Come on." Hellhound opened the liftgate of the Forester, and together we hoisted Armstrong's flaccid body into the cargo bay.

I crawled in beside him. "I'll get the restraints on him. Get us out of here."

Hellhound nodded and closed the liftgate before hurrying around to the driver's seat. "Where to?"

"Back to the park." I shoved Armstrong onto his face and zipped the steel-reinforced nylon restraints onto his wrists and ankles. "If nobody heard me screaming out there, they won't hear him, either."

Hellhound put the vehicle in gear and we rolled away. "Uh, darlin'..." He hesitated. "Don't wanna tell ya how to do your job, but... if we're gonna do anythin', uh... serious... we prob'ly shoulda been a bit more careful about DNA evidence."

What a guy. He had my back even when he thought I

was going to torture and murder a man. I wasn't sure whether to be touched or horrified.

"It's okay, I'm not planning anything serious," I assured him. "I just want to scare him a bit, and then we'll take him into Sirius and put the lie detector on him."

"Oh, okay." Relief warmed Arnie's voice. "Wasn't sure, when I saw ya kickin' him when he was down."

"I just wanted to make sure he had a bruise so he'd think he'd fallen and knocked himself out. I don't like to advertise that our trank pistols exist."

That was true; but it wasn't the only reason I'd kicked him. Shame congealed in my stomach.

"Makes sense," Hellhound agreed, sounding even more relieved.

God, now I felt even worse. When your violence level shocks a professional assassin, you've got to take a damn hard look at yourself.

Later.

Plying my flashlight again, I gave Armstrong a once-over. A trank dart was lodged in the back of his coat, and another had pierced his gloved hand. Fluke shot. He'd still be running otherwise.

"The aerosolized trank didn't touch him at all," I complained.

"Yeah, he was runnin' into the wind. An' I'm surprised the dart went through that big coat."

"It didn't. I hit him in the hand."

"Nice shootin'."

"Sheer dumb luck." I dropped the spent darts in my pocket. "Is it okay if I use one of your blackout curtains for a blindfold?"

"Sure, 'long's it doesn't end up in a murder

investigation."

"It won't."

By the time Hellhound turned the corner into the parking lot, I had Armstrong's head wrapped in dark cloth.

"Back in," I said. "I want to dump him in the park, and I don't want to carry him any farther than we have to."

He complied, and after a rapid survey to make sure we were unobserved, we hauled Armstrong's limp body out of the vehicle and lugged him a few yards into the darkness under the trees.

"There, behind those evergreens," I panted.

We dumped our burden into the snow and stood in silence while I caught my breath.

"So what's the plan?" Hellhound asked.

"I just want him to wake up cold and uncomfortable." Leaning into Hellhound, I grinned up at him. "Not curled up on a nice warm mattress that smells like fresh sex."

He chuckled. "Got it."

"Then I'm going to ask him a few questions, and with any luck, scare the piss out of him..."

"Another good reason not to have him on my mattress," Hellhound put in.

"Very true." I sighed. "It might not work. I won't hurt him. I'm just hoping he'll be scared enough to talk when we get him into Sirius. We'll take him through the secret bowling alley entrance directly into the secured area, and keep him blindfolded the whole time so he doesn't know who we are or where he is. Once he's in the interrogation room I'll trank him again so I can get him shackled to the table with the lie detector set up, and then we can take the blindfold off so I can see his expression while I question him from the observation booth."

"Okay." Hellhound consulted his watch, the small glow bright in the darkness. "He's gonna be out for another ten minutes or so. I'll put everythin' back to normal in the shaggin' wagon..." He grinned. "Unless ya wanna take another ride."

"That was a ride to remember." I gave a pleasurable shiver and reached up to kiss him. "Both rides. But it seems to me you still owe me an orgasm."

"Oh, yeah?" His wristwatch's backlight had blinked off, but I could hear the grin in his voice. "How d'ya figure?"

"You bet me an orgasm that Dipshit here wouldn't make his move until after midnight."

"Guess what, darlin'. Ya gotta pay up." He turned the backlight on again and held out his wrist. "One AM."

"What?" I stared at the glowing evidence. "But it was only ten-thirty... Shit, I fell asleep."

"Yep." He dropped a kiss on my lips. "Ya needed it."

"I did; I just didn't expect to get it." The unintentional double entendre made me smile. "Thanks. For all of it."

"My pleasure. Literally." He chuckled. "This time; an' next time when I collect on our bet."

"Brace yourself," I warned him. "I owe you a really good one."

"No such thing as a bad one." He turned toward the Forester. "Back in a few minutes."

Right on schedule, Armstrong regained consciousness. Hellhound and I waited until his twitching and mumbling changed to frantic panting as he fought the restraints. I handed my small flashlight to Hellhound and kicked Armstrong in the shoulder. Not too hard.

Pitching my voice deeper, I snapped, "Shut up."

He yelped. "Who... what... where am I? Who are you?"

"I said *shut up!*" This time I kicked him in the ass.

It felt good.

A black urge swelled. Stop holding back. Unleash all my fear and fury and frustration on his eminently deserving body...

Hellhound stood silently beside me, featureless in the darkness. The shape of my conscience.

I didn't kick Armstrong.

"Why were you sabotaging Lola's shop?" I demanded.

"I didn't! I wasn't even there, you've got the wrong guy-"

Rage seized me and I snatched my Glock from its holster. As Hellhound's hand flew out to stop me, I grabbed it and placed it lightly on top of my gun.

Aiming safely at the ground with my finger well clear of the trigger, I jacked the slide noisily. "That little lie is going to cost you a knee."

As I had hoped, Hellhound caught the ejected cartridge.

"NO! *Shit-sorry-okay-yeah-I-was-there-I-did-it!* I'm sorry, I'm sorry!" Armstrong blubbered.

"That's more like it." I reholstered my weapon and pocketed the cartridge Hellhound handed me. "So let's try this again. Who sent you?"

"Nobody..."

"You really don't like your knees, do you?" I growled.

"*Nobody-sent-me-I-did-it-all-myself-I'm-sorry-it's-the-truth-honest!*" Armstrong thrashed on the ground, attempting to squirm away. Without speaking, Hellhound placed his large boot on Armstrong's neck. The man squeaked and went still, whimpering, "I'm sorry! I didn't mean anything by it!"

"You fucking well *did* mean it. You set a tripwire. *Why?*" I accompanied the question with another kick to his ass, holding back with every ounce of restraint I possessed.

"I just wanted to teach her a lesson! That interfering old cunt! She fucked up my marriage..."

"I heard you fucked up your own marriage."

"Her and her fucking old-fart CRAPS cronies took *pictures!* I could have talked my way out of it like always, if they hadn't taken those goddamn pictures! It's all their fault!"

Comprehension hit me like a two-hundred-pound sack of shit.

Because that's what Armstrong was. And that's how much shit I was in right now.

"And you iced Pearl's sidewalk, and she fell and broke her ankle," I said. "And you put a mouse in Eddy's kitchen because he hosts the CRAPS meetings..."

And Tom... Of course. Tom had said 'I'm late' when we'd met him outside Eddy's. He was on his way to the CRAPS meeting. It was exactly the kind of civic-minded group he'd join.

"...and you left a trap outside Tom's door and shot up his sign," I finished.

Armstrong's voice took on a whine. "Okay, yeah, so I did a few things to the other CRAPS idiots, too, but I just wanted to scare them, I didn't mean any harm..."

"You fucking sack of *shit!*" I kicked him again, and this time I wasn't gentle. While he was still flinching and snivelling, I cut the restraints on his ankles and snapped, "On your feet!"

Hellhound removed his boot from Armstrong's neck and Armstrong stumbled awkwardly to his feet, fruitlessly fighting the bonds that pinned his hands behind his back.

"We're going for a walk," I said. "If you say anything, or

if you try to run, or if you do anything at all except shut up and walk, I'm going to kill you so slowly and painfully that you'll wish you'd wrapped that tripwire around your own neck and pulled it tight. If you do exactly what I say, I'll let you live. Got it?"

"I got it, I got it, I'll do what you say-"

"Shut up. Walk."

Hellhound and I each took an elbow and escorted him back to the Forester. I got in the back with Armstrong, and Hellhound handed back my flashlight before sliding into the driver's seat to pilot us to the bowling alley.

Our trip to the secured area was silent except for Armstrong's snivelling and the ever-increasing voice in the back of my brain screaming, '*You are completely fucked!*'

I ignored it as best I could.

Standing in the soundproof observation room, I stared glumly at the video monitor. Armstrong slumped in the interrogation room, unconscious from the latest dose of tranquilizer I'd administered, shackled to the table and hooked up to the lie detector.

"I'm fucked," I said.

Hellhound frowned. "Why? We got him. We'll get a confession an' call the cops, an' Lola's gonna be fine."

"Except that it has nothing to do with me." I sank into one of the chairs with a groan. "I just wasted Department resources and a whole shitpile of time barking up the wrong tree and ignoring my real missions." I slumped forward and thumped my forehead against my fists. "And I forgot to call Nora after my nine o'clock briefing. She was going to wait up for my call. She'll be totally pissed, I won't get anything more from her, and Dermott is going to fry me. I'm going to prison for the rest of my fucking life."

Panic squeezed my chest.

Run.

Run now!

"But, darlin'," Hellhound began.

"He's awake." I nodded at the monitor, which showed Armstrong jerking frantically at the shackles. "Time to ask the questions."

I flipped on the voice filter and pressed the intercom button. "Armstrong."

He twitched, staring wildly around the featureless interrogation room. "What? Where am I? What is this place?"

"Shut up and answer my questions with yes or no."

He nodded, his eyes white with fear.

"Is your name Bob Armstrong?"

"Yes."

The green light confirmed the truth.

"Have you ever used any other name?"

"No."

Green light.

"Were you targeting CRAPS members to get revenge?"

"Y-Yes..."

Green light.

"Were you working with anybody else?" I held my breath.

"No."

Green light. Shit.

"Did anybody else prompt you, or pay you, or encourage you to do this?"

"No..." He stared around the room, sweat trickling down

his temples.

"So it was all your own idea."

He gulped. "Y-Yes."

More green lights. Fuckity-fuck.

"Have you ever heard of Arlene Widdenback?"

"No."

Green light. Hellhound and I exchanged an unhappy look.

"Have you ever heard of Aydan Kelly?"

"She's Nora Taylor's daughter."

It wasn't a yes or no so the light didn't flash, but I didn't need clarification of that particular statement.

"So you know Nora Taylor?"

"No..."

The red light flashed.

"Try again, asshole," I snarled.

"*Okay-yes-I-met-her* but I don't *know* her," he babbled. "She's just this old broad I met at the hotel, I was trying to charm her into buying my dinner and drinks but she stiffed me, that's all, I swear!"

My heart plummeted.

"Had you ever met Nora Taylor before you met her at the hotel?"

"No."

"Did you have any reason to communicate with her other than to try to con her out of a meal and drinks?"

"No."

"Did she ever ask you to do anything for her?"

"I drove her to the hospital to visit a friend."

"Was that all she ever asked you for?"

"Just my car keys."

"Did she ever ask you for anything else besides your car

keys and a ride to the hospital? Yes or no."

"No." He was beginning to sound puzzled.

Green lights all the way. Oh God.

Clinging to the ever-diminishing hope that I might still be able to save my own ass, I asked, "What did she tell you about her daughter?"

"Wh-which one?"

I couldn't quite prevent my wince, and Hellhound reached over to squeeze my hand.

"Rebecca," I said on impulse.

"N-nothing much; she's a nice girl, they get along great, that's about it."

"Did she talk about Rebecca's work?"

"No."

Green light.

Dammit, I was getting nowhere. "What did she tell you about Rebecca?" I barked. "I want to know *every... fucking... thing!*"

Armstrong flinched. "I don't know anything, honest! She just said she has a daughter in England who's really nice and that's all she said, she only mentioned her because she was comparing her to what a bitch her other daughter is!"

Hellhound winced on my behalf and squeezed my hand again, but this time I didn't even twitch. Cold purpose filled me.

"Is that the truth?" I asked.

"Yes!"

The green light flashed.

"So Aydan Kelly is a bitch," I said. "What else did Nora tell you about her?"

Armstrong sat up like a student who finally knows the right answer. "Nora had to go into witness protection when

Aydan was a teenager, and finally after thirty years she got out and contacted Aydan, and Aydan's being a total bitch about it. Always making these nasty remarks, and blaming Nora for leaving when Nora was only trying to protect her all along. Nora's still trying to get along with her but it's not going well and she's getting sick of it. I said she should just go back to England and to hell with the bitch, but Nora doesn't want to quit on her just yet. I don't know why. If my kid treated me like that I'd kick him in the ass."

He didn't know it, but he was kicking me in the guts.

Unable to let it go, I asked, "So why do you think Nora's sticking around?"

Armstrong shrugged. "She loves her kid, I guess."

I was about to shrivel up and blow away in a tornado of guilt when he added, "Or she wants something."

"What?" I snapped. "What does she want?"

He tensed, staring anxiously around the room. "I don't know, I'm just guessing! Money, maybe. She said something about getting security for her retirement, but she said it like she was joking."

Security for her retirement. Maybe the kind of security that comes from selling classified intel gathered unwittingly by her daughter?

"What exactly did she say?" I demanded. "What were her exact words?"

"I don't know, I don't remember!" Armstrong jerked at the shackles, sweat beading his forehead. "Come on, let me go! She's just some old lady, she's nobody to me! I swear I don't know anything else about her or her kids!"

"Is that the truth?"

"YES!"

The green light flashed.

"So you're only staying at the hotel because your wife kicked you out."

"Yes!"

"You're only being nice to Nora because you're hoping to get a free meal."

"Yes!"

"And you threatened Lola and iced Pearl's sidewalk and planted a mouse in Eddy's kitchen and left the trap at Tom's door and shot up his sign, only to get revenge on CRAPS," I said, feeling doom descending on me.

"Yes!"

Green lights all the way.

I turned off the intercom and collapsed forward to beat my forehead against the table in time with my words.

"Fuck, fuck, fuck, fuck, *fuck!*"

CHAPTER 45

Our return trip through the bowling alley had the grim silence of a death march.

Back in the park, I escorted the blindfolded Armstrong out behind the evergreens again. "I'll be watching you," I snarled. "If you say anything to anybody about this, *ever*; or if you cheat in your business or miss an alimony payment or even step a *toe* out of line in any way; I'm going to pay you a visit and cut you into pieces small enough to feed a goldfish. Got it?"

"G-Got it."

"Good." I broke open a trank dart in front of his face. He collapsed after one inhalation and I hurriedly removed his restraints and blindfold, holding my breath. Leaving him crumpled in the snow, I returned to the Forester.

"Sure ya wanna leave him out here?" Hellhound broke his silence at last. "He could get frostbite an' hypothermia if he's down for twenty minutes."

"I just gave him a sniff of aerosolized trank. He'll be awake in five."

"Then we better scram. Meet ya in the Sirius parkin' lot."

I slid into my car and followed his taillights.

A few minutes later I parked at Sirius and shivered over to the Forester. Gratefully climbing into the warm passenger seat, I let out a long sigh.

"So, ya gonna call the cops on him?" Hellhound asked.

"I can't. I'd love to see him charged, but we don't have any actual evidence except his confession, and the lie detector is classified so we can't release the footage. And even if we did give it to the police, they'd never get a conviction in a civilian court because we didn't follow due process and we can't even testify without blowing our covers." I sighed. "I put the fear of God into him and that'll have to do."

"Well, at least Lola an' her buddies are gonna be safe." Hellhound squeezed my hand. "Ya did good, darlin'. It ain't your fault it turned out the way it did. Ya hadta follow the leads. Dermott's gotta understand that."

"Back in the days when he still liked me he might have cut me some slack," I mumbled. "But after I showed him up in that briefing last week, he's howling for my blood."

"Fuckin' asshole. But the chain a' command's gotta know that, right?"

"I sure hope so. Because if it was up to Dermott I'd already be rotting in prison. And when he finds out about this clusterfuck..." I slumped in the seat. "Well, at least he still needs me tonight. I'll have a few more hours of freedom." A thought struck me and I added, "Maybe Nora called. She said she didn't care how late I was. If she's still waiting up for me, I might be able to pull this out of the fire..." I extracted my cell phone, hoping against hope.

The message on the screen made every drop of my blood turn ice-cold and drain into my suddenly-sticky socks.

Frozen, I stared at the phone. "Oh... shit..."

"What, darlin'?" Hellhound demanded. "What's wrong?"

Wordlessly, I turned the screen toward him so he could read 'Call home' and its damning timestamp: 10:45 PM.

"Aw, fuck." He fell back in his seat.

"Yep," I said faintly. "I was so busy vibrating, I didn't notice my phone."

He swallowed audibly. "Well, maybe it ain't that big a deal. Ya were s'posed to sleep, right? Ya can just say ya were sleepin' an' ya missed it."

"Cross your fingers and hold that thought." I pulled out a secured phone and reached for the door handle.

"Never mind, darlin', stay in here where it's warm. I'll wait outside." Hellhound got out and closed the door behind him.

I hesitated for a long moment before pressing the speed dial. When the analyst's wide-awake voice answered, I said, "It's Aydan" and held my breath.

"Nora Taylor was attacked, sometime after nine-thirty this evening. She was admitted to the secured wing of the Silverside Hospital at ten-thirty PM."

The air vanished from my lungs as though I'd been punched in the chest. "Wh-What happened? What's her condition?" My voice was a bare ghost.

"It appears she was drugged and abducted, but escaped from her captor or captors. She was found semi-conscious in the driver's seat of Bob Armstrong's car after running it off the road near the hospital. She's uninjured, and they're keeping her for observation and running tests to determine what she was given."

"Does she remember anything?"

"Only that she borrowed the car, intending to visit Agent Rand in the hospital."

"What about the bugs and cameras?"

"She was alone when she left her hotel room at nine twenty-seven and she looked normal on the surveillance cameras. She hadn't spoken to anyone on the phone inside her room; and the bug on her purse didn't pick up any conversations, either. When she got in the car she turned the radio on, and the bug recorded it uninterrupted until she was found in the car. There was no other conversation, no cries or sounds of struggle, and no sounds of doors opening or closing."

"But how could she have been abducted and drugged if nobody opened or closed the car doors?"

"Unknown. They may have been hiding in the back seat."

"Shit. Is she conscious now?"

"Yes, she regained full consciousness around midnight."

I glanced at my watch. Two-twenty AM. "I'm going over there to see what I can find out. I'll be back in time for the three AM meeting."

"Noted."

"Anything else?" I asked, because why the hell *wouldn't* there be something else? Could this night get any worse?

"That's all."

If only I could believe that.

"Thanks." I disconnected and got out of the Forester.

"So?" Hellhound gave me a worried look. "How bad is it?"

I grimaced. "Don't ask. Nora got abducted and she's in the hospital. I'm going over there now."

"Shit, I'm sorry, darlin'. This's all my fault. I shouldn't'a talked ya into the shaggin' wagon."

"It's not your fault," I protested. "If I'd said I didn't want to, you wouldn't have even tried to talk me into it. And I should have checked my phone. This is all on me."

"But..." He trailed off at my vehement headshake, apparently deciding that there were more important issues at stake than assigning blame. "Were ya s'posed to be protectin' Nora?"

"Not officially, but I'm sure Dermott will find a way to make it my fault." I hugged Hellhound, absorbing his strength as his arms came around me in return. "Go back to my place and get some sleep," I added. "I'll go straight from the hospital to my meeting at Sirius, and that'll likely take hours. With any luck I'll make it home for a shower and change of clothes before I have to leave for Calgary in the morning."

"You're goin' to Calgary tomorrow?"

"Uh-huh." I tightened my arms around him, trying not to think about it.

"What for?"

Yeah, I had to think about it.

I sighed. "A sting. Holt figures the best way to catch Grandin's contact is to use me as bait."

Hellhound's arms tightened around me. "D'ya need backup?"

"Holt doesn't think so."

"Holt's a fuckin' idiot. Where's the drop?"

"You can't be there," I argued. "Holt says he's got the whole place locked down and wired, and it shouldn't be that big a deal. I'll be armed, and as soon as the buyer makes contact Holt's team will come down on them like a ton of bricks."

"'Makes contact'." Hellhound drew away, holding me by my shoulders and frowning down at me. "That could be anythin' from puttin' down a suitcase of money an' backin' away, to mowin' ya down with an automatic weapon. Tell me where you're gonna be."

"But if anybody spots you..."

"I've been doin' this for thirty fuckin' years. Nobody's gonna spot me. An' if anybody steps outta line..." The Killer stared grimly from his eyes. "I'll take 'em down before Holt even gets his thumb outta his ass."

I hesitated. If Dermott found out, he'd crucify me.

But if Hellhound had to act, it meant the mission had already gone to hell anyway; and Dermott would be the least of my worries.

"The drop is at ten-thirty, at a nursing home." I gave him the address. "The buyer shouldn't even get near me, but even if it all goes to hell and they capture me..." Somehow I managed not to shudder. "...I'll have a bug and a locator in my wristwatch, and Holt will have a team on standby if they need to retrieve me. He's sure they won't hurt me after going to so much trouble to capture me."

"He's *sure*." Hellhound snorted. "That an' five bucks'll get ya a cup a' coffee. I'll be there."

"Thanks." I burrowed into his arms again.

He held me for a few moments, then drew away and dropped a kiss on my lips. "Can ya get me those spy glasses ya were testin' for Chow last summer?"

"I can try."

"Good. An' wear that bulletproof jacket, too, if he'll give it to ya."

"I'll see if he's still got it." I kissed him again. "I have to go. I'm running out of time."

"Okay. I'll go get the cameras from Lola's place an' take 'em back to Stores."

"Thanks," I said again, the word completely inadequate to describe the gratitude swelling in my heart. "Have I told you in the last few minutes that I love you? In a completely anti-commitment way?"

He chuckled. "Love ya, too, darlin'. Good luck with your meetin'."

Driving over to the hospital, tension wound up in my belly while thoughts whirled in my brain.

Who would attack Nora? Had somebody targeted her as a way to get to me? Or was this something to do with her role as Weapons Director for the UK? Or was it something else entirely?

And where had she really been going? Visiting hours at the hospital were over by the time she'd left her hotel room; and she knew Ian couldn't have visitors anyway. So it must have been an excuse to borrow Armstrong's car; but why?

Had she gone somewhere to do some secret thing or see some secret person between nine-thirty and the time when she was found? But if her car doors hadn't opened and nobody had spoken, what could have happened?

And why would she have left at nine-thirty, when she should have been expecting my call?

As I turned into the hospital parking lot, all the questions converged into an answer.

Nora had been jealous of Lola from the start, and when I had abandoned her because of the threats to Lola, she'd been miffed.

So that was it. She had faked an abduction to get my attention. Or to punish me for my inattention. That's why she had left just when I was supposed to call. She wanted me to run to her rescue, to feel guilty for ignoring her and to prove I loved her as much as Lola.

Juggling equal parts hope, fear, and anger, I jogged across the parking lot to the hospital doors.

When I strode up to the nurses' station in the secured area, Linda met me. Despite my churning emotions, my tension eased. Thank God there was someone on duty I could trust without question.

"Aydan! Thank goodness you're finally here! Your mom's in there." She indicated the room two doors down from Ian's, each manned by a burly security guard.

A fresh wave of fear swept me at her worried expression. "How is she? Is she worse?"

"No, she's stable, just upset. I told her you'd be here as soon as you possibly could."

I gulped down guilt. 'As soon as I possibly could'. After I finished screwing my boyfriend, sleeping on the job, and chasing unrelated clues.

"Have the tests come back?" I asked. "Do you know what she was given?"

Linda's smooth brow furrowed and she lowered her voice. "The tests came back negative for all known drugs. I'm sorry, but they must have used some new drug we can't detect."

Or maybe there was never any drug at all.

"Or maybe..." Linda said uncertainly as though reading my mind, "...I thought maybe she hadn't been drugged at all; that maybe she'd had a reaction to her medication or something, but her only medication is eye drops twice a day for glaucoma; and they can't cause that kind of reaction. And the doctor said there's no evidence of a TIA, either."

"A what?"

"Transient ischemic attack. A mini-stroke," Linda clarified. "That can cause temporary confusion and loss of motor control, and then it passes without causing any permanent damage."

"But the doctor said it's not that."

"No."

But I should still give Nora the benefit of the doubt.

"You said her eye drops couldn't cause side effects like she had, but could skipping them cause a problem?" I asked.

"No, nothing like she experienced. And don't worry, she had the drops in her purse, so I put them in for her tonight. Her hands were too shaky and she said she'd put them in herself later, but you don't want to get off-schedule with those. I'll make sure she gets them on time tomorrow morning, too."

Nora was faking the whole thing. I knew it. Wasting hospital resources and jerking us all around for her own selfish purposes. As usual.

Despite my rising anger, I gave Linda a smile. "Thanks, you're such a good nurse. I'll go in and see her now." I headed for Nora's door.

The guard checked my retinal scan before stepping aside to allow me access. They were obviously taking no chances. I gave him a nod and swung the door open softly.

Nora froze, standing in the middle of the room with a small object in her hand.

"Going somewhere?" I asked evenly. "What's that in your hand?"

She stiffened. "I nearly died, and all you can do when you finally show up is interrogate me like a common criminal?"

It took all my will not to snap 'Maybe that's what you are'.

"Sorry, I didn't mean it that way," I said instead. "I just

thought you'd be sleeping. I was surprised to see you out of bed."

Nora drew herself up. "I am allowed to go to the bathroom," she said coldly. "And these are my eye drops." She opened her hand to display the small vial with its prescription label.

Icy certainty slithered down my spine.

If I was going to smuggle a lethal poison through customs and security, I'd put it in a prescription bottle and forge a label with my doctor's name on it. Nobody would ever question it.

Maybe she hadn't been trying to get my attention after all.

Maybe she'd figured out a clever way to smuggle herself and her poison into the secured wing, right next to Ian's room.

And maybe I'd caught her making her move.

CHAPTER 46

Fighting a blaze of adrenaline, I held my voice completely level. "Linda already gave you your eye drops this evening."

"No, she didn't."

I kept my tone conversational. "I just talked to her a minute ago, and she said she had."

"Oh..." Nora tottered back to the bed and slumped onto it. "Are you... sure? Oh, no." Tears rolled down her cheeks. "I... I don't remember that. Oh, Aydan, I can't remember *anything* that happened to me tonight! What... what drugs did they find in my system? Will they be gone soon?"

Damn, she was a good actress.

Doubt wormed into my righteous anger.

What if she *wasn't* acting? She was a director in MI5. If somebody was going to drug and abduct her, it was plausible that they'd use a designer drug. And surely she wouldn't have let Linda put poison in her eyes.

Shit.

But I'd still like to get my hands on that vial.

"They didn't find anything conclusive," I said. "But at least they know you didn't have a mini-stroke." I hesitated. "Why don't you give me your eye drops? I'll take them to

Linda and she'll make sure you get them on time in the morning. That way you won't have to worry about forgetting again."

Nora wiped her tear-reddened eyes and gave me a brave smile. "That's all right, Dani-dear. Here..." She dug into her purse and came up with a scrap of paper and a pen. "Took... drops... Tues... evening," she said as she wrote. Then she wrapped the paper around the small vial and returned everything to her purse.

Damn.

"Are you sure you want to keep your purse here?" I asked. "There's a secure storage area at the nurses' station. I could take it down for you."

She gave me a hard look. "I know what you're trying to do, you know."

I faked puzzlement. "Um... sorry, what?"

Nora's face softened into a maternal smile. "I know you're trying to make sure I don't double up on my drugs, and it's kind of you to be concerned; but really, I'll be fine now that I've written myself a note." Her smile took on a tinge of embarrassment. "And I may have been forgetful about my drops, but I am still quite certain that I need to use the bathroom. Would you excuse me for a moment, please?"

Defeated, I said, "Of course. And I'm sorry, but I can't stay. I have to be over at Sirius in fifteen minutes for a meeting. I just wanted to see for myself that you're all right."

"Oh, thank you, Dani-dear." She came over to hug me, and somehow I managed not to tense. "Will you still pick me up at eight tomorrow morning for our trip to Calgary?" she asked.

"As long as the doctor says it's okay for you to travel."

Hmm, there was an idea. Maybe I could convince the

doctor to keep her for a day or two.

"I'll see you tomorrow, then, dear." She made for the bathroom, and I left.

Outside her door, I lowered my voice so only the guard could hear. "If she leaves this room, you stick to her. Don't leave her unsupervised for an instant."

"Understood."

"Agent Kelly?" I looked up to see the guard at Ian's room beckoning to me. "Agent Rand left instructions to send you in immediately if you came by. It's urgent."

I checked my watch. Dammit, unless Ian got straight to the point, I was going to be late.

When I went into his room, he was sitting bolt upright in the bed. His usual flirtatious smile was gone, replaced by a hard accusing frown. "What the bloody hell do you think you're playing at?" he demanded.

"What the fuck are you talking about?" I snapped in return.

"I was counting on you and your Department to keep my Weapons Director safe while I was incapacitated."

A few fast strides brought me up beside his bed. He didn't flinch, but I could see the flash of anxiety in his eyes as I shoved my face at him.

"She wasn't attacked," I whispered next to his ear. "I think she faked the whole thing either to manipulate me, or to get close enough to poison you; or both. She's two rooms down from you, and I think she might be carrying the poison in her eye drop bottle. I can't get it away from her without making a big scene, but I've told her guard to stay with her no matter what; and I've told your guard not to let anyone in here, and to make sure that all your food and drink comes directly from a nurse."

He said nothing.

When I straightened, his expression was unreadable.

"I see," he said. "Well, first thing tomorrow morning it won't be your problem anymore. I'm officially taking charge of Nora now. I'll drive her to the airport, and we'll fly back together on her two o'clock flight so I can make sure that nothing *else* happens to her."

"What the fuck?" I ground out. "Earlier today you were all, 'Oh, Storm, please protect poor helpless me from the evil witch' and now you're suddenly all cured and protecting the evil witch from *me*?"

"It's my duty to protect my Weapons Director," he said stiffly. "And no, I'm not cured. I still have a horrible headache and nausea and I likely will for some time, but I don't need to be hospitalized anymore. I'm perfectly capable of flying home; and I certainly think I've been an agent long enough not to eat or drink anything dodgy. So thank you for your concern, but it's rather too belated."

I stared at him for a long moment.

"Fuck you," I said, and strode out.

The drive to Sirius wasn't nearly long enough for me to finish mentally throttling Rand, but by the time I arrived at the security wicket my irritation had been replaced by dread.

If even Ian had decided to blame me for the so-called attack on Nora, Dermott would be positively rabid. And I was five minutes late for this meeting. That was probably enough justification for him to order me gutted and hung.

I plodded up the stairs wondering what fresh disaster awaited me. When I walked into my office only Spider and Holt were present, and I let out a breath.

"Where's Dermott?" I asked.

"Not coming," Holt said. "No reason for him to sit here

for hours watching you stare into space." He shrugged. "No real reason for me to, either, but Webb thought it might help if I came into virtual reality with you and held your hand."

There was no contempt in his voice. Surprised into momentary silence, I stared at him.

He shrugged again, looking uncomfortable. "Only if you think it'll help. If not, I can leave. I've never done this before so I don't know what you need."

A tendril of warmth eased my beleaguered heart. "Thanks, Greg. It'll help."

"Okay. So what's the plan?"

I lowered myself to the sofa with a long sigh. "We'll both go into the VR network and I'll start from the file repository. Your avatar will hold onto my avatar's hand, and then I'll turn invisible and slip into the network. You'll still be able to feel my hand, but it'll stretch, maybe to almost nothing. If everything goes okay, you shouldn't lose me entirely. If it doesn't..." I grimaced. "If you can still feel my hand, you can start trying to pull me back. If I'm gone entirely, Spider will send out continuous internet searches to guide me back."

"So we'll basically just be sitting here not knowing what's happening or whether you need help."

"Yeah." I shrugged, trying to convince everyone including myself that it was no big deal. "And even if you *know* I need help, there's still nothing you can do."

"It sucks," Spider said tremulously. "I hope you'll be able to find Rebecca, and..." He swallowed. "I hope she's still okay. She's been in there nearly three days..."

He trailed off and we both shuddered.

"I hope dumping her out a portal will throw her back into her body," I said. "If it doesn't..." It was my turn to trail off.

"You'll figure out something," Spider said. "You always do."

That didn't make me feel any better.

He went on, "I pinpointed a few potential IP addresses based on what you told me about the last time you collided with Rebecca, and I've been monitoring them ever since. They could be 'way off base, but at least it's a place for you to start looking for her."

"Okay."

We sat in silence for a moment.

"So are we going to do this, or what?" Holt demanded.

As I clenched my network key in my fist and leaned back on the sofa, Spider sprang up and hurried over to fling his arms around me. He was trembling.

"Good luck," he said shakily. "Come back safe."

"Thanks." As he stood back, I turned to Holt. "Let's go."

When we stepped into the white void of virtual reality, an unsettling buzzing hiss surrounded us. Half-formed shadows undulated at the edges of the void.

Holt spun, his gaze snapping from one to the next as they writhed and vanished like smoke. "What the hell is this?" he barked, his gun already in his hand.

"Just my nightmares," I said grimly. "Come on." I visualized the file repository for all I was worth, and it sprang into being.

Holt glanced warily around us. "This is freaky."

"Yeah." I probably should have said something to make him feel more comfortable, but I was fresh out of reassurance. I grabbed his hand. "Wish me luck."

"Luck."

I dissolved into invisibility. For a long moment, I floated in the familiar traffic of Sirius's internal network gathering my courage.

I could do this. Really, I could. I'd just go and find Rebecca and somehow convince or coerce her to materialize inside the VR network created by Stemp's portable generator, and then I'd walk her avatar to the portal and shove her out. Easy-peasy.

Fortunately I had no body or voice inside the internet, because my whimper would have been pitiful.

Just shut up and go.

Bracing myself for the devastating impact of collision, I slipped out into the internet.

The first IP address yielded no result. Nor did the second, nor the third. Dammit, I had only memorized four of the complex numbers Spider had given me. I'd have to go back and get the next batch if-

Millions of hurricane-driven razor blades shredded my consciousness in a fraction of an eyeblink.

One instant I existed. The next-

too-much-LOUD-make-it-stop-WHERE-WHY-getoutgetout-TOO-MUCH-stop-stop-TOO-MUCH-please-make-it-stopstopstopstopSTOP ear-bleeding shriek of a turbine driven far past its limits gut-wrenching moan of failing steel soul-shattering wails of the damned writhing in eternal torment-

Then nothing.

CHAPTER 47

I floated.

Gradually I became aware of data packets hurrying past me, leaving me bobbing gently in their slipstream.

Almost afraid to try, I sent cautious probes throughout my consciousness, nudging here and there as if testing for broken bones.

I seemed whole.

Or maybe I had been so thoroughly destroyed that I didn't even know pieces were missing.

At last I turned my attention beyond myself, extending fearful tendrils down the data tunnels.

Where was I?

When was I?

All sense of time had fled.   Rebecca's terror had magnified her electronic exile into eternity, and I had no time reference.

One of my tendrils encountered something and jerked back.

Something... familiar.

Me.

But I was here/now. How could I be there/then?

Oh God no...

Dread slowed my progress to a crawl. Data packets flicked by like schools of tropical fish pursued by sharks.

Shrinking into myself, I pushed out my trembling tendril again.

The Thing was closer now. Ahead of me, unmoving. It still felt like me, but *not* me. Like an amputated limb lying cold and dead.

At last mere data bits separated me from the Thing. With no eyes to see, I could only flow around it, sensing.

It was me.

A lump of me.

And yet...

I sent a questing tendril deeper-

TOO-MUCH-make-it-stopLOUD-

Recoiling from the shock of pain and terror, I jerked into a fetal ball of data bits.

She was in there. Rebecca was in there. In *me*.

Or in a piece of me.

Flowing fearfully back, I surrounded the Thing again. After a few more terrifying probes that flayed my tendrils, I retreated again.

Somehow I had completely encapsulated Rebecca inside a vessel of my own consciousness and then detached the vessel from myself.

What did that mean?

Were we stuck here forever?

Panic crackled through me, but I beat it back.

I wasn't stuck. I could still move.

But the Thing...

I tried to nudge it forward, but my data bits simply flowed around it.

The Thing wouldn't move.

The Thing was me.

Stuck forever in this place that might cease to exist in an eyeblink if a line went down or a server turned off. Obliterated...

Panic swelled again, and again I fought it.

If you panic, you'll end up like Rebecca.

Don't panic.

Think.

I couldn't push the Thing.

Could I pull it?

Flowing past it in the data tunnel, I imagined a magnetic force drawing it along with me... *no! Magnets destroy data!*

Yes, idiot, but you're not creating actual magnetism. You're just visualizing the same attraction that holds data bits together in packets...

I tried again.

The Thing moved.

If I'd had eyes, I would have wept in relief.

Towing the Thing behind me, I crept down the data tunnel, aiming for Stemp's VR network and hoping it was still active.

What if I'd been in here for days?

What if they'd given up?

What if...

Don't think about it.

Just keep searching.

Creeping down another seemingly interminable data tunnel, I nearly missed the sudden glimmer of the VR node.

But was it the right one?

It shouldn't matter. I should be able to go into any VR network, step out any portal, and end up back in my own body at Sirius.

Pulling the Thing behind me, I slipped through the node and willed myself visible.

An involuntary scream ripped from my throat as I sprang back, reeling.

Falling.

Unable to stop myself.

Both my arms had been torn off at the shoulders, leaving only thin gory strings of twitching muscle. Arterial blood sprayed in fierce gouts with the pounding of my heart.

Rebecca was horribly deformed, my own missing arms somehow woven into the mutated lump of flesh topped by her distorted shrieking face.

Blackness swooped in.

Blood loss.

Only a moment left...

No, it's a sim. I'll only die if I *think* I'm dying.

No matter how hard I visualized, my arms refused to rejoin my body. The whole void dripped with my blood.

My control fading, I imagined a giant scoop whisking down from the virtual ceiling. It wobbled, but solidified and shoved the Rebecca-Thing across the void and out the portal.

She was gone.

My dismembered arms vanished with her.

My mangled body still pumped blood.

Screams strangled me. Blackness suffocated me...

I dove back into the internet.

Safely inside the data tunnel, I hung vibrating in sheer horror.

My arms. My arms were gone.

Why couldn't I visualize them back into existence? Had something terrible happened to my physical body?

No-no-no...

I had to get back to Sirius.

But Holt's tether was long gone *because my arms were gone, omigod, omigod...*

Calm. Down.

Of course my physical body still had arms. It was sitting safely in my office in Silverside, Alberta, and no amount of virtual reality could make my actual arms disappear.

Unless there had been a bomb blast that ripped my body apart and that was why my consciousness couldn't recreate it...

I rocketed down the data tunnel, frantically questing for Spider's searches.

Oh, please let him still be alive and sending searches...

Aydan-Kelly-Aydan-Kelly-Aydan-Kelly...

Redoubling my speed, I fled along the lifeline and burst into visibility in the blessed familiarity of the Sirius file repository. Tumbling across the room, I screamed again at the sight of my blood cartwheeling along with me.

No arms no arms omigod...

"*Jesus Christ!*" Holt sprang across the file room as I fell in a blood-drenched heap. "Hang on, Kelly!" He stripped off his shirt, wadding it up and jamming it into my gaping wounds.

"GET HER OUT!" Spider's frantic voice boomed out of the virtual ceiling. "BRING HER OUT THE PORTAL, NOW!"

Holt hoisted me into a fireman's carry and ran. As the portal loomed up Spider yelled, "SLOW-"

The rest of his words burned away in an inferno of agony.

"Aydan..."

The voice was distant but familiar.

"Wha...?" I mumbled.

"Aydan, wake up..."

"No, Mom. S'not time for school yet," I slurred.

"Aydan, wake up." The voice sounded terrified.

Not Mom.

I knew that voice.

I bolted upright. "Spider, what's wrong?"

He let out a sobbing laugh. "Nothing. Nothing's wrong now." He flung his arms around me and I hugged him back.

Hugged him.

With my *arms*.

"Oh, thank God!" Now I was watery-eyed, too, gulping air and barely clinging to control. "Thank *God!*"

"What happened?" Spider demanded. "Your physical body started twitching and you were making these weird noises, but you were still unconscious. I thought you were having a seizure or something, but I was afraid to call the ambulance in case..." He trailed off. "I just... didn't know what to do."

"I think a small part of my consciousness went through the portal with Rebecca and came back to my body before the rest of me," I said.

"Never mind that," Holt snapped. "You're fine now, and we have to report to Stemp. We just wasted twenty minutes waiting for you to wake up." He glared at Spider, who flushed but raised his chin defiantly.

"I don't care," Spider retorted. "You brought her through the portal too fast and she was going through hell. I wasn't going to let her suffer like that." He turned to me. "I'm sorry, I panicked. My hands were shaking too hard to get a dart out and break it open, so I just shot you."

I took in the spent tranquilizer dart lying on the coffee table with my trank pistol beside it. "Thanks, Spider. Let's call Stemp."

Stemp picked up on the first ring. "Status?" he barked.

"Is Rebecca conscious?" I snapped back.

"Ah."

It almost sounded as though he'd sighed in relief at the sound of my voice; but that couldn't be right. Stemp didn't show emotion.

"Yes," he added. "Ms. Stile is conscious. And you are well, I presume?"

"Not one of my more pleasant trips, but I made it."

"Good. And what is your evaluation of Ms. Stile's mental state?"

I hesitated, swallowing hard. She was absolutely bugfuck crazy. But if I told Stemp that, he'd execute her as coldly and efficiently as I would swat a mosquito.

But if I didn't tell him, she could run amok. A giant security breach just waiting to happen...

"Agent Kelly?" Stemp prompted. "Were you successful in removing classified intel from her mind?"

Something dark and heavy lodged itself where my heart used to be.

"No." The death warrant issued from my lips in a monotone. "I couldn't even find any coherent thoughts in her mind. She was... completely insane. I couldn't get near her without getting torn apart. I... I tried..." I had to stop and draw a calming breath.

"Kelly barely survived," Holt said flatly. "She was torn to pieces when she got back to our sim. Literally... dismembered." His expression was impassive but his voice vibrated on the last word. Old ghosts darkened his eyes.

Silence hung heavily on the line.

"I see." Stemp's two words said it all.

Despair bowed my back.

All that effort; all that pain; for nothing.

My bruised heart tore at the futility of it all. Right now Rebecca's poor parents would be celebrating her return to consciousness, but they would lose her to death in mere minutes. It would have been kinder if she'd never woken.

"Thank you for your service, Agent Kelly," Stemp said quietly. "Go home and get some sleep."

In the silence after he disconnected, Spider stared at me, his eyes wide and dark in his pale face. "What's wrong?"

I couldn't speak.

Didn't need to.

His face crumpled. "He's going to kill her, isn't he?"

CHAPTER 48

Spider's question echoed in my mind while I struggled to say something comforting that wasn't an outright lie.

I found nothing.

Spider hid his face in his hands, his shoulders shaking.

I dragged myself to my feet and went over to rub his back.

"I'm sorry." My voice came out clogged with unshed tears of my own.

"It's not... your fault." His words jerked out between sobs. "I just... she was innocent! I was hoping... so hard..."

He trailed off and I kept rubbing his back.

Holt hissed out a breath and rose. "Sorry, Webb," he said gruffly. "We have to move on." He braced his hands on his hips and arched his back, grimacing at the cracks and pops that emanated from his spine. "Kelly, are you riding with me and Grandin and the security team tomorrow?" He glanced at his watch and sighed. "No; in a couple of hours."

"No." My voice came out completely flat. "If I have to look at Grandin this morning, I'll puke." I didn't mention that I might puke anyway. "I'll drive myself."

"Okay. Just remember to come to the staging area at ten, not the drop zone." Before I could speak, he flung up a defensive hand and added, "I'm not saying you'd fuck up; it's just a reminder. We're both wiped out, and we can't afford mistakes."

"It's okay. I'm too tired to get mad."

We exchanged grim smiles, and he left.

Spider sat up, sniffling and mopping his face. "I'm sorry," he whispered. "I'm so..."

"You don't have to apologize." I squeezed his shoulder. "Go home and get some sleep. I'll email Dermott and tell him I put you on stress leave, so he won't expect to see you in the morning."

He turned a tearstained face up to me. "But you don't have the authority..."

"That's between Dermott and me. You have your orders."

He drew in a hitching breath and stood. "Thanks, Aydan. I'm..." He hesitated, fatigue in every line of his trembling body and pale face. "Just... stay safe, okay? I... I can't..." He hugged me fiercely, then turned and fled as tears flooded his eyes again.

I should be crying, too.

But the dark weight in my chest absorbed all emotion. Nothing remained but leaden weariness and a slow deep current of rage.

I fired off a terse email to Dermott and plodded out the door.

As I descended the stairs to the lobby, the entrance door opened and Reggie strode in. As usual, his confident gait belied the prosthetic legs concealed by his pants, but a memory-flash of blood and torn-off limbs nearly folded my knees. My hand flew to the railing as I stumbled and regained my balance.

"You okay?" Reggie called across the lobby.

The truth jumped out of my mouth before I could stop it. "No."

As concern flashed across his face, I added, "I need a favour. Two favours. Can I talk to you in your lab?"

He nodded, his brow furrowed. "Go on down. I'll sign in and be right behind you."

Giving silent thanks that he understood my need to be alone in the cramped time-delay chamber, I cranked my lips into a semblance of a smile and headed for its door.

Inside, I counted down the long thirty-second delay, forcing myself to stand with my hands at my sides instead of flailing wildly. My prison cell would be about the same size as this...

Don't. Even. Go. There.

Clamping down on my thoughts, I mentally recited multiplication tables. One times one is one. One times two is two...

That carried me to Reggie's lab. Unwilling to face any other early-bird employees, I loitered outside the door until Reggie strode up.

"Can't you get in?" he asked.

"Didn't try. I was just waiting for you."

He flashed his prox card at the reader and opened the door for me, and I preceded him into the lab.

"You're here early," I said, making an effort at normalcy.

"I've started coming in at six. Honey gets the kids off to school in the morning, and then I can leave work earlier in the afternoon to pick them up."

The frozen place in my chest warmed. Life went on. Even when awful things were happening to some people, good things were happening to others.

"I'm glad it's working out for you," I said, and meant it with every shred of my being.

"Thanks. Me, too." He ushered me into his office and closed the door. "Have a seat." As I perched on the edge of the chair, he added, "So I'm guessing you're here about the drug dose I issued to Stemp?"

I froze. "J-just before he left?" The words barely cleared my lips.

"Yeah…" Reggie gave me an anxious look. "Shit, didn't you know? I shouldn't have-"

"No, it's okay, I knew," I lied.

I should have known. Or guessed.

Rebecca.

"I'm just…" All my guilt and misery rushed out in a sigh. "I just know where he used it, that's all. But that's not why I'm here. Do you still have those video-and-sound-enhanced sunglasses I tested last summer?"

"They're in production but not available yet." My heart was sinking when he added, "But I still have the prototype. It's yours if you want it."

"Thank you. I do." I hesitated. "Do you need to know why?"

"Nope. Forgot to ask." He gave me his scar-twisted half-grin. "You said 'two favours'. What's the other?"

"That bulletproof, blade-proof jacket."

"Done. Anything else?"

"No, but I owe you big-time for this."

He shrugged. "No, I'll just log it in the development documents as additional testing." Mischief sparkled in his eye. "Lucky for the Weapons Department that you're so dedicated."

I fell back in my chair with a sigh. "I could kiss you right now."

"Whoa, baby!" He held up a restraining hand. "That's off the table now. You blew it. You should've jumped me while you had the chance."

Grinning at our old joke, I rose. "Damn. I can't believe I let you slip through my fingers like that. Now I'll never get to know your left nut up close and personal."

He snickered. "Don't worry, I'll always have a special place in my nut for you. Come on, I'll gear you up. Are you on your way to work, or on your way home?"

"Home," I said as I followed him out. "And if I speed all the way, I just might get an hour of sleep before I have to leave again."

"Fucking crazy life." Reggie leaned down to trigger the retinal scan on one of the storage lockers. Opening it, he extracted the sunglasses and jacket and handed them over. His too-perceptive gaze flicked over me. "If you can't sleep when you get home, take a sniff of tranquilizer from one of your darts. When you're this exhausted you'll fall asleep in the five minutes you're out, but it won't leave you drowsy when you wake up."

Relief coursed over me. "Thanks, I never would have thought of that." Caution whispered in my ear, and I added, "Don't tell Jack, though. She'll give me hell if she finds out."

The undamaged side of Reggie's lips quirked up, but his gaze stayed serious. "I won't. I love that brilliant mind of hers, but she doesn't quite understand that when you're in the field you do what you have to do."

"Let's hope she never has to." I headed for the door. "Thanks, Reggie."

"No problem. Good luck."

When I crept into my house fifteen minutes later, the bedroom lights were already on. Disappointment made me slump. I had been hoping for a few uncomplicated moments cuddled up to Arnie's sleeping bulk.

As I walked into the bedroom he came out of the ensuite bathroom, a few droplets of water still glistening on his naked tattooed shoulders.

"Hey, darlin'." He folded me into his arms and I pressed my face against his warm moist skin, inhaling the fresh scent of his soap. "How'd it go?" he asked.

Tightening my arms around him, I mumbled, "Shitty. Can't talk about it." Before he could ask any questions, I added, "Why are you up so early? We don't have to be at the drop zone until ten-thirty."

"Yeah, but I want some time to scope it out an' get set up." He took my hand and led me to the bed. "Come on, darlin', ya look dead on your feet. What time d'ya wanna get up?"

"Never," I muttered as I yanked my sweatshirt over my head. "Seven-thirty," I added as I emerged.

"That ain't even an hour."

"It's all I get. I want time to shower and eat something, and I have to leave by eight."

Arnie frowned. "Ya gonna be able to sleep?"

"No idea." I yanked off the last of my clothes and crawled under covers that were still warm from his body. "But Reggie suggested I should take a sniff of aerosolized trank, and by the time it wears off I should be asleep."

"Hm." Arnie considered for a moment. "Good idea. Set your alarm, darlin'. I'll stick around, an' if you're sleepin' after five minutes I'll just sneak out."

"Thanks." I set my phone's alarm for seven-thirty and extracted a dart from my trank pistol. Lying back on the pillow, I said, "I left the sunglasses on the kitchen table for you. Goodnight."

"G'night, darlin'." He leaned down to kiss me, then drew away to regard me seriously. "Just remember, even if everythin' goes to hell this mornin', I'll be there for ya. No matter what."

My heart warmed. "Thanks. I love you."

"Love ya, too."

I broke open the capsule.

The beep of my alarm made me levitate about three feet off the bed. Patting my chest over my thumping heart, I turned off the alarm and headed for the shower. Half an hour later I was in my car, still chewing the last bite of my granola bar.

The two-hour drive was a paradoxical combination of sharp fear and dull fatigue. I fought the drooping of my eyelids all the way, even though my pulse hurried in an unsettling rhythm.

When my secured phone vibrated at a quarter to ten, I twitched violently and risked death by pulling out of the heavy traffic to stop on the shoulder of Deerfoot Trail.

"Kelly," I snapped.

"Holt here." Tension strained his voice. "The buyer just changed the drop zone."

"Shit. Can we cancel?"

His frustrated breath hissed over the speaker, dashing my hopes. "Negative. Grandin bought us an extra half hour, but that's all the buyer would agree to. The new location's out in the middle of nowhere."

The fear I'd been holding at bay crashed over me like an icy wave. "Wh-what kind of 'nowhere'?"

"A fucking field out by De Winton. I hate this fucking stupid redneck province! Back in Toronto we'd-"

"*De Winton?*" I interrupted. "I'm already northbound on Deerfoot! I'm going in the opposite fucking direction and I'm at least forty minutes away!"

"I'm pretty sure that's what they want," Holt said grimly. "They want Grandin scrambling. No time to set up an ambush."

The dull red anger at the bottom of my soul welled up, glowing brighter. "Well, fuck them. If they want me, they'll just have to stick around until we get there."

"I'm pretty sure they will, but we have to play the game. They want to meet where Highway 552 swings south and crosses the river east of Highway 2. South of the bridge there's a pulloff where you can drive down next to the river."

"It's an ambush," I said flatly. "They're planning to kill Grandin and take off with me; or just kill us both. Forget it."

The thump of a closing vehicle door was followed by the hiss of wind blowing across Holt's phone as he lowered his voice. "I already called Dermott and said we should abort, but he gave us a direct order to go through with it."

"He's a-" Remembering at the last moment that they were friends, I didn't complete my sentence. "So we're going ahead?"

"Yeah."

"But where are you and your security guys going to be?" I demanded. "The buyer will have eyes on the new drop zone already, so there's no way you can go in and get set up there without him seeing you. And if Grandin and I go in alone,

Grandin will make a break for it and I won't be able to do anything because I'm supposed to be the unconscious hostage."

"You're not going to be pretending to be unconscious anymore, and I'm going to play Grandin's driver. The security team is already on their way. There are lots of little trails in the bushes along the river, so they'll sneak in from upriver. There's a sportsplex on the north side of the highway just after you turn off Highway 2. Meet me there."

"But what if the buyer's only expecting Grandin and me?" I persisted. "Or what if they decide to eliminate all the witnesses and shoot you and Grandin? That's what I'd do." The words were out of my mouth before I considered them. "I mean... not that I'd kill people in cold blood; I just meant if I were them-"

"I know what you meant," Holt said. "And we're just going to have to take the chance. I'm wearing a vest. I'll just hope they don't go for a head shot."

"But if you're sitting in the driver's seat, that's pretty well the only shot they've got," I argued.

"If you've got a better idea, spit it out. We're wasting time."

I didn't have a better idea.

"See you at the sportsplex," I said.

CHAPTER 49

As soon as I disconnected from Holt's call, I hit the speed dial for Hellhound. The call went directly to voicemail.

Shit. That meant he was in position already.

"It's Aydan," I said rapidly after the beep. "The buyer just changed the drop point. We have to be south of town near De Winton by eleven." I described the site to him in as much detail as I could, hoping I wasn't missing anything.

My heart sank as I talked. He wouldn't make it there in time. The original site was in the north end of Calgary, so his travel time would be a good twenty minutes longer than mine; and I was barely going to make it. There was no way he'd be able to take down his setup, pack up, drive to De Winton, and be ready for action.

"Thanks for trying," I added. "And don't bother calling me back; I won't be able to pick up anyway. I love you. 'Bye."

I disconnected and got back on the highway, taking the first exit to get onto the southbound side.

Navigating the traffic with only half my attention, I racked my brain for a safer way to accomplish this meeting. By the time my exit rushed up, I still had no inspiration.

I couldn't drive us to the drop. I couldn't control

Grandin and look as though I was his captive at the same time. And if we cut Grandin out of the loop entirely and Holt impersonated him, and if our buyer knew Grandin by sight, Holt was pretty much guaranteed to get shot.

Dammit, dammit, dammit!

What would Kane do? Surely he'd have a better plan.

Should I phone him?

I growled and thumped the steering wheel. No. He had made it clear where his priorities lay. And after all my lofty talk about not influencing him, it would be pretty damn hypocritical to call him now and ask for help. He'd feel obligated to rescue me again; and if this meeting ended up being as fatal to witnesses as I feared...

No. Just no.

The sportsplex loomed up on my left, and I turned in.

Holt was standing beside a white panel truck splashed with a gaudy 'Fitz-Rite Fine Flooring' logo, his phone to his ear. When I parked beside him, he headed for my passenger door. I popped the locks and he slid in, pocketing his phone as he did.

"Where's Grandin?" I asked.

"Back of the truck." Holt jerked a thumb in that direction. "I've been keeping him sedated. This kind of situation is his best opportunity to escape, so I'm taking extra precautions. We'll get him into your back seat before he comes to." He hesitated, not looking at me. "So, did you think of any better plans?"

"No. Sorry."

He shrugged. "Okay." Glancing over, he added, "Where's your vest?"

"This is it." I plucked at the light jacket Reggie had given me.

"Are you fucking nuts?" Holt barked. "Put on a fucking vest!"

"This is better than a vest. It's bulletproof and blade-proof, too. It's a prototype I tested last summer for the Weapons Department."

"No shit." Holt poked a tentative finger at my sleeve. "So you're saying I could stab you and the blade wouldn't go through this? Bullshit."

"It stopped a broadhead from a hunting bow at point-blank range."

"Wow." His eyes narrowed thoughtfully. "No wonder you suck up to Chow."

"Fuck off," I said without heat. "Are your security guys in place?"

"Yeah, I was just talking to them. The site's clear except for some old farts ice-fishing down on the river, but it's too late to clear them out. They've got coolers and lawn chairs and a campfire, so they're probably not going anywhere in the next half hour; and we're not going near them anyway. They should be pretty safe. The bushes block their view, and the way they've got their radio cranked they won't notice us, or even hear gunshots if there are any." He grimaced. "And if they're working with the buyer, they're too far away to be much of a threat. Our sniper will take them out before they can get to us."

I eased out a shaky breath. "I guess that's the best we can do." A glance at my watch did nothing to calm my nerves. "It's time."

"Bring the car around the back of the van and help me with Grandin."

Holt got out and I followed his instructions, pulling in close to the double rear doors as he opened them. My heart thumped as I surveyed the parking lot and nearby highway. A cluster of parked vehicles huddled near the building's entrance, but none were close to us. The sparse traffic on the highway whisked by, oblivious to the drama about to be enacted. We wouldn't get a better chance.

I hopped out and joined Holt in the van where Grandin lay sprawled on the floor in leg shackles and handcuffs.

"Cover me," Holt said. As I drew my Glock, he raised his voice and added, "Grandin, if you're faking it, just remember that Kelly's holding a gun on you. If you try anything, she'll be really happy to blow your brains out."

He seized Grandin's feet and dragged him to the doors of the van, then stepped down to the ground. Stooping, he draped Grandin over his shoulder, then pivoted and flopped Grandin's inert body into my back seat.

Swearing under his breath, he wrestled Grandin roughly upright and removed his restraints, then drew his weapon and jerked his chin at me. "Grandin, I've got you covered and Kelly's getting in the other side with her gun drawn, so don't get any ideas."

Hurrying around to the other side of the car, I sucked in a deep breath in the hope of gathering any stray courage that might be floating around in the frigid air.

I didn't find any, so I dropped gracelessly into the back seat and fumbled on my seatbelt left-handed.

Holt closed Grandin's door, locked the van, then rounded my car and got behind the wheel. We sat in silence.

A couple of minutes later, Holt twisted and reached over the seat to give Grandin's shoulder a rough shake.

No response.

Holt checked his watch. "He should wake up any minute now." Enviably calm, he threaded an earpiece over his ear and tucked the transmitter into his jacket. "Black Team, this is Base, do you read?" He waited, then said, "Black Team One, report."

Another pause while he listened.

"Black Team Two?" Holt asked. He listened again, then said, "Radio silence unless there's a change." Turning to me, he said, "Still no sign of the buyer, and the area's clear except for the old farts. Our guys have a sightline to the road, so they'll let us know if anybody arrives before we get there."

I nodded and silence fell again.

A couple more minutes crawled past. Tension ratcheted my shoulders up to the vicinity of my ears. God, waiting was far worse than action.

What if the buyer had spotted our men and aborted?

Or worse, what if the buyer had brought a team? What if they had killed all our men and were even now slaughtering the old fishermen to eliminate any potential witnesses? My stomach lurched at the memory of Dirk's bright blood spraying across white snow.

Grandin twitched and mumbled, and I nearly jumped out of my skin.

Holt raised a sardonic eyebrow in the rearview mirror. "Don't shoot him by accident."

"If I shoot him, it'll be on purpose," I growled.

Grandin groaned and his eyes opened halfway. More long moments oozed by as he gradually regained consciousness. At last he straightened in the seat, his eyes focusing.

"Grandin," Holt said sharply. "It's showtime. Tell me again what you're going to do."

Grandin shot him a look that blazed with pure hatred. "I'm going to sit here in the car until the buyer drives up," he said in a monotone. "Then Kelly's going to hold her gun on me until you come around and open her door. You'll lean in as though you're dragging her out but you'll actually be aiming your gun at me. She'll holster her weapon and stand up, and you'll hold her in front of you to hide your weapon from any observers. I'll get out and pretend to grab her and push her forward. You'll be right behind me with your gun on my spine. As soon as the buyer gets out of the car, your team will take him down. Then we'll go back to the car and you'll put the shackles and handcuffs back on me."

"Very good." Holt gave him a short mocking round of applause. "And if you do *anything* besides what you just described, you'll be spending the rest of your life in a wheelchair."

"Whatever," Grandin snarled. "Let's get this over with."

Holt shifted into gear, and my pulse accelerated along with the car.

I could do this.

I wasn't in any actual danger. They wanted me alive.

But not necessarily uninjured...

Blocking that thought out as best I could, I reviewed our plans again.

So many ways this could go wrong...

The drive took exactly seven minutes. In that blip of time I aged ten years.

I couldn't do this. I was only a middle-aged bookkeeper, for fucksakes, not James Fucking Bond. I should be sitting behind a desk bored out of my mind right now, looking forward to leaving my boring job and going home to my boring life-

"The team just spotted a guy moving into place under the bridge on the north side," Holt said as we coasted down the hill. "But we don't have time to clear him out."

My heart rattled against my ribs. "That's only about a hundred yards. No problem for a rifle. Does he have a clear shot?" I tried to crane my neck without taking my eyes off Grandin as we rolled onto the bridge.

"We'll park where he doesn't." Holt hesitated, listening to his earpiece. "No sign of a weapon and he's scruffy. Might be a homeless guy just holing up..."

As he listened again, my heart rose with momentary hope. Maybe that was Hellhound moving into place.

"Okay, he's curled up with his garbage bags," Holt said. "Easy shot for our sniper. If he makes a move, he's toast."

My guts froze. My mouth was already half open to tell Holt it might be Hellhound when I realized that if Holt and Dermott found out I'd involved Arnie, we'd both be up Shit Creek.

But what if Hellhound didn't know he was in the team's crosshairs?

Oh, God, what if he took out his rifle...

Maybe it wasn't Arnie. Maybe it was an enemy.

Would that be worse or better?

Shit, shit...

Holt slowed for the turn, and my back prickled with the knowledge of eyes watching us.

And eyes *not* watching. The fishermen were strung out along the riverbank in a loose group, their attention focused on the river and their unprotected backs turned toward our rendezvous point. Even through the closed car windows, I could hear the country music blaring. They must be deaf as posts. As I watched, one of the figures limped over to the campfire, red jacket bright and white hair almost invisible against the snowy backdrop. A whiff of wood smoke reached my nose, and I imagined them joking and laughing, enjoying their retirement, probably swigging a few beers kept frosty in a snowbank.

Unaware that death was rolling up behind them.

I lost sight of them as the car bounced down the twisting snow-rutted trail that descended to the river. Scrubby bushes surrounded us, their winter-bare branches dark against the snow and thick enough to completely obscure our view. The dead-white sky crowded down, creating an oppressive monochrome landscape far too much like the VR void.

Suppressing a shiver, I glued my gaze on Grandin. One moment of my inattention was all he'd need to overpower me and grab my gun.

My heart thumped in my ears.

Around a bend the trail opened up into a wider section. Holt braked to a bumpy halt, then turned the car around to face back the way we'd come.

"Good as it's going to get," he grunted, and shifted into Park.

My hand was icy on my gun and shivers rolled through my belly. "Turn up the heat," I croaked.

"It's already a fucking sauna in here," Holt complained, but he complied. Sweat glistened on the back of his neck.

Was he as scared as I was?

Hell, he should be more scared. He was a lot more likely to be killed.

But it probably wasn't possible to be more scared than I was right now. Dammit, this was far worse than anything I'd ever been forced to do in my unwanted new career. Car chases; gunfights; hell, even getting beaten up; any of it was better than this ever-mounting pressure-cooker of suspense and dread.

Run.

Run now.

Shut up. Shut up shut up shut-

"Incoming." Holt's single word forced another spurt of adrenaline into my already-saturated bloodstream. A moment later he added, "One driver. Surely he wouldn't be stupid enough to come alone. Maybe it's not our guy..."

A vintage cream-coloured Lincoln Continental wallowed around the corner and slid to a stop in front of us.

Blocking the road.

"It's an ambush!" Grandin's voice crackled with tension.

"Probably," Holt agreed. He pressed a finger against his earpiece. "Black Team?" After a listening moment, he said, "Okay, we're on."

A phone rang, its sudden sharp tone making me jump.

Holt pulled it out and toggled the speakerphone. "This is Mr. Grandin's phone," he said primly.

"Let me talk to Grandin."

Holt passed the phone back to Grandin with a warning look.

"Yeah?" Grandin snapped.

"Bring her out where I can see her."

"Where's my money?"

"You'll see your money when I see her."

Grandin let out an irritated sigh. "Fine." He disconnected.

"Let's do it," Holt said.

CHAPTER 50

Time slowed as Holt got out of the driver's seat. Approximately an eternity later, he reached for the door handle on my side. The door swung open and his gun appeared in his hand, concealed between his body and the door panel.

Staying out of his line of fire, I holstered my own weapon. My fingers didn't want to release the Glock's handgrip, and I struggled for an instant against the panicked urge to leap out of the car and open fire.

"Come *on*, Kelly," Holt gritted, and somehow I managed to let go of my Glock and slide out the door.

Holt grabbed me roughly, his arm across my throat, and my hands flew up instinctively to loosen his grip. His other arm was jammed against the small of my back, and I knew the muzzle of his gun would be trained sideways on Grandin as we stepped away.

"Out," Holt growled, and Grandin slid across the seat and obeyed.

His gaze flickered as he stood up. He was going to try something...

Holt shoved me into Grandin, who staggered back, cracking his head on the roof of the car. In an instant Holt was behind him and Grandin stiffened as Holt jabbed the gun into his back.

"Just give me an excuse," Holt snarled.

Grandin didn't. He let out a resigned sigh and grabbed the back of my neck to steer me ahead of him as we stepped out from behind the car door.

The buyer sat unmoving behind the wheel of the Continental, his face obscured by dark glasses. Standing there feeling as though I had a giant target glowing on my chest, I suppressed the hysterical urge to wave at him. My knees trembled so hard I could barely stand.

Everything went silent in my mind except the godawful racket of the fishermen's radios. Good Lord, they must have tuned every one of their truck radios to the same station and turned up the volume to maximum. They could probably hear the damn noise all the way to Calgary.

After an interminable moment, the buyer gave a slow nod and reached for something on the seat beside him. Grandin tensed and yanked me closer.

Thanks, asshole. I always wanted to be a human shield.

The buyer raised a black case so we could see it through the windshield, then opened his door.

As he slowly exited the car, Holt muttered, "Wait... wait...", apparently instructing his team. The man straightened and rounded the car door, leaving it open with the motor running.

The raucous country music bounced crazily in my head, creating an incongruous soundtrack as the buyer paced forward in slow motion.

Holt's tension-laden whisper came from behind me "...wait... wait... NOW!"

Black-clad men rushed out of the bushes around us.

Shouting. Guns trained on the buyer.

Grandin's fingers ground into the nerve cluster in my shoulder, yanking and spinning *oh no you don't you asshole...*

My right arm hung paralyzed by the momentary nerve disruption.

Holt couldn't shoot, Grandin had jerked me into his line of fire.

He was getting away...

Going with Grandin's spin, I hooked my left arm around his and dragged him down as I fell.

"*Bitch!*" he roared.

He was on top of me.

Raw panic blinded me. Heaving and thrashing and straining with my one good arm...

"*I got him, Kelly, it's o-*" Holt's shout of reassurance cut off abruptly as I bucked Grandin's limp body off me.

Holt fell beside me.

Crazed panting whistling in my throat, I snapped my head first one way, then the other.

Shitfuckdamn! The buyer had backup.

Over a dozen men, all wearing snow-patterned camo. They must have been hiding in the bushes surrounding us and our team.

Wrinkled faces grim, weathered hands steady on rifles and shotguns, they held their aim as the fishermen from the river roared up in quads. In moments they had trussed up Holt and Grandin and the security team with an economy of motion only achieved by men who'd spent their lives securing struggling calves with a twist of rope in less than eight seconds.

All our weapons, all our preparation, useless.

At least I had that locator in my wristwatch. But the whole team was down. Who would even know this had gone wrong?

My Glock lay heavy in my ankle holster, but there were too many of them. They'd get me first.

The ringleader paced toward me, his heavy boots at my eye level. Vicious treads tortured the squeaking snow.

He crouched down beside me, removing his dark glasses.

"Are you okay?" he asked.

I blinked.

Blinked again.

"*Mr. Nielsen?*" My voice cracked.

Oh God, my childhood had been an even bigger lie than I had ever realized. Another frantic glance around the circle of men told me more than I'd ever wanted to know.

Most of our old neighbours, plus a few men I knew from my teenage waitressing job at the coffee shop.

The whole town had been in on it all along.

Mr. Nielsen grinned, revealing the missing tooth I'd known since I was a child. "Yep. The one and only. But you can call me Lars now that you're all growed up."

"But... but..."

I couldn't help it; a sob escaped me and I squirmed away from him even though I knew it was futile.

"Calm down now, Punkinhead," Mr. Nielsen soothed, the old pet name falling off his tongue with horrifying familiarity. "You're okay. You're safe now. We rescued you. We'll have you back to yer mama in two shakes of a lamb's tail."

"Rescued... *What...?*" My voice cracked again.

"Yep." His chest expanded with pride. "When yer mama called and said you'd been kidnapped and she needed me to pay these dogs..." He spat contemptuously on Grandin. "...to get you back, I just couldn't hand over the money like a yella-bellied coward. And I knew all the boys would help out." He grinned up at them.

Shoulders straightened and chests puffed around the circle, along with murmurs of 'yeah' and 'dang right'.

I sat up, hoping the movement would somehow shake some sense into my head. Fear arrowed through me at the sight of the blood-darkened hair on the back of Holt's scalp, but he seemed to be breathing all right. Alert steel-blue eyes glittered between those motionless lashes.

Releasing my fear on a shaky breath, I was seized with a new fear before I could even inhale.

Nora had told them I'd been kidnapped.

Nora was the buyer.

And if I blew our cover, there was no hope of containing it. Small-town gossip travels by telepathy. The instant these men found out the truth, the whole town would know. One day, rural Saskatchewan; the next day, the world.

"Wh-what happened?" I stammered. "What did Mom tell you?"

Thank goodness my ragtag band of heroes had no concept of securing a site and getting out fast. Mr. Nielsen grinned and hunkered down, preparing for a grand tale.

"Welllll..." He paused, drawing out the drama. "Turns out yer mama didn't die in that car wreck like we all thought. Turns out she got mixed up in some trouble and had to go into witness pertection. They finally let her out and she came straight back to Canada to find you, but the same dirty dogs were lyin' for her and they grabbed you right up."

He stopped to spit on Grandin again, and a memory flash from my childhood almost made me smile. He'd always had deadly spitting aim through that gap from his missing tooth.

"So yer mama called me in a flap last week," Mr. Nielsen went on. "She was willin' to pay whatever they asked but she couldn't get the money in time, bein' as her money was all tied up in England; and anyway she was afraid they'd grab her, too, when she showed up with the cash. She was fit to be tied. They said they'd kill you if she called the cops, and she didn't know where else to turn."

I rubbed my right arm, flexing my fingers as the nerves tingled back to life. "So she asked you to pay the kidnappers and collect me," I prompted.

Smart, smart Nora. She had bribed Grandin to kidnap me last week instead of extraditing me to the U.S. beyond her reach; and our staunch well-meaning neighbour was her middleman and alibi.

But after Grandin got arrested she must have altered her plans without updating Mr. Nielsen. After all, if Grandin couldn't call him, who would?

"Yep." Mr. Nielsen beamed. "And I told her not to worry her head none. We take care of our own." Pride glowed in his face as he nodded at the black suitcase lying beside his faithful Lincoln. "The whole dang town pitched in for the ransom, just in case these dogs..." Another blast of spittle landed on Grandin's deserving head. "...counted it before they'd hand you over."

"The whole *town* donated the ransom money?" I suppressed a groan and pasted on an expression that I sincerely hoped would look grateful. "I can't believe you did all this for me!"

Maybe that's why Nora hadn't cancelled the kidnapping scenario. Maybe she was working on a Plan B that would let her walk away with a suitcase full of our friends' and neighbours' cash.

"Yep. But we weren't gonna let them get away with it. We figgered out a plan, and we were just waitin' for the call. Soon as we got it, we convoyed up and hightailed it here." Mr. Nielsen rose, his knees creaking and popping. Straightening painfully, he reached down to help me up. "And now it's time to call yer mama and the cops."

"*No!*"

They all stared at me.

Shit! If they called Nora now, I'd lose the element of surprise. By the time I questioned her, she'd already have a slick new story manufactured. And if the RCMP showed up, it would be a total circus and my cover would be blown for sure.

"Don't call Nor- ...um, Mom!" I snapped. "Or the cops!" As their puzzlement dissolved into frowns, I added hurriedly, "Mom could be in danger if we lead anybody to her. And we can't call the cops because you threatened these men with guns and that's illegal. I don't want you to get in trouble with the law."

Muttering rose from the circle. "What kinda cockamamie law is that? Kidnappin's illegal, it shouldn't oughta be illegal to get somebody back."

Mr. Nielsen frowned. "Well, we ain't gonna just let these dogs go."

I waited. Sure enough, another well-aimed gob struck Grandin in the same spot. If I kept Mr. Nielsen standing here long enough, Grandin would drown in spit. That thought probably shouldn't have been as gratifying as it was.

"No cops," I repeated.

The muttering increased in volume. Mr. Shepherd

leaned over to Mr. Newsome. His confidential tone might have been more effective if he hadn't been forced to half-shout into Mr. Newsome's famously deaf left ear. "She got that Swedish Syndrome or somethin'?"

"Swedish sin?" Mr. Newsome's rheumy gaze scoured the landscape as though hoping to spot Nordic beauties cavorting naked in a snowbank.

"*Syndrome*, you old fool! Swedish Syndrome!"

"It's Stockholm Syndrome," old Mr. Evans contradicted. "You're both dopes."

Mr. Nielsen was still frowning. "Wellll..." he said slowly. "I reckon maybe you're right, Punkinhead. Nobody's gonna miss a bunch of dogs..." Splat. "...like this." He shot a significant look around his band of cronies. "Seems like we might be doin' the world a favour if we just shoot, shovel, and shut up."

"NO!" I clutched his sleeve. "I don't want you to be murderers!"

Oh God, no. Eight good men lying helpless in the snow, depending on me to pull their asses out of this increasingly deadly fire...

Mr. Engel stepped forward, his rifle at the ready and his dead eyes every bit as terrifying as when he used to drive our school bus. Nobody *ever* misbehaved on Mr. Engel's bus.

"I'll do it," he said flatly. "Won't matter to me. I did two tours in 'Nam. I'm already a murderer."

I could only stare, open-mouthed. I had never known he was a veteran. That explained all those bus evacuation drills he made us do.

Mr. Evans stepped up beside him, his firm gait belying his thin limbs. I had thought he was ancient when I was a kid, and he had to be in his high nineties now. Reduced to leathery sinew and unyielding bone by decades of harsh weather and harsher life, he stood straight and proud beside Mr. Engel.

"World War Two." Mr. Evans presented arms, then slapped the rifle back on his shoulder, his motions as precise as if he was still on parade all those years ago. "I'm in."

"No, no, this is a really bad idea!" My voice was lost in the rising mutters of 'right, let's do it' and 'heck, yeah' as other friends and neighbours stepped forward, egging each other on.

Shit, I had to tell them the truth.

But how many innocent people would die as a result?

Fuck, fuck...

My phone vibrated and I yanked it out and checked the call display. Hellhound.

Should I ignore him? The farmers were milling around, hands twitchy on their weapons, voices rising.

But Arnie wouldn't call me unless it was important...

I punched the Talk button and snapped, "Hello?"

"Tell 'em ya got a friend that's an ex-cop," Hellhound said urgently. "Tell 'em your cop friend can be here in a coupla minutes an' he'll round these fuckers up an' get 'em to the cops. Quick, before they lynch our guys!"

I disconnected and bellowed, "*Listen up!*" over the rumble of male voices.

They fell silent.

"I've got a friend, an ex-cop. He can be here in a few minutes, and he'll make sure these dogs..." Somehow I managed not to spit on Grandin just out of sheer ritual. "...end up in jail. You guys leave before he gets here, and everything will be fine."

"Sorry, Punkin, we can't do that," Mr. Nielsen said

regretfully. "We ain't gonna take a chance on one of these dogs..."

Splat. Right on target.

"...gittin' loose and having another go at you. But you go ahead and phone your friend," he encouraged. "If he's really your friend, he won't turn us in."

No choice. And the longer we stood around here, the more chance that somebody would see us and involve the real cops.

I punched Hellhound's speed dial again.

"Hi," I said when he answered. "I've got a bit of a situation here."

"I'm hearin' it all with the glasses," he said. "Just pretend you're tellin' me where ya are an' what happened. Kane's on his way."

Kane?

Shit, he'd gotten sucked into another one of my disastrous missions.

Somehow I managed to babble something that must have sounded plausible to Mr. Nielsen. When I disconnected from the call, he patted me on the shoulder.

"You done just fine, Punkin. Come on and sit down now, you're shakin' like an aspen in a tornado."

CHAPTER 51

Kane really was only a few minutes away.

When he came striding down the path in his snow-patterned camouflage, I realized that Hellhound must have called him when he'd received my original voicemail. If Kane had been at his condo in the deep south, he could have easily gotten here and concealed himself before Holt's team arrived.

Holt was going to tear a wide bleeding strip off the team for not spotting Kane and the farmers, but that really wasn't fair. The team had been geared up for an urban op, not sneaking around in the snow. And Kane had been the top agent in the Department for years. They'd never had a chance.

"Aydan, are you all right?" Kane swept me into an embrace, playing the concerned friend to the hilt.

"Fine." I clung to him, hiding my smile in his broad chest. This was why the 'damsel-in-distress' fantasy was so popular. Damn, he felt good.

Kane raised his voice. "All right, men, you can clear out now. I'll take it from here."

None of them moved.

"How do we know we can trust you?" Mr. Nielsen

demanded.

"Aydan trusts me."

Emerging from Kane's arms, I gave the group my best reassuring smile. "It's true, you can trust him. Everything's fine now."

"Maybe so..." Mr. Nielsen locked gazes with Kane. "...maybe not. You got some proof that you are who you say you are?"

"Yes," Kane said. "And you're very smart to demand it. I used to work with the Drumheller RCMP detachment. Why don't you call there and speak to Constable Birch or Constable Peters, and ask them if they'll vouch for John Kane."

Murmurs of approval greeted that, and Mr. Nielsen nodded. "I'll just do that." He pulled out a smartphone and poked tentatively at it. "Dang thing, I can never remember how to get on the goldurn interweb and find a phone number..."

Old Mr. Evans stalked over like an emaciated heron, smartphone in hand. "Here, Lars, I've got it." His fingers whisked deftly over his phone's screen and a moment later he held it to his ear. "Hello. May I speak to Constable Birch or Constable Peters, please? It's urgent."

A few moments later he spoke again. "Hello, Constable Peters. Thank you for taking my call. I'm dealing with a gentleman named John Kane, and he says you'll vouch for him." He listened for a moment. "Certainly. Just a moment." He handed the phone to Kane. "She wants to speak to you."

Kane accepted the phone. "Kane here." Peters's end of the conversation was inaudible, and I stood straining my ears in vain as Kane replied, "Yes... no... yes, please. I'd appreciate it if you'd get the Okotoks detachment to send a cruiser and van. This phone's location is correct. Thank you. I'll pass you back now."

He handed the phone back to Mr. Evans, who said, "Hello?" in hopeful tones. His bony shoulders squared. "Yes, ma'am. I appreciate that. Thank you for your service, and have a good day." He disconnected and turned to the waiting group. "He checks out."

Exhaled breaths and a general shuffling of feet indicated their relief.

"All right, men," Kane said with authority. "The RCMP will be here in less than fifteen minutes, and you need to be gone by the time they get here. I thank you from the bottom of my heart for saving Aydan..." He squeezed my shoulders, holding me close to him. "...but please, don't ever do anything like this again. These men were heavily armed..." He indicated the weapons lying on the ground. "...and they wouldn't have hesitated to kill you if they had spotted you sneaking up on them."

Mr. Nielsen laughed. "Son, we been huntin' since before you were born, and these dogs..." Kane winced as another load of spit joined the slimy puddle oozing off Grandin's head. Mr. Nielsen went on, "...show up like cow patties in the snow with their black clothes. The day me and the boys can't sneak around a bunch of city slickers in the bush is the day we hang up our rifles for good." He turned to address the group. "Clear on out! Meet you at Denny's for all-day breakfast!"

"And thank you!" I added. "You're all heroes!"

With a few 'aw-shucks' mumbles, the old men faded into the undergrowth. The racket of the radio masked the sound of their movements, and I smiled up at Mr. Nielsen.

"You guys had this all figured out."

"Yep." He rocked back on his heels, grinning. "That'll be the day, when a bunch of old farmers can't outsmart yella-bellied dogs like these."

Splat.

Grandin twitched and groaned.

As the quads roared off toward the river, Mr. Nielsen added, "Sorry we scared you, Punkin. You know we wouldn't've actually shot 'em, don't you?"

I stared at him. "I, um... no, actually, I didn't..." As the old familiar glint rose in his eyes, I let my head fall back with a groan. "Oh, for shit's sake! You did it again, after all these years! I could never tell when you guys were pulling my leg at the coffee shop, either."

He laughed. "Well, when you weren't gonna let us call the cops, I figgered we better throw a good scare into these dogs."

Grandin flinched, but the well-aimed gob of spittle struck him with uncanny accuracy anyway.

Mr. Nielsen offered me a grubby feed store receipt with a number scrawled on the back. "Here's yer mama's phone number. Are we ever gonna see the two of you around town again?"

Bitter reality crashed down on my head.

My mother was a ruthless criminal. She'd only been using me.

My sigh held enough unhappiness to make Mr. Nielsen's timeworn face soften in sympathy.

"I doubt it," I mumbled. "Mom will have to go underground again, and I'll probably have to stay away, too."

"Well, then, you tell yer mama to take care; and you take care, too." He patted me awkwardly on the shoulder. "Guess

I better skedaddle." Locking gazes with Kane again, he added, "You take care of her, you hear?"

"Yes, sir," Kane said gravely.

"Mr. Nielsen?" I stopped him with a hand on his sleeve as he turned away. "Say thanks to the town for me." I glanced meaningfully at the briefcase as he picked it up.

"I will, Punkin. They were all proud to help." He winked and hefted the suitcase. "And they'll be right glad to see their money again. 'Bye now."

Within minutes a cavalcade of half-tons crept up the snowy slope, some of them pulling trailers with quads. They all waved as they went by and I waved back, feeling as though I was presiding over a particularly bizarre Christmas parade.

When the sound of the last engine had faded, Holt mumbled, "Are they gone?"

"Let me check." I was reaching for my phone when it vibrated. I smiled at the sight of Hellhound's number on the call display and accepted the call.

"Nobody's got eyes on ya, darlin'," he said. "Ya can untie everybody now."

"Thanks." I disconnected and said, "All clear."

"Fuck, finally," Holt growled. "Get these fucking ropes off me."

My sharp jackknife made short work of his bonds and he sat up, rubbing the reddened skin on his cheek where his face had been pressed to the snow. "Fucking old redneck fuckers!" He explored the bloodied patch on his head with cautious fingertips. "That old fart nailed me with a fucking rifle butt!"

Grandin groaned again and flopped over, his arms and legs still tied behind him. "At least they didn't spit on you," he griped.

I left him bound and hurried over to release the rest of the team, who rose and sheepishly collected their weapons. Nobody said much.

The faint sound of sirens drifted to my ears and Holt scowled. "Why did you tell them to send units? It's a fucking waste of their time, and we'll all have to push an extra ton of paper."

Kane eyed him. "I'm willing to bet those old rednecks aren't as dumb as you think. They're probably waiting just around the corner, making sure everything happens the way we promised."

Holt subsided into muttered obscenities, but he didn't argue.

"I'm going to call Ian," I said, pulling out my cell phone. "Now that we know Nora was the buyer, I've got some brand new questions, and there's still time before their flight leaves."

"And I want to know who she owns in our government. *Somebody* high up sent me those orders," Grandin said.

Holt glared at Grandin. "Shut up." He transferred his glare to me. "And you stay out of it. I'll call Rand, and he can damn well bring Taylor down to the secure facility for questioning. She's not getting on that plane today."

"She has diplomatic immunity," Kane reminded him.

"Ask me if I give a rat's ass," Holt snarled, and stomped away, phone to his ear.

I let him go. He probably needed to feel in control right now; and after my confrontation with Ian last night, it was probably better if Holt did the talking anyway.

When a cruiser and a police van slithered down the hill a few minutes later Holt negotiated a ride to the sportsplex, or farther if any of the farmers were still in evidence. The team piled into the back of the van, and Holt shoved Grandin into the back seat of the cruiser.

"Meet us at the sportsplex," Holt snapped, and got in beside Grandin.

When silence and solitude surrounded us again, I wrapped my arms around Kane. "Thank you. That could have gone really badly."

His lips quirked up. "Yes, it could have... Punkinhead."

"Shut up." Pulling out my phone, I hit Hellhound's speed dial.

"Hey, darlin'," he said. "Should I meet ya at the sportsplex, too?"

"Yes. You're still listening? Where are you?"

"Yeah, these glasses are great. I'm up under the bridge on the north side of the river. Wave to the homeless guy." A bulky figure detached itself from the shadow under the bridge and waved. "Sorry I didn't call earlier an' let ya know what was goin' down, but your message said 'don't call' an' I didn't wanna fuck anythin' up."

"It's okay, it all worked out fine. So that *was* you," I said as I waved back. "I was wondering if it was, but the team said they didn't see any weapons."

"An' they wouldn't'a, unless they made a wrong move," he said. "Lucky I could hear everythin', though. If I'd just been watchin' without hearin' the talk, there woulda been a lotta innocent dead men down there."

I shuddered. "I still can't believe they did that, but it's completely in character. Only people from Saskatchewan would take up a collection from the whole town, hit the road in an all-night convoy, and risk their lives to help somebody they haven't seen in thirty years. They're all fucking nuts."

"You're from Saskatchewan."

I grinned. "See?"

He laughed and imitated Lars Nielsen. "Yep." Switching back to his usual voice, he added, "Hey, tell Kane he was right. Your Mister Nielsen was sittin' up around the corner in his big fuckin' boat of a car, watchin' for the cops. The coast's clear now, so ya better get to the sportsplex an' hook up with Holt. Go nail the mother-bitch."

"Right." My amusement drained away. Surviving Holt's sting was going to be the easiest part of this day.

And if I couldn't make Nora slip up and say something incriminating, these could be my last moments of freedom.

I shivered.

Don't think about it.

At the sportsplex, I parked beside the Fitz-Rite Fine Flooring truck again, and Kane's black Expedition and Hellhound's Forester pulled in beside me. We all got out, and I hugged them both in turn while Holt looked on with a scowl.

"Thank you for coming," I said to Kane. "And thank you for calling him," I added, turning to Hellhound. "You guys saved my ass again."

Hellhound shrugged, grinning. "It's a pretty nice ass. Wouldn't wanna waste it."

I feigned indignation. "Oh, sure, it's all about you."

"What's your plan now?" Kane inquired. "Do you really think you'll get to question Nora?"

"I sure hope so. I'm in deep shit if I can't."

His brow furrowed. "How deep?"

"Very deep. Stemp's out of the country and Dermott has

a hate on for me after I made him look bad in the debriefing last week. He's just looking for an excuse to lock me up."

"Does he have one?"

I exchanged an unhappy look with Hellhound. "Probably."

"Oh." Kane's frown deepened. "Is there anything I can do to help?"

"No. But thanks again for everything."

"You're welcome." He hesitated. "If everything goes well, would you like to come for supper tonight? Dad would love to see you again, and I could probably convince the real estate agent to let us in and have a look at my new house."

"You got the house!" I faked excitement for all I was worth. "Congratulations!"

"Thank you." His smile was wide and warm. "I feel as though I'm finally moving in the right direction after spinning my wheels for most of this year."

"Well, that's great..."

Holt cleared his throat loudly and tapped his wristwatch.

"I guess we'd better go," I said. "Thanks for the invitation. I'll call you after I finish with Nora."

"All right. Good luck." Kane drew me into his arms and lowered his lips to mine.

I had expected a light friendly kiss.

What I got was deeper, darker, and deadlier. My knees weakened.

When he disengaged our lips, a silly giggle fell out of my mouth. "Wow. Nice to see you, too," I joked feebly.

"See you soon," he promised, and swung into the Expedition.

Conscious of Holt's sardonic grin, I turned to Hellhound as Kane pulled away.

"I'll be down at Kane's condo visitin' Dad, too, so I'll see ya later," Arnie said. When I wrapped my arms around him, he hesitated, his gaze flicking to Holt. Nudging me around to turn his back on our audience, he whispered, "Is it okay if I kiss ya?"

"Yes. And it's *not* okay if you don't."

He chuckled. "Just checkin'."

His kiss weakened my knees, too. Where John was fire and passion, Arnie was sensual unhurried bliss. Sinking into his embrace, I let my mind go blank-

"For fucksakes, let's go!" Holt barked. "Move it, Kelly!"

"He's just jealous of me," Hellhound murmured against my lips, but I could barely manage a smile.

"See you later." I gave him an extra squeeze before letting him go.

He waved and drove away and I returned his wave absently, my mind already on Nora and her lies.

How could I have believed her when she'd seemed so furious that Sam had hurt me? All her little hesitations seemed magnified in my memory now, so blatantly incriminating that only an idiot could miss them.

I stiffened as Nora's voice replayed in my mind. *But then I found out you were an agent...*

"Kelly! Wake the fuck up!"

I twitched, refocusing on the parking lot and Holt's scowling face.

"You going to stand here in the fucking freezing cold all fucking day?" he demanded.

"No. I just figured out the whole thing."

"What whole thing?"

"Why Nora would kidnap me instead of just pretending to be my loving mommy and slowly sucking me in."

"If you're going to tell me, get on with it." Holt shoved his hands into his armpits. "I'm freezing my fucking ass off and I've got a headache that'd kill a fucking horse."

"She had to keep me quiet. When she first arranged to meet me she thought I was a civilian and she could just feed me some lies and get me to skim sensitive intel that she could sell for profit. But when she found out I was an agent..."

"She was afraid to risk it," Holt finished.

"Yeah. But she's broke, and I was her retirement plan." I wrapped my arms around myself. "Kidnapping me solved everything. Grandin would keep his mouth shut because he'd taken the so-called 'cash bonus' that was obviously a bribe. Ian would be dead, so she was rid of the only person who suspected her of murdering Howard Coleman-"

"Who's Howard Coleman?" Holt interrupted.

"The Weapons Director she replaced. And Agent Dirk was just collateral damage, but if the Department thought I'd murdered Dirk and Rand and attacked Grandin and fled..."

"They'd issue a 'kill on sight' order for you," Holt said flatly.

"Yeah. But by then Mr. Nielsen would have delivered me to Mommy Dearest, who'd spirit me out of the country before anybody could find me. I could never go near the Department again because of the kill order, so she'd have as much time as she needed to convince me."

"But you could tell the Department the whole story, and the lie detector would confirm everything," Holt objected. He shivered again. "Fuck this. Let's get in the back where it's warmer." He strode to the truck and opened one of the rear doors, motioning me ahead of him.

"But Nora didn't know the lie detector existed when she

set up the kidnapping," I explained as I stepped inside. "She thought it would be Grandin's word against mine, and my fingerprints were on the bullet casings. I have to question her again. Did you talk to Ian?"

I turned to face Holt just as his hand flew up.

"Wha-" I began, but the jab of his tranquilizer dart turned my tongue and knees to rubber.

"...th'fuc..." was all I managed before everything went away.

CHAPTER 52

...trapped-trapped-trapped-*TRAPPED!*

I tried to fight but my body wouldn't move. My screams were only dull mumbles leaking sluggishly from between my slack lips. When I finally managed to drag one eyelid half-open, a white room swirled nauseatingly around me.

Holt. That bastard, I'd kill him.

Just as soon as I could move, I'd find him and kill him.

My eyelid fell shut again and I abandoned the struggle temporarily. In a few more minutes the trank would wear off and I'd be able to move again. In the meantime, I didn't seem to be in immediate danger...

Except I was trapped-trapped-*trapped*...

My breath jerked in and out, too fast.

Shut up. Calm down. Think.

My glimpse of the room plus the silence told me I was alone, and I had a pretty damn good idea where. One of the holding cells at Sirius. About six feet wide by nine feet long...

An involuntary scream tightened my throat, but it only emerged as another useless mumble.

Stop panicking.

Stop.

I fought my breath into a slow calming rhythm,

visualizing ocean waves as hard as I could.

I might never see ocean waves again...

A sob wrenched my chest, but I wrestled it into submission.

Breathe.

In-two-three-four... Out-two-three-four...

My heart hammered inside my chest, three heartbeats for each of my counts.

Slow down.

Calm.

In-two-three-four... Out-two-three-four...

My eyes opened more easily this time, and the room stayed stationary around me.

The reality was as bad as I had guessed.

Standard Sirius holding cell. All white, except for the grimy-looking drain in the middle of the floor. Transparent polycarbonate panel with air holes for a door. Plastic shelf bolted to the wall for a bed; seatless, tankless toilet in the corner. Nothing else except the malevolent eye of the small camera tucked into the corner of the ceiling.

In-two-three-four... Out-two-three-four...

I tried to divert my terror. Take stock.

They'd updated these cells. The last time they'd stuck me in one, I'd torn the old security camera off its mounting bracket. Now I wouldn't even be able to snag a fingernail on the smooth plastic dome, even if I could jump that high. They must have realized the old-style cameras were a hazard after I'd tried to cave in Stemp's skull with my makeshift weapon.

I'd love to see Stemp coming through that door right now. How times change.

In-two-three-four... Out-two-three-four...

At last I managed a finger-twitch, then a toe-twitch. A long minute later, I was able to drag myself semi-upright on the narrow bed.

Jingling and an unaccustomed weight made me look down, and panic nearly flattened me again at the sight of the shackles on my wrists and ankles.

A chain between my feet, just enough for half a stride. A chain between my wrists. No way to spread my arms. A chain between my wrist and ankles. I couldn't even raise my arms unless I drew up my knees *no-no-no-NO-NO!*

With every ounce of will I fought the compulsion to scream and struggle. To batter my head against the wall until merciful unconsciousness took me again.

How long would they hold me here, without explanation, without trial, without hope?

Maybe my trial had already happened.

Maybe I'd already been tried, convicted, sentenced, and imprisoned *for the rest of my life...*

Don't-scream-don't-scream-don't-scream...

Jerking my knees up into fetal position, I raised my bound hands. Thank *God.* My wrists reached my mouth.

I could tear open my veins with my teeth.

But I'd have to be smart about it. I'd wait until they gave me a blanket so I could hide my actions under a pretense of sleep. I'd be dead before they realized anything was amiss.

The thought gave me an eerie calm. I could escape any time I wanted. Permanently. They couldn't hold me. Would never recapture me.

Safe. I was safe.

I swivelled on the bed and lay down on my back.

I breathed.

"*Kelly!*"

A rough voice jerked me awake, and I sat up to see Dermott's nasty grin outside my door.

I let my mouth gape open in a thoroughly ill-mannered yawn. Then I did it again, rolling my shoulders and putting everything I had into it.

"What do *you* want?" I asked at last, injecting as much boredom and contempt into my tone as possible.

"Enjoying your little vacation?" he gibed.

"Hell, yeah. This is the best sleep I've had in days."

Sadly, I was telling the truth. Sometimes total exhaustion is your friend.

"This is a nice firm mattress, too," I added.

A vicious light kindled in his eyes. "Too bad about your claustrophobia."

I yawned again. "What claustrophobia? Haven't you read my psych reports? I'm over that."

"Rawling thinks you're lying."

"His problem, not mine." I stretched out on the bed again and closed my eyes. "Buzz off. I was in the middle of a great dream."

"Tough," he snapped. "You've got a meeting to go to. Take her."

As I sat up again, the door-panel slid open and two burly armed guards stepped inside, shrinking the cell to the dimensions of a coffin.

An icicle of terror stabbed my guts. *trappedTRAPPED...*

Don't panic.

Don't give Dermott the satisfaction.

Desperate for a distraction, I studied the guards' faces. Both were members of Holt's erstwhile security team. Too bad my spy career was over. I'd gotten good at this facial recognition stuff just a little too late.

I stood and offered my elbows to them with a grin. "What, *two* prom dates? Thanks, boys. All this attention's going to go to my head." I fluttered my eyelashes at them. "I hope you each bought me a nice corsage."

They looked away and stayed silent as we shuffled out of the cell. Slowly, to accommodate my chain-shortened stride.

Don't. Panic.

"Wow, tough audience," I said brightly. "Well, that's okay; I've got lots more where that came from. Stick with me, folks, I'm here 'til Saturday!" I imitated the '*bup-pup tschhhh*' of a classic comedy rimshot.

"Shut up," Dermott growled.

"Make me," I retorted. Not the smartest rejoinder, but my brain was only firing on one cylinder while the rest was engaged in full-throttle panic. With nitrous boost.

"Oh, I will," he purred. "Believe me, I will."

None of his usual bluster. My blood chilled.

A few moments later we passed through the security checkpoint and I realized why he looked so smug.

I wasn't in Silverside. I was in the secure facility in Calgary.

Where the long-term prisoners were kept.

Don't-scream-don't-scream...

The rest of our walk was silent except for the jingle of my chains and the frantic shrieking inside my brain.

When we arrived at one of the conference rooms, Dermott pushed ahead of us through the door. Then a guard, then me, then the last guard.

As the first guard stepped aside, I got a full view of the conference room.

The whole chain of command was there, along with Holt.

Shit, Dermott must have had this planned right from the start. At least half of these people would have had to drive more than two hours to get here.

I scanned the faces around the table. All were serious. Half looked puzzled and a couple looked outright annoyed.

My gaze flew to General Briggs's stern face and upright posture. I didn't know much about the rest of Command, but I knew Briggs. He was tough but fair. This was no kangaroo court.

At least I hoped it wasn't.

My momentary relief vanished as my gaze travelled past Briggs's face to the clock on the wall behind him.

Two-thirty.

Nora's plane was in the air, winging her forever beyond my reach.

When she realized I'd uncovered her kidnapping scam, she would never come back to Canada. And she would never be prosecuted in the UK because we couldn't reveal classified intel as evidence.

She had shattered my world again.

And I had failed. Completely and irrevocably.

A choking lump lodged in my throat. Thank God I'd kissed John and Arnie. None of us had known it was our final goodbye.

I dragged my attention back to the proceedings. Pointless now.

Don't scream...

"Are the restraints really necessary?" General Briggs snapped. "This is a meeting, not a trial."

"She's an agent. She's dangerous," Dermott growled.

"All our personnel are potentially dangerous. Has Agent

Kelly given you any reason to believe she poses a threat?"

"Flight risk," Dermott said stubbornly. "Everybody knows she's so claustrophobic she can't even go through the time-delay chamber without freaking out. She'll do anything to avoid being imprisoned."

Briggs studied me, and I projected as much composure as I could fake. It wasn't as difficult as usual, since my mind and body had gone numb with despair.

"She seems calm enough now," Briggs observed.

He had always treated me fairly. Maybe he'd stand up for me. I should at least do something to help my case.

I made a show of smothering a small yawn in my shoulder. "'Scuse me. I just woke up."

Brigg's eyebrow rose fractionally, reminding me of Stemp.

God, I missed Stemp. He would slice and dice Dermott with such speed and precision that the cuts wouldn't even bleed until all his pieces collapsed in a twitching heap.

"How long were you asleep, Agent Kelly?" Briggs asked.

"I don't know. I fell asleep a little while after the trank wore off and I woke up in the cell. So I guess... an hour or so?"

"So you were obviously quite agitated," Briggs said dryly.

I avoided a direct lie. "Well, I wasn't *happy*." I shot a small scowl in Holt's direction. "Especially since I don't even know why I'm locked up. But at least I was pretty sure I was with the good guys. Supposedly." Somehow I prevented myself from glancing pointedly at Dermott.

"You haven't been informed of the accusations against you?" Briggs frowned at Dermott.

"No," I said hurriedly before Dermott could get started. Focus on the one successful part of this whole benighted clusterfuck. I widened my eyes a bit, going for 'injured innocence'. "My mission with Holt was a success. We identified the middleman, and Nora was Grandin's buyer. But when I got into the truck for what I thought was a debriefing, Holt knocked me out and I woke up here in a cell." I jerked my hands, rattling my shackles. "In chains."

"Holt?" Briggs prompted.

"Dermott's orders," Holt muttered, not looking at me. "He said to relieve Kelly of duty and take her into custody as soon as our sting was complete."

"Dermott." Briggs turned to him. "Please inform Agent Kelly of the allegations against her."

Dermott rose, his pseudo-grave expression brimming with triumph. "Misuse of Department resources. Inappropriate conduct. Insubordination. She issued orders she had no authority to give." He drew himself up to deliver the coup de grâce. "And she intentionally botched two missions to benefit her mother and her boyfriend. That's wilful dereliction of duty. We can't trust her to perform as an agent, and her classified knowledge makes her too much of a security risk. Our only option is to imprison her for life."

CHAPTER 53

Imprison her for life.

My worst fear, spoken aloud in front of the chain of command. Even though I had always known this day would come, the reality nearly shattered me.

A scream rose deep in my belly, clawing the back of my throat.

If I started, I wouldn't stop. I'd still be screaming when they trussed me in a straitjacket and chucked me in a cell for the rest of my life.

Clenching my teeth, I fought the scream back.

"Those are serious allegations," General Briggs said. "Do you have evidence?"

Dermott gave me a gloating smirk. "Yes, I do."

Briggs sighed and settled back in his chair. I was pretty sure I wasn't imagining the disappointment in his eyes when he looked over at me.

"All right," he said. "Let's start with misuse of Department resources."

"Kelly used covert cameras and monitoring software to resolve a petty small-town dispute. And she brought a civilian into our secured area and let him see highly-classified technology while she wrongfully interrogated him."

Dermott shot me a triumphant look. "*And* she abandoned her official mission to do all that."

I half-expected him to tack 'inappropriate conduct' onto that, but apparently he didn't know about my tryst with Hellhound.

But this was bad enough.

"Agent Kelly, would you like to respond to these allegations?" Briggs inquired.

I cleared my throat, hoping my voice wouldn't come out in a squeak or a croak. Lifting my chin and squaring my shoulders, I said, "I didn't know it was a small-town dispute at the time. As my reports show, I was afraid Grandin's buyer might be trying to keep me, or Arlene Widdenback, off-balance by targeting my friends and business associates. Holt can confirm that Grandin said 'they know how to get to Kelly', so I had reasonable grounds for that line of thinking."

I swallowed, trying to moisten my dry throat. Damn, I was thirsty. And hungry. I hadn't eaten for hours...

Yanking my attention back to my rebuttal, I added, "I did run out of a meeting with Nora when I thought one of my clients was in danger, and I did interrogate Bob Armstrong because I caught him in an act of criminal mischief targeting that client. It turned out he didn't know anything about me or Arlene Widdenback; but at least I gained some intel about Nora as a side benefit. But I had no way of knowing ahead of time whether any of that would advance the mission. That can only be determined in retrospect."

Big words.

Were they convinced?

"Do you have copies of Agent Kelly's reports?" Briggs asked.

Dermott looked momentarily at a loss, but Holt opened

the folder in front of him and passed several sheets of paper down the table to Briggs. Dermott straightened and smirked.

Holt wore his impassive cop face.

Was he covering my ass? Or Dermott's?

Probably Dermott's. They'd been friends long before Holt and I had worked together.

If Holt was against me, too, I was completely screwed.

Panic raked my insides.

General Briggs skimmed the report and passed it to the man beside him. "Next allegation," he said.

What did that mean? Did it mean he accepted Dermott's accusation? Or my explanation?

Dermott drew himself up. "Inappropriate conduct and insubordination. She was sneaking off to cuddle with Agent Rand in his hospital bed and pretending it was work-related, and listen to this." He pulled out his phone and touched a button. My voice blared out of the speaker. "*...stay the fuck out of my way and let me get the job done!*"

My mouth fell open. That fucking slimeball.

The look he shot me was pure poison.

"Which part is insubordination?" General Briggs asked.

Dermott frowned. "Didn't you just hear her yelling at me?"

Briggs matched his frown. "I heard a woman who sounded like Agent Kelly yelling. We don't know who she was yelling at, and without voiceprint analysis we don't even know whether it was Agent Kelly. And a single phrase without context isn't evidence. Do you have the entire conversation recorded?"

Dermott flushed dark red.

I held my breath. Did he want to bury me badly enough

to let everybody in the room listen to me rip a strip off him?

"I don't have it all," Dermott muttered.

Hooray for his giant ego and miniscule balls.

General Briggs swept an authoritative gaze around the room. "No context, therefore no evidence; and in any case, insubordination is the refusal to carry out a direct order. I heard no refusal. Are we agreed?"

Nods all around.

"Then that allegation is dismissed. Agent Kelly, would you respond to the allegation of inappropriate conduct?"

Fury momentarily swallowed up my fear, stiffening my backbone. "I already explained this to Dermott. Agent Rand needed to communicate sensitive information to me while he was confined to bed in the hospital. I told him there were no bugs, but he was afraid of passive listening devices so he insisted on whispering as quietly as possible. I couldn't get near enough to hear him, so I lay down on the bed beside him. I explained that to Dermott; Agent Rand corroborated what I'd said; and I offered to take a lie detector test to confirm it. Dermott didn't take me up on that, so I assumed the subject was closed."

Briggs frowned. "And are you still willing to take a lie detector test?"

"Yes."

"But that's not all!" Dermott interrupted. "She's been screwing her boyfriend, too..."

Oh, shit, he *had* found out about the shaggin' wagon.

Dermott was blustering on. "...and she's supposed to be recruiting him back to the Department..."

My sigh of relief escaped before I could stop it. He was talking about John, not Arnie.

"...so it's a clear conflict of interest. Inappropriate

conduct *and* dereliction of duty!" Dermott finished.

General Briggs frowned. "When you talk about Agent Kelly's boyfriend, do you mean John Kane?"

"Yes. And she's on record saying that she's screwing him." Dermott gave me a smug look. "It's in her psych records."

General Briggs rested an elbow on the table and massaged his forehead. Then he straightened again and met my gaze. "Agent Kelly, I apologize on behalf of the Department for this invasion of your privacy."

He turned to face Dermott. "Dermott..." He paused as if holding his temper in check. "...the whole point of a recruitment mission is to build a relationship with the subject. Even if Agent Kelly's relationship with John Kane weren't already a matter of record, it would be an acceptable technique for her to cultivate that level of intimacy. It's not a conflict of interest, it's a mission strategy." He looked as though he wanted to say more, but pressed his lips together instead. "Next allegation."

"Dereliction of duty and insubordination," Dermott growled. "She obviously hasn't been trying to recruit Kane. He just gave up the lease on his office in Silverside and bought a house in Calgary." He eyed me, his lips curling in a sneer. "Guess you're not very good in bed, honey."

"Dermott!" General Briggs's voice snapped out like a whip. "That was inappropriate. Consider this an official reprimand which will be added to your record."

Dermott's face went scarlet. "But it's true! He's leaving town and she hasn't done a damn thing to stop him!"

Briggs stiffened. "Agent Kelly," he said without taking his gaze off Dermott. "When were you assigned the mission to recruit John Kane?"

"Um..." God, it felt like a year ago. "...Sunday."

"And at that time, were you aware that he was considering a permanent move to Calgary?"

"No. I, um... we don't really see each other that often. He's not really my boyfriend; just a... good friend." I hesitated. "That's in my psych records, too. We're not in a committed relationship."

"So you're not involved in his daily decisions."

"No."

"Dermott..." Briggs drew a breath as though holding his patience in check. "People decide more than three days in advance to buy a house. Kane had probably made the decision before Kelly was even assigned. And recruitment missions like these typically take months, or longer."

Holt rose quietly and slipped out of the room.

Smart man. Dermott wouldn't be kindly disposed toward anyone who had witnessed his humiliation.

Briggs went on, "Not getting results in three days isn't dereliction of duty or insubordination; it's just a fact of the job. If this is all your accusations against Agent Kelly-"

"Oh, don't worry, it's not," Dermott interrupted. "It's just the beginning. She also gave unauthorized commands to subordinates."

General Briggs eyed him in silence. After a moment, he said, "These unauthorized commands had better involve illegal actions or nuclear launch codes."

Dermott frowned. "No, she usurped my authority. She told an analyst she was putting him on stress leave when she had no authority to-"

"Next," Briggs snapped.

"But-"

"*Next!*" The look in Briggs's eye would have quelled a

much braver man.

"Fine," Dermott said. "The main dereliction of duty charge is from her so-called investigation of her *mother*." He infused the word with contempt. "Kelly was supposed to be getting close and building a rapport. Instead she was constantly rude to her mother, when she wasn't ignoring her and walking out on her. And before you ask, yes, I have surveillance logs as evidence." He shot me an ugly glare. "Then she let her mother be attacked, and ignored her in the hospital. So her mother gave up and left the country; and no surprise. Now we'll never know whether she's involved in espionage, because Kelly did everything she could to drive her away. The whole mission was botched from the start."

The door opened and Holt slipped through again carrying the lie detector.

Nausea twisted my guts. He hadn't been avoiding Dermott's humiliation; he had been preparing to orchestrate mine.

Because no matter whether General Briggs was on my side or not, I had no defense against the accusations Dermott had just levelled. Over and over I had let my emotional involvement influence my words and actions with Nora, and now she was gone forever.

And I would have to admit all of it under the lie detector.

CHAPTER 54

With despair turning my guts to lead, I watched Holt hurry over to General Briggs and whisper in his ear. Briggs frowned, then nodded.

As Holt turned in my direction, Briggs addressed the assembly. "There is a new development which is pertinent to this meeting..."

Holt was coming toward me. I was doomed.

He walked past.

Afraid to hope, I stared at his back while he went to the door and opened it.

Nora walked in, followed by Ian Rand.

The shock folded my hunger-weakened knees and I staggered. The sudden rattle of my chains drew everyone's eyes to me.

"Aydan! Heavens, Dani-dear, what have they done to you?" Nora rushed to my side. "My poor baby..." Her chin came up in that familiar imperious gesture as she glared at the assembly. "Bring her a chair! Can't you see she's going to faint?"

A chair appeared behind me and somebody lowered me into it. Maybe Holt; I wasn't sure. I was too busy gaping open-mouthed at Nora.

"Wha...? I thought you were flying out at two," I stammered.

"Change in plans," Ian said crisply. "Nora, would you please take a seat?"

"Yes, of course. Bring me a chair." She shot a contemptuous glance around the room. "I'll sit with my daughter."

Ian placed another chair beside me and Nora sat, taking my hand.

"Holt? If you please?" Ian said.

Holt nodded and brought over a third chair, placing the lie detector case on it. It took every ounce of my strength to hold my head up while he opened the case and unfurled the headdress of electrodes.

This was it.

I'd have to speak the truth. Nora would know all my guesses and suspicions, and her brilliant mind would have an alibi concocted before they'd even finished questioning me.

As Holt advanced with the headdress I stared at the floor, unable to bear the sight of Holt the Magnificent in the depths of my failure.

"What?" Nora's startled exclamation jerked my gaze up again.

Holt was putting the headdress on her.

Frozen, I stared.

"Oh, for heaven's sake," Nora snapped. "Take this foolish device off me. I made it clear last week that I cannot answer any questions due to MI5 security protocols, and in any case my diplomatic status gives me immunity from questioning."

"That's right," Ian seconded, and Nora gave him a satisfied nod. "However..." Ian went on, "...although the receiving country may not hold you or question you, you are still subject to all the laws of the sending country that granted your immunity in the first place. And..." He exchanged a wry look with Holt. "We don't have a lie detector as good as this one. So you can answer my questions right here and now."

Nora blanched white. "What..." Her colour came back in a flood. "You lied to me! You said Aydan had been terribly hurt and she needed me immediately!"

Ian's beautiful deceitful lips curved up as he met my gaze. "Yes, well, that's technically true. She was hurt. By you. And she does need you urgently; or your testimony, at least." His smile widened. "It's really all about the game, you see."

"Holt!" Dermott barked. "What kind of bullshit is this?"

"You told me to relieve Kelly of duty and take over the mission," Holt said. "So I did. As soon as we had proof that Nora had bribed Grandin to kidnap Kelly, I called Rand and filled him in; and I told him he was welcome to use our lie detector if he wanted." Holt's steely gaze pinned Nora to her chair. "I guess he wanted."

"And now we know that she murdered the former Weapons Director and an MI5 chemist, too," Ian said conversationally. "Isn't that right, Nora?"

"No!"

The damning red light flashed.

Nora went redder. "No!" she repeated. "I wasn't answering the question, I was just..."

"Actually, you were answering the question, weren't you?" Ian purred.

"No!"

Red light again.

"Oh, Nora. You're a very bad girl." Ian wagged a playful finger at her. "And you bribed a CIA agent to kidnap your own daughter. Such a pity he didn't manage to kill me in the process, isn't it?"

"Yes, it certainly is." She glared at him, the green light underscoring her sincerity. "You're an odious man, and you're also wrong. I didn't bribe anybody. I received a ransom note-"

"Cut the crap," Holt snapped. "We know you're lying; Nielsen spilled the whole story this morning and Grandin confessed."

"They're lying!" Nora's face was crimson. "They're trying to frame me!"

"Right then," Ian said briskly. "We can clear this up very easily. All you need to do is answer yes or no. Did you set up Grandin to kidnap Aydan?"

"No."

The green light flashed, and my heart froze in my chest.

How could that be true?

How could I have been so wrong?

Ian frowned, and Nora gave him a look of pure triumph.

A slow smile eased Ian's lips. "Oh, nicely done. Let's try another one. Did you get someone in the U.S. government to set up Grandin to kidnap Aydan?"

Nora glared up at him in silence.

His smile widened. "Now, now; that's not very convincing," he admonished. "Come on, give it a go. Did you get someone in the U.S. government to set up Grandin to kidnap Aydan?"

"Why did you even bother?" I blurted. "You didn't need me as long as you had Rebecca."

Her eyes widened. "Dani-dear, I told you; Rebecca could

never replace you. She's a lovely girl, but I only have one daughter. You."

"I wasn't talking about blood relationships," I snapped. "I was talking about somebody to do your dirty work in the internet. When you figured out what Rebecca was, you headed out of here on the next damn plane. The only reason you came back here in the first place was to recruit me, and the only reason you're here now is because you found out Rebecca's dead and you still need me."

"No!"

The green light flashed.

Truth.

My jaw dropped as all my theories evaporated.

"Rebecca's not dead!" Nora protested.

My heart plummeted. For a moment there, I had actually thought she'd meant she loved me.

What an idiot.

"Yes, Rebecca's dead," I said quietly. "She died last night. You didn't get the news because you were in the hospital; and in transit this morning."

"No!" Nora's eyes brimmed. "Oh, no..." She hid her face in her hands.

I almost felt sorry for her.

But not quite.

"So the only reason you came back was to recruit me," I snapped.

She lowered her hands and gazed at me through her tears, her lips trembling.

"No."

Her choked denial was so quiet I had to strain to hear it, but the lie detector flashed instantly.

Green.

I stared.

"You see, Dani-dear," Nora said softly. "I love you. I truly do. I always have. Always will. I've been telling you the truth all along. About Sam, about what happened with your father all those years ago, about how I left to protect you. It's all true."

"Is... that all true?" I croaked. "All of what you just said about my past? Answer yes or no."

"Yes."

The green light flashed again and my heart twisted painfully.

"You're lying," Holt snapped.

"Your infallible machine begs to differ," Nora said sweetly.

"Not about loving her," Holt growled. "I believe you about that. But it's not the only reason you came back, is it?"

"No, of course not," Nora said, and the green light corroborated her statement. "I wanted to reconnect with old friends; I wanted to consult a lawyer regarding the ownership of Sirius Canada-"

"And one of your reasons was to recruit Aydan. Yes or no?"

She said nothing.

"You might as well give it up," Ian said. "We've already got you on two murder charges, bribery, conspiring to murder two agents, misappropriating classified technology and a host of other lovelies. Go ahead and answer."

She crossed her arms, her lips trembling and cheeks still flushed angry red. "I have nothing to say."

Ian shrugged. "It's enough. Nora Taylor, you're under arrest..."

Nora swayed, her face going slack.

"...for the murder of Howard Coleman and-"

She toppled out of the chair.

Her body hit the floor with boneless finality.

CHAPTER 55

I sat.

The wail of sirens and crackle of emergency radios still echoed in my memory.

The waking nightmare replayed in my mind over and over. The futile efforts of the paramedics performing CPR; the horrible laxity of Nora's pale hand flopping over the edge of the stretcher as they carried her body out.

I sat.

The chains still on my body; my mind floating in that numb grey place that precedes pain.

Somebody sat down beside me.

Where my mother had sat only half an hour ago.

Where she would never sit again.

"Here." A firm hand took mine and folded it around a warm paper cup. "Drink."

I sipped mechanically, hot sweet chocolate jolting me back to reality.

"I put a lid on it so you wouldn't spill," Holt said. "The way your hands are shaking, I figured you'd end up wearing it otherwise."

"Thanks." I sipped again. Then again. Each mouthful drew me back to myself. Back to pain.

Ian strode over and lowered himself into the chair across from me. "Terribly sorry about all this, Storm."

"Liar." I didn't even try to stop the accusing word.

He looked taken aback for a moment, but his flirtatious smile quickly reappeared. "Yes, well, you're right. I'm not sorry about *all* this; I'm actually quite pleased that we solved the case. But I did want to apologize for that little scene in my hospital room last night. You caught me on the line with my superiors, and I needed to make a good show. I didn't mean any of it, of course." He gave me one of his debonair shrugs. "You know how it goes."

I just stared at him.

He hesitated. "Also, it seems you were right in your suspicions. Nora tried to deter the nurse who put in her eye drops this morning, so I rang Nora's doctor in London and discovered that she didn't have glaucoma." He gestured at the place on the floor where Nora's body had lain. "I expect it was Substance X in her eye drop bottle. I called our chemists, and they said the effect would have been slowed because she absorbed it through her eyes instead of swallowing it. And when her blood pressure skyrocketed under questioning and the bad news about Rebecca…"

He didn't need to finish the sentence. The result was still far too clear in my mind.

I had killed my own mother by telling her Rebecca was dead.

Innocent Rebecca, whom I'd also killed with my incompetence.

Ian was still talking. "Do let me know as soon as your lab finishes its analysis on the eye drops." He eyed me inquisitively. "Who was this Rebecca, by the way? What did you mean when you said Nora found out 'what she was'?"

Holt rose. "Time for you to go, Rand. We need to finish our meeting here, and get Kelly out of these fucking chains."

"Of course." Ian laid a gentle hand on mine, his beautiful green eyes going solemn. "I am terribly sorry you were hurt, and I'm sorry for your loss. Please accept my deepest sympathies."

I turned to study his handsome face, his utter sincerity.

"Sure," I said.

"Au revoir, Storm. I hope we meet again soon."

I managed a twitch of my lips, and he left.

General Briggs called the meeting to order immediately. "Agent Kelly, we offer you our condolences. We realize this has been very traumatic for you, and we'll wrap it up as quickly as possible. The chain of command is convinced that there has been no wrongdoing on your part-"

"That's bullshit!" Dermott interrupted. "She botched the whole mission, and the only reason she's getting off the hook is because Holt pulled it out of the fire for her!"

"That's what team members do," Briggs snapped. "And Holt only had to take over because you relieved Agent Kelly of duty and imprisoned her so that she couldn't complete the mission herself. Now, as I was saying-"

Dermott shot me a hate-filled look and interrupted, "She's going to botch the mission with Kane, too! And you're just going to keep on making excuses for her, aren't you, because she's so goddamn fucking *special*-"

"One more word, and you'll be the one in chains," Briggs said quietly.

Dermott turned purple, but didn't retort. Even he had finally figured out that it was over.

Except that it wasn't.

He was never going to let it go now.

And the chain of command still expected me to deliver Kane.

A bleak future stretched ahead in my imagination. Me, pretending with less and less conviction to be recruiting Kane. Dermott sowing vicious lies and damaging truths in Command's minds; gradually convincing them that I had never intended to carry out the mission.

And at last we would come full circle. I'd be in chains again with the lie detector wrapped around my head, forced to admit that I had never actually tried to convince Kane to trade his only child for a job.

Briggs had spoken but I hadn't heard what he'd said. The guards were unlocking my chains.

"Wait." The word came out of my mouth in a dry croak.

The guards froze with my shackles half off. Briggs turned, frowning, as a surprised murmur went around the table.

"Agent Kelly, do you have a question?" Briggs asked.

"Not a question."

God, this was probably the stupidest thing I'd ever done, but I was just so damn tired. I couldn't go through it all again.

"What would you like to say?" Briggs asked kindly.

"Dermott's partly right."

Dermott stared open-mouthed.

Briggs's eyes narrowed. "In what way?"

"I don't think I'll be able to get John to come back to active duty, and I don't think it's in anyone's best interests for me to try."

This time the murmur that went around the table sounded considerably more hostile.

"Explain," Briggs said, his tone completely flat.

I sucked in a deep breath. "I know John pretty well. His son is the most important thing in the world to him, and he won't compromise on that. There are lots of ways I could try to manipulate him back into the Department, but he's a top agent. He'll recognize any tactics I throw at him. And if I keep hammering away at him, he'll get pissed off and then you'll have no chance at all."

"That's why we assigned the mission to you. Your relationship with him gives you the best chance of success, and it's your responsibility to develop a strategy that *won't* alienate him." Briggs's voice was dangerously quiet. "Do you refuse the mission?"

Trapped-trapped-TRAPPED...

"I'm not refusing!" The cowardly words sprang from my mouth before I could stop them. "I'm just saying that if you're willing to allow some leeway in your interpretation, I've already accomplished the mission."

Briggs's eyebrows rose. "How?"

Shame burned my heart, but the terror was too strong.

My weasel-words poured out. "Have you read my last two mission reports?"

"Skimmed. I don't know all the details."

"But you do know that in my last two missions, I involved John and he was a key component in the success of the missions."

"Yes. That's why we want you to bring him in."

"Well, I've done it," I said. "He came to my rescue in this mission, too. He's done it three times in a row."

The murmuring started again. Briggs sat in silence, frowning.

"So you're saying..." he said slowly, "...that if you call for help, Kane will come. We gain the benefit of all his expertise, just not through official channels."

"That's what it looks like," I replied, hating myself. "I don't know whether it'll last, but it seems like the best deal you're likely to get. I can pretty much guarantee that he won't come in if you offer him anything directly."

"That's true," Briggs agreed. "We've already tried every inducement we could think of."

I sighed. "He won't change his mind."

"And what happens when the success of the mission depends on him and he doesn't show up?"

Swallowing hard, I raised my chin and looked Briggs square in the eye. "I told you, this is a crapshoot. He might respond to me every time, or he might never respond again. Don't make the success of the mission depend on him. The first time you do, he'll figure it out; and then it'll be over."

Briggs sat in thought for a long moment, then straightened and swept his gaze around the table. "I think Agent Kelly's proposal is our best course of action. All in favour?"

The show of hands was unanimous.

"Good. Agent Kelly, thank you for your service, and for the successful completion of both your missions. You are free to go, and I'm placing you on leave until Monday, January 2. Have a restful vacation." Briggs rose, nodded to me, and strode out, taking the last of my self-respect with him.

The guards finished unlocking my shackles and removed them, and Holt handed me a bag containing my waist pouch, wristwatch, boots, and weapons.

"Good work, Holt," Dermott said as he stalked out, ignoring me.

My verbal filters finally gave up the battle.

"How did you ever end up being friends with that assclown?" I asked as I bent to tie my boots.

"Long story," Holt replied. "He was the class bully in grade school and I was the wimpy little kid. I paid him protection money until I outgrew him, and then he made out like we were best friends. I was flattered. Kids are stupid."

I straightened, shocked that he'd shared such a personal snippet. "I can't imagine you as a wimpy little kid."

Holt grinned. "Gotta love martial arts." His smile faded as he added, "We stayed buddies through university because we were drunk most of the time, and then we lost touch after graduation. When I got transferred here, we picked up where we'd left off. I thought he'd make a good Director because he's tenacious and decisive, but I'd forgotten what a vindictive son of a bitch he is. He holds grudges forever."

My belly hollowed.

Holt waved me toward the door. "Come on, let's get the fuck out of here." As I hurried out ahead of him, he added, "Oh, and Rebecca's not dead."

I jerked to a halt and he ran into me.

"Christ, Kelly!" He detoured around to face me. "You need brake lights."

I gaped at him. "Wh-what did you say?"

"You need brake lights."

"No!" I flapped a hand at him. "The other thing. Rebecca's *not dead?* But... Stemp told me he was going to... He said if I couldn't clean the thoughts out of her brain... When did he... How..."

"Shut up," Holt said tolerantly. "He called in and told Dermott this morning, but I just found out. Remember how you said you couldn't find any thoughts at all in Rebecca's mind?"

My heart shrivelled. "She's a vegetable, isn't she?"

"No, she's fine. She repressed the memories. Stemp said she woke up, screamed her head off for about two seconds, and then sat up and smiled and hugged her parents and blah-blah-bluebirds-and-happiness bullshit."

"She's... fine." The words didn't make sense. "And... he's not going to kill her?"

"Why would he?" Holt said impatiently. "She just thinks she had some weird dreams while she was unconscious. Stemp pretended to be a newspaper reporter and interviewed her along with a dozen other fucking tabloids about how she fell into a coma and then woke up; all the usual dramatic shit. She's been thoroughly questioned. She's not a threat." He shrugged. "And anyway, Stemp's got her network keys now. Even if she's faking the whole thing and secretly planning to go back in, she can't. And Nora was the last person who knew she could."

"So... Rebecca gets to live." The idea slowly sank into my brain, warming my chest and easing my aching heart. "She'll be fine. Her parents will be fine..."

A lump closed my throat. Rebecca's parents would be fine. Mine...

"That's good to hear," I croaked.

"Oh, and..." Holt took a secured phone from his pocket and handed it to me. "Stemp wants to talk to you. He'll call you later."

Oh shit.

I pocketed the phone, turning away to hide my fear. Holding my voice level with all my strength, I added, "And Grandin confessed?" as Holt fell into step beside me.

"No, I lied." Holt shrugged. "He still swears he was under official orders, but he's not our problem anymore.

U.S. agents picked him up an hour ago. And speaking of picking shit up, I called Kane and he said he'd get your car from the sportsplex."

"Thanks." I plodded down the hallway toward freedom. "Guess I'll get a cab to his place, then."

"No, he's waiting for you in the lobby."

"Thanks," I lied.

Kane was the last person I wanted to see right now.

Coming to a halt, I turned to face Holt. "Don't be too hard on your team. They got blindsided. Wrong location, wrong equipment, wrong strategy, wrong everything."

He scowled. "I know. We should have aborted. Fucking Dermott risked all our lives just because of his stupid vendetta against you. You're right; sometimes he's an assclown." He hesitated. "But you didn't hear it from me. I don't need the kind of hate he's got for you."

I snorted. "I don't blame you. Keep your head down."

Holt nodded. As I turned away, he added, "I'm sorry about your mom."

I swallowed hard and kept walking. "Thanks. Me, too."

Not really true. I didn't know how to feel about Nora. I had believed that either she loved me and was innocent; or she was an evil murderer coldly manipulating me. How could I deal with 'she loved me *and* she was an evil murderer trying to manipulate me'?

But there was no uncertainty in my feelings about what I'd just done to Kane.

Bitter shame twisted my guts. After all my high-and-mighty talk about doing what was best for John, I had sacrificed him to save myself.

And now I had to face him.

CHAPTER 56

I couldn't do it.

My feet trailed to a halt at the lobby door.

That door was the only thing shielding me from John's anger and contempt when he found out what I'd done.

And when Arnie found out how I'd betrayed his best friend...

Oh God, no. I was going to lose both of them.

"Forget something?" Holt asked from behind me.

"No." My voice came out in a croak. "See you later."

I gripped the door handle and opened the door to my fears.

When I stepped into the lobby, Kane rose from one of the chairs and strode over.

"Aydan." His arms closed around me. "Holt told me what happened," he murmured against my hair. "I'm so sorry for your loss."

The loss of my mother was a dull ache.

The loss of my integrity seared like a raw wound, and Kane's warm embrace weighed me down with guilt.

I pulled away, unable to meet his gaze. "Thanks. We need to talk."

"All right, but first you need food. Holt said you hadn't

eaten, and you nearly fainted."

"I'm not hungry."

"I understand, but..."

No, he didn't. But he would, far too soon. And when he did...

"...just a bit," Kane finished as he nudged me gently out the door. I let him guide me, too numb to argue even if I had actually heard what he'd said.

As we got into the Expedition I tried again. "John, there's something I have to tell you."

"Will a half-hour delay change it in any way?"

"N-not really..."

"Then it can wait until you've eaten," he said firmly.

My stomach rebelled at the thought. When I opened my mouth to tell him that, he shushed me.

I gave up.

He drove a few blocks, creeping along through the rush-hour traffic to a below-ground parkade. Minutes later we were going up in an elevator. When the doors opened on the softly humid air of the Devonian Gardens, he guided me to a seat beside a small pool.

"Wait here," he said.

I slumped wordlessly on the bench, staring at the splashing fountain without seeing it.

Maybe I nodded off, or maybe my mind went mercifully blank, but it seemed as though Kane was back in seconds bearing a plastic soup bowl, spoon, crackers, and napkins from the food court.

"Here." He handed me the bowl and spoon, and sat beside me with his arm warm around my shoulder. "I know you're not hungry, but just try a bit of soup. It will help."

What the hell, if that was what he wanted, I'd try. I

certainly owed him far more than that.

I spooned in the soup without tasting it. When the bowl was empty I set it aside.

This couldn't wait any longer. Every additional second struck me like a hammer-blow.

"I sold you out," I said flatly.

Kane frowned. "What are you talking about?"

"In the debriefing. I sold you out. I traded your life for mine." I couldn't meet his gaze. "I'm..." My throat tightened and the soup threatened to come up. "...sorry. I'm so, so sorry..."

My stomach heaved.

"Gonna puke," I choked, and fled for the bathroom.

I didn't make it.

Fortunately there was a large open-topped garbage bin around the corner. Hands braced on its sides, I retched over and over. Kane's strong arms were the only thing holding me up.

"I'm sorry..." I sobbed between retches. "I'm sorry, I'm sorry..."

"Shhh. It's all right. Hush, it's all right. It's all right."

Just let me fall headfirst into the bin. Huddle in there with the rest of the garbage...

"All right. You're all right now," Kane soothed when the spasms eased at last. He handed me the paper napkins, and I mopped the tears and snot and other unappetizing things off my face.

"All right. Come on..." He turned me to face him, wrapping his arms around me and rubbing gentle circles on my back. "You're all right. Everything's all right. I'm sorry for making you eat."

"Don't apologize to me." I pushed him away, balancing

precariously on my own trembling legs. "Didn't you hear what I said?" My words came out in a harsh rasp, as ugly as the taste of bile in my mouth. "*I sold you out!*"

"I heard you and I'd like you to explain, but I don't want to have to take you to Emergency. Will you please sit down before you fall down? There's a bench right here..."

I let him guide me to a bench beside another picturesque fountain. The beautiful greenery made me feel even worse.

Kane sat sideways to face me and took my clammy hand in his big warm one. "All right. Now tell me what happened. Just take it slowly."

Sheer force of habit made me check my bug detector. Green light. And the splashing of the fountain would blur our words if anybody was listening.

"I was supposed to recruit you back to the Department." Shivers shook me, long rolling spasms that threatened to turn my stomach inside out again.

"Yes, you told me that," he said gently. "I'm sorry that the timing coincided with me buying the house. Did you get in trouble?"

"Y... No..."

He waited, his thumb gently stroking the back of my hand.

"Dermott..." I swallowed hard. Stay put, stomach. "...he's got a hate on for me, and he tried to convince the chain of command that I was wilfully disobeying orders and not trying to convince you to come back."

Kane's brow furrowed. "Only three days after you got the assignment? That's ridiculous."

"That's what General Briggs said."

Kane's shoulders relaxed. "Briggs is a good man. So you're off the hook."

"No. Well... yes..." I had to gulp again. "But only because I sold you out."

"You keep saying that. How did you sell me out?" he asked patiently.

"Dermott... he's going to keep at me. Forever. Before, he might have let it go; but now it's a blood feud. And sooner or later I'd end up in front of the same tribunal, on the same charge. Because I wouldn't try to manipulate you. And they'd put the lie detector on me, and I'd have to confess and go to prison for the rest of my life, and I..." Another wave of nausea cramped my stomach. "I just... I... c-couldn't."

"So what happened?" Kane asked quietly.

"I told them..." My heart trembled in my chest. Unable to escape.

Trapped.

I couldn't look into Kane's steady gray eyes. I focused on his thumb instead, softly stroking across my hand back and forth, back and forth.

"I told them I had already completed the mission," I mumbled. "I told them you had come to my rescue on my last three missions, so you were already effectively working for the Department." Shame boiled up like acid in my throat, choking my voice to a bare whisper. "And I told them that if they wanted you to keep working for them, you'd probably come if I called you and said I needed your help."

Kane's thumb stilled on my hand.

"You told them I'd probably come if you called," he repeated, his voice dangerously flat.

I could only nod.

Afraid to look at him. Afraid to see his contempt for me.

Still a damn coward.

"And if I don't respond?" There was no emotion in his

voice.

Somehow I forced myself to reply.

"I told them you might not come next time or ever again; but it was the only chance they had." I swallowed hard, but my voice still came out in a pathetic croak. "And they took it. I'm off the hook, and you're on it. I'm so sorry."

Stupid words. Pointless and inadequate.

Choking silence swelled between us.

My heart wailed, dashing itself against my ribs again and again in raw and futile grief.

Over.

It was over.

"Oh, Aydan." It could have been laugh or a sob in Kane's voice as he gathered me close, pressing his lips to my hair. "You're so honourable it's almost embarrassing."

"I'm not *honourable*!" I shoved him away, shame kindling into anger. "Haven't you been listening to anything I said? *I sold you out!*"

"No!" He caught my hands. "No, you didn't. Aydan, listen to me. You did the right thing. You immediately told me about it. That's not selling me out. If you had lied to me about it, pretended it never happened, that would have been selling me out. But this..." A smile spread over his lips, his eyes lighting up. "...you've given me exactly what I wanted."

"*What?*" Flummoxed, I could only stare at him.

His grin widened. "This is perfect. This is better than I ever dared to hope."

"What the ever-loving fuck? But you said..."

Sobering, he squeezed my hands. "Aydan, it nearly killed me to leave the Department. My whole life has been in military service or police service or secret service. It's all I was; the only way I defined myself. Leaving it behind was like tearing off my own arm."

I shuddered violently at the memories.

He tucked me against the warmth of his body, holding me close. "The Service was my life," he repeated. "But Daniel is what I live for now. And..." He hesitated, a smile in his voice. "You were right when you called me an adrenaline junkie last year. Being a father is a huge and wonderful challenge, but it's... uneventful." He chuckled. "Usually. Except for the stomach flu." The smile faded from his voice. "I knew I could never go back to the Department. There's no room for compromise there. When orders came down, I would have had to leave Daniel for days; weeks; months, even. Never knowing when... or if... I'd be back." His arm tightened around me. "But with this... you've given me a way to keep doing a job I love and believe in; but only on missions I want to accept."

Kane pulled away to face me again, his hands on my shoulders, his smiling gaze holding mine. "Missions chosen by a dear and caring friend who always puts my welfare first, and who lets me refuse without consequences."

I gaped at him in silence. After a few long moments I got my voice working again. "Are you lying to me right now? Because you're a spook and I can't tell."

"I'm not lying. I promise I'm not lying."

"And you're not..." I swallowed, my throat scratchy with emotion and too-recent vomit. "...angry? Disappointed in me?"

"Oh, Aydan." He pulled me into his arms. "Never."

I hugged him at last, locking my arms around all the warmth and strength I thought I'd lost.

After a long moment, he spoke.

"If I buy you another bowl of soup, do you promise not to

throw it up?"

I half-laughed-half-sniffled into his shoulder. "Yes."

CHAPTER 57

"Close your eyes." Kane was grinning like a little boy with a big secret.

I obeyed, smiling as the Expedition made one last turn and pulled to a stop.

"Keep them closed," he warned. The suspension bounced as he got out, and his footsteps crunched around the front of the vehicle to my door. "All right, watch your step here..." He helped me out of the passenger seat and closed the door behind me, then guided me several steps through the crisp snow.

His hands closed on my shoulders, turning me.

"All right, open your eyes!"

As I did, he added eagerly, "What do you think?"

I was facing a well-kept bungalow, creamy stucco with smart charcoal trim. Snow-laden evergreens flanked the tastefully dark red door, and terraced lumps under the snow promised flowerbeds in the spring.

"It looks like a Christmas card!" I pointed at the large SOLD sticker on the real estate sign. "And that's the prettiest part."

"I'm glad you like it so far." He took my hand. "Come on, I'll show you the inside."

"Shouldn't we wait for Arnie and your dad?" I asked as he towed me forward.

"They've already seen it once, so they won't mind if we go in before they get here. And I want to show it to you before the real estate agent arrives. She said she wasn't actually supposed to let me in unsupervised until the transfer was complete, but since it's unoccupied..." He stopped on the front step and turned to grin down at me. "...she lent me the keys for a few minutes."

"You flirted unmercifully with her, didn't you?"

"Maybe."

The devilish glint in his eyes made me laugh out loud. "The poor woman never had a chance."

"All my training should be good for something," Kane bantered as he unlocked the door.

When I stepped into the warmth of the foyer, I stopped to take in the open plan and gleaming hardwood floors. "It's beautiful!"

"Wait 'til you see the kitchen!"

We kicked off our boots and Kane took my hand and led me forward. When we turned the corner into the kitchen, I caught my breath.

"Oh... wow! It's gigantic! And look at those gorgeous granite counters!"

"And it's got a professional-quality gas cooktop." Kane tugged me over to see. "I love cooking with gas. And look, a double oven! And there are three bedrooms so I'll be able to set up my office, and I can put a gym and family room in the finished basement. And the back yard is big enough to make an entire playground for Daniel and his friends."

I slid my arms around him, his happiness warming my heart. "It's perfect for you."

He sobered, holding me close. "Not just for me. For Daniel, too. And..." He hesitated. "...for you... if you want."

My stab of instinctive fear didn't surprise me.

But an instant of wistful longing did.

"Don't panic," Kane added hurriedly. "I'm not asking for anything. I just want you to know there's space in my new life for you."

"Thank you." I reached up to kiss him lightly. "That means a lot to me."

His lips found mine again, warmer and hungrier. "I hope you'll come for a private housewarming," he rumbled. Another kiss weakened my knees almost as much as the one he had given me at the sportsplex...

I tensed.

Kane drew away, frowning. "It's all right, I promise I'm not asking or expecting anything from you."

"No, it's okay," I assured him reflexively.

Holt's sardonic grin hovered in my memory.

I sighed. "All right, yeah. There's something bothering me."

Kane stiffened. "What is it?"

I had intended to be subtle, but the words jumped out of my mouth before I could stop them. "Holt says you're pussywhipped because you share me with Arnie."

"Holt is an idiot."

"Well, I know, but..." I gnawed my lip. "Even an idiot says something insightful every now and then."

Kane's eyebrow quirked. "So you're saying I'm pussywhipped?"

"No! I'm just... I wondered whether... maybe you felt that way...? Or it might bother you that other people might think that?"

"No." He eyed me with a frown. "When are you going to stop trying to take responsibility for my emotions?"

"I didn't mean that; I just meant..." I blew out a breath at his skeptical look, my shoulders slumping. "Okay, you're right. When he said that, I felt like I was this sleazy whore sneaking around on you, and that you were secretly hurt and angry even though you were pretending it was okay, and that I was a total shithead for making you feel that way."

"Oh, Aydan. You're so smart, but so..." He hesitated.

"Fucked up?" I supplied.

He chuckled. "I was going to be more tactful than that." He sobered. "I don't care what anybody thinks of our relationship. And if I was so insecure that I needed to own your mind, body, and soul, I'd be long gone from your life by now."

For a moment I just stood there in silence.

Too good to be true. He had to be lying.

And yet, somehow, for the first time...

"I think... I might... believe you...?" Surprise lifted my words like a question.

His laugh was as warm as his arms as he gathered me into a hug. "Now, don't panic, because there's no expectation attached to this," he whispered against my hair. "But... I love you."

"Don't read anything into this, because there's no commitment attached to it," I whispered back. "But I love you, too."

My jacket pocket vibrated.

The secured phone.

Stemp.

My stomach clenched.

Oh God. For just a few sweet moments I'd forgotten

about his impending call.

Pulling away from John, I fumbled the secured phone out of my jacket pocket and pressed the accept button.

"Kelly," I said faintly.

"Stemp here."

His voice was as flat and deadly as ever. I shuddered.

"Can we talk without being overheard?" he asked.

Of course he wouldn't want an audience while he gutted me. I gave Kane an unhappy grimace and padded into the bathroom, closing the door behind me and flipping on the ceiling fan to mask my voice.

A reflexive check of my bug detector showed all clear, and I sucked in a small breath. Stop postponing the inevitable.

"Go ahead," I said.

"Have you been freed?" The dangerous note in his voice made my heart plummet.

He had turned against me. I might as well shoot myself right now.

"Y-Yes..." My shoulders hunched, bracing for the blow.

"Good. General Briggs assured me that he would do his best for you, but the chain of command can be unpredictable at times."

A long moment later, his words penetrated my mind.

Stemp. On my side.

Shock and gratitude made me stammer. "Uh... what... you talked to... how did you...?"

"I am up to date with your situation," he said. His crisp tone softened. "My parents and I offer our condolences to you for Nora's death."

"Th-thanks... I..."

I pulled myself together. I was afraid to ask, but I had to

know. Just in case Holt had gotten it wrong. "What happened... with Rebecca?"

I squeezed my eyes shut. No more bad news. Please, no more bad news...

"I am in a sensitive location, so I will keep this brief," Stemp said in his usual emotionless tone. "I determined that Ms. Stile is not a threat. This morning at zero nine hundred I called Dermott with my decision, and asked him to inform you. When he revealed his intention to relieve you of duty, I called General Briggs to ensure that you received fair judgement. Dermott's antagonism toward you has been noted and the chain of command will take it into consideration if issues arise in the future."

"Th-Thank you." I hesitated. "Is that... all?"

"Only one more thing."

Oh no...

Stemp's voice softened. "I thought you might like to hear this..."

Momentary silence filled the line, followed by an increasing babble of voices as though he had left a quiet room to walk toward a happy crowd. I identified Karma's warm rumble embellished by Moonbeam's gentle grace notes, but the next voice made the corners of my mouth lift.

"Baba, you're funny!" The child's clear voice dissolved into a cascade of silvery giggles that lilted above the laughter of the adults.

The sounds faded and a moment later Stemp said softly, "Baba is Bulgarian for 'grandma'."

No bad news.

Nothing but good.

Happy tears trickled into my grin, and I scrubbed them away.

"Thank you," I whispered when I could speak again. "That's the best Christmas present I've had in a long time."

"I am glad." His voice was warm. "It is the best Christmas present I have ever had. We all thank you for it. Have a merry Christmas. Goodbye."

The connection closed and I stood staring at nothing, savouring the glow of Stemp's hard-won happiness.

The thump of boots on the front step pulled me back to the present, and I hurried out of the bathroom.

Kane met me in the hallway with a worried lift of his eyebrows.

I smiled at him. "Everything's fine." My knotted muscles relaxed at last, my grin widening. "In fact, everything's really, really good!"

"Thank goodness." He gave me a short, fierce hug before adding, "Come on, Dad and Arnie are here."

"Merry Christmas!" Doug Kane's jovial voice greeted us as we rounded the corner hand in hand. His warm smile creased into deep laugh-crevices around his mouth and the gray eyes so much like John's. "It's wonderful to see you again, Aydan."

He gave me a hug as firm and strong as his son's, then stepped aside so Arnie could come in behind him.

"Hey, darlin'." Arnie greeted me with a smile, too, but his gaze searched my face anxiously. "Are ya okay?"

The week's fear and pain and betrayal fell away as I stepped into his arms.

I kissed him. A tender unselfconscious kiss, knowing I was free from judgement here.

Somewhere in the world was another mage. Somewhere in the U.S. government was a person who would lie to their allies. And in Silverside, Dermott would risk innocent lives just to get to me.

But John and Arnie would cover my back.

And sometimes my front.

"Yeah." I gave Arnie a private smile before turning to include John and his dad in this one precious moment. "I'm just fine."

Book 15 is available!

Visit my Books page at www.dianehenders.com/books for progress updates and announcements.

A Request

Thanks for reading!

If you enjoyed this book, I'd really appreciate it if you'd take a moment to review it online.

Here are some suggestions for the "star" ratings:

Five stars: Loved the book and can hardly wait for the next one.

Four stars: Liked the book and plan to read the next one.

Three stars: The book was okay. Might read the next one.

Two stars: Didn't like the book. Probably won't read the next one.

One star: Hated the book. Would never read another in the series.

You can help prospective readers by writing a few sentences about what you liked or disliked about the book.

Thanks for taking the time to do a review!

About Me

Before I started writing fiction, I had a checkered career: technical writer, computer geek, and interior designer. I'm good at two out of three of those. Fortunately, I had the sense to quit the one I sucked at (interior design).

When my mid-life crisis hit, I took up muay thai and started writing thrillers featuring a middle-aged female protagonist. ('Walter Mitty', you say? Nope, never heard of him.)

Writing and kicking the hell out of stuff seemed more productive than more typical mid-life-crisis activities like getting a divorce, buying a Harley Crossbones, and cruising across the country picking up men in sleazy bars; especially since it's winter most months of the year here in Canada.

It's much more comfortable to sit at my computer. And Harleys are expensive. Come to think of it, so are beer and gasoline.

Oh, and I still love my husband. There's that. So I stuck with the writing.

Diane Henders

And here's my "professional" bio, in case you need something more suitable for mixed company:

Diane Henders is the Kindle best-selling author of the NEVER SAY SPY series: Sexy thrillers packed with tension, laughs, profanity, and sometimes warm fuzzies.

The first book in the series, NEVER SAY SPY, has had over 450,000 downloads to date, and stayed on Kindle's 'Women Sleuths' Top 100 list for 60 consecutive months.

Diane enjoys target shooting, gardening, auto mechanics, painting (art, not walls), music, and martial arts; and loves food and drink almost as much as she loves her husband. They live in the wilds of British Columbia, Canada, where they get all the adrenaline rush they could ever want by growing fruit trees in bear country.

Want to know what else is roiling around in the cesspit of my mind? Drop by my blog and website at dianehenders.com, check out the extras, and don't forget to leave a comment in the guest book to say hi – I love hearing from you! Or you can connect with me on Facebook at:
https://www.facebook.com/authordianehenders.
See you there!

www.ingramcontent.com/pod-product-compliance
Lightning Source LLC
Chambersburg PA
CBHW020624020726
47494CB00001B/40